GALAXY IN FLAMES

THE LAST STEWARD

GALAXY IN FLAMES
I

NEW YORK TIMES BESTSELLING AUTHOR
NICHOLAS SANSBURY SMITH

Copyright © 2021 by Nicholas Sansbury Smith

All Rights Reserved

Cover Design by Tom Edwards

These books are works of fiction. Names, characters, places, and incidents are either products of the author's imagination or used fictitiously. Any resemblance to actual events locales or persons, living or dead, is purely coincidental. All rights reserved. No part of this publication can be reproduced or transmitted in any form or by any means, without permission in writing from the author.

BOOKS BY NICHOLAS SANSBURY SMITH

HELL DIVERS
Hell Divers
Hell Divers II: Ghosts
Hell Divers III: Deliverance
Hell Divers IV: Wolves
Hell Divers V: Captives
Hell Divers VI: Allegiance
Hell Divers VII: Warriors
Hell Divers VIII: King of the Wastes
Hell Divers IX: Radioactive
Hell Divers X: Fallout
Hell Divers XI: Renegades
Hell Divers XII: Heroes

SONS OF WAR
Sons of War
Sons of War 2: Saints
Sons of War 3: Sinners
Sons of War 4: Soldiers

ORBS
Solar Storms (An Orbs Prequel)
White Sands (An Orbs Prequel)
Red Sands (An Orbs Prequel)
Orbs
Orbs II: Stranded
Orbs III: Redemption
Orbs IV: Exodus

E-DAY
E-Day
E-Day II: Burning Earth
E-Day III: Dark Moon

GALAXY IN FLAMES
The Last Steward
The Last Ship
The Last Lion

EXTINCTION CYCLE (SEASON ONE)
Extinction Horizon
Extinction Edge
Extinction Age
Extinction Evolution
Extinction End
Extinction Aftermath
Extinction Lost
(A Team Ghost short story)
Extinction War

EXTINCTION CYCLE: DARK AGE (SEASON TWO)
Extinction Shadow
Extinction Inferno
Extinction Ashes
Extinction Darkness

TRACKERS (SEASON ONE)
Trackers
Trackers 2: The Hunted
Trackers 3: The Storm
Trackers 4: The Damned

NEW FRONTIER (TRACKERS SEASON TWO)
New Frontier: Wild Fire
New Frontier 2: Wild Lands
New Frontier 3: Wild Warriors

STANDALONE TITLES
Savage Skies
The Biomass Revolution

For Mark Boyett and Khristine Hvam—thank you for bringing this series to life with your talents!

"One meets his destiny often in the road he takes to avoid it."

JEAN DE LA FONTAINE

PROLOGUE

Over the course of 50 harrowing years in the 22nd century, humanity bore witness to the slow death of the Earth and the extinction of most animals larger than a field mouse. Forests and dense impenetrable jungles dwindled, in many cases, to nothing but noxious little weeds. The verdant cradle of humanity shriveled into toxic deserts, barren mountains, and vast dead oceans matching the color of the abrasive brown atmosphere.

Surviving humans with the means to escape took to the stars, building colonies on Mars and Europa. These artificial habitats became new cradles of civilization, but they were temporary solutions, way stations on the road to the future. Knowing this, refugees from Earth joined together in the most important mission in the history of their species—to create faster-than-light (FTL) engines that would allow them to escape extinction by sowing the seeds of human civilization across the vast canvas of the cosmos. With the help of artificial intelligence, they reached this monumental achievement.

In the end, humanity fled the Solar System with these revolutionary engines, breaking free of their colonies, and primordial

Earth in packed vessels like rats on seafaring ships. A few remained in remote sanctuaries that could still support life. People too poor, too stubborn, too tired. And some who hid from someone or something, too frightened to leave.

They were the last of the Earthlings, and ten-year-old Axel Finn was among them.

Dressed in a windbreaker and wearing a breathing mask and goggles, he stood on a rocky bluff overlooking a wide valley seemingly devoid of life. A river the color of rust meandered between eroding banks and a dying forest of skeletal trees. Normally, the filthy clouds on the horizon blocked the view of an ancient skyline beyond the valley, but it was dusk, and the setting sun was a burning back light illuminating the oblique structures. The leaning rectangles reminded him of a set of childhood building blocks he used to knock over in fits of anger.

He pictured a giant fist smacking the distant buildings down in rage, howling in victorious destruction. There were monsters out there, his mother had told him. But he knew the constructs on the horizon weren't toys, and that it was humans that had broken them.

Axel stared at the massive steel structures, some as tall as mountains. It was hard to believe, but his mother had also told him people used to live and work in those buildings. That the surrounding city had been a vibrant, bustling hive with thousands of places to eat and shop. There were parks for kids to play at, green and safe, and schools for them to learn.

None of that existed anymore.

He couldn't even remember the last kid he saw. Couldn't remember much of anything besides the old bunker inside the mountain where he lived with his mother, Mira, and his aunt, Julia.

Tiny blue lights suddenly flickered on the horizon above the dilapidated city.

Axel crouched behind a rock and pulled his binoculars from his backpack. By the time he brought them up to his goggles, the lights were brighter. The cool blue glow illuminated the dull grey hull of a wingless ship lowering from orbit.

It was a Junker vessel, the size of a city block, crewed by people who came to salvage relics from the old world and cart them away in their heavy barge. The same barges were once lifeboats, salvaging people from this horrible world and transporting them to a new system of planets teeming with alien life.

The Junker flew slowly over the skyline. Orb shaped drones buzzed down from bay doors opening in the hull, searching for antiquated treasure.

Rocks crunched behind him, and Axel spun from the view to see his mother and aunt approaching. They both wore hooded coats and pants to match the brown terrain. It wasn't a surprise to see Julia carrying a laser rifle. She raised that weapon toward the distant vessel and peered at it through a scope while his mother ran to him.

To his surprise, she too carried a rifle, or an ancient "flesh burster," as they referred to guns that still fired bullets.

"Axel," she called out. "We've been looking everywhere for you!"

"I—" he started to say.

"I've told you—how many times—not to venture this far from home."

She crouched in front of him. Using her glove, she bent down and wiped his goggles clean.

"I know you're curious about the world, but it's not safe," she said. "There are bad people that hunt in the darkness."

"The Junkers? They just want... junk, right?" he asked.

He looked back over the skyline, watching the vessel moving between the tower blocks. She spoke of the bad people often, and of monsters, but he never saw any. He only saw the bulky

Junker ships. They were ugly, but they didn't look scary. Not like the pictures of warships he had seen so many times.

"Why can't we leave Earth like everyone else?" This was a question he had asked a hundred times, and each time, his mother had told him that one day maybe they could. Only it was not *this* day.

Axel looked at the darkening sky above, seeing the first twinkles of stars. "I want to see the colorful planet again," he said. "There was life there. Life everywhere."

In his mind, that planet wasn't much more than a flash of scattered images. Like faces, things you forget over time. He wasn't even sure whether the images were real or if he'd only made them up. He strained to remember, but like grasping a slippery fish, the moment he thought he had it, it slipped from his mind.

After struggling for several moments, he relaxed. Blooming memories surfaced of red trees with purple leaves, a crystal clear stream, and kids. Kids with moms and dads.

Yes, that was all real.

"I want friends. I want to know about dad," he said.

"Axel..." There was frustration in his mother's voice. There always was when he asked about his father, something she never talked about. Ever.

Had he left them? Had he died?

Axel longed to know.

His mother sighed. "I wish I could give you those things, I do, but someday you'll understand. Now come."

She stood and reached out, but Axel stepped back. For a fleeting moment, he wanted to tell her he wasn't going anywhere until she told him the truth. But he knew she was just trying to protect him and loved him deeply. That she would have given him the life he wanted, if she could have, even at the cost of her own.

So he took her hand, and she guided him away from the bluff. Julia remained close, eyeing the sky, always eyeing the sky.

Many years ago, she had been a soldier, one who had fought in bloody battles in a war before he was born. It reminded him that just days ago he'd found a box of toy soldiers in an old storage closet. He was looking forward to playing with them tonight.

They trekked through the forest, passing what few living pine trees remained, their branches drooping. The vertical rock face of the mountain loomed above. A hidden entrance to their home wasn't far, burrowed deep inside the safety of solid granite.

The path guided them on a slope overlooking a road below. Bulging, cracked asphalt went right up to the derelict gate of an ancient tunnel. That passage led to a blast door, but they never took that route.

Instead, his mother guided them up the hill along a trail that wrapped around the mountain to a hidden entrance, or perhaps, exit.

She opened the door when they arrived. "Don't forget to get cleaned off," she said.

Axel went inside the clean chamber, its disinfectant nozzles aiming at him, while his aunt remained behind to cover up the hatch. The cleansing process took thirty minutes. First, they hung up their outside clothes. Then they showered, and finally, they went into a smaller chamber that sprayed chemicals to kill any toxins still left on their flesh.

Happy to be done, Axel dressed in the shorts and t-shirt left out on a bench. Then he hurried down a hall and through another door into a large communal room. A cozy space full of couches, scratched desks, and worn down tables. The ceiling had already transformed to a nighttime image of the Milky Way, rotating overhead. There were other places where the walls changed images. According to his mother, they did this to keep people happy.

From what he knew, the bunker was designed to house a population hundreds of years ago in the event of a bomb going off. In a way, this place was like a lifeboat that never came ashore. A place you lived *all* your life.

Why would anyone have wanted that? Pretty pictures couldn't have kept them happy for long. Sure didn't make him happy at all. In fact, the sight of so many stars only made him feel small.

He wanted to leave. To seek adventure, see new planets. He wanted to be free.

This place was a prison.

"I'm going to my room," Axel announced.

"Okay, but dinner in an hour," Mira called back.

Her voice was kind again, soothing. Axel suddenly felt bad for making his mother worry. He walked over to her before she could leave the chamber and go to the connecting kitchen.

"I'm sorry," he said. "I didn't mean to upset you. I just want to see things."

She smiled her nearly perfect set of straight, white teeth. He had always seen her as beautiful, and still did, but she was changing in ways he didn't understand. He heard her sighing more. One time, he found her with her head in her hands. There were grays in her brown hair. Stress lines on her face.

This place was getting to her too, even though she would never admit that. She had to be strong for him. He knew that, too.

She came over and wrapped him in a hug. "It's okay. You are a curious, smart boy, and I would expect nothing less."

"Thanks, Mom."

Axel went to his room and looked under his bed for the box

of toys. There was something else under there he had hidden—a map of the Hironia System. He slid it out, unfolded it and blew off the dust, examining the planets where the rest of humanity had gone many years ago.

Nearest the sun was the blazing hot planet of Furia. Then the gas planet of Tecca, and after that two larger worlds called Eern and Corinnia. Someone had circled the center of the map and written, "Goldilocks Zone." Five planets were inside that sector: Azuri, Honi, Runi, Hex Prime, and Dari. He tried to recall which one he had lived on when he was just a baby, but none of those names sounded right. His eyes went to the outer rim of colder planets, including Jolia.

Axel wished he could remember more, but maybe it was for the best to not remember. He slid the map back under his bed and pulled out the box of toys. Inside were plastic space marine figures in bulky armor with helmets and laser guns, like the one his aunt carried. He lined them up in front of his bed, creating two opposing forces. At first, he wasn't sure which side to choose, but then he decided he wouldn't favor either. He smashed two of the figures against each other, repeatedly, until one of their heads popped off. He tried to put it back on, but the plastic had broken.

Anger surged through his body, warming his chest. He hated the feeling, and it seemed to be happening more often. Maybe it was this place, or maybe it was something else. Although he was young, he knew the feeling was rage.

And while he knew what it was, he did not know how to control it. That made him even angrier. The heat spread and he smashed the remaining soldiers together until their plastic arms and legs were scattered across the carpet. He never heard his mother come to get him for dinner until she was inside the room.

"Axel? What are you doing?"

Slowly, she sat on the side of his bed.

He breathed rapidly, heart pounding, the anger barely in check. His mother put a hand gingerly on his arm.

"It's okay," she said. "It's okay to be angry, but you must learn to control it."

He looked up at her. "Do you get angry? I never see you get angry."

"Yes, of course, everyone gets angry, Axel. Me, your aunt. It's a natural human emotion."

"My anger...it's not like that. And it seems to be changing."

"How so?"

He glanced back at the mayhem he'd caused, trying to understand a way to explain it.

"Axel..." She got down on the floor and sat in front of him, putting her hands on his shoulders. "Look at me, Axel."

He avoided her gaze another moment before meeting her dark brown eyes.

"The anger is getting stronger, I can't—" Again he searched for the words. "I don't like the heat in my body. It's like someone is trying to take control of me. Is there something wrong with me, Mom?

"No, no, no," she replied while shaking her head. "You're a sweet boy, Axel."

He surveyed his destroyed toys, disappointed and ashamed of himself.

"There's something I'd like you to repeat when you get mad," she said. "Something that your father wanted for you."

"My dad?"

She nodded. "He wanted a peaceful life for you."

"Where is he?"

"He's gone, but he loved you *deeply*."

Axel felt that anger again, but a sadness slammed into it with a cold force that made his heart hurt.

"Repeat after me, okay?" she asked.

He swallowed, then nodded.

"Peace is my way. I will not hurt what can't be healed. I will not take what can't be replaced. Violence only leads to more violence. All life is precious. I will be the peace that I want to see in the galaxy."

Axel repeated each line, but he was confused. How could all life be precious?

"If there are monsters, then I should learn to fight. Maybe Aunt Julia can teach me."

"No... Axel—"

"But I want to protect you, Mom."

"There are some fights that are impossible to win. Do you understand that? Some monsters you must hide from instead of fighting. Okay?"

"I guess."

Deep inside, he had a desire to fight, a longing, but more. A compulsion, like thirsting for water on a long day's hike in the mountains.

"Come, let's eat dinner," she said. "We can talk more about this later."

Axel got up and followed her to the dining room. Julia set bowls of soup out on placemats. They sat around the table, bowing their heads and giving thanks.

He felt guilty thinking it, but he hated this soup. It was the same broth they had almost every single night.

"Eat, Axel," Julia said. "You need strength."

His aunt smiled at him and waited until he picked up his spoon before she dug in. As he spooned in the warm soup, he thought of questions that he couldn't resist asking. "Aunt Julia, did you fight monsters?"

Julia looked at Mira, who then nodded. "It's time we tell him," she said.

Setting her spoon down, Julia leaned forward. "Before you were born, an alien race invaded the Hironia System, where humanity fled many years ago," she said. "They were fierce beings, made of rock and fire..."

Again, Julia looked to Mira, clearly nervous about describing these monsters.

Mira took over. "The aliens had one purpose—to eradicate all life," she said. "Your father fought them alongside many soldiers. Eventually, these brave warriors pushed the aliens back, but the threat of their return still remains."

Axel considered everything he had just heard. He had more questions now than ever.

"Did Dad die fighting them?" he asked. "The alien monsters are still out there? That's why we're hiding here?"

Mira looked him in the eye, her lips moving slightly when a warning chirped from a small monitor on the counter.

Julia shot up from her chair and grabbed her rifle leaning against the wall. Mira snatched up the monitor and tapped it.

"What is it?" Axel asked.

"A drone," Mira said.

"One of the Junker orbs?" Julia asked.

"Maybe," Mira said. "It's flying this way."

Axel got up from the table.

"Go to your room and stay there," Mira said. "I'll come shortly."

"But Mom—"

"Axel, just do it, please."

He hurried away as his aunt ran down the hallway back to the clean room. A few minutes later, he heard the hatch opening and his mother telling her to be careful. He waited at his bedroom door until his mother arrived.

"It's okay," she said. "Nothing to fear from a drone."

Axel could tell by her careful tone that she wasn't being fully honest.

"What kind of monsters use drones?" he asked.

His mother pressed her lips to the side, something else she did when she didn't want to tell him the truth.

"Mom, I'm old enough to—"

"The human kind, alright? Not aliens," she said. "The kind we don't fight. The kind we hide from. Okay?"

"Okay."

"Let's fix your toys. How about that?"

She pulled out something she had in her pocket. "Glue," she said. "I found some in storage."

By the time they had pieced the toy soldiers back together, Julia had returned.

"It's okay," she said with a smile.

A forced smile, Axel could tell.

"I'll be right back," Mira said.

"Where are you going?" he asked.

"I'm going to talk with Aunt Julia."

She left the room and walked down the hallway with her sister. Axel stepped up to the door and put his ear to it.

"They're closing in on us," Julia whispered. "Only reason a drone would come this way..."

Her words trailed to silence, broken by his mother speaking a few seconds later.

"It might be time," she said. "Did you contact the Junker crew?"

"Yes."

"And you trust them?"

"I know they will look after him and keep him hidden."

Axel felt his heart kick again as he realized they were talking about him.

A sigh followed from his mother. "He isn't ready. There's so much he needs to learn, so much I haven't taught him."

Axel didn't understand what she meant by that. About the monsters? His father?

"He can never see a doctor. No scans. No tests," she said.

"I know," Julia replied. "He will have a flawless bio ID, I've already made sure of that."

There was a long pause.

"When does this Junker arrive?" Mira asked.

"Soon."

"Okay, I will tell him. Soon."

Axel felt that heat rising inside of him again, but this wasn't from anger. It was from fear. He was finally leaving Earth and heading back to the Hironia System, something he always wanted, but it seemed he would be going alone.

CHAPTER 1

TWENTY-THREE YEARS LATER

"We're almost broke, Axel," said Lieutenant Luna Gervasi. "Like running on fumes broke."

Luna followed Captain Axel Finn into the cargo hold of their salvage ship, *Trash Squid,* currently parked in the Blui City Spaceport on the tropical water planet, Honi. Most of the secured crates inside the stowage were empty. Their supplies were almost exhausted. Food, fuel, equipment—and everything else they needed.

"It's five in the morning," Axel said. "Why aren't you asleep?"

"Did you not hear what I just said? Are you not worried at all?"

Axel turned and lowered his eyes to meet Luna's dark brown gaze. She was over a foot shorter than him. Braided locks of hair that looked almost auburn in the dim lighting hung down her back. Her freckled face tightened, both dimples almost vanishing. Her youthful features and small stature often led to the thirty-three-year-old powerhouse being underestimated, but Axel knew better. They'd met fifteen years ago, when she was assigned to the *Jabbith* for junior officer training. It was the same Junker ship they had sent him away on.

Holding out a HoloMatrix pad, she said, "I've found three new salvaging contracts within range. They might be enough to keep us flying for another run, but there is another option."

"Nope," Axel said.

"Captain, just one of these bounty contracts would erase all of our financial problems."

The problems she knows about, Axel thought. The debt he had racked up to keep them afloat wasn't on the books.

He walked through the hold, noting the crates of scuba gear he had used on their last salvage run in the ocean about fifty miles from where he stood now. A yacht, chartered by a wealthy human family who owned mines on some distant moon, had sunk at sea while carrying a pair of forgite nuggets. The bright red mineral with its mesmerizing metallic luster was the most valuable rock in the galaxy.

After locating the yacht, Axel had dived to recover the loot. The owners were lucky he was an honest man. A single shard of nugget was enough to clean his slate and then some.

He'd handed the rocks over, only to find out the owners *weren't* honest. When he went to collect the fee from the estate's handler, the man dodged him. A week later, Axel realized they had stiffed him entirely.

His pulse had raced, beating in his neck and rapping in his ear as the old rage warmed his chest.

He'd wanted to rip the bastards limb from limb.

But the words of his mother had echoed in his mind, as they always did in times like these.

Peace is your way, Axel thought. *Violence only leads to more violence.*

He pushed on through the cargo hold with the tap of Luna's boots behind him.

"You looking for some solar coins I don't know about?" she called after him.

If she'd known he was actually looking for his surfboard, and not solars, the common Colonial Alliance currency, she would be furious.

"Just hear me out," she said. "I found an Eagle bounty for a Wooly that owes twenty million in back taxes."

He ignored that. She knew his rules. No bounties. Nothing to do with the Colonial Alliance Naval Defense Force (CANDF).

It wasn't just the danger of a bounty job—where your bounty might shoot back—he had to remain hidden from authorities, especially the ruthless CANDF.

"Axel," Luna said, dropping his formal title.

He let out a sigh.

"Are you listening to anything I'm saying?" she asked.

"Yes, I'm just thinking."

Axel finally located his yellow surfboard tucked behind two crates.

"All due respect, boss, but we're out of time for thinking," she said. "After those assholes ripped us off, we can barely keep the lights on."

He thought for a moment then removed the two crates to free his surfboard.

"Wait a second." She laughed, but not her typical fun giggle. Her tone was laced with shock.

"You've got to be kidding me, Axel. You're really going surfing right now?"

"Going to be epic waves after yesterday's storm," he replied.

She folded her arms across her chest.

"You know how important this ship is to me, and the crew,"

he said. "I get that you're upset, but I have rules, and you knew those rules when you agreed to be XO."

"Yeah, yeah, no bounty contracts, too dangerous. But times have changed, Axel. We aren't teenagers anymore, and we're seriously about to lose our home."

"Have I ever led us astray?"

Luna shook her head without hesitation.

"Then trust that I won't now," he said. "The best way for me to come up with a plan is to get out there, surf, and clear my head."

Truth was, he needed the escape to fight the darkness he felt growing inside of him now—a darkness that would lead him to lose his temper, to unleash the constant anger he kept pent up. It was a curse that no one on his ship knew about, not even Luna.

"Okay, fine, you'll do your own thing regardless." She smirked. "Just be careful."

"Sure thing."

Before dawn, Axel left the ship quietly to not wake the rest of his crew. He walked out of the port, gripping his surfboard under his arm, stopping to look over his shoulder at the orange hull of the *Trash Squid*. The two-hundred-foot-long ship was once a Plasma-31 military transport with an attached Tech-N. A small, two-winged fighter ship they called the *Hammerhead* could eject from the top aft section.

Axel had owned the retrofitted former warship for a decade and put every profit into making it lighter, faster, and more agile than any ship in its class.

His heart raced faster at the thought of losing her to his creditors in a hostile repossession. Not only was he out of funds, but he had borrowed a substantial amount to fix his FTL engine, and from a Corinn investor, no less. Not the type you wanted to piss off.

A metallic taste emerged in his mouth.

He knew what would happen next... he could feel the tingling in his muscles and prepared to hear that voice... that *rage* filled voice.

Axel had to get his anger under control.

He jogged all the way to a bluff where the view refocused his mind. A beautiful wave, eighty feet tall, climbed into the sky. In the respite of the crashing waves, chirping sounded.

Axel turned to see Cricket, a Marka, an alien that looked like a large dog—aside from the green fur, the two tails, four eyes (one set on the front, and one set on the back of their head), and webbed paws. The creature served a variety of functions on the *Trash Squid*, but the most important, to Axel, was as his best friend.

The earpiece Axel had translated the chirps. His words, in turn, were translated into an earpiece Cricket wore.

"You're not thinking about surfing that are ya, Commendatore?" Cricket asked.

Axel smiled at the nickname that Cricket used from time to time. "I thought I'd clear my head," he said.

"By yourself? Okay, I understand."

Just as the alien turned, Axel whistled. "No, come on, pal. I could use your help."

The Marka wagged both of his tails. Cricket had been his companion for the past decade. They had met when Axel found the alien as a pup, digging through trash of a port city like this one. His siblings had all been sold off to work various jobs, but as the runt in the litter, Cricket was abandoned, left for nature to intervene.

Survival of the fittest.

You would never have known the Marka was once a runt. The lean muscle on his three hundred-pound, six-foot-long body flexed as Cricket ran alongside him.

Axel checked to make sure no one was out there watching. If someone saw him ride one of these record waves, it could cause unwanted attention.

Something his mother had warned him to avoid two decades ago.

You are very special Axel, in ways other people won't understand... they might fear you. Stay hidden, and you will remain safe.

He had never forgotten those words.

There was no one on the shore that he could see. And there was no lineup of surfers in the water, as there often were. Most men would not dare try these waves. But Axel was no average man.

Even as a child, Axel had known he was different. Stronger and faster than other kids. And there had always been this anger inside of him, like a demon seeking possession. He knew what would happen if it ever got out, how he would hurt people.

Peace is my way. I will not hurt what can't be healed.

A sense of calm washed over his body at those words, the words his mother had taught him to repeat whenever he felt the heat of rage building like a volcano about to erupt. She was no longer with him, but he could hear her voice repeating those words, and he could see the loving smile on her face.

The purple horizon brightened with a fiery glow. The sun would be up in moments. Perfect time to catch a wave.

Exhaling, Axel hiked to an entry point down the beach where the waves were smaller. Cricket led the way into the surf, leaping as a wave crashed against the shore and turned to foam. Axel waded out with his board. Once he was past the shallow set, he got down on his board and paddled after the Marka, who extended his tails to Axel. Holding on tight, Axel rode the surfboard as the creature used his powerful legs and webbed feet to tug them out to deeper water. He watched Axel with the eyes set on the back of his head.

One thousand feet from the beach, Axel let go.

"Thanks, pal!" he shouted.

"Be careful, Commendatore!" Cricket chirped. He ducked down, vanishing into the water.

Axel felt the powerful force of the wall of a swell under him. That power humbled him like looking at the vast galaxy from the darkness of space, knowing he was just a miniscule part of this seemingly infinite universe.

The mammoth waves broke against underwater rocks, crashing over the beach in the distance. Another set hit, then another. He watched them come, waiting for that singular moment when it felt *right*.

Instinct struck at the sight of a gigantic wave farther out, already forming a sheer face and curling lip.

This was it.

He paddled toward it, the board rising with the water. The shape of this wave was different, choppy looking. His gut was right about this being the biggest, but it was also the most dangerous.

Axel pushed himself effortlessly to his feet and dropped into his stance, riding down the growing mountain of water. He carved a diagonal line, his board cutting over the surface, leaving a trail he couldn't see, like a razor across flesh. The wave curled as the bottom broke against the rocks.

Behind him, the crest would form the barrel. The frothy white peak would quickly wrap over, threatening to wipe him out and bash his body against the rocks. He didn't dare look over his shoulder.

His speed increased, hitting terminal velocity as he rocketed down the side. The power of this wave was unlike any he had surfed before. He knew how special this was, and how deadly.

Axel improvised his line, trying to pick up some speed as the pipeline began to collapse. Judging by the crash behind him, he wasn't far away from the crushing waterfall.

He glimpsed the shoreline in the distance. If someone had been there watching, they would have seen a six-foot tall man with lean muscle, his head thrown slightly back, his long blonde hair flying behind him. They might mistake his smile for that of an egotistical maniac—or an idiot. But he wasn't either.

He moved with elegance, with grace, hunching as the barrel crashed closer behind his board. The sheer strength of the wave sent a rush of fiery bliss through him like nothing else could.

This was his therapy. His religion. His way of bonding with the galaxy. More importantly, it kept the demon inside him silent and his body at peace.

Axel cleaved through the pipeline, the white crest now folding overhead, the noise growing louder. An approaching train preparing to swallow him and batter his body.

He kept his focus on the end of the tunnel. The big board carried his lengthy frame toward the end as the water crashed behind him, spraying his hair.

A moment of pure terror broke over the bliss. *I'm not going to make it*, he thought as he ducked under the wall of water practically over his head now. The pipeline closed above him.

He was a half-second from shooting through when the wall collapsed on him with the force of a building. One moment he was looking at the shore, the next, he was underwater, tumbling topsy-turvy like a chuteless skydiver through turbulent storm clouds. The overwhelming force of the water was impossible to fight.

He kicked and pulled, trying to right his body, but could not find the surface. Panic set in at the feeling of being absolutely powerless, at the mercy of the natural goddess he had bonded with moments before.

Through his blurred vision, he saw the bottom, then a rock. Pain cobwebbed across the side of his skull as if a Corinn bull had kicked him.

The world went dark, and he was transported to the main habitat of a space station. A rusty, shadowy space of 3D printed quarters stacked on top of each other like dilapidated toys. Voices, music, and the hum of human engineering filled the massive chamber. There was nothing remarkable about this place, but he remembered it well.

It was here he'd first gone insane.

He was just eleven years old when the Junker ship docked at the station for supplies. Axel had snuck out, despite strict orders. He'd wanted to meet other kids. To have a friend.

But the six kids he found kicking a ball across an artificial green field stared at him like he was an unidentified life form. They were about his age, maybe a bit older, all of them wearing black suits with a sun logo on the breast.

"Can I play?" he asked.

They all laughed, the sound rising as they crowded around him in a circle. Then the name calling started.

Dirty Earther. Soil rat. Bug eater.

The largest kid pushed him into another kid, who also shoved Axel. It became a back-and-forth game until they knocked him to the ground. His heart raced, his breath came in short bursts, and he tasted the metal in his mouth.

That big kid towered over him and spat in his hair.

That was when Axel had first heard the voice in his head.

Break his nose! Gouge his eyes out!

He could hear it perfectly now, that gruff male voice, its barely tempered rage commanding him to violence.

Axel lost control of his body, as if his limbs were on wires pulled by a demon. He leapt up, throwing an uppercut into the boy's nose. The kid dropped like a rotting tree in an Earth forest, and Axel pounced, going for his eyes.

It took three adults and a droid to pull Axel off the boy. Screaming, Axel ripped free and ran back to the *Jabbith*, hiding in the shadows until the ship took off into the darkness.

Wake up and fight! You must fight!

The rough voice wasn't from the memory, wasn't just in his head.

Axel opened his eyes to a radiant, bruised sky that seemed to bob up and down.

"I got you, Commendatore!" Cricket chirped.

Axel gripped tufts of fur on his friend who swam through the surf. Once they hit the beach, Cricket bucked him off into the sand. He lay there gasping.

Over the clap of waves, he heard the rumble of engines. He turned as a shadow passed overhead. The orange hull of the *Trash Squid* lowered from the sky.

Axel reached up to his head, feeling a welt under his long, wet hair where he had kissed the rock. He glanced up at the logo on the side of his ship: a chunky Wooly wearing a red bandana, a bandolier of explosives around his furry white chest. Gripped in one curled arm was a glowing cigar stick. In the other five arms, he held plasma grenades.

A dual hatch opened on the port side, and the real-life face of the logo appeared. Salvage Chief Uga Bir, just three feet tall, had what some called the face of a koala, until he opened his mouth of razor-sharp teeth to eat, or in this case, speak in his low-tone barking.

All six of his short, furry arms were gripping a cable and a harness. The two hanging from his chest were telescopic, but he kept them stubby now, holding one end of the cable close to his muscular torso. Woolies often used these top arms for eating, which they loved to do, partly because of their fast metabolism.

Two more sets hung from his sides at his shoulder and under his armpit. These were used to build, fix, and create things. The species was known for being excellent engineers.

"Capa is okay, no? Bump on a rock knock a little sense in?" Uga barked in his normal deep tone. He gazed down with large black eyes, feeding down a cable with a harness to Axel.

"Commendatore is fine," Cricket chirped up. "Don't see a scratch on him."

"No owies or boo-boos at all?" Uga asked.

Axel might have grinned as he rode up to the cargo hold, but he was slightly embarrassed. He also knew his XO would not be happy.

"Have fun?" she asked.

"Yeah, a blast," Axel said.

"Good, because it's time to get to work. Brayton found something for us."

Thirty-nine-year-old Chief Engineer and Technology Officer Brayton Jones walked over with a smart-pad. Next to him was the last member of their crew, a retrofitted war droid with only one arm that Axel had bought on the black market and restored. He programmed the once emotionless killing machine to adopt a personality, and it had emulated Spartacus, the ancient Thracian gladiator who had escaped slavery and fought the Roman Republic.

"Not a scratch, eh?" Spartacus said. "Right. Let me have a look at you."

The bulky black droid strode over on long legs. He leaned down, his hunched back and small head coming in close to examine Axel through electric blue eyes. A memory of what his mother had said to his aunt twenty years ago surfaced.

He can never see a doctor. No scans. No tests.

Those blue eyes flashed, running a basic medical scan over his body. Little did the rest of the crew know, Axel had programmed Spartacus to only run external scans, which would appear normal. He could only hope he never needed a more invasive treatment.

"Oh no, this isn't good," Spartacus suddenly said, making an electronic clicking sound to mimic a tongue.

"What? What's wrong?" Luna asked.

The droid tilted his head toward her. "I am sorry to inform everyone that the Captain has *severe* brain damage."

Axel had also programed Spartacus to have a sense of humor, though he sometimes regretted that decision. The droid broke out in his trademark chuckle. "He-heh, he-heh."

"Capa already had de brain damage. S'no other excuse to surf out there, no?" Uga said.

Spartacus rose back up to its full seven feet of gleaming metal. "Cricket's assessment is correct, Captain Finn, not a scratch on you, just a nasty bump on your noggin. You would have made a fine gladiator, with your strength and—"

"Luck," Luna said. She tossed a towel to Axel.

He caught it and wiped his face off. Then he looked at the screen Brayton brought over, noticing right away that the cargo manifest read *Classified*.

"A cargo ship went missing overnight, and whatever's on it is going to fetch whoever finds it a big payday," Brayton explained.

"It's not far," Luna added. "And that's lucky because this'll draw a lot of other salvagers, going after this contract."

"Only crazy ones willing to set course into an asteroid field," Spartacus said.

Cricket, Uga, and Luna all looked at Axel for his orders.

He tried to consider his options, but deep down, he knew there was only one. If he wanted to keep the *Trash Squid*, he had to take some risks.

"Get to your stations," he said. "Let's go find that ship."

As his crew moved out, Axel stood there thinking about the

dream sparked by hitting his head. It wasn't the first time. There had been several events in his adult life where injuries prompted these memories, and the voice.

He didn't understand them, and probably never would.

His entire life he'd believed he was just crazy. That nothing his mother had told him could ever fix him, and that was why she had sent him away. Because she knew the truth, that he was broken like those toys in the bunker.

He used to hate her for abandoning him, but he had accepted it as he got older, coming to the rational conclusion that it was to protect them both. But something told him that someday he would have to reckon with this demon inside of him —and with the monsters his mother had kept him hidden from all those years ago.

CHAPTER 2

The vast Hironia Star System had entered a time of peace, but the blood that coated the stars had never been forgotten.

For thirty-five years, humans had prepared for the return of the Wrath by building massive spaceships. Goliath Destroyers, heavily armed metal barges manned by AI and a skeleton crew of sailors, patrolled the sprawling system of planets. The Hammer Rail Guns and laser turrets stood ready to blast anything that emerged from unchartered space.

Orbital cannons guarded the colonial worlds as a second line of defense. In military camps on every continent, a new generation of soldiers trained to fight a foe they had never seen, instructed by aging warriors that had survived battles with the enemy.

Entire fleets of Ironclad warships and Warhorse transports had been constructed and were prepared to drop these soldiers into battle, should the mysterious Wrath ever emerge from the pitch black in which they had spawned.

Average citizens assumed that humanity was prepared to fight, but three decades without a major conflict had made the

Eagles of the Colonial Alliance Naval Defense Force (CANDF) complacent. Many of the young soldiers believed war would never come.

Twenty-six-year-old Sergeant Jacqueline "Jax" Brito was not one of them. Standing five-foot seven, she was one of the shortest members of Hatchet Platoon, made up of mostly men. She wasn't as strong as most of them, despite spending most of her free time in the weight room. Nor was she as fast. But she was the best shot, and what she lacked in height, and speed she made up with sheer determination.

Strong and steady was her motto. Something her farmer father had taught her at a young age. They called him the Ox for his size, strength, and steady speed, just like real life Oxen. The species was known for their strength and extremely hard work ethic, especially in difficult terrain. That was her dad to a T, never giving up no matter how hard things got. Jax had that same burning grit inside of her.

She stood in the shadows of a tunnel with Hatchet Platoon, waiting to start the march up the streets. Since she was young, she had wanted to join CANDF as an infantry Eagle. To fight for places like this, Aritrea, the capital city of the human world, Hex Prime.

"March!" commanded platoon Lieutenant Folkert.

The Eagles surged out of the tunnel. The rap of their heavy boots echoed up the cobblestone road that wound steeply toward the Bronze Keep built atop a massive bluff of rock that towered over the city.

Jax looked up at the cathedral reaching into the bright sky. Her visor tinted to help shield her eyes from the glow, allowing her a visual of the stone walls and parapets surrounding the keep. Pinus resinosa, red pines, a hundred-feet tall, grew in the halo shaped terraces jutting away from the fortress walls. The rounded green canopy swayed in the wind, carrying a fresh evergreen scent across the city streets below. Their hybrid seeds had been transported here from Earth, along with dozens of species, stored in vaults aboard the life barges. These long-range vessels had carried humanity from Earth, transplanting people and their trees to the sprawling Hironia System, which was already teeming with life on a handful of planets orbiting a sun in the Goldilocks zone that could sustain human life. Hex Prime was the largest, but there were others, like the mountainous planet of Azuri, the ocean world of Honi, the agriculture planet of Runi, and the Wooly world Dari that all boasted gravity, atmosphere, and temperatures similar to the old Earth. Fortunately for the first human colonists, the most advanced race in the system, the Corinns, had preferred warmer planets like Eern and Corinnia, located in the inner rim of the system.

Unfortunately for the Corinns, the Wrath had invaded those worlds first. The bulk of the survivors now lived in a space station, but some had moved to places like this city, which probably looked completely alien to them.

Architecturally, Aritrea looked like a medieval Earth city during a time of prosperity with its whitewashed stone walls, tiled and wooden shake roofs. There were parks with statues of great explorers, warriors, and politicians, water features, and verdant gardens. Each painstaking detail made this city feel ancient and beautiful.

The crowning stone fortress was as old as the Colonial Alliance, having just celebrated its five-hundred-year anniversary.

Today was another anniversary, the thirty-fifth year since the victory over the Wrath, and all across the colonies, citizens stood in the streets with their heads bowed and hands over their mouths to symbolize the silence of billions of souls that had perished during the invasion. Soon the city would erupt in celebration, but first, its people spent hours standing in silent remembrance.

Slowly, the Eagles marched up the streets, their visors reflecting the gaze of citizens who joined the festivities. Some stood on balconies or on the streets outside cozy cafes, eateries, and shops. Markas trotted along, their heads down, keeping to themselves. Woolies stood around in pairs or groups, their furry, squid-like arms gripping every sort of food and drink.

All eyes were on the white helmets and the black matte armor fashioned from high-grade Tani Flesh (T-Flesh), a durable, off-world-mined metal that bulwarked the Eagles. A pair of human teenagers pointed at the black automatic laser rifles equipped with barbed guard rails on the barrel that could crush a skull. Another kid gestured at the fire swords sheathed over Jax's back.

While they looked archaic, the Corinn-made weapons relied on a core energy source housed within the hilt, which channeled energy through a network of thermally conductive filaments woven up into the serrated blade. When activated, the filaments became so hot they created a thin plasma field around the blade, visible in a flaming effect that earned the weapon its name.

Jax felt pride as the Eagles entered a section of the city known as the "Road of Shadow" due to the draping canopy of gigantic ferns that blocked out most of the sunlight in the narrowing street.

Aritrea wasn't just the capital of Hex Prime, it was the capital of the Colonial Alliance. Hex Prime was the new Earth.

Jax had seen pictures of the home planet. She understood by the wastelands that dominated the surface why it wasn't habitable. She came from a third-generation family of farmers on an agriculture world called Runi, which was the next closest planet to Hex Prime in the Hironia System.

Runi was lush and bountiful like many places on Earth had once been. The peaceful planet was the human breadbasket of the system, but best known for a single crop called the Ash Root. The green plant looked like a tiny bonsai tree and was popular for its medicinal and health benefits.

Farmers on Runi were regarded as pacificists. They were kind people living hard lives. Generous people. The type that would help a stranger. What money was collected after a harvest first went to pay taxes to the Colonial Alliance, often leaving very little to pay for maintenance of droids, supplies, and money to support a family. Unfortunately, the past decade had seen years of damaged crops from invading insects that had hitched rides on transport ships.

No matter how hard her father worked to keep things going, he always fell behind. Jax felt a constant guilt for not being there to help, but she helped in another way by sending part of her monthly solar coins to her mother, who ran the farm finances. The extra funds helped pay for servicing the many droids, purchasing feed for the livestock, and everything else that went into the large operation. Her father was too prideful to accept coin from a child, and didn't know about their arrangement. He spent his days in the fields trying to keep the things running, working right next to the harvest droids.

Jax felt it was her duty as a child who had left home to become an Eagle instead of staying to help run the vast farm. Both of her parents had hoped she would reconsider her decision.

They viewed the Eagles as having deviated from protectors and peacekeepers into tax collectors who showed little respect for hardworking colonists, squeezing every drop they could from their own people, who were just trying to survive. It didn't matter that Eagles had cleaned up most of the pirates and hardened criminals that once had free rein in what was then an almost lawless system. Or that they were still there to put the scoundrels down when they emerged.

Jax had taken a few of them out herself, including a bounty hunter that had gone rogue. But people on worlds like Runi had a short memory. They had been far enough away from the Wrath invasion that it felt like they were safe.

But Jax knew that if the aliens returned, no planet would be safe.

The people on Hex Prime seemed to understand that. Even though it was the most protected human world, there was tension in the air. Many of the people in the streets were old enough to remember the invasion. Theirs was the nearest planet to the Corinn worlds that had burned in the attacks.

Every year near the anniversary, the same rumors about the Wrath returning spread like wildfire, building volume until the day came and went. Another anniversary devoid of the invaders. Those worries subsided, but never fully left. Especially for Jax. In her mind, it was better to prepare for the worst, than to fear it.

The platoon arrived at the Bronze Steps, a wide stone path that went up five hundred steps to the top terrace. Hundreds of Eagles marched their way up in unison, the rap of their boots echoing throughout the city. At the top, a sturdy bronze gate had opened to allow the soldiers onto a terrace replete with fountains, bronze statues, and rose gardens.

The office of the Galactic Minister, with its bronze columns and cathedral roof, stood straight ahead. On the right was the domed building supporting the parliament, and to the left, the three-story Castle of the Court.

Perfectly manicured red pines stood next to the buildings, providing shade from the blazing sun. In the center of the terrace, the largest fountain was centered in a pool of water surrounded by more of the bronze statues. She recognized some of the memorialized politicians, including the great Galactic Minister Giada, who had died a decade earlier.

There were statues of noble warriors too, Eagles who had earned their place here through valor in battle. Stone wings that in life contained energy capes protruded from their upper backs. These had replaced the monuments to the former guardians of the Colonial Alliance—the Stewards—who had been all but erased from history. In their stead, statues of men and women who had hunted them down, like Admiral Rex Jessup, were erected, obscuring evidence of the once elite soldiers who had defeated the Wrath.

Today, some of that evidence reemerged as memories. The elder population remembered cheering the warriors as they marched through the streets up to the Bronze Keep, just like Jax had done today.

History was an odd thing. A hero one day, a villain the next.

She didn't have any bold vision of earning a place on this terrace in the form of a statue. Jax was just proud to be here. Proud to be serving the Colonial Alliance and protecting those who could not defend themselves. Loyal, hardworking people like her family.

Hatchet Company moved down an aisle framed by other companies that had already arrived. Jax took up her place in the fifth row back from a raised platform.

A bell rang once, twice, then a third time. The chime echoed across the courtyard.

Every Eagle came to attention in unison, their boots thumping the ground with a tremor that vibrated over the keep as the brass arrived. Jax stared ahead, catching movement in her peripheral.

Four Royal Eagles escorted a man dressed in a blue suit with red shoulder plates. This was Admiral Rex Jessup, who had gained notoriety for fighting the Wrath, and then for hunting and eradicating the Stewards. Both accomplishments were represented by the medals on his chest. But he had paid deeply for one of those medals by losing one of his twin sons, Nathaniel, in the bloodiest battle against the Stewards, on the desert planet Furia, located in the inner rim. The young Eagle had been slain by the Lion of the Galaxy, Steward Captain Leon Kahr.

But by the time the battle was over, Kahr and his forces were dead. The last major Steward force erased from the ranks.

The eighty-five-year-old admiral mounted the raised platform and looked out over the thousands of Eagles gathered here. He was tall, with white hair slicked back, and gleaming blue eyes that swept over the warriors before him like a droid scanning them for injuries.

The double bronze doors of the Galactic Ministry offices swung open, and the Minister himself, Troy Goodwall, strode out in his black suit adorned by a bronze collar and cuffs. A dark brown beard with hints of gray clung to his cheeks. He was a fit man, his muscles pressing against the well-tailored suit.

This was the closest Jax had ever been to the minister, probably the closest she would ever be again. That her unit had been selected to be here today was an extreme honor.

Goodwall stepped up onto the podium with Admiral Jessup just behind him.

"We all know why we're here today," Goodwall said in the smooth, rehearsed voice of a politician. "Thirty-five years ago, a fleet of black ships emerged from the abyss. Admiral Jessup and hundreds of thousands of Eagles stood and met these foes, fighting against the abominations until we pushed them back into the darkness in which they bred. We mark this day to remember those lost, and to celebrate victory. But this year...this year is different."

He stepped back from the podium and lifted his bearded

chin toward the sky. As if in answer, a squadron of three Bloodhogs roared across the horizon. The fighters curved toward the city. The thin, but well armored ships were the pride and joy of the Colonial Alliance Navy, some of the most versatile fighters ever designed.

They blasted overhead, leaving a red trail across the blue sky to symbolize those lost.

As Jax began to look away, another squadron of fighters shot across the sky. But these weren't Bloodhogs. These were Lancers. *Corinn* Lancers.

Several Eagles around Jax shifted where they stood. Others mumbled in hushed voices, confused. The purple two-wing fighters flew over Aritrea for the first time… ever.

Minister Goodwall moved back to the podium.

"Thirty-five years ago, we were allies of the Corinns," he announced. "We faced the Wrath together, and today we are announcing a new partnership that will ensure we never lose another soul to the aliens—should they dare return."

Jax felt her heart kick, not from pride, but fear. She wasn't ashamed to feel it, either. Perhaps there was something more to the rumors this year—perhaps those who whispered them knew something she didn't. Was it possible the Wrath were coming back to finish what they had started?

She had prepared so many years for this day, but she wasn't sure she was ready, or that CANDF and their Corinn allies were ready.

Clanking echoed in the distance. Jax resisted the urge to turn around and look for the source. She didn't have to wait long before the stomping of boots and clatter of armor moved down the aisle toward the platform.

A legion of Eagles in modified, bulky T-Flesh armored suits with red shoulder plates and helmets strode past. Leading them was Admiral Jessup's surviving twin son, Gabriel. The general was dressed in matte gray armor, mounted in the saddle of a robotic horse with red eyes.

Jax couldn't help but turn slightly to stare at the infamous Dark Horse Company. They had earned fame under then General Rex Jessup during the Wrath Invasion. And of course, when they had hunted the Stewards down.

In the years since, DHC had become best known for their brutal tactics, putting down rebellions, collecting taxes, and taking out any perceived threat to the Colonial Alliance with extreme prejudice.

These were the most feared Eagles in the galaxy, and the soldiers her own parents despised for their brutality. Jax had mixed feelings. On the one hand, they had done a vast amount of good, but on the other, they had left a trail of corpses, sometimes innocent people who simply got caught in their crossfire, or their crosshairs.

General Gabriel Jessup stopped his horse, removing his helmet from a long, square face with piercing blue eyes that matched his father's.

"My son Gabriel, General of Dark Horse Company, will lead the new Colonial Alliance Expeditionary *Defense* Legion," Rex said in a gruff, aged voice. "But don't let that name confuse you. If the Wrath return, we will be on the offensive, striking at them hard on first contact."

Jax held her head high, shaking away her trepidation and fear. She would stand her ground no matter what evil came from the darkness of space. To protect people like her family, their homes, their lands from burning.

She watched in awe as Admiral Jessup drew a long-bladed fire sword, clicking a tactile button on the hilt to activate the core. A lustrous plasma sheath lit up brightly around the razor edge.

He raised the glowing sword over his son and thousands of Eagles.

Jax drew her own blade, clicked the button, and angled the flaming tip toward the sky, repeating after the admiral who now yelled the war motto that had started thirty-five years ago:

"We guard the gates of Hell and strike with the vengeance of a thousand worlds!"

The shouts echoed across the Bronze Keep and the city below, fading away at last to silence.

CHAPTER 3

"We're the first ones here," said Luna. She was busy studying radar monitors on the port side of the bridge. "Ready for a look, Captain?"

Axel nodded.

The meter-thick shields covering the viewports on the oval-shaped bridge of the *Trash Squid* lowered, revealing the sprawling asteroid field. Rocks of all sizes, many much larger than the ship, spun across the view.

Axel sat in his cracked leather chair, his long hair still wet from surfing. He held the flight controls, expertly guiding them around the exterior of the belt at a safe distance. Somewhere inside, the cargo vessel *Cyprus* had gone missing the night before. Fortunately for the *Trash Squid*, they'd been close to the last known location and had arrived here just hours after Axel got out of the water.

He was still a bit shaken up—more from hearing that demonic voice in his head than from hitting his head on the rock—but he had to push that all aside for now.

This was the opportunity he had been waiting for. With his finances a mess, success was imperative. He had to find the ship and tug it out of the asteroid belt or remove whatever classified loot was on it.

The slow dance of tumbling rocks was soothing to Axel, but it had everyone else on edge.

Uga, Luna, Cricket, and Brayton all watched from their stations, staring anxiously.

"Drop me here. I not go through that, okay?" Uga barked in his deep voice.

"A gladiator does not fear death," Spartacus said. He raised his arm and balled his skeletal fingers. "They embrace it through strength and honor."

"Food and wine," Uga grumbled back while grabbing his stomach.

"Cut the banter. I need to think," Axel said firmly. He took a few moments, then rotated his chair to Brayton. "Have you located the *Cyprus*?"

"Still searching for it," Brayton said. He scratched at his puffy hair, a sign he was getting agitated. "And trying to figure out what's so important inside that cargo hold."

Axel had complete faith in his Chief Engineer and Technology Officer, whose checkered past included being one of the top human hackers in the galaxy. Those skills had earned him multiple offers to work for the infamous Colonial Alliance Intelligence Division (CAID), the top agency of the Colonial Alliance military. But Brayton had chosen a life of adventure over what he had told Axel would have been a life as a wage slave.

As Brayton worked, he tapped his favorite pair of red sneakers against the deck. He didn't look much like a stereotypical nerd hacker. The young man spent as much time on the ship's treadmill and lifting weights as he did behind a HoloMatrix screen—and it showed. He was solid ropey muscle with a square jaw.

"What I know is the transponder for the *Cyprus* went offline out there about ten hours ago, but they did not issue an SOS," Brayton said.

"Means whatever happened, must have happened fast," Luna said.

"Maybe." Brayton didn't sound convinced at all. Axel wasn't either, but it was too early to guess what might have happened. Could have been an asteroid, pirates, a mutiny? It was a big universe. The possibilities were literally endless.

"What were they doing out there in the first place?" Luna asked.

Another good question, Axel thought. From his experience, a captain that risked going into an asteroid belt was hiding or searching. Both indicated trouble.

They were taking a major risk, and that was probably the reason they were the first crew to arrive. But it was this or chase a bounty that could end up getting one of them shot—or worse. None of his crew were trained to bring in fugitives, they were trained to run salvage missions, and a decade of working together had made them damned good at it.

"Idea," Uga barked. "Why don't we send Sparty in there? Gladiators not fear, no? Probably not fear big space rocks either."

Spartacus raised his arm at Uga, balling robotic fingers. That fist had no doubt killed many times before the droid had ended up in a black market junk pile. Axel had reprogrammed Spartacus to kill only in order to protect the crew of the *Trash Squid*, which meant he would never harm Uga, and the Wooly knew it.

"Get that metal mitt away from me," Uga barked as he leaned away. "You really need to wipe some of that aggression, Capa, he's psycho!"

"He-heh," Spartacus said. Then he lowered his arm and

looked to Axel. "I hope you won't consider this blasphemy, but you simply don't mess with art."

"Nobody's reprogramming anybody around here, okay? And Sparty's not going into the blender," Axel said. He paused for a moment before adding, "I'm going."

Everyone turned from the view of the asteroids to Axel.

"I'll take the *Hammerhead*," he said. "Once I locate the *Cyprus*, I'll send the coordinates back and Spartacus will chart a course to get the *Trash Squid* there safely."

"*If* you locate it. I know you're an excellent pilot, and the *Hammerhead* is agile, but if you hit something..." Luna said.

"I won't."

"Chances of you surviving in the *Hammerhead* are..." Spartacus did some unsolicited calculations as his blue eyes studied the belt. "Fifty-one percent."

"Over half, I'll take it," Axel said. He was confident in his piloting and was eager to get to the wreck before someone else.

"We're wasting time," he said. "XO, you have the bridge."

The tap of four webbed paws followed him out of the hatch. He turned to Cricket, his normal co-pilot. "Don't play the 'I'm going alone' game again,'" chirped the Marka. "If you'd had your way back on Honi, you'd be fish food."

Axel smiled and jerked his chin.

Uga got off his raised stool, gripping his furry pannus hanging over his belt with two arms as a growl resonated through the bridge.

"Where are you going?" Axel asked.

The stench that drifted off the Wooly as he waddled away implied the alien's nerves had gotten the best of him.

"You should consider eating less," Spartacus said.

"And you should consider speaking less, mech-man," Uga barked back. "This beautiful, athletic body requires a lotta nutrition, but thank you for concern."

"He-heh, athletic by the standards of old Earthers, perhaps. Some of those fatties could hardly move."

"I move like lightning!" Uga raised all his arms at once and spun around. As he twirled a third time, he tripped and fell to the deck.

"Owie, owie, boo-boo!" he roared, holding an arm.

"Very impressive, he-heh."

"Guys, come on," Axel said. "You okay, Uga?"

Uga cursed something about dumb metal nuts as he climbed back into his seat.

Spartacus shrugged his large, curved shoulders. "I have said my piece. Not my problem if Uga eats through the rest of our supplies. I will not starve."

Though the droid spoke in jest, supplies were a problem constantly on Axel's mind, being so low on food. Wooly appetites were a difficult thing to satisfy, and Cricket, who doubled as the ship's cook, was often exhausted trying to keep Uga full. The Wooly species had incredibly fast metabolisms, requiring six meals a day—one for each arm, was the galactic joke.

Axel and Cricket left the bridge with Uga. The alien squeezed into the closest head and hardly had the hatch shut before he let it rip.

"That's your fault," Axel said to Cricket.

"*Me?* I don't force him to eat everything in sight," Cricket chirped. "Besides, I think Spartacus got on his nerves. Uga's definitely got IBS."

Axel laughed and ducked to avoid the bulkhead he had hit too many times to count. Switching from boots to sandals years ago had helped.

Loose power cables hanging down from the exposed maintenance tunnels were the next thing he had to avoid. They had been in the process of installing new cabling before they ran out of funds. It was one of many things that needed replacing on the run-down ship.

Axel didn't care that the vessel looked like something you'd find in a junkyard, or in the dusty warehouse of some rich mining tycoon who collected archaic warships, then forgot about them. This was his pride and joy.

His home.

They made their way through the aft section, entering a hatch that opened to a large cargo hold. Axel pictured the fifty Eagles that would have once waited in here with their two all-terrain armored vehicles, when the *Trash Squid* had been a military transport, moving special forces in and out of hostile zones.

His crew had retrofitted the expansive space for their cargo and salvaging equipment, which included cable winches, two mech-suits covered in graffiti, and a mini-mining crawler rig with drilling equipment.

Originally the bay was equipped with middle-range armor, but Spartacus had removed much of it, allowing them to be more maneuverable when not in FTL travel. On days like today, Axel would have taken the extra armor over the extra speed.

But that was why he was taking the Tech-N fighter, aka the *Hammerhead*. He walked through the cargo hold packed with chained down equipment to a connecting corridor. The ladder to the combat ship wasn't far. First, though, Axel had to swap out his uniform, or his version of one: sandals, blue t-shirt, and shorts for his dented armored space suit, boots, and helmet.

He folded the t-shirt so that their logo (the stocky six-armed Wooly smoking a cigar stick and holding grenades) faced up.

As Axel dressed, he pictured the salvage run that had given Luna the idea for the logo. It went down five years ago, on a desert world called Ori. They'd had to blow through the hull of a ship partially buried in a mound of sand. Uga had burned half his facial hair off and was covered in soot. Axel still smiled about it from time to time.

Once he finished getting into his flight suit, he took the ladder extending up a vertical tunnel to the *Hammerhead*. Cricket followed him up to the top, where Axel popped the hatch to the two-seater cockpit.

Two laser turrets were attached to the dual wings, which had earned the ship its name. Axel used to wonder how many lives those turrets had claimed during her service. He had used the weapons a handful of times, but never to kill.

Might need them today, he thought.

As he climbed into the seat, he activated the weapons, just in case he needed to nudge any asteroids out of his path. He put his headset on and flipped the switches across the dashboard. Once all systems were online, he tapped the screen in front of him.

"XO, you copy?" he said.

"Copy, Cap. All systems look good from our end," she said.

"Good to go. Preparing to eject in three, two, one..."

Axel hit the button, resulting in two heavy clicks from the attached locks, and the *Hammerhead* drifted off the main ship. He gripped the yoke and then turned the vertical thrusters to horizontal. The combat craft blasted backward from the *Trash Squid*, providing a view over the much larger transport ship.

From the outside, it looked rough from the damage it had sustained in war, and because salvaging was a rough job. Dents from space debris and laser rounds marked the orange exterior like scars and scabs. He hoped to avoid any further damage today.

While she looked like a trashcan on the outside, beneath the hood, she had a modified engine that made her one of the fastest ships in the galaxy at speeds below FTL.

The *Hammerhead* wasn't too shabby either. He steered the

small fighter toward the asteroid belt. Cricket chirped rapidly as the stern rotated toward the vast stretch of tumbling asteroids.

"That's a lot of rocks," Cricket chirped. "But you're the Commendatore, don't forget that."

Axel smiled. The creature was kind, funny, and loyal. Sometimes he found it remarkable how much Markas were like Earth dogs.

Cricket was part of the family and a valuable member of the crew as the chef and assistant to maintenance issues. Not to mention a companion for Axel on his adventures.

This would be one for the books.

"Here we go," Axel said. "Hold on to your tails, pal."

The thrusters blasted them toward the asteroid belt. Where some pilots might feel a twinge of trepidation, Axel felt the rush of adrenaline. He knew the tempered glass wouldn't do much to protect him, that a direct impact with a large rock would leave him a smear on its side, but he trusted his skills as a pilot.

Axel entered the belt, experience taking over as object indicators popped onto his visual display. He used the device in conjunction with his own eyes and instincts to weave around the larger rocks. Smaller pieces pinged against the hull like a heavy rain.

As the *Hammerhead* flew deeper into the belt and obstacles became denser, his focus narrowed to calculated precision. He carefully dodged the biggest pieces until there was nowhere else to go.

Grabbing the controls, he prepared to activate the turrets. Blasting one of the big bastards to pieces would be expensive, but maybe a quick burst might nudge them out of the way.

Lining up a shot to the bottom corner of the largest rock, he fired.

"Pinching pennies, Commendatore?" Cricket chirped. "I didn't realize we were that broke."

Axel squeezed off another burst with clenched teeth, trying to figure out how to explain they were beyond poor, they were in a hole so deep he couldn't see the top.

The red laser bolts lanced through the darkness, slamming against the bottom of the rock and finally pushing it out of the flight path.

Cricket chirped as an asteroid the size of a CANDF Warhorse transport ship tumbled toward them from behind the one they had just moved. This one was way too big to move.

Instead, Axel rolled away, diving below it—right toward another boulder. He jerked the controls, turning them upside down and then roaring upward. They shot past the tail end of the mammoth asteroid they had just dived under. A proximity alert warning blared, and Axel fired both turrets at a rock the size of the *Hammerhead* coming right at them. The flurry of rounds slammed into the rock, bursting it into hundreds of chunks. They shot through the debris, pieces clanking across the cockpit.

"So much for pinching pennies," Cricket chirped.

"Yup, kind of gave up on that to avoid becoming pulverized space dust," Axel replied with a chuckle.

Cricket raised a gloved paw at something off their port side.

"Look over there!" he chirped.

Axel rotated the fighter. Beams illuminated yellow and black shards. It took only a second to see this was no asteroid—this was, or had been, a ship.

"I got eyes on a wreck," Axel reported over the team comms. "Standby."

Using the thrusters, Axel maneuvered closer toward the aft section of a gold ship. It was much smaller than the *Trash Squid*, but that was because it was split in half.

He pulled up to the cockpit, where the glass viewports had shattered. Only ten feet away, Axel could see the pilot still strapped into the seat, his face distorted in shock from the freezing vacuum of space—or perhaps from something that had happened before the glass broke.

"Poor lug," Cricket chirped. "Looks like he was taking a painful shit when they hit that asteroid. Maybe that's what caused it?"

Axel couldn't help but chuckle, but quickly grew serious out of respect for the crew that could have been his own. There was nothing funny about dying out here.

"Sorry, mate," Axel whispered.

He focused his attention on the ship. Judging from the damage, the *Cyprus* had hugged the asteroid.

"Wait a second," Axel said. As they coasted farther, he read a different name on the aft of the vessel.

"Wreckage is not our target," he said into the comm. "This is the *Gold Fish*."

There was a brief delay in the response.

"Copy. Any survivors?" Luna replied.

Axel rotated the thrusters again, but there was no way someone could have survived this impact. "One popsicle, but that's all I can see," he said. "We'll keep searching."

After another temporary delay, Luna came over the comms. "Copy, umm," she replied. It seemed like she wanted to say something else, but she held her tongue, trusting that Axel knew what he was doing.

He looked over at Cricket.

"Guess we weren't the first ones to come for the *Cyprus* after all," Axel said.

Cricket nodded slowly as they pulled away from the wreckage.

"Poor bastards," Axel said.

He turned the *Hammerhead* and flew deeper into the belt.

"You sure about this?" Cricket chirped. "I trust your piloting, I mean, you're the Commendatore, and all, but..."

Axel studied the sprawling field of rocks. Somewhere out there, the *Cyprus* held the key to their financial salvation. But it wouldn't be any good if they ended up like the crew of the *Gold Fish,* which had been after the same loot.

"We came this far, but if you want to turn around, I'll understand," Axel said.

Cricket shook his head. "It's okay, just don't shit your pants, and I'm sure we'll be fine."

Laughing, Axel pushed down on the thrusters and blasted back into the field.

CHAPTER 4

At midnight, under the dense cloud cover blocking out all three moons of the planet Azuri, a small, curved ship flew toward a mountain range. The vessel was named the *Nicane*, according to transponder codes, but those were forged. The real name was the *Beak*.

It descended into the blue fog using near-silent conical thrusters. Landing pads extended from the black hull onto the rock with a muffled thump. A dorsal hatch opened, and a man shrouded in a brown, weather-worn duster climbed out onto the stern in a confident, but slightly bowed stance, an effect of countless injuries over the years. Wind blew his gray beard and dreadlocks of gray hair, exposing a missing right ear. Piercing blue eyes swept over the terrain.

He secured a helmet over his head and then shrugged off the duster. After folding it neatly, he placed it back into the ship. Then he jumped down to the rocks, his vacuum rated suit shifting from black to gray to match the terrain. Bulwarking his chest and abdomen was a T-Flesh rig, mottled with plenty of scars from relentless use. Armored wrist and leg guards showed more signs of wear and tear. Each piece encompassed an exoskeleton vital to help him move in a variety of environments and gravity.

His birth name was Rangnar Soki, but he had an alias, like his ship. Most people that he encountered knew him simply as "Phantom."

Some would say it was a miracle he had stayed alive fifty-eight years. It certainly was an amazing achievement for a bounty hunter. Especially a human. Most didn't make it to see their forties. But this man was different—this man lived by a code, what he called his "Five Death Rules."

Number 1: *Never* trust a human.

Rangnar had survived into his middle age partly due to hiring a crew of Markas, who were loyal beyond question. Three of them had joined him today and were preparing the gear inside the *Beak*.

They had landed here to extract, some might say *steal*, Wrath technology that had been recovered from one of their buried ships and then smuggled into Lark territory. Those smugglers had gone missing, probably killed by Larks who were reportedly seen moving the Wrath tech into one of their mounds. Or so said the intel he had paid a hunk of solars for from a Wooly bounty hunter named Circa.

Circa, like most bounty hunters, preferred to take the solars rather than attempt this heist.

"You crazy," Circa had barked when Rangnar purchased the intel. "You will die and end up Lark shit."

That was entirely possible. The Lark mound he had to penetrate was guarded by hundreds of drones, and not the metal crafts powered by AI that fired missiles from the sky. These drones were Lark female warriors who could fly and were driven by a single purpose: to protect their colony. This specific mound was a monstrosity, easily ten stories high, carved out of the rust-colored hills at the base of the mountains.

Rangnar had landed above and couldn't see it now because of the perpetual blue fog obscuring the way down. He knew better than to approach the bottom, where the drones lurked. For some reason, they avoided the fog. Perhaps because of the chemicals that colored the steam venting from the inner core of the mountains. Or maybe they were simply superstitious about it.

The Larks were an odd species, considered to be the fourth or fifth most intelligent in the Hironia System, depending on whom you asked. Some "scholars" would rate humans that far down the brain chain, although Rangnar believed them to be a close second, right behind Corinns.

Personally, he thought Larks were the dumbest and most brutal of all the "intelligent" species. He knew them well enough to make that decision, having lived on their home world of Azuri for a decade and having traveled the entire Hironia System extensively over his life.

In the cities on Azuri, the Larks followed galactic laws for self-preservation, and in that sense, they were smart. But out here, in their territory, those laws didn't apply. The Lark drones would kill you on sight. The Larks were granted this reserve not long after waves of human colonists had moved in, three and a half centuries ago.

Larks only lived twenty-five years on average, but they had excellent memories, and held animosity toward their conquerors.

Any alien, especially a human, who approached a Lark mound could expect to be speared by their razor-sharp claws or their six-inch fangs. A bite released a unique poison that paralyzed the victim, allowing the Lark drone to rip their prey apart.

Not pretty. Rangnar had seen it happen.

It would not happen to him, though. He fully planned on living up to his nickname today with the help of his Marka companions, Lucid, Saber, Nuke, and Billy Bob. The four-legged creatures trotted down the ramp of their vessel, carrying packs and climbing gear. Each wore a heat-reducing suit with camouflage and light boots to further mask the sound of their webbed feet.

They were expert hunters with excellent vision and sense of smell, and muscular bodies that could run faster than the extinct species on Earth known as cheetahs. It was only modifications to his aging, chronically injured body that allowed Rangnar to hunt with them. Artificial hips and knees helped him keep up, and gel pads reduced his pain. Contact lenses enhanced his vision, allowing him to see in the dark, and he could zoom in or out with a few blinks. An auditory system was threaded in his dreadlocks behind his ears. The tiny speakers allowed him to amplify sound, such as the buzzing coming from the Lark mound thousands of feet below them.

"All set, boss," Nuke chirped. He was a giant creature with bulging muscles, and Rangnar thought of him as a large pit bull, though he'd never say that to Nuke's face.

Then there was Billy Bob, the huskiest crewmember by far, with a belly that hung close to the ground and chubby cheeks. Billy loved to eat and had an appetite that could match a Wooly's.

Saber, on the other hand, was long and lean, with ropey muscles and glistening metal canines. He was a calculated killer.

Rangnar whistled to Lucid. She was the fastest of the three and vanished into the fog to scout out a path down the mountain while he did a weapons check.

Hand cannon (a holstered laser pistol), check.

Two sheathed fire hatchets that could cut through metal, check.

"Nuke," Rangnar said.

The Marka had just finished snapping a long-range laser rifle into a single piece. He tossed it to Rangnar, who caught it. With an attached scope that connected to his heads-up display, the thing practically fired itself.

Next, Nuke tossed out a drum containing the cable they would need to get Rangnar from the trail down to the mound. He snapped the drum onto the rifle, then attached the firing spear to the barrel. By the time he finished his weapons and gear prep, Lucid had returned, chirping.

"I found a path," she said. "All clear to the mound, but I count thirty drones at the bottom."

"We should have brought more firepower," Saber said.

"Not going to need it," Nuke replied. "We're gonna be Phantoms, like the boss here."

"All of us but Billy Bob," Saber said.

"Fat but fast," Billy chirped back.

"True, but I'd like you to stay back with Saber at the *Beak*," Rangnar said. "Lucid and Nuke, you're with me."

"Come on," Saber whispered.

"Want a snack?" Billy asked. "I've got some jerky back in the hold."

Saber grunted. "Surprised you're not trying to eat Lark."

"Who says I'm not saving that for dessert?"

Rangnar chuckled as he headed out with Nuke and Lucid into the fog. She had left a trail of glowing gel to lead the way down the rough terrain. The trail would be invisible to the Larks because of their sensitivity to light. They couldn't see nearly as well in the dark as humans, but it was a fair evolutionary trade-off for their 360 vision.

Rangnar used the light to guide him around the loose, sharp rocks. Steam vented from cracks along the path as boiling teal liquid bubbled in pots of raised orange dirt with veins of yellow.

Everywhere, the blue fog rolled off from the mixture of cold air hitting the heated chemical water.

The buzzing grew louder during the trek, as if they were about to enter a swarm of bees. As they carefully navigated the mountainside, the fog dissipated. Rangnar's contact lenses provided a green-hued visual of the mound below. Lips of dirt platforms protruded from tunnels in the honeycombed side of the mound. A steady flow of male workers buzzed out below. They looked harmless enough, frail bodies, no claws.

Then he saw one of the female drones flying inside the blackness.

Four wings buzzed behind her humped back. In front, the six-foot-tall insect-like creature had four arms and twice that many breasts hanging on her wrinkled chest. It was an ugly being with carmine leathery flesh capped with chitinous armor over joints. Three hairy trunks were attached to its jaw. Compound eyes on stalks allowed them their three-hundred-and-sixty-degree view.

Fortunately for Rangnar and his Marka hunters, those eyes would have a hard time seeing them moving, which is why they'd waited until dark. Lark vision, like their intelligence, provided no special offense, but the claws and fangs of a drone could kill the most elite galactic warrior.

You're not gonna get close enough, sweetheart, he thought.

Rangnar raised his wrist computer and brought up the time schedules he had calculated by watching the drones when he'd scouted the area days earlier. The fearsome bugs operated like clockwork, and each was assigned to multiple entrances in the mound. When one shift was up, they rotated to their next station, leaving temporarily unguarded entry points as the changes were made.

That gave him seconds to get inside without being seen. Once there, he could move freely in the nearly pitch black interior. As long as he didn't make a sound, he would get in and out with ease.

He aimed his rifle at the top of the mound and fired. The wire uncoiled and the tip speared into the dirt.

With a strong yank, he confirmed it was secure, then handed the weapon to Nuke to hold steady. The Marka had already set out a cable rider from his pack. After clicking it into place, Rangnar wasted no time. He kicked off, sliding down the cable to the curved top of the mound, five hundred feet below. As soon as his boots slammed against the hard, clay-like dirt, his suit took on a rusty color, a perfect match. He unhooked from the cable and got onto his stomach with his pistol in hand, just in case his landing had attracted any hostiles.

The buzzing now formed a solid din that was hard to track. For all he knew, there was a Lark drone just ten feet over the edge—or not for a hundred. He waited a few seconds, got up, and walked over for a look. Below, a train of male Larks buzzed out of their tunnels, zooming off into the forest.

A tap of his boots activated his climbing spikes, then a pull to activate the tiny nanoparticle hairs on his gloves, allowing him to cling to surfaces, much like a chameleon.

Lucid slid down as soon as he gave the all clear. She landed without making a sound. Nuke remained on the bluff with the sniper rifle, ready to extract them or headshot any drone that reared its ugly face.

Getting down on his knees, Rangnar looked over the edge, hoping not to see one of them, but there it was, a winged monstrosity guarding the top tunnel entrance he had selected from his scouting missions.

He pulled back to check his clock. If his calculations were right, it would be two more minutes. The seconds ticked by, and just before the mark, he looked again, watching as the beast buzzed away to the next position.

"Go time," Rangnar whispered.

He turned around and began the twenty-foot climb down the side of the mound with the wind whistling across his body. Lucid followed, and together they entered the tunnel shaft. The outside was dusty, but the inside became damper and more humid with each step.

Buzzing sounded behind them from the next shift approaching their station. The female Lark drone landed at the tunnel lip and climbed inside faster than he had expected. Rangnar flattened his body against the moist wall while Lucid curled up.

The drone strode inside, wings folding inward. All three of the ribbed, hairy trunks peeled away from its wrinkled face, the mouthed ends sniffing the air while both compound eyes searched the darkness from tiny stalks. Rangnar stared right at those eyes, confident they wouldn't be able to see him.

He was right. The stems rotated the orbs in the other direction, but the hairy trunks remained wiggling outward.

Can it smell me and Lucid? he wondered.

Their hearing was far superior to their vision. Maybe that was it—maybe the sentry had picked up an unfamiliar noise.

Rangnar held in a breath and slowly reached over his shoulder, touching a sheathed fire hatchet, prepared to use that silent weapon over his pistol. The creature stepped toward him, tilted its head, made a clicking noise, and then turned away.

The wings fluttered, launching it back into the night.

Rangnar didn't waste time flashing a hand signal to Lucid. She rose from the dirt and kept moving, leaving behind the gel path so they could find their way out. Using her excellent vision, she guided him through an intersection, taking a right. Another passage curved into a second junction. This time they went left. The journey took them into a variety of different-sized labyrinths, caves, and passages.

The current tunnel had ribbed walls covered in some sort of fungus. Lucid trekked through another intersection, halting at the end of the passage to the sound of running water. Slowly, she advanced with Rangnar to an edge that overlooked the central chamber of the hollow mound. A waterfall was the source of the noise they had heard. It rushed out of a gap across from them, pouring into a stream that formed a moat around the bottom of the chamber.

Larks drank with their trunks, filling up their humped backs to transport the water to their offspring. The tiny Larklings were all housed in smaller honeycomb mounds across the clay floor, and there were various other mounds, some with foreign-looking objects protruding from them.

Rangnar pulled out his scanner and set it to detect the minerals in Wrath tech. Sure enough, the fuel rod was down there in a pile of dirt. This was their dumping ground, where they discarded everything, including their feces.

This should be fun.

He motioned for Lucid to follow him down the hundred-foot drop to the bottom. She rolled all four of her eyes and sighed.

Halfway down, a drone flew overhead, shrieking.

Rangnar clung to the wall. Frozen, he carefully glanced up at the creature. It lowered to a mound he hadn't seen from above. The drone landed outside the only hole in the exterior but did not enter. Out of that hole came two Lark heads attached to the same body.

This was their leader, the father and mother of every Lark in the kingdom.

Rangnar felt his first chill of fear since arriving. If that thing somehow saw him and Lucid, they would be in a world of trouble.

He considered climbing back up and fleeing after considering his death rules.

Number 2: *Never risk your life for loot.*

Perhaps most people would say he broke that rule every time he laced up his boots. But they would be wrong—or so he hoped.

Seconds ticked by. With each one his gut told him to abandon the mission. Right as he was about to dump the job and start climbing back up, the King-slash-Queen ducked back into its mound. The drone flew off with whatever orders it had received.

Rangnar and Lucid finished their descent. He moved at a hunch, keeping to the wall and following the stream that he would have to cross to get to the Lark dump. As he got closer, his scan revealed the rod was inside a ten-foot-tall mound. Steam rose from one side where a maintenance Lark had just dumped feces.

This was gonna be gross, but he had to prove the Wooly bounty hunter, Circa, wrong. Rangnar "Phantom" Soki wasn't dying down here.

He followed the water until he was right across from the mound.

Here goes nothing.

With a running head start, he jumped. As he sailed over the eight-foot gap, he saw the mud on the other side, but by then it was too late. He landed and slid, falling on his back with a gurgling splash.

Clacking answered as three smaller figures walked around one of the honeycombed mounds next to the dumps. The Lark children bent down to investigate the noise, their compound eyes roving and trunks flickering.

Lucid prowled across the stream, ready to pounce, but Rangnar raised a finger to keep her from attacking. The eldest of the three creatures was a female, obvious by her size compared to the smaller males. She came within a foot of his boots, leaning down to sniff with her trunks.

Rangnar closed his eyes, unable to watch.

When he opened them, she was directly over him. Lucid didn't wait another second. She sprang across from midstream. By the time the eyes of the young Lark drone spotted movement, Lucid had knocked it to the ground. The other two turned to flee but got only a foot away before her two tails whipped out, wrapping around their necks and yanking them to the mud.

Rangnar pushed himself up and ran for the mound, throwing his gloves to the side and punching through to search for the Wrath fuel rod while Lucid restrained the Larklings. He knew he had only moments to find it. Desperate, he dug through the organic matter until finally, he found a hard object.

"Yes," he whispered.

He wiped off a... rock.

"Dammit," he said.

It went over his shoulder.

Rangnar reached back in, pulling out two more hunks of rock before he found a piece of the Wrath ship. It wasn't what he was looking for, but it told him his sensor was right. He punched back inside, moving systematically around the base of the mound. Goo and grit coated his suit, warming his body. Feces smeared across his faceplate.

Arsed-face alien twats!

Getting frustrated, he resisted the urge to curse out loud. The digging continued until he felt something solid and spiked. A prideful smile formed on his bearded face.

He pulled out the log and wiped it free, revealing a cylindrical metal object with spikes in a perfect circle around three sections. The smile fully formed now. This tech was a fuel rod with four crystals inside that were from another galaxy. Extremely precious treasure, indeed.

"Hell yes," he whispered. He should have had a Death Rule for premature celebration.

Shrieking came from over the mound in sync with a chirp warning from Lucid.

It was almost too late.

Rangnar backed up just as a clawed arm swooped down, narrowly missing his helmet. He smacked the drone that dove onto him, hitting it in the face with the cylinder. The three trunks peeled back to expose a mouth full of fangs. One of those fangs bit down and pierced the arm holding the rod, sinking deep into the muscle.

In that instant, all he could think was that Circa had been right after all—he was gonna die in this Lark shit mound.

But not without a fight.

Rangnar pulled out a hatchet, activating the core with the click of a button on the hilt. The weapon instantly warmed hot enough to ionize the air and create a field of brilliant plasma around the blade.

He swung it into the side of the wrinkled face. Simmering fluid squirted out. He withdrew it as the creature reared back, tentacle-like trunks whipping at his face. He slashed with the blade, severing two of the hairy appendages. By now, his other arm was already going numb and the poison entering his bloodstream forced him to drop the cylinder.

He used the crest of his helmet to smash the beast back to the ground.

"Stupid," he said with a swing of his hatchet that hit it in the chest. "Ugly," he said with another swing that took off an arm. "Alien. Bitch!" The third hack severed the head.

Chest heaving, he stumbled away from the carcass and deactivated the blade. The internal cooling mechanisms clicked on, and it was ready to go back into its sheath. He went straight for his med-pack next, pulling out a syringe the length of his middle finger. He found the wound and jammed the needle right through the bleeding fang holes and into his poisoned flesh.

The pain was masked only by the fear of what would happen if the poison spread. This wouldn't stop it altogether, but it should slow it down long enough to get to his ship.

He hoped.

As he tossed the hypo and leaned down to scoop up the cylinder, a wave of lightheadedness hit.

"Ah, thunder tits," Rangnar muttered.

His knees gave out, and he collapsed to the ground. Lucid released the three children, who scrambled away.

"Don't let them getttt...rphm..." Rangnar grumbled, his words turning to gibberish.

Lucid whipped the drone with a tail, sending the juvenile crashing into the mound of feces. As it slumped off the side, she barreled over to Rangnar, nudging up under him. He flung his good arm over her back, and, holding the Wrath treasure, he let her take over.

The powerful Marka bolted away, hurdled across the stream, and jumped onto the vertical mound wall. She clambered up the side, Rangnar hanging onto her and the cylinder with all his strength.

By the time the first alarm shrieked from the drone guards, they were back in the tunnel. Rangnar had lost all feeling on his right side now, and his neck tightened. He had to get back to the ship—back to the meds.

"Sabbberr, Bill—y," he mumbled through numb lips. "Need evac."

"Copy," chirped Saber.

Faint buzzing came from the chamber, but Rangnar knew it

was his failing senses. The buzzing wasn't faint. Lark drones were already closing in on Lucid's two tails. The tunnel narrowed as Rangnar's vision dimmed.

He focused on the end of the passage, where moonlight had broken through the cloud cover. His vision blurred further.

Stay awake, man, stay awake.

His chest tingled, the poison closing in on his heart. He couldn't even hold up his own head. It rolled to the side, providing a view behind him. Unfortunately, he could see the fuzzy bodies of six drones...or maybe it was three? Two?

I'm done. This is it. I'm not gonna make it.

After all his perilous missions, hunting Stewards, shootouts with the worst pirate scum in the galaxy, underwater encounters with dinosaur-sized sea aliens on Honi, and man-eating sand snakes in the seemingly bottomless canyons of Tor, he had run out of luck.

He would die by the sting of a bloody insect.

He turned as the world fizzled, seeing two familiar forms in the passage ahead of Lucid. Chirping rang out.

"Let's barbecue us some Lark!" Billy Bob shouted.

Growling answered, that was definitely Saber.

The two Markas barreled past Lucid and Rangnar as his vision faded to red. He closed his eyes, unable to resist.

When he opened them again, he saw a bright light and heard humming. Rangnar swung his fist out of instinct.

"Stop!" came a chirp.

That was...Lucid?

Batting his eyes, he saw the face of his friend, who had saved him.

"Am I dead?" he asked.

"Judging by the smell, I'd say you've already rotted."

Rangnar tensed back up at the human voice. His vision cleared to the interior of the *Beak*, where he lay with cords hooked up to the medical units on the hull. He tried to focus on a human shape standing just outside the open cargo door. Billy Bob, Nuke and Saber prowled beyond the man.

Slowly, Rangnar's vison cleared to the black and white armor of an Eagle.

Captain Joshua Weston. The only man who knew his real identity, and the closest thing Rangnar had to a human friend. They went back all the way to his early twenties, when Weston was hunting down Stewards. Rangnar had met him on a mission where he was hired as a bounty hunter to track one of the genetically modified warriors with a blend of human and Corinn DNA.

Rangnar had worked off and on with Weston ever since.

That didn't mean he broke Death Rule One and trusted the guy. They both had a lot to lose with Weston skimming off the top whenever Rangnar brought him tech like this.

"You're covered in Lark shit, Phantom," he said.

"It was worth it," Rangnar said.

"Yeah?"

"Yeah." Rangnar sat up with Lucid helping him slightly. "I extracted the fuel rod. Billy Bob will give it to you after you pay *double* my initial fee."

"Double? What the galactic snot nugget, Rangnar?"

Billy Bob trotted over, his belly practically dragging the dirt. He bared his teeth, saliva dripping off his maw.

"No need to be a dick," Weston said with a scowl.

"No?" Rangnar asked. "I can't feel the right side of my body, including my testicle, and if you want the rod, you're paying for my pain and suffering, or you can pay me the fee and let me keep one of the four crystals."

"You had that planned all along, didn't you?"

Rangnar held back a smile. Of course he had, though he

hadn't planned on a near death injury to blame it on. He'd lined up a buyer for that crystal before they even left the city.

Weston scoffed. "Fine, but only because I need to get back to base quick," he said.

Billy Bob used a tail to remove the fuel rod from a pouch on his back. Then he used his other tail to pluck out a crystal, which he tossed to Rangnar.

Reaching out cautiously, Weston grabbed the rod with the three crystals still inside. He held it up, looking it over. "Still don't know what the Corinns want these for. They got us working with them now, did you hear about that, Phantom?"

"What? Since when?" Rangnar asked.

"You been off the grid or what?"

"Yeah, been out scouting the Lark mound for three days and waiting for cloud cover, like tonight. So break it down for me."

Weston shrugged. "All I know is that something big is brewing, and the brass got something planned with the Corinns. If I were you, I'd get rid of that last crystal as soon as you can then find a new line of work. Maybe even retire on some distant planet."

"Why distant—" Rangnar's vision suddenly became crystal clear. "The Wrath?"

The captain examined the rod, not answering.

"Weston, are the Wrath—"

"I don't know, but if they are, I wish I could say we're ready." Weston glanced over, looking Rangnar in the eye. "But you and I both know that'd be a lie."

CHAPTER 5

Two days had passed since the ceremony to mark the anniversary of the victory over the Wrath. Sergeant Jax Brito had spent that time on the Ironclad battleship *Epoch* with the other Eagles of Hatchet Platoon. The ship orbited the mostly frozen planet Jolia on the outer edge of the system.

It was almost midnight, and she lay in her bunk still trying to sleep in the quiet barracks. Worries about the future had her too tense to drift off. To relax, she closed her eyes and transported herself back to her home world of Runi. She thought of the first brisk nights of late summer, when she would head out into the fields with her brother Nico, and their father Tim, whom they called the Ox. He had worked those fields his entire life, right alongside his droids, and his father, and his grandpa before them.

Under the bright moon, they would dig the first pale roots and place them into woven baskets, much like their ancestors had their tuber crops on Earth, centuries ago.

Nico would always compete with Jax, trying to fill his basket first. The roots weren't exactly easy to pluck free of the dirt. It required a careful extraction to ensure the entire root was harvested and none of the plant went to waste. Of course, they had droids to do this, but the first batch was always done by hand. It was tradition.

Jax enjoyed life on their third-generation farm, but she knew early on, before she reached her teens, that she would leave Runi someday. She wanted to see the other planets, and to keep them safe. When she saw her first Eagle, she knew right then she wanted to be a soldier.

Her father didn't discourage her, but he didn't exactly encourage her either. She had a feeling he hoped she would change her mind.

It had nearly broken her mother the day she shipped out.

"You're a good young woman, Jacqueline. You have a kind heart," she had said through tears. "Don't become a killer. It will damage your soul."

"I'm joining the Eagles not to kill, but to save lives," Jax had said.

"Sometimes things blur out there," her father had replied. "The galaxy is a rough place, you must always be on guard."

"I will, I promise."

At some point she drifted off into a dream. In it, she was in the vast fields of Runi with Nico and their dad, harvesting the first ash roots of the season.

A sudden bright light, greater than any sun, flashed across the horizon. The fertile soil shook hard, cracking open in places. Nico ran, stumbling and dropping his basket. Jax came from behind and helped him up just as a dark cloud bloomed in the distance, blocking the moon. Flames stretched along the border, lightning flashing inside.

"What is that!?" Jax asked.

Her father turned, screaming, "Run!"

Jax awoke to a blaring alarm and shot up in her bunk.

"All hands to their stations," came an automatic voice.

She shook off the sleep, jumping down. All across the barracks, Eagles were gearing up, some already flooding out of the hatch into a passage.

Jax quickly donned her black-clad armor over her muscular body. She activated the battery pack on her T-Flesh rig, bringing online the intricate system of thermal regulators and exoskeleton that allowed seamless adaptation to varied environmental extremes. Whether exposed to the crushing gravity of a massive planet or the bone-chilling cold of the void, the suit adjusted in real-time, recalibrating its internal systems to maintain optimal mobility.

Picking up her helmet, she slipped it over her brown hair, buzzed on one side. The HUD came online in the upper corner of her display. All green. Good to go and ready to roll.

"This it, Sarge?" asked Corporal Eli Krish. "You think the Wrath are back?"

Corporal Aleksandra Ostovich clicked her armor into place. "If they are, we're ready."

"You say that now," remarked Private Martin Keyes.

"Move it," Jax said.

The Eagles of Hatchet Platoon flooded into launch bay 19 of the ship. Four Clipper assault ships waited on a pad across the vast room, their landing gear still locked into the deck. They were a tenth the size of a Warhorse dropship and were used to drop a fire-team into a hostile zone quickly.

That told Jax they were about to see some combat. She fell in line in front of Hatchet Platoon Lieutenant Trey Folkert. The forty-eight-year-old man had seen his share of it over the years. He was supposedly one of the oldest living Eagles to have fought against the last of the Stewards. In fact, Folkert was just out of training when he was thrown into the meat grinder in the battle on Furia against Captain Leon "the Lion" Kahr and the last of the Steward forces. A scar crossed his face from his left cheek, over his nose, and all the way to his right ear from a fire sword that had deformed him during a battle.

"Listen up! We're heading to Jolia, home to ice, snow, and not much else," Folkert said. "But what looks like a frozen shithole to us is a sacred place for the Ino Tribe. Unfortunately for them, the Corinns claim this planet as their own, and they have long wanted the Inos out."

He glanced across the hold where six Corinns waited with their hands behind their backs. Dressed in black suits that fit their tall, muscular bodies snugly, they were armed with two daggers in beautifully carved sheaths strapped to their long arms. Their elongated skulls were tipped back slightly, their green eyes roving across the space.

"As you know, Galactic Minister Goodwall announced a new partnership between us and the Corinn Empire," Folkert said. "As part of this agreement, decrees were drafted to collect specific Wrath artifacts previously assumed safe by the lab jockeys."

He stepped closer to the platoon.

"An advance team, two of our Eagles and a dignitary, were deployed to inform the Inos that they are harboring Wrath bones that need to be turned over," Folkert said. "The message was delivered to tribal leader Minnor Jikk personally."

Folkert held up a HoloMatrix pad in one hand and clicked it. A translucent video showed Jikk in a thick coat with fur around the collar. The heavily tattooed face came into focus as Jikk held something up in a large glove. It only took a moment to identify the object as a severed human head. Jikk spoke in his native tongue, but a translator relayed the message clearly to the Eagles.

"Anyone that dares step foot in our territory will meet this same fate!" he shouted.

Folkert lowered the HoloMatrix pad. "We're here to carry out the decree with extreme prejudice," he said. "However, we have special instructions to not disturb the Torq population."

"What's a Torq?" asked Corporal Krish.

"Some sort of water cow with a crazy valuable twisty horn, and meat that costs more than us grunts earn in a month," Folkert said.

Jax had heard of the pink-fleshed mammals which spent most of their lives paddling around the icy water with their large flippers. They were best known for their single horn, which could grow up to ten feet long. The shimmering silver bone twisted gracefully at the tip. Sometimes they were called unicorn cows.

He looked over at the Corinns, who were crossing the room, still unsure why exactly they were here.

"Hatchet Platoon has been charged with this important mission," Folkert said. "I'm sending three fire teams. Before we bring the pain, we'll give 'em one chance to surrender—but don't expect that, and don't expect this to be easy if they do fight. Inos are well trained, and this is their ancestral home."

Hoots and *oorahs!* echoed through the troop hold, including Jax. They were all happy to face a human enemy, rather than the Wrath.

"Wayne, Tannis and Jacobs will lead the assault," Folkert said. "Brito, Spear Team's in charge of watching the Torqs that will be on the beach. We'll take care of any guards before you land."

With quick salutes, the other three squads took off toward their Clippers, but Jax hesitated.

"You got a problem with your orders?" Folkert asked.

"No, LT," Jax lied. She turned and followed the rest of her team, resenting once again being left out of the potential action.

How was she supposed to prove herself if she was continually left behind?

"We're glorified babysitters of livestock," remarked Krish.

Jax couldn't help but feel the irony of the young man's statement. Krish had graduated from training just a year earlier and was still very much green.

"I'm the babysitter, have been ever since you got assigned to my team," Jax replied.

But that wasn't the reason she was getting passed over. It was due to her background as the daughter of a farmer. It didn't matter she was the best sharpshooter in the entire platoon or that she continued to work her ass off. Despite everything she gave, she still got held back, even now. Despite over seven years of hard work, sweat, and blood.

She wasn't the only one capable of combat. Corporal Aleksandra Ostovich was a tough woman with thighs of solid muscle thicker than most of the men's, and Private Martin Keyes was one of the best hand-to-hand fighters in the platoon. Krish, on the other hand, was inexperienced, and pretty much useless. He had zero killer instinct and wasn't a great shot. Jax recalled he had once told her that he had never experienced adrenaline once in his life.

She didn't even know how that was possible.

Jax had served with them for two years now, and she could tell by their body language that they weren't pleased with their assignment either. They followed Jax over to their ride, climbing inside the four-seater behind a pilotless cockpit.

An alarm blared, and the room cleared. A message surged over the comms from the flight commander. "All teams prepare for deployment."

The massive cargo doors opened, revealing the white ball of Jolia. The birds lifted off and blasted out of the bay, swooping toward the planet's atmosphere. A floor of green clouds greeted them.

No one spoke until they pierced the clouds and saw the snow-capped mountain chains and frozen terrain.

"Why the hell would anyone want to live here?" Krish asked.

"Sounds like these Inos are religious nuts," said Aleksandra. "I get respecting and even being fascinated by weird creatures and cultures, but worshipping these Torqs and collecting Wrath bones?"

"Honestly, I'm just glad we're not being dropped into Hell to fight those Wraths," Krish said.

Jax gave him a side-glance of disgust. He was nothing but dead weight.

The Clippers roared over the terrain, blasting up a wave of snowy grit behind their thrusters. Spear team's AI pilot suddenly curved away from the other assault crafts, increasing speed toward the village, taking them toward the ocean. From there, they dipped down, hugging the sheer cliffs overlooking the shoreline.

Hundreds of feet below their craft, waves crashed against a beach littered with patchy green vegetation. *Some sort of seaweed, perhaps,* Jax thought. She wasn't familiar with the flora or fauna of the planet, but she did know it was their summer. The ice had receded from the shoreline, and much of the snow had melted over the lower rocky terrain, exposing pink moss.

"Entering Ino territory in t-minus one minute," came the robotic confirmation of the Clipper AI.

"Lock and load, Spear Team," Jax said. She pulled her laser rifle from over her shoulder and charged the weapon. The others did the same as the attack craft rose up toward the crest of the jagged bluffs.

Jax spotted something moving in one of the outcroppings.

Yellow and white stains waterfalled down from a nest made of hardened vegetation, the same color they'd seen on the beach. A bird the size of the Clipper suddenly flapped out of a crevice in front of them. The AI pilot adjusted slightly, pulling away from the cliff and rising, accomplishing the maneuver much more gently than most human pilots.

"Holy shit that was close," Krish said, letting out a huff.

The viewports provided a visual of the target, the village of Norii. Even from afar, Jax could see the colorful buildings constructed against the near vertical walls of a bluff overlooking the ocean. Some of the dwellings were studded into the side of the mountain, presenting a variety of red, blue, green, and yellow among the stark white landscape.

Orange explosions burst along the exterior of the village bordering the port. Jax watched on her mirrored feed, which showed the other squads, as the Clippers zoomed over a collapsing border wall and the guard towers they had targeted. Return fire lanced away from another tower along the perimeter before it, too, vanished in a fiery blast.

"Guess they didn't surrender," Aleksandra said.

Missiles thumped away from elevated locations along the bluff. The Clippers deployed flares against the archaic heat-seeking projectiles. Explosions burst in the air as the dropships avoided the almost useless weapons.

"Prepare for Lightning Missiles," Folkert came over the comms.

Not ten seconds later, missiles screamed out of the sky, fired from the Ironclad, *Epoch*, still in orbit. Each one targeted the Ino anti-aircraft defenses in the rocky bluff.

"Exterior defenses neutralized, preparing to engage hostiles on the ground," Folkert said. "All teams, be advised of possible IEDs and traps. Looks like someone gave them a heads up we're coming."

"Brito," Folkert said. "You're clear to land at the LZ. Make sure not a single flipper is harmed on those Torqs."

"Understood," Jax replied. "Not a single gorgeous flipper, LT."

The Clipper came in over the ocean, flanking the port to the west while the dropships lowered the Eagles into the village to put down whatever resistance was left. As their vessel began to descend over the bay, Jax got a visual of the Torqs and their corkscrewed horns. Most of them had waddled off an enclosed portion of beach and entered the water, which appeared to be fenced off to keep them from escaping.

"Here we go," Jax said. The Clipper began to lower over the beach where the corralled Torqs had been sleeping. Two Inos had been standing guard where a crater now marred the landscape. There wasn't much left of them, just a few limbs, one still gripping a crossbow.

The Clipper set down and Jax grabbed the handle. "Move it!" she shouted.

Aleksandra went first out the port side while Krish and Martin jumped out the starboard. The Clipper began to pull away before Jax had even jumped out. Explosions rocked the ground as her boots hit the gravelly sand. She cleared the beach with another quick scan, then turned to the ocean. The Torqs were easy to spot in the clear sea, their pink bodies gliding under the water, and horns piercing the surface. A flipper suddenly breached the surface, splashing water toward them.

"Yeah, we don't want to be here either," Jax said. She faced her team. "Martin, you and Aleks hold security here. Krish you're with me."

Jax started toward the metal fence surrounding the beach, looking for the best position to hold back anyone that might be coming from Norii, a quarter mile away. A rocky garden separated them from the view of the lower part of the village, but the vibrant colors of the buildings constructed in the rocky walls were within sight. Smoke curled away from the aerial defenses the *Epoch* had erased in seconds.

"Spear Team in position," Jax said over the team comms. "Torqs are secure."

"Copy that," Folkert said. "Hostiles are hunkered down in the caves with the artifacts."

The line went silent and Jax again found herself brooding. The crack of gunfire and laser bolts echoed in the distance. Over that tumult came the whisper of the sea wind.

Jax pulled out her infrared binos and brought them up to her faceplate. Then she scanned the rocks in front of her, searching for any sign of hostiles.

"Shit! My boot!" Krish whined.

Seeing nothing, Jax lowered the binos to check on her rookie. He had stepped in a pile of what appeared to be Torq shit made chunky with cracked shells and fish bones.

"This is why we're held back—" Jax began.

A choked cry cut her off. She turned toward the water to see Martin holding onto something protruding out of his naval. The glowing blue blade came into focus just as another pierced his back and skewered him to the ground like a kebab.

Six Ino insurgents wearing green Ghillie suits that looked like seaweed rose out of the water. Breathing masks covered their faces, muffling their screams of rage as they fired at Aleksandra. She cried out as laser bolts streaked in her direction, one of them hitting her in the shoulder. She spun behind a Torq scat-coated rock about ten feet from Jax and Krish.

"Stay down!" Jax shouted.

Her voice drew attention from the enemy. There was a split second to yank Krish out of the way from a barrage of gunfire. They flattened their bodies against the sand behind a rocky outcropping.

Jax immediately got up and squeezed off some cover fire, peppering the leading Ino with bolts as the man waded out of the surf. The other five warriors stopped to fire back at Jax. She hit the sand with her back against the rocks and activated the comm.

"We're under attack by multiple contacts!" Jax shouted. "Martin and Aleksandra are down! Requesting reinforcements—"

A distant explosion cut Jax off. The ground rumbled from a blast that felt like an earthquake. Sand shifted under their boots.

"What the hell was that?" Krish asked as he visibly shook.

"Get your shit together and focus on covering fire for Aleks when I tell you," she said. "Got it?"

Krish nodded.

"Aleks, when I tell you, run to us. We'll cover you!" Jax shouted from cover.

"Got it!" she called back.

"On three," Jax said. "One, two..."

Holding in a breath, Jax popped up and fired with Krish at the Inos who were now out of the water and advancing up the beach. Two of them collapsed under the fire, but the others went for cover.

"Now, Aleks!" Jax yelled.

She bolted for their position then followed as Jax led them into the high-walled rock garden separating the shore from the village. When they got inside the fortress of stone, Jax tried the comm, but got nothing.

"I think we lost command," she panted.

"What? How?" Krish asked.

"That explosion," Aleksandra offered.

Jax looked at heavy plumes of smoke coming from the village. "Screw the Torqs," she said. "We've got Eagles to help. On me."

They took off through the rock formations toward the village, the distant sound of gunfire and laser chatter guiding them.

You wanted action?

You got it.

Jax led the way toward the battle, realization setting in. Their comms were down, Martin was dead, Aleksandra was injured, and they had no idea how many hostiles were out there. It was an ambush, and a damn good one.

God, this is going to be a nightmare.

"Strong and steady, Jax," she whispered.

CHAPTER 6

Axel flew on, easily navigating the variety of rocks, until the life scanner crackled, causing him to jerk the yoke. He eased off the thrusters and slowed, checking the screen before he turned the fighter toward the signal.

The route took him toward a huge asteroid that looked like a floating mountain. It wasn't unusual to detect life on a rock this big. Chances were good it was home to space maggots.

Cricket chirped again in a low tone. It was too late to fire at a smaller rock that came hurtling toward them from behind the monster asteroid, but thanks to his trusty companion, Axel had an extra second to pull back. The jagged piece had nearly taken out their starboard wing and turret.

"Thanks, pal, you just saved us from being space jam," Axel said.

"That's why I get the big bucks," Cricket chirped. "Except for lately, when I get no bucks."

"That's gonna change soon, bud."

The *Hammerhead* lurched as Axel turned the ship for a visual of the formerly shadowed asteroid. Sure enough, the cratered exterior was home to space maggots.

The purple segmented bodies of the human-sized creatures swaddled a section of the rock, very close to a spread of wreckage. The slow-moving maggots were definitely on their way to look for a meal.

"*Trash Squid*, do you copy?" Axel said over the team comms. "I've located the salvage of what I'm guessing is the *Cyprus*. Maggots present. Heading in for a closer look."

Ever so gently, he rotated the thrusters, gliding the *Hammerhead* through space like a sailboat in a calm sea, coming up along the bow.

Unlike the *Gold Fish*, this one looked damaged from something other than the hurtling space rocks. Axel felt a stab of fear as he examined a blackened scar surrounding a jagged opening in the hull that was caused beyond doubt by a missile. Two more marked the bulbous dual cockpits, taking out the glass and making them look like empty eye sockets.

Realization sank in—someone had attacked the *Cyprus* then stolen their cargo.

"Someone killed them," Axel whispered.

"You think they are still out there?" Cricket asked, scanning the field of rocks.

"Doubtful. Question is, did they leave anything for us?"

It was unlikely, but Axel wasn't ready to give up yet. Giving up meant going home emptyhanded. They would be lucky if they had enough fuel and supplies to pick up another salvage op.

He carefully rotated the *Hammerhead*, seeing another gaping hole where a missile had slammed against the hull.

Had to be pirates, he mused.

But pirates armed with missiles? Most preferred good old-fashioned MACH Spears, or railguns. These were professionals, probably a merc crew of former soldiers.

He flew toward the aft, passing directly under the cargo

hold. Cricket craned his neck and suddenly broke into frantic chirping. Axel yanked the yoke hard to pull them away from a jagged opening.

The interior was filled with space maggots, some of them coiled up, others munching away with their square teeth. If there'd been any cargo left, it was gone now.

Axel shook his head, disappointed.

"It's gonna be okay, Commendatore," Cricket replied.

Axel turned and hit the comms to share the bad news with the crew.

"We're too late," he said. "Maggots got whatever was left."

Silence filled the cockpit, then Luna said, "Damn."

Axel prepared to pull away.

Brayton came on the channel. "Captain, we've got four contacts closing in on the asteroid belt."

"Contacts?" Axel asked.

"Probably salvagers...hold on."

The comm crackled, and a few seconds passed.

"These aren't salvagers," Brayton said. "They look like Slicers."

"Bloody pirate scoundrels," Axel said. "Oh shit," he whispered offline. The sleek single cockpit pirate vessels were fast, with a dorsal wing and two side wings that could retract against the hull. The sharp vessels sported a variety of devastating weapons, making them extremely deadly, but they weren't built for distance. There was a larger vessel out there somewhere that had deployed them.

He looked back to the wreckage. He should have seen this coming. The red Slicers had already attacked it, taken the cargo, and were covering their tracks by coming after the *Gold Fish*, and now they were after the *Trash Squid*.

"Captain, they're locking on!" Luna cried.

Axel leapt into action. "You'll have to lose them in the belt, it's the only way. Don't wait for me."

Axel backed away, steering with one hand and using the other to tap the HoloMatrix screen for a larger map of the asteroid belt, showing his position relative to the *Trash Squid*. It also showed the four Slicers advancing—following them into the belt.

"Hold on, Cricket!" Axel said. He pushed the thruster down, blasting away. The *Hammerhead* picked up speed as he swerved around rocks almost recklessly.

"Two missiles incoming!" Luna reported.

Axel felt a rush of heat in his chest, but not just from anger. Two heavy rocks were spiraling right toward him, threatening to crush the *Hammerhead* into dust. A quick jerk of the yoke had them slip sideways between the asteroids, which smashed together not two seconds later. The fighter plowed onward at full speed. Axel checked the screen to find the *Trash Squid* was taking damage as Spartacus tried to navigate the big barge.

Each new impact made Axel flinch. His ugly but prized ship was getting beat to hell. But it was better than eating a Slicer missile. Each hit would send an armor piercing second projectile to detonate inside the wound to kill crews.

Waves of anger washed the fear away. Axel tasted copper in his mouth, felt his heart pounding in his neck. The rage was trying to claw its way out and unleash the insanity that was locked in his mind.

Axel pushed the thruster to the max, flying on pure instincts. He gritted his teeth, waiting for a view of the ship. He saw the orange barge a moment later, and the red Slicers gaining on it.

"Another missile on our six," Luna said.

Cricket whipped his two tails and chirped in the adjacent seat. "Oh gods! We're maggot food!" he said.

Axel stared, his vision narrowing into a tunnel of swarming red.

The rage-filled voice broke through the final prison bars in his mind.

Vaporize them! Blast them into space dust!

Axel lined up the sights on the leading Slicer. He could blast it to pieces with the accurate laser cannon, breaking his code to preserve life and never take it. But today he knew he had to choose to protect his life and that of his crew through violence.

It should have been an easy choice, but for Axel it wasn't.

Hesitation is death, growled the voice in his mind. *You must kill, so others can live.*

Axel exhaled as he tried to find *another* way, a path without violence.

With only seconds to act, he saw that path. Gripping the turret controls, he squeezed the triggers, sending a storm of bolts at two goliath asteroids. Explosions burst across the visual range as the lasers chewed them apart and spat the hunks out toward the Slicers, forcing them to pull up.

He then lowered over the top of the *Trash Squid*, noticing the faded logo of Uga had been dented by an asteroid. The fighter set down and locked into place.

"Go, Sparty, go!" Axel yelled. He opened a hatch that connected the two vessels. Then he dropped down five feet and ran for the bridge. The crew was strapped into their seats, eyes on the screens showing four Slicers spread out in the belt, still pursuing them.

"Spartacus, deploy a trash pod to distract them," Axel said. "I'll take over the flying."

He slid into the cracked leather of the captain's seat and grabbed the controls. The pod deployed, streaking away into the darkness. One of the four Slicers took the bait. It peeled off after the decoy.

Rocks pummeled the light armor of the *Trash Squid* as Axel pushed the thruster down. He banked hard to the right, narrowly avoiding a Slicer missile. It ripped past the port side and slammed into a rock, shielding them from the brunt of the blast.

"Watch out, Capa!" Uga barked.

Axel jerked the controls again to avoid a Corinn bull-sized rock that came hurtling right toward the bow.

He turned the controls hard, but the bulkier vessel was much slower to react than the *Hammerhead*. They flipped sideways, the bottom of the asteroid scraping against their portside hull with a gnashing grind.

Emergency lights winked on and a klaxon wailed.

"Owie, owie, boo-boo to *Trash Squid*," Uga grumbled. He gripped his guts with three arms and howled while his other three arms whipped back and forth over his bandana.

Axel tried to fight the anger swarming his mind, tried to regain control. They were almost out of the belt, but with danger on every side, clear space might as well have been lightyears away.

Another missile streaked through the rotating boulders, closing in on the *Trash Squid*. Axel watched it advance on the dashboard screen.

"Multiple contacts ahead," Spartacus said.

"Yep," Axel acknowledged.

The asteroids were thick here, and he couldn't see a clear path through.

Fight back! Kill them!

Axel flipped the turrets without thinking, as if his finger was no longer his own and the voice had taken control of his body. A prickling sensation climbed his legs, his torso, and went down his arms.

"Peace is your way. Peace is your way," he chanted.

Axel closed his eyes, trying to picture the loving smile of his mother and hear her soothing voice. The anger subsided enough that he was able to consider a sudden idea.

"Captain, are you with us?" Luna asked.

"Yeah," he replied. "I'm gonna try something. Everyone hold on!"

"Uga, button that furry ass of yours!" Spartacus said.

"Screw the bolts tight on your metal mouth hole!" Uga barked back.

Axel shoved the throttle toward the spinning barrier of rocks.

"XO, prepare for FTL jump," Axel shouted.

"On it, Captain," Luna replied.

Axel pulled down on the trigger to the laser cannons. Bolts crisscrossed over their flight path, pounding into the oncoming projectiles.

"Here we go!" he shouted.

The ship barreled right into the cloud of dust and gravel. Debris slammed against the hull, pounding like a Steward was hammering the ship on an anvil.

The cameras went dark. Alarms screamed and red lights swirled across the bridge. Axel held on to the controls, the turrets still firing. A violent impact rattled the ship so hard he felt his back pop.

The debris cleared and suddenly, they were clear, shooting out of the final stretch of the field. The Slicers had changed course, but Axel knew they were just looking for a safer way to pursue.

"Get us out of here, Spartacus!" Axel shouted.

The ship groaned and rattled, but nothing happened.

A warning flashed on the dashboard: *FTL Drive Damaged.*

Anger cut through Axel, returning like a tidal wave. His recently repaired FTL was broke dick again! He brought his fist down on the HoloMatrix screen, cracking the glass.

"Captain," Luna said in a voice shy of a shout.

He shook his head, trying to re-focus, but she wasn't calling him out for smashing the dashboard. She was pointing at a planet in the distance. Not just any planet. Eern. A Corinn colonized world wiped out during the Wrath invasion. But before all that, almost a millennium ago, this was the home of the Marka species. They had been the Apex predators, the top of the food chain before the Corinns, and then the Wrath.

Cricket stared with his front eyes at the brown ball that was once a thriving, beautiful planet for his species.

"Contact!" Brayton yelled.

Axel saw them on the radar. Two Slicers had emerged from the asteroid belt and were increasing speed. He rotated the turrets, acknowledging that violence would be the only way to save his crew now.

Heaving a sigh, he pulled the trigger, unleashing a spray of lasers.

The Slicers spread out, easily avoiding what Axel had meant as a warning. He couldn't believe it worked.

"I think they're retreating," Luna said.

Axel waited until he confirmed then slowly looked around the bridge.

"Everyone good?" he asked.

"Yeah," Luna said, holding her head.

"My stomach, it hurts so bad," Uga grumbled. "Owie, owie—"

"Boo-boo, yeah, we get it, but you're fine," Cricket chirped.

"I'm okay, but we're in the open," Brayton said.

"I know," Axel said. "Sparty, do we have enough fuel to get to Eern?"

"It should be adequate, with some slight reserves left," replied the droid.

"Tinus is closer," Luna said. "Perhaps we should make for it? Park it in a crater?"

She brought up an image on the cracked screen next to Axel. He nodded. That would at least save fuel.

He curved around the other side of Tinus, blasted toward the surface, and lowered into a crater. Darkness swallowed the ship.

"Life support only," Axel said.

The lights clicked off, and their systems shut down. They waited in silence, with only the sound of their breathing and Uga's stomach rumbling. Axel kept his hands on the controls, watching the stars above, knowing full well the enemy could still be out there.

"Captain," Brayton whispered.

"Quiet," Axel said.

"You need to see this. Check your screen."

An image of the four Slicers flying through the darkness came online, a live view from the trash pod that was lingering at the edge of the asteroid belt.

"Are they really going there?" Luna asked quietly.

Axel narrowed his eyes at Eern. A theory emerged as he studied the barren terrain from space. "I think whatever the *Cyprus* was carrying came from the surface," he said.

"So, it's been stolen twice?" Luna mused. "Unless the Corinns gave the *Cyprus* permission to enter."

"Who cares?" Brayton said. "The treasure's gone and those pirates just tried to kill us! I say we tuck our tails and run as soon as it's clear."

That sounded logical, but there was still so much anger

coursing through Axel he couldn't think properly. Between the pirates, his debts, the broken FTL drive, *and* the demonic voice in his head that he couldn't seem to shake.

It should have quieted, but it hadn't, and he feared he wouldn't be able to keep it contained. He looked down at his hands, remembering the moment he had almost lost control, as if the voice had taken over his body.

It was rare, but it *had* happened. The image of breaking the bully's nose when he was just a kid flashed in his mind and he closed his eyes.

"You okay?" Luna asked.

Axel looked up, back to the viewports. "Fine," he said.

"Captain," Spartacus said. "Please tell me you are not thinking what we all know you are thinking."

"What's Capa think? Think it's time we eat?" Uga barked.

"That he wants to take a closer look at these scoundrels," Luna said with a raised brow. "Right?"

Axel shot Uga a glance. "You want to eat?"

"Yes! Yes, Capa! Eat!" barked the Wooly, raising three arms.

"Then buckle up," Axel said quietly. "We're all out of options."

Smoke billowed out of the side of the vertical cliff where the Ino had built their houses. The command channel was still down, and the chatter of laser rifles and crack of gunfire had all but ceased over the past hour.

That was a bad sign for the Eagles of Hatchet Platoon. Especially since Command seemed content to leave them down there without reinforcements. For now, Jax, Krish, and Aleksandra were on their own.

They had escaped through the rock garden and made it to

the eastern side of the village, keeping to the exterior buildings, which the Ino had fled hastily. In the dwelling they had just entered, there was fish stew bubbling over on a hearth.

Jax entered a living room. A rug covered a smooth, stone-tiled floor with a fireplace in the corner, the wood also still burning.

These people lived like ancients from Earth, but what they lacked in technology, they made up for in strategy. Whoever was in charge had taken Hatchet Platoon by surprise in the tunnels. It was the first time in her service as an Eagle the locals had managed to ambush them this badly.

Krish came out of the other room. "All clear," he said.

Nodding, Jax flashed hand signals, taking point, and guiding them up a set of creaky wood stairs. Various pictures hung in frames on the wall. In one, a mother and father stood with two small children on an icy ledge, all dressed in white snowsuits with fur collars. They looked out over the ocean, where a Torq had surfaced.

In another picture, the family was among other villagers, gardening, fishing, or singing hymns. They looked so peaceful.

Or so we were told, Jax thought.

She signaled to the top of the stairs. Aleksandra went to the left with Krish while Jax went to the right. As she stalked down the creaky hallway, she thought of Martin lying there with two spears sticking out of his back. The man didn't even have a chance to fire off a shot.

Jax had watched Eagles die before. The first time was in the jungles on Honi, where Hatchet Platoon was sent to track down a pirate crew. The bastards had put landmines in a swamp the platoon was forced to cross. Their scanners had missed them until it was too late. A new recruit stepped on one and was blown sky high in a red and brown sludge tower of gore. Jax was the one to write to the kid's parents.

The next was when they were deployed to a metropolis to help local authorities take out a drug cartel. A sniper took out their lieutenant. That was Hawkins, the head of Hatchet before Folkert.

Folkert was the third platoon leader since Jax had joined. The first ate the barrel of his laser pistol after his wife left him and he gambled away his life's savings.

Now, it was likely they were going to need a fourth.

The team met up in a second-floor bedroom that had a view of much of the city. A central square with a statue of a Torq was within visual. Huge candles, the size of a man, surrounded the chiseled rock of the sacred creature.

Beyond the houses framing the square they could see the rock wall that rose up two thousand feet, with more houses and structures built into the stone. The smoke streaming upward had to be coming from the tunnels Folkert and the other squads had entered. The Inos had likely blown it, probably killing—or trapping—most of them.

"Where are our reinforcements?" Jax asked. She looked to the sky, still expecting Warhorses to lower, or perhaps even the *Epoch* to descend over the village.

"They must be trying to figure out what happened before sending more of us to..." Aleksandra grunted from pain.

Jax stepped back from the window to check her out. They had buttoned up the plate of armor, but she had already lost a lot of blood. Dried red streaks clung to the smooth connecting plates covering her chest.

"You good?" Jax asked.

She nodded. "I'm okay."

She could tell by Aleksandra's labored breathing that wasn't true. She was in shock.

"Krish, you stay here with her. I'm going to look for survivors," Jax said.

"Wait," Krish said.

"That's an order, dammit."

"But Sarge, I think I already got eyes on survivors."

Jax turned to Krish who held a pair of binos up to his helmet visor. Rushing over to the window, Jax used her own binos to zoom in on a flurry of movement in the village square. A team of ten Inos wearing snow-colored full-body suits and helmets rushed across the stone streets. They were all armed with machine guns and spears.

Behind them, a group of ten soldiers in gray were being led, chained together. It wasn't until Jax zoomed in that she saw these were her fellow Eagles, their black armor covered in soot and grit. Some of them limped, others were helping each other. One man was missing a leg and was being helped by another Eagle. He suddenly tripped, both of them falling and bringing the chained-up line to a halt.

"That's LT," Krish said. "We have to do something."

Jax moved the scope to see Folkert didn't have long for this world. Blood gushed from a stump above his knee, and the entire back of his armor was ripped open, like an angry Marka had pried it off.

An Ino with spikes on his helmet turned and started screaming. That was their leader, Minnor Jikk, and would be the first one Jax would kill.

But first, she had to come up with a plan.

She brought up her rifle and extended the barrel. The lengthened barrel would allow her a more accurate shot, when the time came. She placed the scope back to her visor.

Minnor Jikk had a crossbow pointed at Folkert. He was on the ground, somehow still conscious despite his devastating injuries. Using the scope tech, Jax was able to translate their conversation to an earpiece she wore.

"We're just one platoon. There are four more in orbit,"

Folkert choked out. "They will keep sending us until you're all dead."

Minnor Jikk turned away, firing his weapon at the same moment. The arrow pierced Folkert's chest. The LT managed to reach up and grab it before going limp. The other Eagles screamed and tried to fight but were quickly knocked down by the Ino warriors who had them under guard.

Jax watched through her scope in horror, her finger hovering over the trigger.

"My god," Aleksandra said.

Krish got up. "We have to get out of here—"

"Sit your ass down," Jax said. "It's too late for LT, but we can save the others if we're smart."

Minnor Jikk yelled something that was answered by his tribe in primal screams.

"What's he saying?" Aleksandra asked.

Jax focused the crosshairs on the Ino leader, seeing a bearded face and dark eyes wild with rage. She could take him out right now if she wanted but resisted the urge to erase his features with the pull of a trigger. More people suddenly flooded into the square.

But these weren't warriors. These were women and children, elders, all of them joining in on what suddenly transformed into a celebration. Some of the kids ran over to examine the Eagles before the Ino insurgents waved them back.

Several Marka aliens with white jackets joined the crowd, chirping in celebration of the captured soldiers. Dogs joined the gathering crowd, barking and wagging their tails, some of them chasing the Markas.

Jax flitted her sights over the Eagles. Half of her platoon was still alive, if you counted her fire team. But she was going to need a solid plan to save them without reinforcements. Especially now, with that swarm of innocent civilians.

She zoomed in on the pale faces of some of these people, an idea forming in her mind.

"Krish, I need you to get to the high ground and establish a link to command. Let them know what's going on," she said. "Aleks, you stay here and stay hidden."

"What are you going to do?" Krish asked.

"Save some Eagles."

"You're going to take out all those insurgents on your own?" Krish asked.

"Not even a Steward could save all of them," Aleksandra said.

"They could have, with a plan, and I've got one that will prove I'm not—" Jax closed her mouth. Truth was, she wanted to prove she was more than the daughter of a farmer. Aleksandra must have picked up on her thoughts.

"Don't throw away your life to prove a point, Jax, because no one is going to remember that point," she said. "Think of your family back home."

Jax did just that, especially what her father had said before she joined the Eagles.

Sometimes things blur out there. The galaxy is a rough place, you must always be on guard.

Never in her career had this been more true.

"You can't take them all," Krish said. "Come with me and we'll radio command together. They'll send reinforcements."

"When? When it's too late?" Jax asked. "We're Eagles. We don't sit by and watch while our comrades are slaughtered like animals."

Aleksandra looked at her and nodded.

Krish hesitated, but then acknowledged the orders with a shrug.

"Stay to the rocks, and keep your head down," Jax said.

She hunched in front of Aleksandra to check her again. The painkillers were definitely starting to wear off.

"You're going to be okay," Jax said. "We're all going home."

Aleksandra reached up when she stood, gripping her wrist.

"Don't do anything stupid," she said through clenched teeth.

Jax went back to the bedroom they'd entered earlier and began to strip off her plates of armor. The entire process took several minutes to finally get down to her vacuum rated suit and take it off. Once she was in her undergarments, she went to a closet and grabbed a colorful robe that looked like it would fit. She looked in a mirror, seeing her fit frame, square jaw, partially buzzed head, and confident brown eyes.

Strong and steady. You got this, Jax.

"That is definitely what I would call stupid," Aleksandra said.

Jax grinned. "And that's why it's going to work."

CHAPTER 7

The weather-worn brown duster did little to protect Rangnar from the torrential downpour of acid rain. His beard was soaked, clinging to his face like a moist towel, stinging his skin. He still couldn't feel his right arm where the drone had poisoned him the prior night, but it was imperative to get rid of the crystal fast. The longer he held onto it, the better the chance some bounty hunter would find him, or worse.

Wrath tech wasn't just illegal, it was so rare, people would kill for it.

As soon as Saber had flown the *Beak* back to their homebase, the city of Optus on the planet Azuri, Rangnar headed out into the slums to meet with the Corinn treasure dealer with whom he'd arranged to sell the tech. Of course his Marka hunters weren't big fans of him working with Corinns after their long history of being colonized by the more advanced species.

But that didn't mean the Markas wouldn't take their money. Rangnar didn't have a problem with it either.

He already felt like he was being watched, and not just by his crew, though the Markas prowled nearby, each of them keeping their multi sets of eyes on the streets for hostiles.

Two distinct pairs of heavy bootsteps had been following him through the streets for the past few blocks. He doubted it was a coincidence.

In his world, coincidences were rare, and were therefore always treated as threats. The sixth sense of being followed triggered his Five Death Rules:

Number 1: *Never trust a human.*

Had Captain Weston betrayed him? Of course, that was entirely possible, even though Weston had to know doing so would mean the end of his life. Even if Rangnar was killed, one of his Markas would hunt the traitor down.

Rangnar considered Rule Number 2: *Never risk your life for loot.*

The problem with that one was, as long as he held the crystal, he *was* risking his life. Not to mention he couldn't well live without loot. So he would proceed with Rule Number 3: *Always have multiple escape routes*—preferably—*none that include public transport.*

He knew these streets like he knew his ex-wife: too well. It didn't take long to lose the boots and find a place to shelter. Across from him was the overhang of a local watering hole. The tall, dilapidated buildings making up this block were just one of hundreds in Optus, a slum city built in a halo around an industrial shipyard that constructed everything from four-passenger civilian cruisers to mammoth freighters that hauled goods across the colonies.

Rangnar kept his back to the wall. If it weren't for the storm clouds, he might have been able to see one of the many ships heading up to the orbiting station, where customers would take possession of their new vessels. Not this evening, though. The storm clouds blocked any hope for a view of a shiny new ship, or the rust colored mountain chain to the east where the Larks lived.

The only things Rangnar could see were the run-down buildings with sad businesses below and sadder apartments above. Shanty metal awnings protruded out of the stucco-like substance coating the exterior to protect from the weather. Tarps covered rows of clay pots or raised dirt beds that locals used to grow whatever they could to help supplement their diets. Some of those people could be seen behind their filthy windows, watching the city Bug Match at the stadium ten miles away, where Lark drones battled each other in a gladiator styled format.

One of those creatures must have died in the current match, because he could see several people inside their apartments howling at a loss. He did a quick scan to make sure none of them were glancing down at him.

That was Rule Number 4: *Blend in.*

To any average onlooker who was paying attention, he would simply appear as an older man seeking refuge from the storm. But Rangnar didn't care about the health effects of the rain. He had spent most of his life exposed to plasma bombs, fire blades of all shapes and sizes, laser bolts, and the fiercest warriors the galaxy had to offer. It seemed something, or someone, was always trying to kill him.

And like always, he was ready for combat.

Death Rule Number 5: *Be prepared for anything.*

Under his duster, he had his sniper rifle, hand cannon, fire hatchet, and a rig of T-flesh bulwarking his organs. He activated the auditory system hidden in his dreadlocked hair and set the range to allow him to hear multiple conversations nearby. The tech made a huge difference, especially with his shitty hearing in the ear that he lost years ago.

He could hear a Wooly arguing with a drunk human at the adjacent bar, something about the Bug Match. A woman standing in a doorway offered a "blazing ride" at a whisper to a passing man. Rangnar used his enhanced lenses to zoom in on a shipyard worker coming home from a shift, covered in grease.

Then he heard the rap of heavy boots. Heavy treads, military style. The same he'd heard from the two guys earlier. They were definitely getting closer. It was time to get a look at their faces.

He pulled his duster hood down over his missing ear and snuck a glance. At the end of the street, the two men in black ponchos rounded the corner. Both were in their forties and shared a honey pipe. They paused to take a drag under the awning of a bath house. Then they stumbled his way, following the scent of barbequing meat to a food stand on the corner.

An umbrella draped over the grill and the cook. Some type of rodents roasted on skewers behind a glass window. The men both placed orders.

"I'm starved," one of them said.

Rangnar narrowed his eyes on their weathered faces. He thought the pipe could be a ruse to throw watchful eyes off, but they were both inhaling the smoke. That told him they were desperate, addicted mercs. That, or they were casual users with the munchies for some rat wings.

Perhaps it was just one of those rare coincidences and he was being paranoid.

As I should be, he thought. Paranoia had helped keep him alive, and he knew these streets. He had grown up in ghettos just like this one, on Hex Prime, in a dump of a city where slumlords doubled as crime bosses, squeezing every solar out of the poverty-stricken occupants through rent, the cost of inflated food grown on rooftops, and of course on the "honey" their associates, their "soldiers" forcibly dealt.

Most people that grew up in places like this never left. Living and dying on the same block they were born on. But by sheer, grinding determination, killer-instinct, and an eager heart,

Rangnar had escaped Hex Prime. Over the years, he had amassed an empire of wealth from bounty hunting both humans and aliens, and then by going after Wrath tech.

It certainly hadn't been easy. He spent much of his youth in a run-down building with other squatters, doing whatever he could to make a living after he fled the orphanage. He never knew his father, but was told he had died serving in the Colonial Alliance Eagle Infantry. His mother had abandoned him.

For years he had longed to find her and give her a piece of his mind. But as he got older, he let his anger go, and when he did get info on her location, it was too late. She was dead from an overdose of the same garbage these men were smoking.

The crystallized nectar, *honey*, came from bird-sized insects on Corinnia. After it was destroyed in the Wrath invasion, the insects became incredibly more valuable until everyone and their grandpa started breeding them across the system.

The finished product was potent, and extremely addictive, but Corinns could process the toxins that came with the intense high derived from smoking the glaze, making it less so. Humans did not have the systems to metabolize it well.

Even now, Rangnar could picture his mother smoking the pipe stuffed with a shining hunk of what looked like honey. It melted as she sucked in breath after breath, her body becoming limper and limper until her head slumped against her chest.

He felt guilt, regret, anger, but mostly now, he felt sadness.

Rangnar watched the two men for another moment. One of them took a seat on the curb with a hunk of meat, not bothering even to get out of the stinging rain. Lucid trekked into sight, one of her sets of eyes on the men, the other on Rangnar.

He gave her a slight nod that it was okay to proceed.

Seeing how careless the two men were told Rangnar these guys weren't bounty hunters, and if somehow they were, they would be no match for his close-combat weapons. He would cut them down with his fire hatchet before they knew what hit them.

He pushed back into the rain, lowering his head, but not too far, so that he could still see under the brim of his duster hood. The meeting area he had relayed in an encrypted message to the Corinn treasurer dealer wasn't far, inside a crowded market with a retractable roof. Tonight that roof was closed off to shield the shoppers from the rain, but there were cracks in the dome, leaking in areas. He could see it streaming down with his enhanced eyes.

Rangnar entered through the western arc, an impressive structure built to look like one of the distinct Arc mountains with the stone at the top forming a fishhook-like peak. Retractable spikes stuck out of the street to block incoming traffic from the pedestrian area. Thousands of human colonists and a variety of off-worlders melted together in a throng within the largest public space in the city. A smorgasbord of smells hit his nostrils, everything from the wet, furry arms of Woolies to the gamey aroma of the most famous Azuri dish—a stew made with the tentacled limb of a carnivorous plant that grew in the warm saltwater ocean.

He didn't care for the chewy meat himself, but his hunters loved it. Nuke and Billy Bob were probably salivating over the smell—especially BB. Both of the Markas were close, perched along the high, wrap-around balcony of the central building in the market.

Saber was also nearby, stalking through the crowds.

"Clear," Lucid chirped over their encrypted comms.

"Ready when you are, boss," Nuke said.

Rangnar waited a moment to check his surroundings. In the building below them were more market stalls, and below those, an extensive set of utility tunnels. That was where he would retreat, if the transaction went poorly. He had other escape routes planned too, but that was the primary.

Satisfied all was set, he moved into the crowd. He reached inside his duster and gripped the handle of his hand cannon in one hand, and a knife in the other.

A group of Woolies waddled ahead, barking in their language, which his translator relayed. They were searching for frog legs tonight. Their species had a thing for Earth amphibians, for some reason.

Just ahead, tanks full of the green creatures along with bowls of colorful fish had attracted some human buyers. There weren't many Corinns here tonight, only a few of the tall, blue beings, dressed in their jeweled robes. Some of them walked with their hands behind their backs, like bored old human men.

Rangnar entered the central building to a corridor framed with stands. One vendor displayed tanks of two-foot long purple crustaceans that humans called river prawns. They were native to the Wooly planet Dari and were one of his favorite treats. A grill sizzled with the shelled creatures, and the server was packing the meat into hotdog buns.

Saber trotted into view just ahead, his muscles flexing around his black limbs and white chest. The Marka lifted a chin, exposing his titanium canines, protruding like a saber toothed tiger. Like most of his species, he was extremely loyal, and could be extremely violent when necessary. Those tungsten-tipped teeth had ripped through the flesh of many unfortunate people who had crossed Rangnar over the years.

Lucid also came back into view on the balcony above, her coat fluffy and gray. She could be violent too, but didn't enjoy it. She was as kind as her four diamond-colored eyes appeared.

She chirped quietly, but the auditory system relayed the message to Rangnar.

All clear. Guest is waiting.

Rangnar proceeded to the rooftop, cautiously stepping out onto a lookout covered by an awning. Standing at the opposite end near a railing was a tall Corinn woman who simply went by D. She had her hands clasped behind her back and was gazing out over the market.

He let the door click to make sure she knew he was there.

The Corinn slowly turned, spreading out her lengthy arms, her sleeves falling downward. "Greetings," D said. "I've been waiting to meet the Phantom for many years."

"You got the solars?"

"Humans," she said with a shake of her elongated head. "Always so quick to business. You know, patience is a characteristic of higher intelligence. Sad you humans never developed much of it. Perhaps that's why you're only—what's your intelligence rating? Fourth? Fifth? I can never remember."

Rangnar let the condescension slide without comment. "Business is why we're here, is it not?"

She reached for the center fold of her robe, and Rangnar prepared to draw his hand cannon. He heard a cracking and saw Billy Bob and Nuke in his peripheral vision, on the roof. The Markas were both ready to pounce.

"Easy," he said.

"Call your dogs off," D said. Dimples formed on her high cheekbones. It was the Corinn way of smiling, and sometimes frowning. In this case, he wasn't sure what it meant.

Rangnar jerked his chin. Both the large Markas backed away into the shadows, but just barely. Their hatred of Corinns showed in their glistening eyes, which pierced the darkness.

"Good," D said. She slowly withdrew a curved metal case, as smooth as a pearl. It cracked open to a disc. "I have half of the agreed upon fee here."

Rangnar raised a brow. "Half?"

"The rest will be sent to an encrypted account on Honi, as soon as I'm safely out of orbit."

Rangnar studied her emerald eyes for a read that would tell him whether he could trust her, or if this was a scam to rip him off. But reading a Corinn was nearly impossible. There was nothing there.

He reached into his vest slowly and removed the crystal shard, enclosed in a scanner blocking case. Ever so slowly, he opened it with one hand, keeping his other on his pistol.

D stepped closer, eyeing the crystal. Her dimples formed again in a rare display of emotion. She handed out the solars and he accepted, exchanging them for the crystal.

"Nice doing business with you," he said.

She bowed slightly as Rangnar retreated, keeping his eyes on her.

"What's D stand for, if you don't mind me asking?"

"Destiny," she said.

Rangnar nodded. "Later, Destiny."

"Until next time."

He went back into the market, stuffing the case into Saber's jacket. The creature took off into the crowd, vanishing with the solars. Lucid remained near Rangnar as they hurried through the patrons. Nuke and Billy Bob went ahead to watch for hostiles.

A pair of Woolies moved in front of Rangnar, every single furry arm gripping crushed frogs, some that had their heads already bitten off.

Rangnar squeezed by on the right side, bumping one of the orangish red beasts. It barked and turned, baring its teeth.

"Apologies," Rangnar said.

Lucid glanced back for a slight second, then up toward the skyline. Rangnar heard the rumble of engines as they exited the dome. Cautiously, he stepped out into the street and looked to the east where the noise originated, expecting to see a new vessel heading up from the shipyard. Instead, he saw the brown hull of a Colonial Alliance Warhorse transport descending from orbit. Flames from the vertical thrusters burned bright over the city as the beast of a ship began to lower over the eastern wall.

Rangnar stared for a long moment, wondering who, or *what*, could have possibly brought an entire company of Eagle Infantry to Optus.

Whatever the trouble was, he wanted to get gone fast.

CHAPTER 8

The *Trash Squid* hung out in a crater on Tinus, the largest moon of two orbiting the Corinn controlled planet of Eern. Axel knew it had to be hard for Cricket to be this close to the former Marka home world without feeling animosity toward the Corinns, which was totally understandable. This would be like Axel looking at Earth, if the Corinns had taken it. Or if they decided to invade Hex Prime now.

He didn't want to say anything to put Cricket on the spot, but Axel did offer a nod to his friend to make sure Cricket knew he was thinking of him. That was all it took for them sometimes to communicate.

Cricket saw the gesture with his back eyes and returned the nod. He kept his front eyes on the HoloMatrix screens. They sure had a great visual of the surface, thanks to the trash pod drone Axel had sent after the pirates. It had entered the atmosphere and was tracking the Slicer fighters on the surface. So far, it didn't seem like any of the Corinn security patrols had detected the pirates or his drone, but the Corinns were down there, and they would blast anything out of the air that dared try to raid the surface of what they viewed still as their world.

He looked away from the screen for a view with his naked eyes. Even from hundreds of thousands of miles away he could see the sad truth. It was difficult to believe the world was once covered in lush purple trees, waterfalls, and deep canyons brimming with life. Now the surface looked like scabs on festering wounds.

The Wrath had all but destroyed the planet thirty-five years ago. The Stewards slowed their advance in several battles, allowing Corinn refugees to escape the major cities, but eventually the decision was made to glass the planet with plasma bombs to kill the aliens that had taken root there, rather than let the Wrath spread.

Gigantic craters marred the surface from those bombs. There were also gigantic cracks that crisscrossed the brown surface like scars on the back of a Corinn bull. The massive, elephant-sized beasts with three eyes once roamed Eern's vast purple prairies after the Corinns had bred them en masse. The beasts had thrived in the pastures of bio-luminous flowers. Axel had seen old images of herds so dense it looked like the ground itself was moving. Before that though, long before, he imagined there had been packs of Markas roaming those fields.

He glanced at Cricket again, noting that he was still extra quiet. Not a huge surprise.

"You think anything is still alive down there?" asked Luna.

"Nothing native to the planet," remarked Spartacus. "The Wrath invasion caused a rapid die-off of all life, as food chains began collapsing. On top of that, the invasive foreign chemicals introduced from the aliens burned through the flora habitats, killing virtually everything."

"They're trying to bring it back," Brayton said. "Just look at those terraformers."

He tapped on a HoloMatrix screen, bringing up an image of a small city-sized blue machine that looked like a spherical bacteria cell. A twisting corkscrew tower extended from the center, rising fifty stories into the sky. Branches draped off the spiral, each equipped with sensors and specialized tools.

"Those machines are currently in their first stage, cleansing the planet," Spartacus said. "However, as you can see, they do not appear to be working."

"Not what the Corinns are saying," Luna said. "They claim to be ahead of schedule in their efforts to restore their planet."

"Our planet," Cricket said.

Axel glared at Spartacus, hoping he wouldn't say anything stupid.

"Sorry," Luna said. "I didn't mean anything—"

"It's fine," Cricket chirped back.

"Honestly, I'm not buying the Corinns will ever bring this world back," Brayton said. "There should just be a bright yellow No Trespassing sign around the whole place."

Isn't that the truth, Axel thought.

Relentless fires burned from the endless tunnels of gasses that vented out of the canyons and fissures across the terrain. He looked away from the view.

"You got that damage SITREP for the FTL drive yet?" Axel asked.

Luna lingered behind a monitor, checking lines of data. "It's not promising," she said. "We can't fix it without additional parts. Good news is the damage to the exterior of the ship is mostly cosmetic, nothing Uga can't fix."

"Uga no fix nothin' 'til I get some food," he barked. "Eat first, fix later."

"We're not repairing the ship right here," Axel said. "Cricket, go ahead and whip up whatever you can find."

"Got it," Cricket said. He trotted off with Uga following.

"Brayton, Luna, you too," Axel said. "I'll stay here with Sparty and keep watch."

"You need to eat too, Captain," Luna said.

"I'll stop by in a bit."

She gave him a worried glance, her eyes flitting to the monitor he had smashed.

Yeah, I know, he thought.

The crew left the bridge and Axel brought up the mirrored view from the trash pod drone following the Slicers across the surface of Eern. They had lowered into a long stretch of gorges, probably to avoid any Corinn radar and their mechanized foot patrols. Fires raged inside the gigantic cracks, venting smoke and gases that further kept them hidden.

"Go eat, Captain," Spartacus said. "I will inform you of any updates."

"Thanks, Sparty," he said.

Axel was hungry but decided to stop by his quarters for a moment of solitude to clear his head. The private space was nestled under the bridge. As soon as he opened the hatch to the small, tidy space, he heaved a sigh.

This was home, furnished with a bunk, chair, and a sturdy desk made from a tree that lived on Earth hundreds and hundreds of years ago.

He liked *old* things. Pencils. Paper.

A recessed shelf in the hull across from him held the leather-bound books he had collected over the years. Some were written by alien races about their histories, others were ancient books from Earth.

The only picture he had was that of his adopted family—his crew—taken a year ago when they had just secured the biggest payday of their career by recovering a CANDF Bloodhog fighter that had gone missing on a backwater planet. Axel was holding a surfboard under one arm, surrounded by his crew on the beach where they had pulled the vessel from the ocean.

He smiled, looking at that old yellow board that he had nearly died on a few days ago on Honi.

Surfing, diving, climbing, rafting, flying—anything that got the adrenaline flowing—were the things Axel loved. The adventures kept the anger at bay, kept him from going insane.

He could feel that heat now, like a snake wrapped around his neck, waiting to hiss venom into his ear. It had almost taken hold of him back in the asteroid field. He glanced now at a tiny slice on his hand where the viewscreen glass had nicked him.

Exhaling, he reached across his desk and pulled out the only novel he owned: *The Adventures of Huckleberry Finn* by Mark Twain. Mira had handed him the book with an inscription when she sent him away at the age of ten. He opened it to the fading words.

Axel, always seek adventure, but don't forget what I've taught you—seek yourself first. I will always be in your heart, my sweet brave Lion, but you must now make your own way.

Sometimes reading it made him sad. Other times it made him angry—angry for her forcing him to be on his own, then never looking for him, never reaching out to let him know she was alright over the years. To this day he still didn't know where she was, or if she was even alive.

Five years ago, after he bought the *Trash Squid*, he had broken his promise and gone looking for her, returning to Earth, but finding no trace.

A knock startled him.

"Come in," Axel said.

Luna opened the hatch.

"What is it?" he asked.

"Checking on you." She didn't mention his actions on the bridge, but she did eye his hand.

"I'm sorry about getting upset," he said. "Won't happen again."

"You're under a lot of stress, I get it. Dinner's almost ready."

They went up to the mess hall where Cricket slaved over the stove with two boiling pots, using his double tail curled over his shoulders to stir the contents.

Uga sat at the table wearing a bib to collect whatever fell out of his mouth so he wouldn't waste a bite. He tapped his utensils in four hands on the table.

"Hold on," Cricket chirped.

Brayton hung out with his back to the hull, reading a smart pad. When he saw Luna and Axel, he walked over with it.

"Lots of chatter over the encrypted CANDF channels in this sector," he said. "I haven't been able to decode any of it, but something's definitely happening out there."

"Related to this?" Luna asked.

"Anything about the Corinns?" Axel asked.

"Radio silent, from what I can tell," Brayton said.

"Supper's served," Cricket chirped. He trotted over with a pot gripped in one tail and a large spoon in the other. He used it to scoop out the broth with boiled Hydro meat into Uga's bowl, which he held up greedily.

"More," Uga barked. "Please."

When it was nearly overflowing with the purple chunks, he brought it down to the table and dug in. The Wooly utilized all six limbs to eat in a chaotic flurry of furry movements with his long arms shoveling food in, and his short top arms wiping any misses back into his mouth. He finished with his bowl before Axel even had a chance to cut into one of the buttered ash roots that Cricket set down on a platter.

Uga snatched a handful of the superfood then retracted the arm swiftly to his mouth.

"Thanks, Cricket," Axel said.

"Yes, good, good," Uga barked while chewing.

Just as Axel raised a fork with a skewered root to his mouth, clanking clattered from the open hatch. Spartacus raised his only arm. "Sorry to interrupt, but I didn't want to use the comms," he said. "Those Slicers have landed on the surface."

Axel shot up, raced back up to the bridge, and brought up a visual from the trash pod to the main monitor. The mounted screen came to life, relaying the feed from their drone. All Axel saw was a wide fissure with what appeared to be a stream of lava snaking across the bottom.

"I don't see—" he'd begun to say when the visual zoomed in.

The gorge in the ground went deep, almost seven thousand feet. At about four thousand feet down, an enormous black Vulture ship had landed on a rocky overhang. Red, feather-like objects protruded around the bow, but these weren't feathers—they were the re-docked Slicers.

"Can you get us lower?" Axel asked Spartacus.

The drone descended until they had a visual of the pirate crew wearing sand-colored, bulky, vacuum rated suits. Four of them rolled a cage on wheels across the terrain with a cable winch system that Axel guessed they were about to use to lower into the cavern.

He noticed a second group with two more pirates and a third person in a blue suit.

"Zoom in on that guy," Axel said.

The trash pod relayed an image of the man's blue suit. There was no mistaking the name on his chest.

Cyprus.

"He's a prisoner," Axel said. "These pirates must have destroyed his ship, taken him, and forced him to bring them back to this original excavation site, whatever it is."

"We should report this," Luna said. "That guy is innocent."

"Maybe, or maybe he sold out his crew, no?" Uga gestured toward the screen with two arms and shrugged with two others. "Joined the pirates."

"Brayton, do you have confirmation of the pirate ship's name yet?" Axel asked.

"Negative, Captain."

Another pirate crossed the ledge to the men at the winches. He was taller and leaner than the others and bulwarked by a type of armor that Axel had never seen before. That fact alone might be enough to get a hit.

"Brayton, see if you can get a match in the system on that armor," Axel said.

"Already on it, standby."

Axel folded his arms over his chest, waiting just ten seconds.

"Sir, I have a match. That is Kian Ka' Ki," Brayton said.

"A Corinn?" Luna asked. "I've never heard of a Corinn pirate."

"Kian Ka' Ki is a former colonel who oversaw an army of war bots for thirty years, but was disbanded when the Stewards were deployed," Spartacus explained. "Kian Ka' Ki remained an emissary, but later vanished—"

"Do we know what they are excavating?" Axel asked.

"Negative," Brayton said.

"I have a theory," Spartacus said.

"Let's hear it," Axel said.

"This canyon was once a key Corinn mining system that employed millions of Woolies to extract forgite veins deep beneath the surface," the droid explained. "Many of those mines were destroyed during the invasion, but due to seismic activity, some have reopened."

"You think these pirates are here to steal forgite?" Luna asked. "And that was what the *Cyprus* was carrying?"

"Uh, guys," Brayton said.

Axel looked back to the drone view of the pirates. Kian Ka' Ki was standing in front of the *Cyprus* crew member, pointing at him. The man went down on his knees, holding up his hands as if to beg for his life.

Kian turned and walked away. Two of the guards remained with the prisoner.

Suddenly, Kian drew a dagger from a sheath on his wrist guard, whirled, and threw it right into the chest of the man. He slumped over into the dust.

"My god," Brayton mumbled.

Luna had a hand over her mouth.

It was crystal clear now that these pirates were ruthless and would do anything for whatever loot they were excavating. The other group of men lowered their cage down into the trench with a Marka-sized spider droid equipped with a variety of tools.

An idea seeded in his mind as Axel watched, but if he was going to risk everything, he needed the support of his crew.

"Who's up for stealing from some thieves?" he asked.

"I was afraid you were going to ask that," Brayton said.

"Deploy me into the flames! I am prepared to meet my fate in the arena," Spartacus said. "I am—"

"Shut it, or we use your metal bones for wind chimes," Uga barked.

"Relax," Axel said.

"*Relax*? Capa, those Slicers just 'bout turned us into maggot food, no? Now you want to go down there and poke them like hornet nest?"

"You better have a damn fine plan for that," Brayton said.

"Spartacus, how are our Bafflers?" Axel asked.

"Operational," replied the droid.

Axel considered his idea—sneak to the surface using their Baffler system to stave off any Corinn radars, then get within visual range of the Vulture. He would drop down, trek in, and steal some of the goods right from under their noses.

"Those scoundrel assholes are doing the grunt work," Axel said. "The plan is simple. We drop in and ruin their day. Then we buy Spartacus a new arm, upgrade the ship, and bring on all the food Uga could ever eat."

"Not possible," the Wooly replied.

"The Corinns might be able to detect us, even with our Bafflers," Brayton said.

"Yeah, and those pirates aren't just any thieves," Cricket said.

"No, but we have a Wooly." Axel grinned.

All eyes flitted to Uga. He growled back, a sign he had an explosive idea, literally.

"Capa, you promise me all the food I can eat, no?" Uga said.

Axel nodded. "You'll never go hungry again."

Uga grinned, showing his two canines. "Get me close enough, and I'll make sure they never fly again. I give them big owie and boo-boos in big *boom*!"

"I'm in, but I'm coming with. That's non-negotiable," Luna said.

Axel held her gaze.

"Someone's got to keep you two scoundrels alive," she said.

"Krish, SITREP," Jax said.

White noise crackled over the short-range encrypted comms. Then came the reply. "Working on re-establishing comms with Command."

"Copy."

Jax glanced over her shoulder at the two-story stone dwelling where she had left Aleksandra. She could see her in the upstairs window with a laser rifle trained on the square.

Smoke tendrilled over the horizon where the Inos had

blown up half of Hatchet Platoon when they had entered the caves to retrieve the Wrath bones. Jax reminded herself that she could have been one of those Eagles if it weren't for Folkert sending her on babysitting duty.

Now Jax was the best chance the survivors had until reinforcements arrived.

She quickened her pace down an abandoned stone street on her way to the village square. She felt naked despite wearing the baggy, colorful garments she had stolen from the closet.

Pulling her stocking cap down to her ears did little to make her feel better. It did little to help her blend in with the long-haired men of the tribe. But if they caught her, she would take a few down on her way out.

The distant excited shouts grew closer. From the sounds of it, the entire village had gathered there to celebrate, perhaps thinking they had beat out the Eagles.

They couldn't be that naïve, could they?

Jax almost felt bad for these people, at least for the civilians. Their tribal leader had doomed them all. It was just a matter of whether Jax would bring that doom, or if Command was going to get their shit together and drop in another platoon with orders to shoot first and ask questions later.

Right now it seemed they were waiting to figure out what had happened on the surface before committing more troops or missiles. Chances were good Command already knew and had sent drones to capture visuals of the town's square. But Jax wasn't going to take that chance.

She hurried down another abandoned street that intersected the square, instinctively reaching for her weapon, but having to resist. She stopped a few minutes later to check in with Aleksandra and Krish.

"I'm just outside the square," Jax said over the short-range comms.

"Copy, I've got eyes," Aleksandra said. "Six of the insurgents took off a few minutes ago."

"How many left?"

"Three, but there are civies everywhere."

"Krish, what's the status on comms?"

"I'm working on an uplink, should only be a few more minutes," he replied.

Jax considered not waiting, heading in now. If there were only three hostiles out there, she could take them out, free some Eagles, and even the odds against anyone else. But only if she moved this second. The other warriors could return at any time.

"I'm going for it," Jax decided.

She moved around the wall and got her first glimpse of the crowd. Hundreds of people of all ages were out here. Markas trotted among them, chirping. The loyal alien species could be extremely fierce to protect their handlers.

Jax approached the crowd, holding a breath in her chest.

Strong and steady, and slow...

An Ino armed with a rifle looked at her for a long moment, but Jax kept walking, avoiding eye contact. She searched for Minnor Jikk, finally seeing the Ino leader standing next to the Torq statue with his glowing fire sword raised skyward as if taunting the Eagles to strike him down with a Lightning missile.

If that happened, it wouldn't just be the tall, proud warrior blasted into a pile of burning pulp. The entire village would be dead or on their way.

Jax melted into the back of the crowd, working her way through. People shouted and cheered at the statue of the Torq. Some of them put their fingers to their necks to make a humming sound.

The gamey scent of clothing saturated by smoke filled the cool air. Not having a helmet on was a new experience, but she remembered her training back on the desert world of Nadi, where she was taught to use her senses instead of relying on technology. That didn't mean she was happy to be striding up without her power armor, but at least she had a voice translator earpiece that would tell her what the hell these people were suddenly so excited about.

She was cautious not to bump into anyone, keeping her head down as she approached the front of the crowd. Just ahead, a man with long golden hair held a young child up on his shoulders. The boy was pointing, but not at the statue.

Jax followed the tiny finger when she heard the same grunting noises she'd heard when they landed. As she turned, she saw it was indeed made by the same source.

You've got to be shitting me, she thought.

"Jax, we got a problem," Aleksandra reported on the comms. "You're about to have company."

The warriors from earlier were returning across the square, but not with more Eagles as prisoners. They escorted Torqs. Four of the pink-bellied beasts grunted and squawked in the back of a cart pulled by a pair of Purlas, white-furred creatures that looked like a cross between a cow and a horse with a black, furry trunk.

The crowd backed up to make way, giving Jax a view of the Eagles. Folkert lay in a fetal position, blood pooled around his corpse. The other men were on their knees with their hands on top of their helmets.

Minnor Jikk swiped his blade over their heads with a whoosh that made the crowd grow wild. Then he raised the burning sword back to the sky, again taunting the enemy.

"The Colonial Alliance and their murdering Eagles have taken from us for the last time! Now we take from them!" he shouted. "Today we sacrifice the infidels who came to take our Torqs!"

Take your Torqs? Jax thought. *The dumb shits attacked my platoon because of that?* Could this all have been a grave misunderstanding? It didn't seem possible.

Jax felt her heart quicken at the sight of more Inos joining the crowd around the wagon. The back gate was open, and two of the soldiers helped herd the creatures down a ramp onto the terrace.

Their leader now had his blade angled at an Eagle at the left end of the line. It was Jacobs, the squad leader for Alpha team, and a man Jax considered a friend.

As the Torqs waddled over, the crowd lowered their heads. The other soldiers did the same thing, bringing their fingers up to their necks to hum. Minnor Jikk raised his spear.

A crackling came over the noise.

"Established connection with Command," Krish said. "I requested reinforcements, but they were denied."

"What? Why? What the hell are they waiting on?"

"I don't know."

She again thought of what her father had said about things blurring out there, in battle, when things weren't exactly clear.

Shouting from one of the captured Eagles rang out. That was all Jax needed to hear. They were out of time, and it was time for her to make her move.

"Cover me, Aleks, I'm going in," Jax said.

She shut off the comm, striding through the last of the crowd. Reaching down, she pulled out both pistols. There was a single beat of hesitation as she raised them at the Ino leader holding up his blazing serrated sword. Two squeezes of the trigger blasted him with a pair of bolts. The impacts seared through his light armor, knocking him off kilter. Yet, somehow, the massive man managed to raise his sword again.

He glared at her with a gaze full of rage.

"You should have surrendered," Jax said. She shot the man

in the chest with two more shots, knocking him off his feet and to the ground.

Screams rang out from all directions, and the Ino warriors charged. Sniper fire from Aleksandra dropped two of them before they could get close. By then, Jax had already tossed a pistol to Jacobs. She aimed the other pistol at the closest Torq and fired.

The skull exploded in a burst of flesh and bone. The twisted horn, easily ten feet long and corkscrewed twice around, cracked against the stone as blood rushed out of the seared neck. That stopped every single Ino soldier on the square.

"Lay down your weapons, or we kill them all!" Jax shouted.

The Inos had frozen in shock but still aimed their weapons at Jax and the other Eagles.

"Enough blood has been spilled!" Jax shouted. "Put your weapons down and go back to your homes. No one else needs to die."

None of the Ino warriors moved. Some of the civilians slowly encroached back into the square. Men, women, even some children.

"What is more important? Your families, or these beasts you worship?" Jax asked. "Did they protect you from me? Do you think they will protect you from what's waiting above the clouds?"

The Inos exchanged glances.

A woman with weathered skin and white hair stepped out of the crowd. Judging by her fancy robe and jewelry, she was some sort of elder, perhaps a council member. Someone important with a voice that carried weight.

"Your minister has long treated us like slaves. The Corinns send Eagles to take our Torqs whenever they want, and for nothing but their flippers," she said. "You may see them as nothing more than beasts, but we are entitled to keep our ancient beliefs, and these creatures are sacred to us."

"Believe what you want, but choose now what's more important to you in this moment." Jax replied. "Your families, or these animals."

Slowly, the Inos began to lay down their weapons, which clanked on the ground. One of the Torqs let out a melancholy mooing noise, as if it understood what had just happened.

Jax felt a wave of relief—until she noticed something in her peripheral vision. She turned toward the Ino leader a few feet away, whom she was sure she had killed.

Before she could move, he slashed with his fire sword, the burning teeth cutting right through Jax's unprotected legs. The ground seemed to give out before her as she fell to her back, a hot and icy pain racing up her entire body.

Angry shouts rose from the Eagles she had freed. Her comrades opened fire. The confused Inos who had just surrendered scrambled for the weapons they had just given up.

Bullets and lasers streaked over Jax as she stared in the sky.

There was something up there...an object lowering. It vanished behind an Ino figure towering over her with a sword. Jax tried to move, but her body felt numb, no longer her own. Her mind still worked though, and it processed what was about to happen.

As the Ino plunged the blade downward, the front of the warrior's chest exploded outward around the dual spear shaft through the center. He was suddenly lifted off the ground by a giant of an Eagle in power armor.

The soldier tossed the Ino away like he was a child. An orange energy-cape solidified around his back as laser bolts pounded the electrically powered shield, an advanced technology that only officers had the fortune to carry into battle.

The Eagle raised a laser rifle and fired it at the shooter.

Then he turned and looked down at Jax, his red helmet displaying the emblem of Dark Horse Company.

She blinked, trying to confirm she was seeing what she thought she was seeing—the leader of not just DHC, but the entire Expeditionary Defense Legion standing above her.

General Gabriel Jessup himself.

All sense of time vanished as he nodded down at Jax. That single action filled her with enough pride to keep her alive for a few more moments. She thought of her parents and brother. They hadn't wanted her to be an Eagle, but they would be proud of her now.

Her vision dimmed, darkness moving in as the battlefield raged around her body. It was her final fight, the end of the road for Sergeant Jax Brito from Runi. She would be going back to the farm in a casket, but she was going home a hero.

CHAPTER 9

"All units, report," Rangnar whispered down to the comm bead in his beard.

Rain beat down on him as he cautiously made his way back to his operations center. The entire time, he watched the skyline over the dilapidated apartment buildings. The Warhorse military transport hovered, the thrusters burning like upside down flare sticks. From what he could tell, they were directly above the spaceport.

The acknowledgements of his Marka hunters watching the Eagles sounded off over their encrypted channel. The fast, agile creatures had spread out through the slums, searching for the targets the soldiers had landed to take into custody—or eliminate.

Rangnar knew there was a slight chance he could be that target. No matter how much he had worked to cover his tracks over the years, it was always a risk. After all, he dealt in illegal Wrath tech. He had broken the law hundreds of times, with the help of Captain Weston, who had broken the law with and without him.

Earlier he had ruled out Weston betraying him, but now he

was wondering again, the paranoia creeping into his brain like a space maggot burrowing into an asteroid.

If his gut was wrong, and paranoia right, then Rangnar had a plan to escape, with Death Rule Number 3. His many routes could take him off the planet, if necessary.

One by one, his trusted Marka hunters replied with the same reports.

"No visual," reported Nuke.

"Negative," added Saber.

"Nffging," Billy Bob said while chewing on something, "err. Nadda."

Lucid kept close to Rangnar, just in case they ran into trouble on the long trek back to their home. They kept to the sidewalk, gazes alternating from the sky for drones, to balconies, the hovering Warhorse, and back again. Rangnar liked to keep close to the street where he could access one of thousands of storm drains if necessary. The Markas knew the tunnels well.

"Eyes on a fire team," Saber chirped over a channel. "Sector 3, shipping yard."

Maybe the Eagles had come to seize a ship. It hadn't occurred to Rangnar until now, but it seemed like overkill. He didn't buy it.

The rain lanced down as he pushed his way through the streets. It was going on midnight, and while there were plenty of people going from bar to bar, traffic was starting to thin.

Saber suddenly chirped a warning over their encrypted comms. "Two fire teams headed this way."

Rangnar searched for the closest storm drain, but a group stood on the curb outside a food stand, blocking it.

He stepped into a lounge to take cover.

All four occupants rotated toward him on their stools, facing away from a tarnished brass trimmed bar. The bartender, a woman cleaning a mug, looked at his reflection in the filthy mirror behind it.

"Help you?" she asked.

It was clear this place didn't get much business besides the locals. Rangnar stepped up as

another update from Saber hit his earpiece.

"Teams have split up. One's heading this way. Moving for better visual."

Rangnar could hear approaching boots. Eight sets.

Wait...no, there are nine.

"You want something, mista?" the bartender asked.

The three human patrons and a Wooly all glared, waiting for his answer.

"Whatever they're having," Rangnar answered, electing to stand instead of taking the spare stool.

The boots tramped closer. Tip. Tap. Tip. Tap.

A radio crackled.

The distant voices of civilians scrambling away or gawking hit his auditory system. Then a voice: "You're gonna regret this!"

The bartender handed a mug of frothy beer that Rangnar paid for with a solar coin. He put his hand back inside his coat, feeling his pounding heart as he gripped his hand cannon, ready to fight. With his other hand, he snatched the mug and rotated to look out the window.

The Eagles marched by, escorting a muscular man wearing energy cuffs. Thin, wet hair tendrilled over his features, but Rangnar recognized him right away.

The guy was a soldier of the gangster Tatt, a local slum lord who had several illegal revenue streams, including Corinn honey. One of the biggest manufacturers in the system.

Rangnar kept his hand on his gun as the troops passed. He watched them through the mirror, remembering a time he had marched with soldiers just like this. It felt like a lifetime ago, when he worked as a bounty hunter tracking the remaining Stewards throughout the galaxy.

Of all his jobs, he hated that one the most. It was one thing to hunt dangerous criminals, but he knew not all the Stewards were evil. Many were heroes from the war with the Wrath, a war that would have been lost without the giant genetically altered soldiers.

Rangnar was a teenager when the aliens invaded the Hironia system. He watched, like many colonists did, in horror as the fiery beasts destroyed the Corinn planets of Corinnia and Eern. But the monsters met their match when the Stewards were deployed. Many of those warriors died, or suffered devastating injuries that left them unable to fight—a curse for someone built for only one purpose.

Now they were gone, just like the Wrath.

The tip tap of the boots slowly faded, and Saber finally gave the all clear.

Rangnar passed the beer to the Wooly next to him.

"Here ya go, pal," he said.

The Wooly extended one of his stubby front arms to the mug, picking it up and slopping it down while Rangnar left the bar. He rushed back to his operations center, which was in an industrial zone of the city abandoned long ago. The factories that once produced wings for the shipyard had been retrofitted into apartments. Deep beneath the structures, in an old utility sector, was the entrance to his lair.

Saber led the way through the streets of warehouses, factories and workshops. By now, most of the locals were asleep, but a few drunks or addicts stumbled down the sidewalks. Randoms loitered in the neglected green spaces that weren't so green. The play equipment for children had been parted out by the many junkies that used the salvage to construct their shacks.

The entrance to the building Rangnar had built his home under wasn't far. He took an alley to a stairway that led down to a basement. Saber was at the secure door waiting. He used one of his tails to open it then went down a stairwell.

"Billy Bob, stay topside and watch our backs," Lucid chirped over the comms. "That means stop eating for a minute."

"You got it," he replied.

Nuke showed up a moment later, following Lucid, Saber, and Rangnar down four flights of concrete steps. At the bottom, he pushed in a keycode and opened the door to a warehouse-sized space with a bathroom, kitchenette, and vast storage areas.

This was home. One of several.

In the center of the space was his desk, salvaged from the hull of his former ship, the *Nork*. The old girl had protected him countless times over the thirty years he'd owned her. Back then, Rangnar was a pro at double-crosses, and even triple-crosses. He wrote the playbook on treachery. But he had made a vital mistake that then became the number one Death Rule. That mistake had been trusting his former business partner and childhood best friend.

Nolan Spear.

Rangnar pictured his freckled face and fiery orange tuft of receding hair. Nolan had a contagious laugh and personality that drew people to him. But deep down, he was a snake, the king of deceit, having spent his entire life scamming, stealing, and hunting.

And Rangnar had been right there with Nolan for most of their lives. They had run the galaxy, making a fortune after gaining fame for tracking Stewards. When the last Steward was dead, they had their choice of other high-target bounties. But it all started to go bad when they got into Wrath tech. Things changed between them when CAID and the Corinns put contracts out on *their* heads. For years they survived by changing the name of the *Nork*, updating their identity documents, and forging all new records.

In the end, it was the human he had called his best friend, brother, and business confidante that stuck him in the back with a knife, so to speak. Cutting him as deeply as if with a steel blade.

When enemies closed in, Nolan had ambushed him, cutting off his ear after knocking Rangnar to the ground. He had sabotaged their ship and left him to be captured while Nolan escaped in a small transport.

Rangnar reached up to his missing ear, anger burning at the memory. He had never trusted people much after his mother left him, but this was the final straw. After that, he had surrounded himself with his Marka hunters, in great part for their legendary undying loyalty.

Nuke trotted over. "Was worried the Eagles were here for your head," he said.

Rangnar grinned and took off his duster, draping it over a chair. "Not today, my friend, not today."

Saber growled and went down on his haunches, on guard, as always. Lucid went to her bed, conking out after a long day of duty. She was getting old. The species normally had a life expectancy of around forty human years, and she was already in her thirties.

Rangnar couldn't imagine losing her. He would make sure she lived far longer, ensuring she had the best care when her joints began to go out, which was typical.

We can be grumpy old assholes together, he thought.

He crossed over to his desk where a bank of smart glass showed security feeds from the many entrances to the building. A few junkies were moving about, but that was it. Nothing out of the ordinary.

"Bring in Billy Bob," he said. "It's time to eat."

He took off his coat and went to the bathroom to shower off. His arm was still swollen where the Lark fangs had poisoned him, but he saw no sign of infection. After a long shower, he put on a clean suit and went back to his desk.

"Tonight we celebrate," he said.

Rangnar went to the kitchen and opened up a double-doored fridge. Inside were four slabs of Corinn bull, thick steaks that he had thawed the day before.

"Been saving this for a special occasion," he said.

One by one, he placed the steaks on plates. Some Markas working with humans had taken on human traditions, eating at tables, using utensils. But Rangnar never forced his hunters to do that. They ate on the ground, where they preferred it. They also preferred their meat raw.

Billy Bob ripped his steak in half. He slurped it into his mouth, hardly even chewing it.

Rangnar patted the big fella on the head then did the same to Lucid and Nuke. He stopped when he got to Saber. The muscular Marka stopped, looked up with a half-eaten hunk in his mouth. He didn't like being treated like a pet.

"It's my way of giving you a hug," Rangnar had said long ago.

"Find a woman for that," Saber had replied.

Rangnar returned to his desk and sat down for some bookkeeping. He checked his accounts, noting that the second half D had promised was there. With a grin, he stood to grab a bottle of wine, stopping as he heard a crackling noise.

The Markas, most of them already finished with their meals, heard it as well. All of them got up quickly, except Billy Bob, who struggled to lift his belly. Their sets of eyes went to the smart glass security feeds—which winked off, one by one.

Rangnar rushed over, looking at the last active video. Two men in trench coats walked down a corridor a few floors above them. He only needed a moment to recognize them as the honey users he thought were following him, just before he met with D. Now he was certain this was no coincidence.

He'd been had.

"Pack up, we're outta here!" he called out.

"I'll cover us!" Billy Bob chirped. The Marka opened the door and charged into the hallway with Nuke right behind him before Rangnar could stop them.

A flare of fire surged through his gut as realization set in. His reason had failed him—paranoia had been correct. He grabbed his duster, tossing it on over his duty belt. Securing that with a click, he then rushed to grab his rifle and fire hatchets.

He froze at the unmistakable chatter of laser bolts a second later. And then came the horrifying cry of Billy Bob. Nuke released a chirp that sounded more like a howl.

"No...no...no!" Rangnar shouted.

He rushed over to the door as flashes of lasers pounded the wall at the end of the hallway, the shooters—and Markas—still in the stairwell. Orange glow from the shots illuminated the husky body of Billy Bob, still and limp on his side at the bottom of the stairs. Smoke tendrils rose off his back and belly.

Rangnar could tell he was already gone, but Nuke was trying to drag his body away.

"Nuke! Back!" he shouted.

Shouldering his rifle, Rangnar fired down the passage to keep the two men from entering. He slung his rifle as he got to Nuke, pulled his hand cannon, and fired again. Then he grabbed Nuke by the collar and tried to pull him back.

But the Marka was in beast mode. He had Billy Bob's scruff in his jaws as he pulled his comrade back toward the open door. All Rangnar could do was fire and hope to hold the men at bay. In the respite of shots, he heard heavy military boots.

Eagles were coming.

Saber and Lucid ran over and helped pull Billy Bob into the chamber. Rangnar shoved the door shut, locking it.

He crouched next to the body of his friend, putting a hand on his still warm body, smearing blood onto his sleeve. The other Markas whimpered in grief.

There was nothing they could do for Billy Bob now.

"We have to go," Rangnar said. "Come on, we gotta get, now!"

He started toward the escape exit across the room and halted, hearing the shouts on the other side of the blast door. It suddenly exploded off the hinges. Eagles in black-clad armor rushed forward.

Rangnar brought up his pistol and fired two bolts into the charging lead soldier. The lasers hit him in the helmet and shoulder, blowing off armor and everything underneath. Gore peppered the wall.

"Suck on this you sons of whores!" Rangnar shouted as he fired at the next soldiers storming the room. They fired back, bolts ripping past him. His desk flipped upwards thanks to Lucid and Saber, both of whom retreated behind it. A storm of lasers slammed into the metal as he hunched down.

Saber leapt over the top with lightning speed. The crunch of metal teeth through armor and ripping flesh followed. Nuke also attacked, plowing into two of the Eagles and tearing at their helmets.

"Run!" Rangnar yelled.

He had just stood up to fire when a trap door opened under his feet, and down he went, sliding a hundred feet in a dark tunnel that dumped him into the bowels of the old industrial zone.

Lucid popped out a moment later. Then Saber.

Screams came from above, along with more laser fire.

"Nuke!" Rangnar shouted. "Nuke! Come on!"

Lucid and Saber looked up the shaft with Rangnar.

Seconds passed by before the laser fire ceased.

Moaning sounded, followed by a crunch and a scream.

Silence took over.

Rangnar fumed with anger. Weston must have betrayed him after all. He would track the man down and nail him by the balls to the side of a trash pod then blast his naked ass into space.

"We have to go," Lucid said.

"No, we can't leave Nuke," Rangnar said.

Please, Nuke...please...

Clanking suddenly came from the tunnel shaft. Rangnar raised his pistol at the opening and moved his finger to the trigger, ready to blast the first Eagle.

But instead of black armor, a furry shape shot out.

Nuke hit the ground, his maw covered in blood.

Exhaling, Rangnar took his finger off the trigger. "Thank god," he said, something he *never* said.

"Let's go," Lucid said.

She led the way into the utility sector under the city. The industrial machines powered the slums far above. Fires raged out of the open-faced ovens that worked day and night to keep the heat on. The Markas knew exactly how to navigate the dark corridors, which became a maze among the equipment. Only service droids and rats lived down here.

The clap of boots echoed behind them. Eagles had found their way there through the shaft.

Rangnar ran harder, heading for the mammoth boilers once used to smelt metals to be tooled for various parts of ships. The sector wasn't far, and the pack of Markas knew the way well. But there was one major problem—if they couldn't shake their pursuers down here, they would be forced into a mile-long passage that would put them within firing range before they could reach the end. He had a plan for that too, but it meant he would never be able to come back.

Heaving for breath, he hesitated when he got to the entrance.

"Saber, blow it behind us," he said.

Saber pulled off grates where they had planted explosives. Rangnar kept going with the Markas.

"Brace yourself!" Saber chirped.

The team hunched down as the explosion boomed behind them. Flames rushed down the corridor, and the top of the tunnel collapsed, sealing the way.

"Keep moving," Rangnar said.

Dust and smoke chased them for a few moments before receding. Using flashlights to guide them, they advanced down the long passage which opened to an extensive industrial space. Heat blasted Rangnar as they moved out among the twenty-foot-tall smelting pots that worked around the clock, melting metal dropped in from above then sending the molten liquid through pipes toward smithing areas of the shipyard.

His escape ship was under one of those tanks. All he had to do was access a door to an underground ladder, board, and then fly it out the top.

Lucid was leading the way.

"Rangnar!" boomed a familiar voice.

He turned to see D, the Corinn he had met with, standing with her hands behind her. She pulled them from her back, holding a fire sickle and a laser pistol. It was odd seeing a Corinn with weapons. They rarely committed violent acts, relying on others to do their dirty work, and even to defend them.

"I'm guessing the D doesn't stand for Destiny," he said.

"Not today," she said, dimples forming. "Today, it means *death*."

"At least I know who sold me out."

"It's over," she said. "Those Eagles will be here soon."

The Markas closed in, snarling at her, eager to get some revenge on the race that had taken their home planet.

"You would have never escaped with your dogs," she said. "I can smell them from a mile away."

"They're not dogs," Rangnar said through clenched teeth.

"They aren't much smarter than a dog, maybe a tiny bit more, perhaps on the same level as a Lark. Conquering Eern was truly the easiest in our history of multi-planetary imperialism."

Rangnar wasn't sure if she was trying to goad him and his hunters, but that insult worked. They charged, and he aimed his pistol as fast as he could.

D did the same, both of them firing at the same time and both of them missing. Her bolt nearly took off his other ear.

"You bitch!" he shouted as he dove to the ground.

She spun with her sickle out as the Markas attacked. The sizzling blade cut Nuke across his back to a wail of pain.

"NO!" Rangnar shouted. He and the Corinn both aimed again, but this time D didn't miss. She fired a bolt right into his upper chest, the laser burning through his duster and into his armor with enough force to knock him to his back.

"Boss!" Lucid chirped. She slid next to him, nudging for him to get up while Saber tore into D's arm, ripping one hand clean off.

She sliced with the sickle in her other hand, forcing Saber back. Nuke lunged, taking a bite of her neck. He hit the ground and turned with fresh Corinn blood dripping from his maw as she fell back.

On her rear, she swiped desperately with the blade in one hand to keep the hunters back.

"Stop," Rangnar choked out. He pushed himself up, stumbling.

D pushed herself up to her knees, gripping her neck where Nuke had torn into her, holding her bleeding wrist close to her chest.

Rangnar limped over to her with his fire hatchet. He activated it, the blade blazing blue over her head. Her eyes met his.

"Who do you work for?" he asked.

The dimples on her face formed again.

"Always business with you, isn't it, Phantom?" she said.

"Tell me what I want to know, and maybe I'll let you live," he said.

The dimple fluctuated slightly, maybe into a frown, maybe into a smile.

"Was it the Eagles?" he asked. "Did they hire you, or are they just your security?"

She shook her head. "This isn't about you. This is about something far greater—"

Footfalls sounded in the distance, and then voices. Time was up. The mystery would have to remain just that. Rangnar had to go.

He pushed the axe closer to her head, drawing her gaze, but she didn't flinch or waver in the slightest.

Slowly, he pulled the blade back. Maybe he would earn some good karma by sparing her. He sure needed some.

But then he thought of Billy Bob.

Good karma, or bad karma, he couldn't let this go.

Baring his teeth like a Marka, Rangnar swung the axe into her neck, severing her head with one powerful strike.

"New Death Rule," he grunted. "Never trust a Corinn."

CHAPTER 10

"Entering atmosphere in ten, nine, eight..." Spartacus sounded off.

On one, Axel pushed the thrusters gently, increasing their speed. The goal now was to get to the surface as fast as possible. The ship carved through the thick, reddish clouds choking the planet.

"No sign of Corinns in the sky or on the surface," Luna reported.

"They're out there somewhere," Axel said. "Deploy a second trash pod."

"Deploying now," Spartacus said.

Another drone fired out of the portside, picking up speed and vanishing into the clouds that lay across the wastelands in all directions, a product of the burning gasses from fissures across the surface.

"All the food I can eat, all the food I can eat," Uga chanted, crunching nervously on a nut bar baked with the shells of insects.

"Bafflers activating," Spartacus said.

The hull of the ship transitioned to match the atmosphere.

Axel pushed down harder, increasing their speed to the max the ship could handle. A plasma wave enveloped them as they came lancing through the sky, but the fire receded quickly, and the surface exploded into view. Dusty, cracked hardpan with a concentration of scattered timber stretched as far as they could see.

"Was that a forest—?" he started to say.

"Those are bones," Spartacus said.

"It's a Marka graveyard," Luna confirmed.

Cricket got out of his seat, staring and letting out a sad whimper.

Axel sank into a visualization that was dreamlike, but vivid, gripping him and transporting him down to the surface. It was as if he were there in the bioluminescent fields, the ground shaking under his feet.

A pack of fifty Markas stampeded away from tendrils of fire as flames raged across the grasslands. The males carried bags with their belongings, and females wore pups in slings.

These were refugees, fleeing the Wrath. Trying to find a place to hide or a way to evacuate. But for millions of these innocent native creatures and others like them, there were no dropships that came to rescue them like the Corinns.

The humped body of a gigantic Corinn bull lay writhing in pain with two broken legs at the bottom of a ravine. Axel went down the bank and extended his hand, but was this his hand? It was clad in the golden armor of a soldier.

One of those hands stroked the blue hide of the magnificent creature, while in the other, a serrated fire cutlass ignited to life.

That blade was thrust into the chest of the mammoth steer. It snorted from flared nostrils set between tusks. All three eyes focused on the soldier, not filled with rage or fear, but with gratitude. As if the animal understood this warrior was putting it to rest.

"Captain," Luna said.

Axel heard her voice, but he couldn't break free from this vision. It was as if he were kneeling right beside the bull. The majestic beast lifted its head to the sky and bellowed an ethereal, melancholy cry.

Then it was gone, and Axel found himself looking at Luna.

"Are you okay?" she asked.

"Yeah, I'm fine," he answered.

Cricket, on the other hand, was not. He sulked in his seat, clearly mourning from the thought of the suffering his species had been through.

"I'm sorry, pal," Axel said.

"Approaching landing zone," Spartacus said. The ship lowered over a gigantic crater that was once a Corinn city. Not a trace remained of the grand towers that had reached for the sky. Ten million citizens once lived here, but there was no trace of them either.

Axel braced himself for another image, but now he didn't see anything—he heard it. All at once, the cries of countless Corinn souls hit his ears. Axel tried not to react, but he winced in pain, and turned away.

"Let's get suited up," he said. "Spartacus, you have the bridge. Uga, get the salvage equipment ready."

Brayton and Luna exchanged a glance that Axel saw on his way out. He hurried through the ship, the cries of the Corinns fading away.

Axel was used to the anger, and some visions, but not like these. He had to get focused, especially now, when they were about to embark on a dangerous mission.

Maybe you call this one off.

Axel shook that thought away. He didn't have a choice. He joined Uga and Luna in the cargo hold where he put on his scratched and dented armored suit. The decade old rig needed updating just like the ship. He further hesitated at the thought of the exoskeleton and thermal regulators failing in a hostile environment like Eern's.

"Something up?" Luna asked.

"No, I'm ready," Axel replied confidently.

Uga struggled to get all his arms into the thick vacuum rated suit. Cricket went over, helping him throw a satchel of explosives across his vest, sling his tech pack, and secure salvaging tools all at the same time.

Luna secured her curved helmet. The interior lights glowed, illuminating her freckled features and button nose.

The ship set down with a jolt.

"Good luck," Brayton said, standing next to Cricket. They both looked more than a little worried.

Axel led the way out onto the cracked, broken ground. Uga and Luna trekked by his side up the slope and out of the crater. At the top, Axel turned to see if the ship was visible, but it blended perfectly with the shadows.

"Stay close," Axel said, starting across the flattened terrain. In the distance, geysers of molten rock burst skyward in red jets. The temperature was a balmy one hundred twenty degrees Fahrenheit. That alone wouldn't kill Luna or Uga, but combined with the low oxygen levels, it might.

The hot ground across the volcanic field made Uga dance a few times, his two retractable arms kept tight against his body. He yelped as a geyser shot up just to his right.

Axel almost laughed. The Wooly stayed close behind him as they closed in on the Vulture site within the gorge ahead.

"Not far now," Axel said.

He moved ahead to the end of the plateau overlooking the

gorge. Cautiously, he knelt and peered over the side, relieved to confirm that the Slicers were still attached to the mothership, about two hundred feet below.

Axel checked the elevator platform where three pirates stood. The cable fed car was being cranked back up. He would need to get down there before it reached the top. The best way to do that appeared to be climbing under the ledge and snatch the loot off the platform. Meanwhile, Uga would rig explosives on the engines with Luna watching his back.

"Get ready," Axel said. "I'll let you know when to set and blow the charges."

Uga nodded and began to prepare his explosives, gripping one in each arm. As Axel picked up his coiled rope, Luna reached out.

"You're sure about this?" she asked.

"It will work," he said. "You trust me, right?"

She nodded. "Be careful."

"Always am."

He jogged away, looking for the best place to rappel down unspotted. Finally, he saw a narrow, vertical rock shaft that would mask his descent. He secured his rope, looked briefly over his shoulder then leapt backward.

His spiked climbing shoes hit the rock with a crunch, shattering chunks. He jumped back again, and again, making great time.

Ten years ago, Axel had climbed the second biggest peak in the Hironia System. After a brutal snowstorm and five days of climbing, he had reached the crest.

Not a single person knew of this daunting feat, nor would anyone know when, someday, he climbed the largest mountain in the galaxy, a summit in the chain called the Four Peaks, on the planet Dari, close to where Uga was born.

Axel usually climbed for himself. Like surfing, it left him free and at peace.

But this climb was for his crew and for their livelihood. It was also extremely dangerous.

Kian Ka' Ki had already proven he would kill for the forgite.

Axel braced himself against a gust of wind. Grit peppered his armor and visor. On his next jump, his boots slid upon connecting, breaking off a chunk of the wall. He reached out to grab a handhold, but his hand found a razor-sharp rock, and the shard cut right through his glove. He held on, clenching his teeth from the pain, causing anger to flare.

He closed his eyes, suppressing it. Once it passed, he was relieved to find himself directly parallel to the ledge where the Vulture perched above. The platform was being raised, and standing in the center was the spider drone. It hadn't come back emptyhanded. The pirates had excavated a steaming, smoldering rocky object, clearly a prize. Unfortunately, he was too late to snatch this one from under their noses.

The encrypted channel crackled in his helmet.

"Captain, we have located a patrol of three Corinn Lancers," Spartacus reported.

Axel glanced to the sky. "Where?" he asked.

"Two hundred miles due west, heading away from your location."

"Copy."

He pulled his hand away from the shard, glancing briefly at a spot of bloodied glove. He checked over his shoulder then rappelled down another hundred feet. Satisfied with his position, he began a sideways climb across the vertical wall, a far more difficult task.

He tried to move fast, but even with the rope, this was precarious. If he fell, he would make noise and scatter debris.

And then he would be dangling from a rope, making him the easiest target in the galaxy.

"Captain, Corinn Lancers have spotted the trash pod and are pursuing," Spartacus said. "What are your orders."

"How far?" Axel asked quietly.

"Ten minutes, unless I increase the speed of the pod," Spartacus said.

"No, see if you can hold them back a bit, but lure them in our direction," Axel said.

"In your direction?"

"Problem with your ears, Spartacus?"

"Technically, I do not have—"

"Shh!" Axel froze at the sound of hoots, *ahahs!* and hollers coming from the ledge. Kian Ka' Ki and his crew had clearly found something spectacular.

That meant they were distracted. Now was his chance.

"Uga, what's your status?" Axel whispered into his headset.

"Boom sticks in place, ready to blow a hole in this bird bitch, Capa," Uga barked back over the channel.

Axel pulled out his grappling pistol. A blast of wind nearly knocked it from his grip. He aimed at the ledge and fired off the hook, flying straight upwards with the attached line as soon as it connected.

As he hit the ledge, an enraged shouting came from above. He put the grapple gun away and grabbed the pickaxe. With the rope still attached to his harness, he began to scale the cliff. The screaming grew louder the higher he went.

"Luna, what's going on up there?" he asked.

"One of the pirates got burned," Luna snickered.

Idiots, Axel thought.

"Uga, disable the ship when I say," he said.

"Boo-boos incoming," Uga confirmed.

Axel climbed swiftly, like a Lark drone. At the crest, he

peeked for a view. The first thing he saw was Uga climbing up the ledge, moving fast for the chunky little fella.

Four of the pirates loitered around the cart where the ball of forgite continued to smolder. The spider drone was hunched down in front of it, missing the bottom part of four jointed legs that had melted off on its descent.

One of the scoundrels was hunched over, wailing, clearly in agony.

Kian Ka' Ki came running with two guards flanking him.

"Quiet, all of you," he snarled.

The hunched man tried to straighten his body. He held up his hands, which were missing all but two melting fingers.

"Oh god—oh god!" he cried.

The sight quieted the other pirates.

"I told you not to touch it, idiot human," Kian said. "Use the drone to secure it in the cargo hold with the other one."

Axel looked to the cliff above the ship. He could now see Luna helping pull Uga up to the ledge. The husky Wooly was flailing, having a hard time. His longer arms found holds, but the two shorter limbs on his chest couldn't pull up his weight high enough to get any leverage.

Luna reached down, grabbed him by the scruff, and pulled him up.

"Uga," Axel said quietly into the comm, "when I tell you to blow it, blow it. I'll grab the loot, the *Trash Squid* will extract us, and hopefully the Corinn patrols will show up to take care of these assholes."

"I like it, except for the part about picking up the bone melting loot," Luna said.

"I'm hoping it cools fast."

"*You're hoping?*" Luna hissed.

"Uga, blow it," Axel said.

"Three...two... Fire in the hole!" Uga barked.

At that, Axel lowered his head just a bit.

Nothing happened.

The moment he looked up, the back landing gear of the Vulture exploded, cracking the hull in half. The attached Slicers burst into pieces in a chain-reaction then both hunks of the ship collapsed to the ground, sending out a wave of grit that slammed right into the unsuspecting pirates.

"*Holy crap!*" Axel wasted no time. He hopped over the ledge, ran forward and grabbed the ball, clutching it like a football against his chest. The thing was still piping hot, steaming against his gloves and armor. It was also extremely heavy, far heavier than forgite—

Not to mention too perfectly shaped.

What in the stars was this thing?

As he reached down for his grapple gun, a vision gripped him. Humming came from overhead, a low, menacing sound. Shadows darkened the ground from something massive in the sky. He glanced up at a fleet of six rough black ships covered in barbs and venting smoke.

A group of Corinns suddenly emerged around Axel, who was dressed in that same golden armor again. Men. Women. Children. All dressed in their robes with encrusted jewels.

The soldier—Axel—waved for them to run as he fired a laser rifle into the sky.

The humming transitioned to a horrible roar that brought the aliens to their knees, their hands over their ears, screaming.

This wasn't a vision, this was a memory.

"Axel, get out of there!" Luna shouted.

Her voice snapped him from the trance. He flinched in pain and looked down to find the ball burning through his gloves. His eyes shot to another voice.

"Who the hell are you?" said Kian Ka' Ki.

The Corinn leader of the pirates came at him with a fire

cutlass in one hand, and a viscerally terrifying Rocket Laser Gun in the other. If the laser didn't kill him, the miniature rocket would blow Axel to smithereens.

He backed away, coming close to the ledge. His entire body prickled and his insides turned to fire as his chest furnace activated.

Don't run! Stand and fight! the confident, masculine voice screamed in his mind.

Axel didn't have time to battle that voice. He ducked beneath the sword that came whirring through the air as lasers pounded the ground around him.

Kian aimed the pistol right at his chest.

"I won't miss again," he said. "Drop the artifact and tell me your name so I know which grave to spit on."

Axel stared at the barrel, still gripping the—*artifact?*

"Incoming!" Luna shouted.

He heard them humming, but these weren't illusionary Wrath ships. Three blue Corinn Lancers swooped down, firing bolts at the pirate crew.

Return fire answered from a tripod two pirates had set up from a weapons crate nearby. The gunner tracked the two Lancers, firing into the sky.

Axel turned to meet Kian's boot to his chest. The impact knocked him on his back. The Corinn pirate loomed over him with the pistol aimed at his head.

Sweep his legs then crush his skull!

The voice tempted Axel to do just that, but there was no time.

Another explosion rocked the ledge, knocking the pirate backwards and sending Axel right over the edge. He plummeted into the steaming gorge, limbs flailing. Jagged shards of rock threatened to break his fall by tearing off a limb or impaling him.

He jerked suddenly upwards, pain lancing his chest. He

swayed for a few seconds before he realized his harness rope had caught. A sense of relief washed over him, until the rope snapped.

Then he was falling again. Right toward the river of magma.

Still gripping the ball, he pulled out the grappling gun but didn't get a chance to fire before he hit an outcropping of rock. The impact knocked away the pistol and sent him spinning downward.

A humped shelf of stone rose up to meet Axel. There was no time to reposition his body. All he could do was bring a hand forward. What should have snapped a human arm like a twig, simply sent a wave of heat and then ice up his bone.

Axel slid all the way to the edge of the cliff, his head and shoulders going over the side. He coughed, blood spackling the inside of his cracked visor. Gasping for air, he managed to fill his empty lungs and hugged the ball against his body.

Slowly, he rolled to his back to the view of an aerial battle between the blue Corinn Lancers and the red pirate Slicers. Explosions burst in the sky over the valley.

"You're a dead man!" Kian shouted.

From the ledge above, he aimed his rocket pistol down. The shelf under Axel trembled suddenly, the rock shaking away grit around his body. The edge suddenly cracked free from the rest.

Axel slid for a second, fell, and then hit something hard. Almost immediately he was rising, like the object under him had sprouted wings. He glanced down to see he was sitting on the upper hull of the *Trash Squid*.

Cricket was inside the cockpit of the attached *Hammerhead*. He popped the lid and dashed over to grab Axel, holding them both steady by gripping a maintenance handle by both tails.

"Spartacus, get us out of here!" he chirped.

A hissing came from above, and while Axel couldn't see it, he knew it was the rocket launching toward them. He dove onto

Cricket, flattening his body over his companion, holding the ball in one arm to the side, pressing them into a groove on the hull as the blast boomed behind them.

Heat slammed over Axel, along with chunks of whistling shrapnel. It was over in a heartbeat, but he remained covering Cricket as the ship blasted away from the shattered ledge.

Axel rolled away, gripping the Marka with one hand and the steaming ball against his chest. They slid down the hull as the ship rose, coming to rest as she flattened out.

Pain trembled through Axel's entire body. Warning sensors beeped inside his helmet, but he could hear the message from Spartacus over the comms.

"Hold on to something."

Axel and Cricket both gripped the outer hull as the *Trash Squid* roared low through the valley, using the cover to escape. He watched for enemy contacts but saw nothing trailing them.

"Oh no," Cricket said.

Axel looked over at his friend, heart flipping.

"Are you hurt?" he asked.

"Not me." Cricket pointed at the *Hammerhead*.

The cockpit of their single fighter was a smoking mess.

"Move your ass, Capa!" Uga barked over the comm. "You too, four eyes!"

Cricket was too busy helping Axel to respond to the insult. He gripped him under an arm with a tail and helped him to a dorsal hatch, using his other tail to pop it open.

"Go, Commendatore!" he chirped.

Axel backed down the ladder to the deck. Cricket dropped next to him.

"We're in—go—*go!*" Axel yelled.

He went down on his knees and bent over, feeling the ship pull skyward and blast toward space. Gripped against his armored chest was what he had risked everything for—a ball no larger than an Earth soccer ball. Perfectly round. Extremely dense.

The words from Kian echoed in Axel's mind.

Drop the artifact.

As the adrenaline waned, realization hit Axel.

This thing wasn't forgite. Nor was it Corinn tech.

It was Wrath.

CHAPTER 11

Jax stood on the wide stone terrace of the Bronze Keep, overlooking the grandeur that was Aritrea, the capital city of the planet Hex Prime. She could smell the fresh red pines and the sweet fragrance of the rose gardens.

Fountains fired streams of water at the statues of great Eagle warriors across the terrace while bells chimed in the distance.

Old-Earth single bolt rifles fired in unison.

Crack.
Crack.
Crack.

A bulky Eagle wearing traditional black armor and a gold cape, a Captain's insignia on his breast plate, strode up to Jax. The soldier's features were all but hidden by his parade armet, decorated with gold trim around the nose.

"Sergeant Jax Brito, we honor your valor and bravery on the planet of Jolia by presenting the Golden Eagle Wings," he said.

Jax kept her gaze on the bronze memorial statues. The pride she felt standing here among them was unrivaled by anything she had accomplished in her life.

"Sergeant Jacqueline Brito."

The firm voice came from somewhere beyond the terrace, muffled and distant. She glanced up at the blue sky as the sun brightened. That pine scent turned to a potent chemical odor.

"Can you hear me, Sergeant?"

The sun transitioned to a blinding white glow that she blinked against.

"Jacqueline," came a voice.

"It's Jax," she replied. She had always disliked her birth-name. Felt too old-fashioned and formal.

"Where am I?" Jax's vision cleared to see—not an Eagle Captain—but a man in a white uniform. She was no longer at the Bronze Keep, but in a small medical space with robotic surgical equipment hanging from overhead.

"Sergeant, I'm Doctor Andrew," said the man. He focused on Jax with kind hazel eyes set between crow's feet. "How are you feeling?"

Jax groaned as she went to sit up. Truthfully, she felt fine, other than not being able to feel her legs.

"What happened to me?" she asked.

"You don't remember?"

This was a new voice. A figure came out of the bright light, this one with eyes not so kind. These eyes were dark. Emotionless.

This was a soldier, dressed in a full-black uniform that had the red CAID logo of a Dragon. He removed a black hat from his buzzed head and tucked it under an arm.

"I'm Lieutenant Zac Ripley with CAID. You're currently being treated for injuries at Shield Base on Hex Prime," he said. "I'm here to debrief you regarding what happened on Jolia."

Jax swallowed down her dry throat, trying to recall. She remembered landing on the beach where they were ambushed by Inos. Then fleeing to the city where she'd come up with a plan to save the captured Eagles. She recalled killing the Ino leader, but everything was blank after that.

She felt pride at killing the barbarian. All sense of trepidation vanished. Not only was she alive, she was a hero, bound to be respected for her actions. Maybe she would even be getting a promotion, possibly even replacing Lieutenant Folkert.

"Do you remember your actions on Jolia?" asked Ripley.

"Yes, sir, I do," Jax said. She nodded and cracked a friendly smile.

The lieutenant looked to the doctor.

"Is she mentally fit for this interview?" Ripley asked.

"Our tests indicate so, and as you can see, Sergeant Brito's very much alert."

"Leave us."

Jax watched as the older doctor opened the door, looked over his shoulder once with a gaze of concern, and then left.

Something's not right, Jax realized.

"You broke direct orders, Sergeant Brito," Ripley said in an official, icy tone.

That voice filled Jax with apprehension.

"Not only did you break direct orders, you put your entire platoon at risk," Ripley said. "You also killed a Torq."

"Sir, I did that to get the..." Jax let her words trail off, knowing how ridiculous they would seem.

"Go ahead, Sergeant, finish your statement, whatever you say will go into the completed After Action Report."

Jax considered her words carefully, knowing whatever she said could be used against her.

"My fire team was ambushed when we landed, with Private Martin Keyes KIA. We were cut off, and unable to reach command," she began. "I led Corporal Krish and Corporal

Ostovich into the city. I ordered Corporal Krish to contact Command and moved forward with a plan I devised to save my platoon. I killed the Ino leader and then the Torq to cause a distraction and buy time to free the POWs."

The officer raised his long chin slightly and walked a step closer to the bed.

"Your actions not only put the platoon at risk, they put the civilian and alien populations at risk, including the Torqs in that square," Ripley said. "And according to your corporal, you didn't heed his warnings. He warned you not to move forward with this plan and instead to wait for orders from Command."

"All due respect, but my LT had been executed, and if I had waited, more Eagles would have died, sir."

"Krish also noted that when he received orders from Command, you ignored them."

"Sir, I received no such orders."

"Krish stated that he sent you orders from Command telling you to stand down and that reinforcements were on the way."

"No, sir," Jax said. She remembered it vividly in her mind. "That's not accurate. Krish relayed to me that command denied reinforcements. I moved in to save lives, knowing it was their only chance."

Ripley shook his head. "I interviewed Corporal Krish, and he gave multiple examples where you decided to be a lone wolf."

"Lone wolf? Maybe because I was the only one that could help, since Krish wasn't willing and Aleks was hurt." Jax grew more agitated, unable to hold back. Krish was setting her up, probably to get his own promotion.

"Ask Corporal Ostovich, she will confirm Krish's lying," Jax said.

"That won't be possible."

"Why?"

"Because Corporal Ostovich was killed after your daredevil actions. Along with all but three of the Eagles in your platoon."

"No," Jax whispered.

"No? So you don't remember?"

Jax slowly shook her head.

"Perhaps a video will refresh your memory," Ripley said. He held up the HoloMatrix pad again. "T-1, this is Lieutenant Zac Ripley requesting permission to view the classified video from AAR file 10991."

A holographic image emerged, showing Jax in the middle of the square. She had just shot Minnor Jikk and was yelling for the Inos to put their weapons down. But now Jax saw something she hadn't recalled—the Ino leader she thought she'd killed was moving on the ground.

Slowly, he gripped his fire sword and then swiped right into—

Jax looked down at the sheets covering her legs in horror, a chill running up from her feet. When she reached down to pull the covers back with a shaky hand, she realized this chill wasn't real. The phantom pain increased as she stared down at her legs, missing below both knees.

Her eyes made their way back to the video of a scene of chaos and carnage. All around her fallen body, the survivors of her platoon fought the Inos. Civilians fell among the crossfire, blood pooling across the stone.

Dark Horse Company dropped down from the sky in bullet pods, slamming into the stone square and bursting out with laser rifles and flaming fire swords, jumping immediately into battle.

"My god," Jax whispered.

"God had nothing to do with that," Ripley said. "That was all you. Command was preparing to take out the targets from orbit, but you jumped the gun, as they used to say."

He turned off the video and then held up the HoloMatrix

pad, which ejected a holographic list, reading the items aloud in turn. "As a result of your actions, you're being charged with the following."

Insubordination: Failure to follow two direct orders.

The murder of an alien creature protected under CE Article 919.

Action(s) deemed harmful to the completion of a mission in wartime.

"Do you understand these charges?" Ripley asked.

Jax wanted to argue, to further explain, but there was nothing else she could say. Someone had to take the fall, regardless of Krish's lies.

This time, that someone was Jax.

"Is there anything else you'd like to say about the operation?" Ripley asked.

"No," Jax said.

The officer studied her for a moment, his nose twitching ever so slightly. He held the HoloMatrix pad back up to his lips.

"I hereby recommend the dishonorable discharge of Sergeant Jax Brito from the Colonial Alliance Eagles, effective immediately," Ripley said.

"Sir—" Jax stammered. She clamped her mouth shut, knowing it would do no good to argue—or beg.

"The case file will be sent to CAID for further disciplinary action," said the lieutenant.

"Disciplinary action?"

"Yes, typically these charges carry a minimum of ten years at a penal colony."

Jax glanced up at Ripley as the man tucked the HoloMatrix pad away.

"Any questions?" he asked.

Jax could hardly breathe, let alone talk. She managed to shake her head, afraid to do any more damage.

The lieutenant took his hat from under an arm and fit it over his head as he left the room. From the hallway, Jax heard him say, "Doctor, Brito is ready for you."

Brito, she thought.

No longer *Sergeant*.

No longer an Eagle.

Now a criminal, it seemed.

Doctor Andrew walked inside pushing an electric wheelchair. "This is only temporary," he said, "until your request clears for prosthetics. It will take longer, due to your situation, but we have people that can help you fill out the proper forms."

Jax gazed at the scooter. Her heart fired like a laser rifle as things began to sink in. Her eyes flitted up to the doctor, meeting his kind gaze. Now it was full of something else—pity.

She thought about her parents and brother and how she had promised she would return some day, planning full well to do so as a hero.

She would never go back like this. Broken, and shamed.

Chances were good she would probably never see home again anyway. Not if she was sentenced to a penal colony, especially in her physical condition.

"Before I go," the doctor said. "Is there someone I can contact at home for you?"

"I don't have a home," Jax lied. She put her head back on the pillow, wishing she had died on Jolia.

From the bridge of the *Trash Squid*, Axel looked out the viewports over the twinkling stars in the endless black sea. They were in the middle of no man's space, drifting with minimal power to conserve fuel.

Dents and scratches marred the hull of the ship, but there was no way to know the extent of the damage from the asteroid belt, nor from the rocket that hit the *Hammerhead* during their escape from Eern.

From what he had seen, the small fighter was a complete loss. It broke his heart seeing his ship like this. But it had saved their lives.

Once again, Axel had proven he could succeed without maiming or killing. But it was a damn close call. He was lucky to have escaped with the Wrath artifact. Also lucky the pirates and the Corinns hadn't killed him and his crew. But they weren't out of trouble yet. Although they had escaped Eern, they were almost out of fuel, had a busted FTL drive, and were defenseless without the *Hammerhead*.

"Spartacus, you're sure the Corinns didn't spot the ship?" he asked.

"We have been through this, sir," Spartacus replied.

"I know, but I want you to go through the video footage again."

"I have, two hundred and twenty-one times. If they had noticed us, they would have pursued us into the atmosphere and beyond."

"I'm more worried about the pirates, after what you did to them," Luna said.

"They won't be going anywhere with that hole Uga blew in their hull," Cricket said.

"No, but if the Corinns captured them, and one of them somehow made Axel or our ship, then we're gonna have problems," Luna said.

"The bafflers were on," Brayton said. "I wouldn't worry, too much. Captain was wearing a helmet."

Luna had her arms across her chest, a tell that she was indeed worried. For good reason. All it would take was a single identification mark, like the distinctive logo of the *Trash Squid* on the outer hull. The baffler would have disguised it, but they still couldn't take chances.

It was going to have to go, for now.

The PA system surged with the unusually panicked voice of Brayton from the cargo hold.

"I've been listening, and I think we should all be more concerned about the fact we have illegal Wrath technology inside our cargo hold," he said. "I'm running scans, but right now, I have no idea what this thing is, *or does*. It could be a bomb, for all I know."

"I'm on my way," Axel said.

He made his way to the cargo hold and stood on a metal platform extending over the storage space. Below him, a dome sealed the spiked Wrath ball. Brayton paced around the dome with his engineering pad, conducting a series of tests. Uga was down there helping, his many arms all holding different tools and a HoloMatrix pad.

"This thing is what you just risked everything for," Axel whispered.

The glass housing the artifact was nearly indestructible, but that didn't bring him much comfort. It likely possessed technology that was beyond even what the best human and Corinn minds had developed. He wasn't even sure anyone understood the tech. Although there was no doubt a bunch of human and Corinn lab jockeys that had been studying artifacts just like this since the invasion.

The hatch to the platform opened, and Luna walked out holding a cup of steaming tea that she offered to Axel.

He shook his head. "Thanks, but I'm good."

"No offense, but are you?"

"Yeah, been intense, and my head hurts a bit from Honi."

She gave him the side-eye, clearly still harboring concern about his outburst on the bridge. It was unlike him to lose his temper, and she knew that. That wasn't all. The visions had gripped him, transporting him into a trance-like state that he knew she had seen.

Stepping up by his side, she took a sip of tea and looked down. "We know what it does yet?" she asked. "Give us invisibility? Maybe let us breathe fire?"

"What can you tell us, Brayton?" Axel called down.

"Not a weapon," Uga barked. "I no think."

"You're not sure?" Luna asked.

"Working on it," Brayton said. "What I do know is we've got something special here."

Cricket trotted into the room carrying a tray on his back. On it was a batch of baked insect power bars. "How special?" he chirped.

"Special enough we won't have to keep buying insects to mix with our food," Axel said. "Once we offload this thing, we can pay off some debt, fix the *Hammerhead* and the FTL drive, and take a nice, relaxing break."

"A break does sound nice, if we're alive to enjoy it," Luna said. "I, however, think maybe we should sit on this for a while. As much as I hate the idea of sleeping within a deck of this...whatever it is."

Axel didn't like that idea at all. He wanted to get rid of it and get paid.

"Spartacus," Axel said.

The holographic image of the droid emerged just below the railing.

"You ready to get a new arm?" Axel asked. "Tell me where we can sell this thing, and it's all yours."

"I've decided I want Corinn bull steaks as my *first* meal, Capa," Uga said. He plucked a bar off the tray and took a hearty crunch.

The hologram of Spartacus walked over to the device, examined it, then looked back up to Axel.

"I ran a complex set of scans using algorithms based on the current black market dealers in our database," Spartacus said. "I have narrowed it down to two names. The first, a Wooly dealer named Maro operating at White Station."

"You know him?" Axel asked Uga.

Uga swallowed the last of his bar, then fetched another. "Do *you* know every human scoundrel in the galaxy?"

"Okay, so, no?"

"Just so happens, I do know him, good for nothing. Real hooligan."

"You couldn't have just said that?"

Uga let out a low cackle, his version of a laugh.

"And the other option?" Axel asked Spartacus.

"A human named Phantom."

"No way," Luna said.

"You know him?" Axel asked.

"Heard of him."

"Phantom is a former bounty hunter who is known for dealing Wrath bones and Tech," Spartacus said.

"Hmmm," Axel said. "I'm assuming this Phantom operates off the grid and might be hard to find?"

"Yes."

"So we go see Uga's third cousin, Maro, instead?" Brayton asked.

"He-Heh," Spartacus said. "Funny. You did not let me finish."

"Continue, then," Axel said.

Spartacus nodded. "Very well, Captain. There is conflicting information on whether or not Phantom is still alive. I intercepted several civilian reports of an Eagle raid in the city of Optus on the planet Azuri. There were Corinns seen with the soldiers. After some deeper digging, I discovered this 'raid' was focused on bringing in some local criminals, but appears to have actually been aimed at a high-level target, a bounty hunter."

"Ah," Axel said. "So the Eagles showed up under the cover of arresting some low-level mobsters while closing in on this Phantom."

"Did they catch him?" Luna asked.

"There are conflicting reports," Spartacus said.

"When did all this happen?" Axel asked.

"Two days ago, shortly after Galactic Minister Goodwall and the Corinn Empire announced a joint effort to bring in Wrath bones, tech, anything related to the aliens." Spartacus put a finger on his chin as if in thought. "For some sudden reason, they are even cracking down on bones, to which they used to turn a blind eye."

"Maybe we should turn this thing over to authorities," Luna said. "This seems above our expertise."

"We the most experienced crew in the entire galaxy!" Uga extended two furry limbs to make his point. "Right, Capa?"

"Sure. But not Wrath tech," Luna countered.

Axel watched his XO begin to unravel slightly. That wasn't like her at all. Normally she was a rock. Calm and collected. Not a single stray hair in her dark braid.

He trusted her more than anyone on this ship. That trust started when they were just teenagers on the *Jabbith* Junker ship. Even back then she was calm in any situation, regardless of danger.

Axel smiled recalling the time he climbed into a dumpster

chamber an hour before it was to be jettisoned—or so he thought. He was searching for scrap and food thrown out by officers. There were always discarded treasures. He had lost track of time and was rummaging through a pile across the chamber when the hatch shut.

Luna had been the first one to the scene, working hastily to disengage the ejection function that would have sent Axel spinning out into the cold, dark space with the trash.

When he climbed out, covered in gunk, she stood there with her hands on her hips and a curious look.

"If you're hungry, you could just ask for more food," she had said.

Axel was taken aback by the innocence on her features. She had no idea how the known galaxy worked for the majority of people.

After that day, they became friends. Then best friends. Eventually, he had opened her eyes to the *real* galaxy. The sweat, tears, and blood that so many species spilled to survive.

"This thing could be very dangerous," Luna said. "I know how dire the financial situation is, but what good is money if we're not alive to spend it?"

"Exactly what the Commendatore said in the asteroid belt," Cricket chirped.

Axel chuckled. "Told you we'd make it through though, right?"

"You're the Commendatore! So what's your big plan now?"

"For now, we stay here, conserve power, and work on finding this Phantom. I'm thinking he's our best bet on figuring out what we have—if that is the route we go."

Below, Uga suddenly broke into what looked like a dance, whipping his arms back and forth and hopping around.

"Something's happening, Capa!" he barked.

From the balcony, Axel could see the Wrath tech glowing

like it had on Eern. But now there appeared to be some sort of hieroglyphics burning on the sides where the spikes had all retracted. Now it was just a smooth ball with a message illuminated across it.

"I think this is some sort of Wrath language," Brayton said.

"Can you translate it?" Cricket asked.

"No, none of us can," Spartacus said. "If CAID ever cracked the code, it has never been hacked."

"Brayton?" Axel said.

"Spartacus is right," Brayton said.

"Of course I am, he-heh."

"This thing shouldn't be sold," Cricket said.

"I have a bad feeling, like hunger, but worse, like bad diarrhea or bad owie," Uga said. "I vote destroy. Chuck it out of airlock."

"Or give it to the Corinns, or CAID," Luna said.

"No deals with the Corinns!" chirped the Marka.

"Or Eagles," Uga barked. "The Eagles are good for nothing bullies. They will betray us! No. Never trust Eagles! Never!!!"

"Everyone calm down," Axel said.

Spartacus stepped up to the glass dome, putting his robotic fingers on it. Then he turned to face the crew.

"The distraught Wooly is correct. If the authorities know we have this, they are likely to kill us all to keep it a secret," Spartacus said. "And right now, we are at extreme risk just for harboring whatever this artifact might be."

"Yup, we're in deep shit," Brayton said.

Axel let out a long breath, trying to find his focus. Everyone stared at him, waiting for orders. Spartacus was right, as usual, but Axel wasn't ready to simply get rid of the Wrath ball inside his cargo hold. There was only one person in the galaxy that could help them. Someone with experience, someone also on the run.

Another renegade like Axel and his crew.

"Locate this Phantom. And find us a safe place as close as you can to make some repairs," he said. "I'll trade whatever I can for some additional fuel in the meantime."

"Safe," Uga barked. "Not sure there's anywhere safe for us now, Capa."

"Wow, I agree with Uga two times in a row," Cricket said. "We're fugitives now."

CHAPTER 12

"Do you think they will find us, boss?" Saber chirped.

"If they are as good as I am, then yes," Rangnar said.

"Good thing no one's as good as you are."

Rangnar might have believed that before he had been ambushed back in the city of Optus. He sighed at the memories that made his wound hurt. Reaching up, he gripped his upper chest, right below his collar bone, where the Corinn had shot him. The bolt had burned through his duster and armor, singeing his flesh. Another inch lower, and he would have been dead.

"I'm a lucky man," Rangnar said.

"Not luck, boss," Saber chirped. "It's cause you followed your death rules."

Rangnar stepped out in the mouth of a cave, surveying the bubbling red sea below the bluff. This hostile planet was Tecca. The uncolonized world was devoid of natural resources, useful minerals, and most life.

Beneath the surface of the boiling water, a graveyard of long extinct beasts lay in the muddy bottom. An asteroid had hit the surface ten thousand years earlier, give or take a few hundred years, reverting the already bare world to what it had looked like during the primordial ooze period, billions of years ago. Only a few creatures had survived.

Rangnar had once come here in search of a Steward warrior that had hidden in these very caves. Now, he was the one hiding.

Two days had passed since they escaped Optus. During those agonizingly slow hours, Rangnar had gone over what had happened piece by piece. The Eagles had finally caught up to him, with the help of the Corinn agent posing as a black market dealer. He had vetted her, but her records had been forged like his own.

Whether Captain Weston was behind any of this, Rangnar wasn't sure. If he was, then he had likely sold Rangnar out to save his own skin. And that wouldn't be the first time. Former friend—best friend, mind you—and business partner Nolan Spear had also betrayed him.

This time though, Rangnar hadn't escaped unscathed. He had lost Billy Bob.

The rest of them were lucky to have gotten away on the *Beak*. Injured from the laser bolt, Rangnar had barely managed to pilot the small vessel into the busy lane of transports in orbit. The fake transponder had helped them sneak past the Colonial Alliance Naval forces watching the lanes.

Saber watched the orange skies, scanning for ships.

"They won't find us," Rangnar said. "Come on, pal."

The Marka trotted back into the cave system, leading the way to a blast door. A pair of Woolies had built it many years ago, off-planet, and Rangnar had brought it here for installation, like much of his tech. He tapped in his code and went inside.

As soon as it clicked shut behind them, he pushed up his

helmet and took in a breath of the cool, toxin-free air pumped in by vents located in a central utility chamber.

Over the years, Rangnar had taken measures to make this place more habitable, just in case he found himself in the situation he did today. Like everything he did, he had made plans on top of counterplans on top of failsafes to ensure his survival. Betrayal will do that to a man. Teach him to be paranoid. Teach him to always try to be a step ahead of his enemies.

This way of life had taken a toll on his mind and his body. And while he wasn't an old man by human standards, the years of running and gunning had caught up to him. The artificial hip, knee, and metal plates in his head were a constant rat race to keep maintained. Now he had another wound to deal with, and judging by the increasing pain, he was going to need to change his bandage soon. The built-in pain-inhibitor had stopped working.

Saber entered the communal living space. Colorful woven blankets and pillows were spread across the floor. Lucid and Nuke woke from their slumbers. Nuke had a bandage on his back with nano-meds designed by Corinns to help rapid healing.

It was a Corinn weapon that had almost killed Nuke, and the irony wasn't lost on Rangnar. A centimeter deeper and the fire blade would have severed his spine.

Lucid and Nuke both lifted their heads, but neither of them wagged their dual tails. They missed Billy Bob.

"I do too," Rangnar whispered.

He walked inside the next chamber where hundreds of storage crates sat. Food, ammo, gear, and medical supplies filled the gray containers with red lids. He walked over to the portable fridge, pulling out a chilled bottle of Corinn wine. The best in the galaxy. He had been saving this for a celebration, but now he was toasting to Billy Bob.

You failed him.
You failed to see the threat.
You failed in your reaction to the threat.

Rangnar bit the cork off with a twist and lifted the bottle.

"Until we meet again in the stars," he said.

He didn't bother getting out a glass, opting to take a long swig right from the bottle. Much like Corinn honey, the wine was far more potent than human wine. Too much, and Rangnar would be on the floor, puking his guts out before ultimately passing out.

After a single drink, he set the bottle down and started on removing his chest armor. The T-Flesh had a charred mark from the bolt. In the center of that black mark, a single hole had broken through and penetrated his flesh.

"Want some help?" Lucid asked.

She had followed him into the room with Saber and Nuke hanging behind them.

"Nah, I'm good," Rangnar said.

He winced as he raised the T-Flesh rig over his head.

Lucid came over to help despite his request. She pulled the armor off then bent down to look at his bandage. Blood and pus had seeped through. He slowly pulled it away to find the burn mark had a ring of infection.

Saber brought over an ointment cream that Rangnar took and rubbed on the wound. He cleaned it, then put a fresh bandage on with Lucid's help.

"Thanks," Rangnar said. "I'm...I'm..."

He couldn't say the words.

This wasn't like him. He wasn't an emotional man but losing Billy Bob had hit him hard. Harder than losing any human, of which he had lost countless over the years.

"I'll be back later," he said. "Stay here."

Rangnar picked up the wine and went down a corridor to

another space he had stored things over the years. He took a second swig along the way, wiping his mouth with a sleeve.

Another custom-built blast door sealed off the entrance to the huge chamber. He tapped in his code. The door clicked open and closed behind him as he entered a clean room, sealed off by a second blast door.

After securing a pair of fire rated gloves and boots, he took a third drink. Then he put on his helmet and waited for the door to open. The last drink pushed him close to the edge of intoxication. He staggered into the room, activating a light that brightened over a sprawling space with fifty various sized safes attached to the walls.

"Welcome back, sire," came a voice.

From around the largest safe came Blaster, a Corinn-built war droid that Rangnar bought almost thirty years ago. The robot strode over in its dull T-Flesh, keeping both laser cannons up at its side.

If only we'd had Blaster back on Optus, Rangnar thought.

He had long ago decided to keep the droid here, to protect his treasure just in case anyone somehow stumbled upon it. Now, he realized, that was a mistake. If Blaster had been back on Optus, maybe they would have all made it out.

"How ya' doin', Blaster?" Rangnar asked.

"Ready to kill at your orders," Blaster replied. "It has been ten years, thirty-one days, twenty-two hours, nine minutes, and thirty-one seconds since I was last utilized."

"That long? We're getting old."

"You are, sire, but I am still in tip-top shape, and ready for combat."

"Might not have to wait too much longer, my friend."

There was a glint of something, perhaps what Rangnar would describe as excitement, that sparkled in the droid's digital display. Although the Corinns had programmed these machines without emotion, it seemed that hearing it might soon be used for its original purpose—to kill—gave Blaster a dash of something extra.

Nah. Just the booze, he thought.

The droid clanked after him as he navigated the vaults within a vault.

He went to the closest middle-sized safe and pulled a keychain with a single universal key from around his neck. He inserted it, twisted it with a click. Next, he spun a wheel handle, and pulled up on the lever that popped out.

An interior piece of the safe opened, revealing a keypad. He tapped in the code. The door clicked open, venting steam from inside.

Rangnar tested the door with a finger to make sure it didn't burn through his glove, as he always did, despite the fact the temperature-controlled safes regulated the contents. Feeling no source of heat, he opened the door all the way.

Inside was the spiked skull of a Wrath Spectre and shards of exoskeleton excavated from the scene of a battle. They were rare finds. Of the millions of beings killed during the invasion, very rarely were any pieces left intact.

Considered the foot soldier, Spectres were the most common Wrath. Their front limbs were a marvel of adaptive galactic evolution, capable of morphing from spike-like protrusions to jagged blades. This, alongside a whip-like tail tipped with a lethal stinger, endowed them with a terrifying agility. Veteran warriors, carrying the scars of past encounters, recounted their movements as a blur, their speed so extreme it was almost imperceptible. Spectres used their transforming limbs for nimble scuttling and adept climbing, while their tail provided the force for rapid, snake-like slithering.

Attached to these appendages was a fortress-like torso, studded with dorsal spikes. From this heavily-armored center, a neck extended like a retractable telescope, encircled by a collar of hardened, chitinous spikes. At its end sat a stretched, barbed head, terminating in a curved jaw reminiscent of a beak. When extended from the protection of its armored torso, this skull revealed an array of misaligned eye sockets, each glowing with a spectral light as if hiding an otherworldly flame within.

Ragnar knew little about the science of their physiology and had never seen one in full form. There was very little footage from the invasion, much of it erased and controlled by galactic governments to keep the species across the galaxy from panicking. Perhaps the leaders thought that by hiding every trace of them, people would forget. This stifling of evidence, added to the erasure of the Stewards, the only warriors that had successfully faced them, putting the Great War securely away in a vault.

Just like this one, Ragnar mused.

But neither the Wrath nor the Stewards that fought them would ever be forgotten. Not with planets like Eern and Corinnia out there as evidence of the devastation these monsters were capable of unleashing.

He closed the vault and looked out over the room. He had several more pieces of Wrath bones, like Krull, flying rock beasts the size of a baby Lark. There were also seeders, spindly worms that carried a toxic venom. And then there was a small chunk of the wing of a Hydra, the goliath beast that could fire a radioactive mist from the eyeless sockets in its deformed head.

The warmth of the wine flowed through his body as he walked around the vaults containing the relics of monsters. This was what his life had amounted to. A collection of bones from dead aliens. Some he had sold off over the years, but these he had kept as a reminder of the ancient evil.

But there was something else here he had kept inside a glass display case: a gold telescoping spear shaft with a fire blade. He could still vividly remember the Steward holding it up. Sergeant Lannon, a seven-foot-tall beast of a man with limbs like oak trees and a jaw like an alligator.

Rangnar opened the case and pulled out the telescoping shaft. The heavy metal felt powerful in his hands. He thought of all the Wrath it had slayed over the years.

And all the men.

He could have been one of those men.

Three decades ago, Rangnar had spent a week scanning for lifeforms in the *Nork* after receiving intel that a ship was seen entering the atmosphere of Tecca. There were virtually no habitable places on the planet, almost nowhere a human could survive. But Lannon was no ordinary human. He was a Steward, genetically modified with the DNA of a Corinn. And while he looked more man than alien, "under the hood," as they might say, he had an arsenal of Corinn properties like rapid healing and robust organs. He could breathe the gaseous atmosphere and survive the blazing heat.

Still, there were only a few places to shelter on this world long-term, and Rangnar had found him, here, in a cave on the border of a mud pit.

Rangnar had hovered in his maiden ship, the *Nork,* afraid to land and face Lannon. The warrior stood on the bluff with the golden spear stretched out in one hand. Opening the cargo hold door, Rangnar had stepped out on the ramp to get a closer look at the "man."

"If you came to kill me, you will fail!" Lannon had called up. "Leave and live, boy."

Rangnar had remained there, watching, knowing the Steward could easily launch the spear the hundred feet and strike his heart.

"You won't escape, no matter how many of them you kill," Rangnar had replied. "There's no need for more soldiers to die."

Lannon had looked to the orange skies, realization setting in that Rangnar was a scout hired by the Colonial Alliance. Soon, the Warhorses would descend over these boiling mud pits. And yet, the warrior remained standing, prepared to meet his end.

This Steward is one of the good ones, Rangnar realized. Not driven crazy like so many others. He just wanted to live out his life.

The Steward turned and ran for whatever ship he had stowed away. Rangnar used a remote to fire the thrusters of the *Nork*, blasting the giant off the cliff and into the mud below. He'd never meant to kill the warrior, only to stop him.

For hours he had searched the mud with his remote claws, but it appeared the bubbling graveyard had swallowed yet another victim. All that was left was the spear he had dropped on the ground. That spear became a consolation prize that the Eagles allowed him to keep after he shared the video evidence of Lannon's death.

The Brass was glad Rangnar had saved them the trouble of combat with the Steward.

The walls of the vault suddenly shook, snapping him from the powerful memory.

"What's that?" Rangnar asked.

"Seismic activity," Blaster replied. "This is the fifth occurrence in the past three months. Nothing to be alarmed by."

"Famous last words." Rangnar pushed a button on the shaft of the telescoping spear which clanked down to the size of a flashlight. He slipped it into his duty belt and saluted Blaster. "I'm going to bed."

"Goodnight, sire," Blaster replied.

He left the vault and went to the security room where Saber was watching the digital displays. "Hey, boss," the Marka chirped. "You feel that quake?"

"Yeah, nothin' to worry about, according to Blaster," Rangnar muttered.

Saber glanced over to study Rangnar with two of his eyes while he kept the other two on the monitor. "You good?"

"Yeah. I'm just tired. Gonna go get some shut eye."

"I'll keep the watch."

"Thanks, Saber."

Rangnar reached out to pat the creature, but hesitated, remembering how much Saber hated it. He pulled his hand back, only to have Saber crane his neck.

"If it will make you feel better, go ahead," Saber said.

"Really?"

"Just don't tell the others. And just once. Don't get all mushy on me, boss."

"I'm not the mushy type, except, I guess when it comes to..."

Saber let out what might be considered a sigh. Markas weren't just loyal to their masters, they were loyal to one another. Losing a brother or sister hurt them to their very core, even though some might not show it.

Rangnar was also used to not showing his emotions, but for another reason—he didn't want to look weak. Weakness, he had learned from an early age, was like bleeding. The more you bleed, the weaker you become.

But Rangnar was old now and he had lost too much. Markas. Humans. Body parts. His heart was hard. If he allowed himself one moment of memory, the pain was too much to bear. As he curled up in his bed, a flood of despair rushed over him, amplified by the potent alien wine. He fought the anguish for a few minutes but then gave up. Pushing himself up, he clumsily made his way out of the room. Dreams would only make the pain more intense.

He grabbed his duster, throwing it on. The burn mark from the laser made his chest hurt just looking at it. Grabbing his helmet, he went to the blast door and flipped the lever. The metal whine opened to a view of the bubbling mud pits.

His Death Rules had kept him alive over the years, but they had also prevented him from fully living life. He had nothing but a vault of dead monsters, and the spear of a desperate man who had only sought peace.

Rangnar stepped close to the edge of the bluff. Maybe he would be better off jumping, ending things his way. Joining Lannon in the roiling morass that would eat his flesh and suck his bones down into the mud.

A second step brought him to the very edge where grit tumbled over the side—but not from his boots.

Another quake rumbled through the rock.

Rangnar glimpsed movement in the boiling ocean. A bubble burst a few hundred feet away, spreading a wave across the surface. The vibrations continued, and more bubbles popped closer and closer.

The scales of a beast glided just out of the sizzling muck. Rangnar had never seen one this big. The humped back of the behemoth surfaced, and an armored hole opened, blasting out a geyser of air and fluid like a giant blue whale on Earth, coming to the surface to breathe.

The goliath monster, over thirty feet tall, rose up out of the mud, planting three tree-like legs like a tripod into bottom of the pit. The bulbous, scaly body connected to a narrowing neck with an eyeless skull surrounded by a beard of ten squid-like arms, each covered in spikes. An ethereal, melancholy wail reverberated from the sucker mouth that could swallow Rangnar whole.

Three rows of needle teeth the length of his spear clicked together. Yellow drool slipped off each of the daggers.

Like the Steward that Rangnar had hunted here, he stood his ground, holding the same spear. But unlike Lannon,

Rangnar was not of sound mind. He was intoxicated from the Corinn wine. Not in any shape to be fighting a creature of *any* size, let alone a legendary abomination.

It was likely that the wine was part of the reason he felt like fighting. Or maybe he simply had a death wish.

With a shake of his wrist, the telescoping shaft extended outward.

The creature lifted its scaly head toward the bluff, the cephalopodic limbs attached to its face flicking scorching mud over the bluff. A hunk hit the ground, splashing against Rangnar's boots. He looked at the steaming pile on his left toe and something snapped.

"YOU BASTARD!" he screamed.

Those draping limbs shot toward him. Normally, he would have been fast enough to get back, but his reflexes were off, and all he could do was counter them by slashing his spear outward. The creature was fast enough to withdraw all but one before his blade cut through a meaty arm, severing it.

A roar burst from its sucker lips as the snaking piece dropped with a splat to the rock, still wiggling. He kicked it off the bluff into the mud.

The blast door opened behind him and all three Markas rushed out in their suits, snarling and barking.

"Get back inside!" Rangnar yelled. "This one's mine!"

He ducked under another swipe while the Markas, well past listening to him, attacked.

Rangnar knew there was no recalling them now. His companions were committed. He needed them, too, he realized dimly, if he had any hope of surviving this drunken battle.

The Markas bit at the whipping appendages as they swung across the bluff. Nuke crunched down on one, and Saber captured another, sinking his metal canines deep into the flesh.

Lucid slid under one, then whipped her tails to capture another of the flying limbs.

The weight of the Markas pulled on the ropey arms, stretching them in a deadly game of tug-of-war. Ducking and stumbling around, Rangnar hacked through them one at a time with his blade.

The creature shrieked, dropping its bleeding skull onto the ledge, sending out a tremor. A tongue the size of a steroidal anaconda thrust forward from its open mouth, attaching to Rangnar and yanking him toward the jaw of wicked teeth. Nuke and Saber fought ruthlessly but were soon swept off their paws.

Rangnar speared directly into the tongue and was dropped, hitting the ground fifteen feet from the mouth. He reached up and caught hold of Nuke by a tail. Saber slammed into them both, knocking them even closer—within ten feet of the gnashing rows of six-foot-long needle teeth. The creature drew back the tongue and sucked in hard, the action lifting Rangnar off the ground as he pawed for something to hold onto.

A whirring sounded, followed by the absolute brilliant flash of dual laser cannons. The creature paused to deal with the new threat, allowing Rangnar to cut Lucid free. She dropped to the ground and he pushed her under the flurry of lasers.

Blaster stood behind them, holding up his dual arm-mounted cannons, both blazing.

The goliath monster roared in agony as those bolts pounded the sucker mouth, shattering teeth and blowing out pulpy fluid. It reared back from the onslaught, but not before smacking Rangnar in the helmet with a limb. He crashed to the ground with enough force that his vision dimmed to red.

Nuke and Saber dragged him away from a probing limb as Blaster continued to fire, aiming at the scaly lips at the center of the head. A powerful burst of gelatinous liquid and meaty hunks exploded, coating Rangnar in goop.

The beast sucked desperately, pulling Rangnar and both of his Markas backward. Each breath became a long, wet gasp as the remaining tendrils whipped lazily and it slumped away.

Rangnar turned onto his stomach and wiped the nameless goo from his visor. Pushing himself up and panting like a dog, he watched the creature sliding back into the muck. All three of the Markas guarded him, growling at the retreating beast.

Blaster walked up to the edge, both cannons disarmed and aimed downward.

"Combat complete," he confirmed in a satisfied tone. "Hostile eliminated."

CHAPTER 13

The *Trash Squid* had limped back to Honi, running on nothing but fumes by the time they put down at Halygen, a very sparsely populated chain of islands on the southern tip of the water planet.

Almost a week had passed since sustaining damage in the asteroid belt and escaping Eern. Axel had spent much of that time working on the ship with his crew. Aside from cosmetic damage—dents, scratches, and broken panels—there was plenty of damage under the hood, electrical, and of course, the FTL drive.

He worked on the top of his ship to the sound of jackals squealing in the distance. The wind howled over the treetops where the scavenging creatures made their homes. Axel looked out over the halo of purple trees on the small island. On the horizon, past the sea, he could see the silhouette of mountains on a large strip of land. The moon glowed in the night sky, casting a bright glow over the snow-capped peaks.

Somewhere out there, five-hundred human colonists had constructed an outpost. Soon, Axel would send Spartacus there with some items to trade for additional fuel, but first he wanted the ship ready to fly. You could never be too careful when dealing with strangers.

Especially humans.

For now, he had deployed a trash pod to watch for any hostiles. Anyone who established a home this far away from civilization, whether all the way out in the frontier like this, or out in the resort cities in the tropical zone of the planet was going to be armed and potentially dangerous. It truly took brave souls to risk being this far from the protection of the Eagles. For as horrible as the soldiers could be, they were often the only authoritative force to help guard people from dangerous life-forms like the jackals.

The frog-faced aliens with the bodies of chimpanzees swung across the thick branches of the jungle around the ship. It was hard to tell whether they were playing or fighting, due to their naturally aggressive behavior. The species were known for being spontaneously violent and had killed more than a handful of human children, and even adult colonists, just in the past year.

Whatever they were doing up there, it was annoying the crap out of Axel as he worked on replacing wiring under a damaged panel. Uga was on the ground with Spartacus, soldering on a new panel beneath the ship.

Axel stood and wiped the sweat from his brow then looked for Cricket. He was out there, out of sight, patrolling in the shadows. Inside the ship, Brayton and Luna continued to search for intel on Phantom. So far they had reported he made it off Optus alive, thanks to a message Brayton intercepted while hacking into the CAID network. That in itself was a crime punishable by time in a Colonial Alliance prison camp, if they got caught.

Brayton was good at covering his tracks, but Axel couldn't help but feel like threats closed in from all sides. For years now he had been living on the edge, hardly making ends meet and chasing dreams—like riding the great wave two thousand miles away from here and free-climbing the tallest peaks in the galaxy.

Now they were at the end of the rope.

But there was still a way out.

He had it inside his cargo hold.

The Wrath artifact, whatever it was, remained secured inside the glass encasement. He had considered mounting it to a trash pod and firing it into the closest sun, and maybe that was what he should do, but no matter how potentially scary this thing was, it was also potentially valuable.

Very valuable.

Axel finished replacing the wire, replaced the panel, then walked to the smashed cockpit of the *Hammerhead*. The rocket Kian Ka' Ki had fired had all but destroyed the exterior. The glass viewports were gone, and the T-Flesh support system was left a tangled mess of beams. The interior wasn't much better. Destroyed consoles. Shattered sensor clusters and analysis screens. Seats burned to their supports.

One of the laser turrets was mangled, but the other had only exterior damage. Axel had run several tests from the bridge, and it was still in working order.

At least that's something.

The only way to get the entire space fighter fixed was by selling the artifact. But a lot of things had to happen before they could do that, first of which was securing fuel. Which he had to purchase.

Axel set his tool case down and began to work on disassembling the laser cannon. He hated selling it off, but it was no good to them right now, and it would allow them to buy enough fuel to buy them some time.

An hour later, a shadow moved in front of him—small, husky, with multiple arms. It had to be Uga.

He glanced up to see the Wooly salvage chief, along with Spartacus, climbing up a ladder.

"Capa, we have to fix me," Uga barked.

"Fix *you*?" Axel asked.

Uga pointed to the dented logo down the hull. "I see orders to scrub me off," he said. "No, Capa. Gotta fix me. No boo-boo. What. You think me ugly now?"

"There is no fixing you. No amount of paint that will make you beautiful, Uga," Spartacus said. "He-heh."

"You think you funny, mech-man?" Uga said, spinning.

Axel groaned.

"It is...the portrait is funny," Spartacus said.

"Why?" Uga barked. All six of his arms whipped back and forth in agitation, the fur standing up.

"I'm sure it is not personal, but people do laugh at our logo." Spartacus shrugged. "I have heard them."

"You not a people." Uga extended an arm with the end shaping into what looked almost like a finger. He poked Spartacus in the torso. "You got no stomach. You eat no food."

"Is that supposed to make me feel bad? He-heh. I would rather have this smooth metal six pack than your furry pannis."

Uga looked down at his gut then growled. He snatched the blowtorch out of his pack and activated the flame.

"Guys, come on," Axel said.

"What do you plan on doing with that?" Spartacus asked, taking a step back.

Uga held it up. "Seal up your dumb word hole."

"He-heh." Spartacus kept laughing. "You are such a primitive, nasty creature, Uga Bir."

Uga became furious, holding the torch up and waddling over toward the droid. He tripped and fell to the hull. "Oowwwie, boo-boo!"

"Clumsy cave rat—"

"I said, *stop*," Axel said firmly. He helped Uga up to his feet. "You good?"

Uga shut off the torch. "Somethin' wrong," he said. "Frog-faces no longer cackle."

Axel looked out over the jungle, noticing the jackals had stopped their banter. A glance in that direction confirmed the entire troop were observing the crew's interactions.

"They watch us," Uga said.

"Yeah, so stop fighting," Axel said. "Both of you."

Spartacus walked away, still laughing.

"Sorry, Capa," Uga barked softly.

"I get it. Sparty can get on my nerves at times too."

"Screw that wannabee gladiator. *I'm sorry* for what I have to show you." Uga pointed another arm. "Come with me, Capa, we got new problem."

Axel climbed the ladder down to an exposed part of the hull where Uga and Spartacus had been working.

"Happy thing we made it this far, no? Ship have very bad boo-boo," Uga said. "We got to replace big section of wire and parts."

Axel ducked under to have a look while Uga waddled away.

"Where are you going?" Axel asked.

"Galley. Robot wore me out, I eat now," Uga said.

Axel looked into the guts of the panel they had removed. A web of tangled, shredded wires hung out. He pulled back, and in a fit of rage punched the side of the ship. Bone struck armor, making yet another dent that fit right in with the hull.

Pain lanced up his hand and blood beaded up across his cut knuckles.

Get it together, man.

Axel felt prickling in his hands and his feet. This wasn't from hitting the hull, it was from stress. He had gotten himself into a real mess, and not just him—his entire crew.

And perhaps even worse, he had left himself vulnerable to that voice, open to the rage inside of him always clawing to get out.

A message hissed in his earpiece.

"Captain, how are the repairs going?" Luna asked.

"Okay," he said. "Any updates on Phantom?"

"Not yet, unfortunately. Still searching for anything that might give us a clue to where he fled after leaving Optus."

"Keep trying."

"Copy that. Good luck."

Axel noticed Cricket trotting out of the forest, heading back toward the ship. He trotted over to Axel, looking at him while he hid his hand behind his back. The Marka said nothing, but Axel knew he was suspicious.

"You good, Commendatore?" Cricket asked.

Axel nodded. "You?"

"Storm's coming in from the west."

He looked toward the swollen storm clouds surging over the water. Streaks of red lightning flashed from a bulging cloud which, for a moment, reminded him of a Wrath ship.

His mind reverted to the visions he'd experienced on Eern. Of the fleeing Marka packs of refugees, the injured Corinn bull and the soldier in golden armor that had ended its suffering. Then of that same soldier helping Corinn civilians escape those barbed ships.

What were those visions?

They couldn't have been memories, but they seemed so *real*.

Axel had known his entire life that he was a bit crazy, but this all felt different. He feared he had been slowly going insane over the years, and it had gotten worse. Now he feared he wouldn't be able to stop that voice from taking over.

He thought about what that voice had told him several times —that sometimes to protect life you must take it.

No, that wasn't right. If he listened to that, he truly would lose all control. He held up his injured hand. That was his future, pain and blood, if he obeyed that rage filled voice.

Axel brought up a different voice in his mind, kind and loving, the voice of his mother.

Peace is our way, Axel
We will not hurt what can't be healed.
We will not take what can't be replaced.
Violence only leads to more violence.
All life is precious.

After a few deep breaths, Axel regained his perspective. He accepted what had happened and was grateful they were all still alive.

A flickering glow pulled him back to the present, multiple lights going on and off. It came from the direction of the beach. Axel turned in the soft rain, seeing blinking, bioluminescent jelly fish-like creatures drifting through the sky. There were dozens of them, hundreds. Their soft bodies glowed a bright blue before fading and brightening again.

The beautiful sight captivated Axel, until the voice of Brayton broke over the comms.

"Captain, we need you on the bridge," he said. "I've found something."

Axel rushed back to the hatch and hurried through the corridors. When he got to the bridge, Brayton and Luna were both crowded around a monitor with Spartacus, examining a map of the Hironia System.

"What is it?" Axel asked.

"A high value target was tracked to the inner edge of the system, where they vanished," Brayton said.

"Bring up the area."

"Not much there," Luna said. "Just three planets that are too hostile to support human life."

"I found something interesting in the CAID files Brayton accessed," Spartacus said. "There is a planet there called Tecca, and thirty-two years ago, CAID documented the death of a Steward on that world."

Axel narrowed his eyes.

"A bounty hunter named Rangnar Soki tracked a refugee Steward named Lannon there," Spartacus explained. "There is more. We know that Rangnar worked with Dark Horse Company to hunt down the last of the Stewards. Then, fifteen years ago, he was accused of trafficking Wrath technology and taken into custody by Eagles, only to escape."

"You think Rangnar Soki is Phantom?" Axel asked.

"If I were a betting man, I would say so, considering the Wrath tech angle to this story," Brayton said.

"Perhaps," Spartacus replied. "Either way, he is a very dangerous criminal and a killer."

"And he's our best shot at figuring out what this thing is," Luna said.

She raised a brow at Axel, scrutinizing him for a reaction.

Truth was, Axel had backed himself into such a corner, that this seemed like a *good* option, despite the risk.

"Luna and Spartacus, I want you to take the good laser turret to the colony and trade for fuel," he said. "I'll keep working with Uga and Brayton to fix the ship. Soon as you're back, we're headed to Tecca to look for this Phantom."

Jax Brito is hereby sentenced to ten years at Ripa Penal Colony.

Two weeks after losing her legs on Jolia, Jax Brito read over her sentence for the hundredth time. Even now, it didn't seem real.

Ripa might just as well have been called RIP. The hard

labor prison colony was located in an asteroid belt rich with minerals. For most inmates, it was a death sentence, especially for a female former Eagle.

Doctor Andrew. The kind man who had helped Jax with her recovery, had explained that they would give her a job in laundry or food processing. But Jax knew those jobs were reserved for droids. She would probably pilot some sort of mining equipment.

The life she had built as an Eagle was over. And clearing her name was going to be impossible in prison. Appealing the decision was a waste of time. When CAID made a ruling, reversing it took nothing short of the Galactic Minister.

She tried to be positive, tried to remember she was still a young woman.

Your life isn't over, she thought. *You will create a new life after your sentence.*

All she had to do was survive. Ten years. Ten, long years.

To keep sane during her hospital stay, she spent her time doing physical therapy and working out, trying to prepare for what awaited her on Ripa.

Sweat beaded down her forehead as she did pushups on her knees over the white floor of her room, replaying the battle on Jolia in her mind, everything that happened, step by step, including Krish questioning her the entire way.

That fucking weasel had pinned everything on her.

Maybe she had doomed lives by moving in, but if she hadn't, Jax was *almost* certain not a single one of the Eagles would have survived.

She was taking the fall for a botched operation.

At two hundred and two reps, the door suddenly opened. Doctor Andrew.

Two Eagle MPs stood in the hallway.

Time to go, Jax realized.

The doctor brought in the wheelchair. "Best of luck to you," he said.

The two Eagles walked inside, wearing helmets that disguised their features. It was hard to believe they now viewed Jax like she had viewed criminals. In some ways, they probably hated her even more.

She was a traitor in their eyes.

They picked her up under the arms and put her into the chair. One of them walked ahead while the other pushed from behind.

Through the hospital they went. All the way to the outside, where Jax felt the sun on her sweaty face for the first time since arriving at Shield Base on Hex Prime. They wheeled her to the raised tarmac where a Clipper parked idly at the top.

She was loaded up a ramp and then moved into the spacecraft. Inside, the Eagles secured her into a bucket seat, fastening a harness over her chest. A half hour later the Clipper rose off the pad, rotating and activating the vertical thrusters that blasted them into orbit.

Jax looked out the viewport once the pilots eased off the gas. The Clipper was heading for a cigar-shaped barge of a ship that most Eagles called "Coffins." The vessel was privately operated by mercs and used to transport expensive goods—and criminals.

Seeing it was a cold, hard reminder.

She was about to become cargo.

"Prepare for docking," announced one of the pilots.

The two Eagles waited until the transport had flown into a bay on the Coffin. As soon as it touched down, they helped Jax out of her harness and back into her chair. From there, they transported her down a ramp into the pressurized cargo hold where two mercs waited in black-clad suits with light armor and mirrored face shields.

One of the Eagles handed her an electronic ID card.

"Former Eagle, you must be a real space maggot turd," remarked one of the mercs.

The Eagles said nothing as they returned to the Clipper.

"Time to meet some new friends," the merc said, grabbing onto the chair.

Jax was wheeled out of the hold into a passage that ended at a closed hatch. It opened to an interior chamber with ten-foot-tall barred cages. Each had four bunks, a toilet, and a sink.

Most of them were already fully occupied.

Jax scanned the human and alien prisoners, her eyes falling on one group in the center of the chamber. All of them were covered in tribal tattoos.

Inos.

The eyes of each prisoner watched Jax as she was wheeled to an empty cage in the middle of the chamber, directly in front of the warriors she had fought on Jolia.

She recognized one of them. A man with a beaded beard and tattoo of a Torq on his right arm. The same arm that had thrust a spear into one of the Eagles from Hatchet Platoon.

Jax may not have been an Eagle any longer, but these were still her enemy.

And they definitely felt the same way.

Four of the six Inos stared through the charged bars at her.

The two mercs locked her chair into place against the deck, and then locked the gate to her single cage. Voices called out as the lights dimmed. Not long after, the thrum of engines reverberated through the vessel.

Jax gripped her harness as the ship pulled away from Hex Prime toward their destination—Ripa.

It felt surreal that she was now a prisoner alongside the enemy killers she had fought against to save her platoon. They continued to eye her through the bars. The man with the Torq tattoo definitely recognized her. He spoke to his comrades, then pointed at Jax's missing legs.

Of course. They were there. They saw their leader cut me down after I shot him.

These men would want her head for what she had done.

Without legs, what could she do to fight them off?

She held up her fists.

She still had those.

As the ship tore through space, she stared right back at the Inos. Showing fear was the last thing she wanted to do right now. And she didn't fear them. What she feared was never being able to clear her name. Krish had betrayed her, made it look like what happened was all her fault. An open and shut case of recklessly disobeying orders to damning effect.

Anger burned through her. Someday she would get her revenge on the coward Krish.

"Hey, you!" someone shouted.

Jax looked toward the voice, spotting a tall, slender man with spiked hair.

"You're an Eagle, aren't you?" the man yelled out.

"Was," someone else said. "Now she's just a crippled civie."

"Guess ya don't have to worry about droppin' the soap where we're going."

Laughter broke out, but there were also angry shouts.

"I'm gonna make her throat smile!"

Realization hit Jax as screams broke out. The Inos weren't her only enemy. It seemed everyone in here hated Eagles. Probably because Eagles had put them in here.

Jax could fight a few Inos, but she couldn't fight everyone. She shook in her harness, heat rising in her chest. No matter how hard she fought, she wasn't going to last long at Ripa.

She thought back to Doctor Andrew, and his offer to contact her parents and brother back on Runi. Her father had always told her things weren't fair in the Hironia System, that they hadn't been fair back in the Solar System either. That life was cheap throughout the galaxy, and humans were plagued by the diseases of greed and war.

They didn't see eye to eye about a lot of things, but he was right about that.

Jax thought more about her family. Eventually they would learn of her fate—a fate that would bring great shame to them all. She could picture her mother, who had been so adamant about her not joining the Eagles.

"Don't become a killer," she had pleaded with her. "It will damage your soul."

Maybe she'd been right too.

But one thing was certain—Jax wasn't meant to be a farmer. She had left to help people, to defend those that couldn't defend themselves.

The flight grinded on, hours passing by at a blur. Jax remembered the trials and tribulations of her training, and in each deployment. The worlds she had seen. The aliens and people she had put in places like this dimly lit cargo hold.

That night, droid carts motored into the chamber with cords hanging off the side. The electrical fields were deactivated to allow the prisoners to reach out and suck out some of the protein paste inside.

When it got to Jax, she couldn't reach the bars. She had a choice. Unbuckle from her chair and scoot across the floor in front of everyone. Or not eat.

She chose the latter.

A merc guard walked by, looking at her but saying nothing. At midnight, the lights clicked off, and Jax climbed out of her chair to drink from the sink. She was used to taking a shit and pissing in front of other people, soldiers shared tight barracks, but not like this. Not without her legs.

As she climbed up onto the toilet, she heard laughter. But then came another noise—a rumbling, as if the engines were reducing their speed.

Were they already at their destination?

Someone else heard it too, and said, "Why are we stopping?"

Crunching sounded. Jax knew that sound.

They were being boarded. She finished her business and pulled herself back into her chair. For a several minutes there was nothing but a few hushed voices, and some snoring from oblivious prisoners.

Then came clanking. Deep echoes that reverberated through the ship.

Muffled shouts broke out, distant, but getting closer.

Lights flipped on in the chamber. Prisoners jumped out of their bunks and gathered in front of the bars. All eyes went to the only hatch in the room, the one they had all been guided through.

Grinding sounded, then the hatch broke open.

Smoke curled out. Through it came an Eagle with a red helmet. They marched down the aisle, cape glowing behind them. Four more followed, each armed with a laser rifle like the one Jax had carried.

Their leader, a lieutenant, according to his insignia, stopped not far from Jax's cage. She looked out as the man took in the view through a golden visor.

"Today's your lucky day, assholes," he said. His voice repeated in multiple languages before he continued. "We're here to offer you a choice. Fight with the Colonial Alliance, or continue to the Penal Colony where most of you will die."

Jax narrowed her eyes at the soldier in front of her.

This had to be a dream. An illusion.

Why would they be offering these people a chance to fight

now? Why commandeer a merc vessel on its way to a penal colony?

Something was off.

Jax squinted, trying to make out the crests on their armor. It was then she realized none of them had any markings.

Were these even Eagles?

"Who are we fighting?" someone asked.

The lieutenant looked in the direction of a scrawny man standing next to the guy with spiked hair who had yelled at Jax earlier.

"An enemy of the Colonial Alliance," he said. "You have one minute to make your decision. Step out of your cage with your hands on your head, if you choose to serve."

Grinding sounded, followed by a whirring noise.

The electrical charges were off.

Several prisoners stepped out as their gates opened. Jax unlocked her chair then wheeled out. The lieutenant looked over at her, but again said nothing.

"I'd rather die than serve the Colonial Alliance," came a voice.

The man with the spiked hair spat through the bars.

"Suit yourself," said the lieutenant. He swiftly unholstered a pistol, aimed it, and fired as the man tried to back away. A bolt fried his spiked hair, and a second tunneled through the center of his forehead, dropping him in a heap of limbs.

"Anyone else?" he asked. "It's a much quicker way to die than where you're headed."

More prisoners stepped out. First ten, then twenty. The Inos, talking among themselves, moved out together. Jax didn't have time to react once she realized what was happening.

All six of them charged the lieutenant, who hit the deck. He didn't have much time to react either, but managed to bring up his pistol and fire off several shots.

Two of the Inos crashed to the ground, maimed, but alive. The man with the Torq tattoo stomped the Eagle's wrist and tried to take the pistol. It went sliding away as the other soldiers unleashed calculated—or not so calculated—lasers killing two of the Inos instantly and hitting other prisoners farther down the aisle. All hell broke loose as the criminals charged the soldiers.

Jax fell out of her chair to the deck near the pile of Inos on the lieutenant.

She reached for the dropped pistol, stretching out her arm and fumbling for it. Her fingers found purchase, and she yanked it over. In a shaky hand, she raised it at the Ino with the Torq tattoo.

Strong and steady, Jax. Strong and steady.

She gripped the handle, and then pulled the trigger, erasing his enraged face.

In a flurry of shots, she took out several Inos, then fired multiple bolts into the overhead. "Everybody back the hell up!" she shouted.

Another squad of Eagles rushed into the room, quickly securing the space.

Jax handed the pistol back to the lieutenant, who pushed himself up from under the heap of bodies.

The man directed his visor at Jax, then nodded. "Get her up," he said.

Two Eagles rushed over and grabbed Jax, heaving her up into her chair. They wheeled her out of the room as the other prisoners were left behind.

It wasn't long before the hiss of laser bolts and the screams of dying men and women echoed from the hold. Jax tried to calm her thumping heart as she was pushed out into the same cargo hold she was delivered to by the Clipper.

Now there was a ramp connecting to a Warhorse. She was

taken up the platform into the belly of the ship. Then she was dropped into a single cell quarters.

Hours she sat there, her heart slowly calming. She was exhausted, mentally and physically, but couldn't sleep.

After what felt like a day, the hatch unlocked. The lieutenant she had saved stood there, helmetless. "Name's Apollo," he said.

"Jax. Jax Brito."

"I know who you are," he said. "Let's go, my new friend."

Jax wheeled out then turned for the lieutenant to take the grips. He pushed her down a passage, into an elevator. After a few seconds, the doors opened to a dimly lit operations floor with officers in black uniforms attending to different stations. The lieutenant wheeled Jax up to a hatch and knocked.

"Enter," came a deep voice.

The hatch whisked open to a small quarters with a viewport looking out over a field of stars. A man sat in a chair, facing the porthole.

"This is Jax Brito, sir," said the lieutenant.

The officer turned in his chair, and once again, Jax found herself looking at General Gabriel Jessup.

"We've met before, haven't we?" Gabriel said.

"Yes, sir, on Jolia."

The general took the pad that the lieutenant handed him.

After reading the file for a few moments, Gabriel shook his head. "Dumb shits at CAID," he said. "They needed someone to blame, so they put it on you, probably the only capable soldier in Hatchet Platoon."

He handed the pad back to the lieutenant, stood, and grunted. "Apollo, find this woman a new pair of legs, the best, and pronto. War is coming, and I need true-hearted soldiers like yourself, Sergeant Brito."

CHAPTER 14

Axel stepped on the scrubbed logo on top of the *Trash Squid* with Cricket by his side.

"Weird not hearing Sparty and Uga squabbling," Cricket chirped.

"Yeah, definitely enjoying the peace and quiet." Axel chuckled and raised his binoculars.

Four hours ago, Luna and Spartacus had taken a small raft to trade the laser turret for fuel at the human colony. He expected them back soon, and Axel had taken a break from repairs on the ship to watch for them.

They were on strict radio silence orders, not wanting to reveal the ship's position. The jackals were no longer the only creatures that knew the *Trash Squid* was on the Halygen island chain. The human colonists would know there was a ship somewhere out there after dealing with Luna and Spartacus.

Axel sat down, dangling his long legs over the edge. Uga and Brayton were down there, working on repairing the conduits beneath the hull.

"I'm going to go watch the beach," Cricket said. "Maybe you should get some rest, Commendatore."

"I'll rest up here," Axel said.

The Marka hopped off the ship and took off to hold watch.

Putting his hands behind his head, Axel stared up at the dazzling, star-filled sky. The storm had blown right through, and it was all clear now. In the rare moments he was alone, Axel would look up to the stars and think about his mother and aunt, wondering if they were out there somewhere.

Closing his eyes transported him to his last memory of them. Over twenty-three years had passed, so long that most humans would never be able to access such a vivid recollection of a single event. But this was another special ability, or perhaps curse. Axel had to witness his past in crystal detail, as if he was reliving it.

In his mind's eye, he saw the inert roadway of abandoned vehicles snaking toward the metropolis back on Earth. He could still smell the plastic scent of the breathing mask he wore to protect his lungs from the toxic air. And he could still remember the crack of bones under his boots when he had accidentally stepped on the skeletal remains of a person partially buried in dirt.

Axel had seen a few dead people, but that was before he understood death was final. He stepped over the corpse. "I'm sorry," he said.

"It's okay, Axel. That person is no longer there," replied his mother. "Their spirit has moved on."

She reached out and he took her hand. They kept walking, following Julia. She had her rifle up, always up, always scanning. From the black ground to the orange sky, from the horizon to the crumbling buildings in the abandoned city. To Axel's surprise, they found life when they entered the first city blocks. Spiders. Beetles. Rats, even a cat. The hardened creatures had all adapted to the harsh environment, living in the ancient relics of the once bustling human city.

With each step his heart rate quickened.

It hadn't sunk in that he was going to be leaving his family until he heard the rumble of the engines roaring over the sprawling city. The rusty hull of the barge lowered over a collapsed stadium, setting down with a thud in the dirt that sent a tremor under his boots.

He turned to his mother, expecting her to tell him this would be temporary. That she would board another ship soon and they would be reunited.

But as she let go of his hand and crouched in front of him, he realized that he was going to be alone. That he might never see her again.

"You must make your own way now," she said in a firm voice.

"My own way?" he replied. "I don't want to—"

"We can't be together anymore." Her voice was even firmer, but then it cracked. "I'm so sorry, Axel."

She brushed the hair away from his goggles. "You must be strong."

"Mom," he said, upper lip quivering. "Please, don't leave me, I won't ask questions again, ever, I promise. I won't complain, I promise!"

"My sweet boy." She wiped the tears from his face. "You deserve a better life, and you will never be safe with me."

"But I don't care. I don't want to be apart! I want to stay with you."

"I know you do, but this is the only way."

"I will protect you! I will fight—"

"You must live a life of peace. And you can't ever look for me, Axel. It will put us both at risk. Do you want that?"

"No, I just want to—"

"Mira," Julia said.

Axel turned to see two men walking across the dirt, both

dressed in navy blue suits and wearing breathing masks. He faced his mother, who hugged him, holding on tightly.

"No, please, mom, please," Axel said.

"I will always be in your heart," she said. "That's where you will always find me."

He looked at her through warm tears.

"You must promise you won't look for me, Axel. Promise me," she said.

He had nodded. But fifteen years later, Axel had broken that promise.

His next memory transported him back to Earth, on the mountainside where he had lived in the bunker with his aunt and mother until that fateful day in the city. Axel searched the dirt for fresh tracks after landing the *Trash Squid* in a valley. His crew followed him into the forest. They were all there, younger, and just starting their adventures.

Axel found the old hidden entrance with the branches and camo tarps disguising the blast door. He opened it, and with the help of Spartacus, they got into the clean room.

The dust told Axel it hadn't been used for some time.

He hurried to his old room, finding the basket of broken space marine toys under the bed. From there he went to the room his mother had slept in. The bed was made perfectly, but her stuff was gone.

Axel had ransacked the bunker for a note, anything that might indicate where they had gone. His crew watched him as he grew more panicked, throwing clothes out of drawers, rummaging through supply crates and tossing books after skimming through the pages for something—anything!

"I'll keep searching the databases," Brayton said. "I'm close to hacking into CAID—"

"She doesn't want to be found," Axel whispered. He had known that. She had told him as much.

"We'll help you," Luna said. She put a hand gently on his shoulder, quelling the anger rising in his heart.

"You a cute lil Capa," Uga said.

"What?" Axel turned to see the Wooly waddling over, holding a HoloMatrix screen in an arm. He held it up to reveal an image of Axel when he was just five or six, sitting with his mother and aunt in the library.

"Where'd you get that image?" Luna asked.

"Follow," Uga said. He went to the command room where he took a seat at a terminal covered in dust. The screen flashed with old security videos.

"My mom didn't delete those?" Axel asked.

Uga shrugged. "She did, but I bring back." He directed a limb at his multi-cased backpack, which had all sorts of tools inside, including batteries and cords to hook up to different technology, some of which snaked out of the pack into terminal ports.

"We got her face and voice on file now, that will really help in our search," Brayton said. "I'll find her if she's out there, Captain."

That had given Axel hope, but his mother had done an excellent job covering her tracks. For years he had searched for her on his adventures across the Hironia System, finding no trace.

"Commendatore," Cricket chirped.

Axel blinked, snapping out of his reverie and sitting up. He grabbed the binoculars and zoomed in on the area of ocean where Cricket directed a long leg.

Under the moonlight, a small raft thumped over the waves. In the bow, Luna sat wearing a hooded sweatshirt and coat. Spartacus was at the stern, manning the outboard engine.

Axel took a ladder down to the beach to meet them.

Spartacus eased off the throttle and the raft rode the surf up the sand.

"How'd it go?" Axel asked.

Luna hopped out as he grabbed a handle and heaved the boat up. Judging by the heavy contents, they had secured a successful trade.

"Great, aside from Spartacus mouthing off," Luna said.

"To who?" Axel asked.

"Asking for a spare arm is mouthing off?" Spartacus asked.

Luna huffed. "Sparty, you asked another droid if you could have their arm."

"I need it more than they do. I am a gladiator. Born to fight!"

Axel shook his head wearily.

"Mech-man was born to be annoying," Uga said, "only not born. Hatched from grease garage." He waddled down the beach with Brayton right behind him. They all surrounded the raft to look at the case of fuel cells.

"Good haul," Brayton said.

"Yeah, let's get them loaded up," Axel said to Spartacus.

Luna jerked her chin, indicating she wanted to talk privately. Axel followed her back to the ship. "Yeah?"

"The Woolies we traded with were working for a man who asked us if we'd heard anything about the Wrath," Luna said.

"Like what?"

"Apparently there are rumors circling, people are scared."

Axel glanced out at the horizon. The colony was hidden, isolated.

"We've been off the grid, maybe something's happening," Luna said. "You think there's anything to it?"

"I don't know." Axel turned back to their ship, considering the cargo they had inside. It was yet another secret. Just like his past and the voice.

"What is it?" she asked.

Axel looked her in the eye.

Someday he might tell her the truth about the demon he battled in his mind, but not today—today they had to start the search for this Rangnar. Their future depended on it.

"Listen up," Axel said. "We've got more than enough fuel to make it to Tecca, where I believe Rangnar is hiding."

"Tecca is not a small planet," Spartacus said. "How do you plan on finding this man?"

"I don't. I plan on him finding me."

"Boss, wake up. Wake up!"

Rangnar felt his body being shaken. He blinked lazily at a furry face. Then two. Then three. Lucid, Nuke, and Saber all crowded around his achy body. But there was one missing.

He remembered then—Billy Bob was gone.

With a sigh, Rangnar managed to sit up with his back against a large metal door.

He raised a hand that was sticky with something *slimy*.

The next thing he saw was the half-empty bottle of Corinn wine on the ground next to him. His pounding head made thinking difficult. Seeing wasn't easy either. His blurred gaze went to his boots, both covered in the same orange slime.

Reaching up, he winced at a random memory of fighting a monster outside the caves. He had slashed off the wormy beard limbs, but it was Blaster that had come to the rescue.

The droid stood at the end of the hallway, both cannons at its side.

"Boss," Saber chirped.

"Rangnar, snap out of it," Lucid said.

Nuke growled. That did the trick.

Pushing himself up, Rangnar looked at his companions. "What? What is it?" he asked.

"We've detected a ship entering the atmosphere," said Saber. "Blaster deployed two of our drones to track it down."

The heat of what felt like fear tore through Rangnar. He suddenly barreled over and vomited on the ground. The Markas all backed up from the splash.

This isn't fear, Rangnar realized. He was hung over. "I'm okay," he said, raising a hand. "I think."

Rangnar fought his way back upward, staggering slightly. "Ship?" he asked. "What kind? Is it a Warhorse?"

"No," Lucid said.

"Show me."

Rangnar stumbled down the corridor, hitting the wall and dropping the telescoping spear that had belonged to the Steward. He picked it back up, clipping it to his belt. He was going to need it again, it seemed.

Saber led the way to their command center where a bank of HoloMatrix security screens showed multiple locations on the surface and inside the bunker. It took a few blinks for Rangnar to clear his vision enough for a good visual of the ship. Right away he could tell this wasn't an active military vessel.

It had been once, though. The decommissioned transport had a detachable fighter on the top called a Tech-N. This one was damaged, with a shattered cockpit and mangled frame. The orange hull of the main ship wasn't in much better shape. Dents marred the exterior.

"We got any visuals on a registry?" Rangnar asked.

"Negative. Whoever it is, they don't want us to know who they are," Blaster said. "They are using all sorts of stealth tech."

Rangnar narrowed his bloodshot eyes. The pilot and crew were smart. Maybe they were here to hide, like him. Or maybe they were hunting for Rangnar. Maybe they wanted him to see them.

A thought crossed his mind: *Could this be Nolan?*

Had his former business partner and best friend tracked him down?

Rangnar looked at the old transport dipping down on the screen. It sure looked like something Nolan would pilot. And the fact it was using stealth tech? It could be him.

Definitely possible, he thought.

"You come to finish the job, you old bastard?" Rangnar whispered.

The last he had heard, Nolan was on the run and hiding in the outer edge of the system after pissing off too many pirates, bounty hunters, and finally—the Eagles.

Rangnar grunted and gestured to Nuke.

"Get me a stim," he said. "And Blaster, get ready for combat."

"Twice in a day," Blaster replied. "Music to my ears, sire."

Nuke trotted back inside with the medical kit, dumping it at Rangnar's boots. He pulled out a stim package, tore off the sealing then dumped two of the jell tablets into his mouth.

"Should we get the *Beak* ready?" Lucid asked.

Rangnar thought for a long moment. All three of his Marka friends looked back at him with their front eyes. They knew this ship's arrival wasn't a coincidence.

The hunters were being hunted.

Rangnar thought about running. He had other bunkers out there. But if this was Nolan, they had a score to settle that dated back decades.

"Boss," Saber said.

"Yeah, get it ready," Rangnar said.

The stims warmed his body as they melted into his system.

He stared at the ship for another long moment, anger fueling his rapidly beating heart.

"*Beak* is fired up and ready to go," Blaster announced.

"Go, I'll meet you there," Rangnar said.

The Markas hesitated around him. It wasn't like them to not follow an order.

"Didn't you hear me?" he asked.

Saber turned and led the way out of the command center. Rangnar took another look at the screen, then followed them out. He rushed to the vault as the stims went into effect, feeling like a young man again.

He looked through the glass port in the blast door at the safes inside the room, the boxes that contained his life's work. This was probably the last time he would ever see it.

Rangnar felt a deep dread, something that not even the adrenaline from the stims could mask. He had given his entire adult life to securing this room. And for what?

"Boss, we're ready to fly," Saber said over the comm.

Rangnar retreated from the vault, not looking back. He entered the supply room and broke open a crate of weapons, pulling out a heavy laser cannon minigun with a rotary barrel. He then grabbed a rifle and slung it over his armor. If it was Nolan, he would need to be well-armed.

With the weapons charged, Rangnar strode to a corridor with a t-intersection. One way led to the cave where his friends waited in the *Beak*. The other way led back to the bluff overlooking the boiling mud pits.

His heart tugged at him to go with the Markas, but his brain knew that would only endanger them.

His days of running were over.

It was time to fight.

He opened a channel to Blaster. "Deploy the *Beak*," he said.

"To where, sire?"

There was one last place that the Markas would be safe, but it meant he couldn't go with them. In this case, Death Rule Number 3 only applied to his crew.

"Hex Prime," he said. "I've uploaded the coordinates."

"Copy."

"And one more thing."

"Standing by."

"I want you to send a drone out within view of that ship." Rangnar paused briefly, then added, "Lead them to the lookout."

"Sire?"

"You heard me."

"May I fight by your side?" Blaster asked.

"No, go with the hunters. Make sure they survive. That is your new mission. I will meet you at the coordinates."

"Understood. Godspeed, sire."

Rangnar opened the hatch and stepped out into the blazing, gaseous atmosphere. As he made his way out to the bluff, the *Beak* blasted skyward, rocketing toward the orange clouds. The comms came to life in his earpiece.

"Don't do this!" Saber chirped.

"Rangnar, don't leave us!" Lucid cried.

"Let us stay with you!" Nuke exclaimed.

"You'll be safer without me," Rangnar said.

He shut the comm channel off.

Be well, my friends, he thought.

His heart pulled at him, but he buried his emotions deep. Weakness would get him killed. He watched the ship until it was out of sight. For a fleeting moment, he regretted his decision. Something about standing here alone, dying alone.

Ironic, he thought. *I'll die the same way Lannon died, all those years ago.*

Holding the laser cannon, Rangnar took a path to the bluff

where he had faced off with the Steward. His career had started here, it was fate that it should end here. Possibly against the man who had betrayed him after their days of hunting Stewards had ended.

The sea of boiling mud stretched across the horizon, popping and gurgling.

On his HUD, he tapped into the mirrored view of the drone that Blaster had sent within visual range of the alien ship. The pilot had taken the bait and was flying in his direction. He was leading them right here.

Rangnar wanted to look the captain of this ship in the eye before he went down in a hail of laser bolts. At the current speed, the unmarked vessel would be here within minutes.

The blink of an eye, in the scheme of things.

He lifted the laser cannon at the sky and took a deep breath.

Memories of his life surfaced from vaults in his brain. As a youth, living as a squatter with other kids in a run-down slum building on Optus. They had formed a gang of sorts, with Rangnar quickly becoming the leader. Days of scavenging, working any job he could find, sometimes stealing when he was so hungry there was no other option.

Then the score that changed everything. He had snuck beneath the spaceport with his two best hooligan friends and popped open a storm drain under a wealthy merchant vessel. They had each taken a black, secure crate, escaped, and opened them back in their freezing apartment. The crates were freezers of their own and inside were Corinn bull steaks.

That was the most decadent meal Rangnar had ever eaten. It was the first time in his life his stomach pain had fully eased. He never realized until that night that the constant ache was from hunger.

After that, his palate changed—and his attitude. Within months of that score, their small crew made extensive advancements in their skills and intelligence. They saved up enough to buy their own small vessel. It was a pile of junk, but it flew. They became better scavengers and used the vessel to become bounty hunters off-world.

It was only a few years later he arrived here to track the Steward.

After that, his life was a blur. Running. Gunning. Victories. Hard losses. And then finding a Wrath crystal worth a fortune.

Nolan and Rangnar became addicted to the treasures, amassing wealth, building a black market trading empire that made them two of the richest hunters in the galaxy.

But Nolan became greedier, and his heart hardened. He would do whatever it took to secure Wrath tech and artifacts for *himself*. That had included betraying Rangnar. It shouldn't have been a surprise when he sold Rangnar out to the Colonial Alliance to save his own hide.

Rangnar pictured the day that Nolan sabotaged his ship. He caught Nolan in the act, which led to a knife fight, and Rangnar losing his ear.

It was only thanks to Lucid that Rangnar escaped into the jungles as the Eagles descended in their dropships. She was a young member of his crew but was braver than any human. Her actions getting him off that planet led to his love for the species as well as his Death Rules.

The distant sound of a ship broke over the wind.

He studied the fiery clouds just as the hull of the vessel burst through. The thrusters kicked on underneath, slowing the descent. A draft of air slammed into Rangnar. He held his ground, keeping his laser cannon aimed upward, but holding off on firing.

"Rangnar Soki!" they shouted over the comm system.

He kept his laser cannon aimed at the cockpit.

"Yeah!" he yelled. "That you, Nolan? I hope it is, you motherfucker! Why don't you come down and face me yourself!"

A troop hold door that had once deployed Eagles and vehicles opened along the portside. From the shadows came a figure. Tall. Strong. Athletic...*young?*

This wasn't Nolan Spear. He would be an old man by now, like himself.

The guy moved out of the shadows, looking down with brown eyes and long blonde locks blowing in the toxic wind.

Rangnar watched in shock. No man could breathe these fumes without choking.

A helmet suddenly activated, rising over his face, but Rangnar already knew this was no average man. Perhaps not a human at all.

CHAPTER 15

"Approaching station."

The grizzly voice woke Jax. For a frightening second, she had no sense of place or time. There was only darkness, a low humming, and a fog over her brain.

It took another moment to realize her eyes were closed. She cracked her eyelids to the sight of a metallic hull with weak lights glowing along portholes. Stars twinkled outside the thick panels. She was in a Clipper, flying through space.

The fog hung over her like the grips of anesthesia after surgery.

Surgery? she thought.

Her gaze lowered to a vacuum rated black suit over her torso and lowered further to robotic legs connected just below her knees. Heart thumping, she stared for a long beat. The gunmetal gray mechanical prosthetics were shaped to look like human legs, muscles and all.

Through her fog, she remembered what she thought had been a dream.

In her mind's eye, she was on the Coffin during the assault.

Killing the Ino, saving Lieutenant Apollo, then meeting General Gabriel Jessup.

War is coming, he had said.

What happened next was a blur, but she had a vague memory of being taken into a medical bay with a droid and human doctor. Next to a gurney were the very robotic legs fastened to her knees now.

That wasn't a dream either. It was all real.

Her heart rate quickened.

"Remain calm, Sergeant Brito," came a robotic voice.

Glancing to the side, Jax saw a new medical droid, different from the one during her surgery. This one looked like a war droid, with T-Flesh, designed to support troops in combat.

"My name is D-4. I have been assigned to oversee your care," it said. "As you may remember from your prior consultation, your new robotic legs, i.e. TIN-A3, are the most advanced model ever designed. They are connected by artificial nerves to your spinal column. The interface is seamless. After only a few hours of using them, they will feel and respond like your natural limbs."

"How long have I been out?" Jax groaned.

"Twenty hours."

"Where are we going?"

"Look up here, Sergeant." That grizzly voice was the same one that had awakened her and came from up front.

Jax craned her neck to the cockpit where two pilots sat. One of them was glancing back at her. "Welcome to the Citadel," he said. "First moving space station of its kind, built for the new Expeditionary Defense Legion."

Beyond the reinforced glass viewports, Jax saw this wasn't just a station, but also a fleet. The biggest Naval Fleet she had seen in her entire life. It wasn't all military vessels out there, either. She spotted two of the cigar shaped Coffins, probably full of prisoners to help support the CAEDL. To prepare for the Wrath.

Six Ironclad Destroyers were docked at the honeycombed station. At least a dozen small Knight Attack Cruisers were also there. A hive of other activity buzzed around the station. Warhorses and Clippers moving troops and supplies. Drones and satellites.

"Prepare for landing," said one of the pilots.

The transport carrying Jax entered the bustling lanes, pulling right toward a goliath Ironclad. On the portside, she made out the name: *Nexis*. Hundreds of small troop and supply hold hatches were open along the aft section. The Clipper dipped down into one of them. The hatch closed behind them, sealing it off.

"Are you ready to use your new legs?" said D-4.

Jax looked at the medical robot, trying to grasp the change of events. Hardly a day earlier she was being shipped off to Ripa with a group of prisoners that wanted to slit her throat. She was trying to figure out how to defend herself. Now she had state-of-the-art legs that worked nearly flawlessly, as if they were her own.

It seemed too good to be true.

She had gotten really lucky. Maybe.

The hatch opened on the back of the transport, and a ramp extended down to the deck of the *Nexis*. D-4 unlatched from the seat, then went over to Jax carrying a bag that she recognized as her own.

The crossbars unlocked over Jax. She got up, finding it effortless.

"Please follow me," D-4 said. The droid picked up the bag, but Jax reached out.

"I can carry my gear."

"Very well, Sergeant."

Jax took the bag, slung it over her shoulder and started out of the Clipper.

"Thanks for the lift," she said.

"Good luck, Sergeant," replied the same pilot from earlier.

Jax stumbled a few times on the ramp but managed to get down to the sprawling troop hold without falling.

"Well done," said the droid. "You will be running soon."

Raising a metal hand, it waved for Jax to follow. Rows of ten Clippers sat idly in the vast room. Crew pushed supply carts back and forth, some of them containing ammunition and missiles. Mechanics worked on the transport ships.

"Come, I will show you to your new CO," D-4 said.

She followed the medical robot through the hold, into an empty corridor. The journey to the barracks took several minutes. By the time Jax got to the space, she had walking down. A smile almost formed on her face, but she didn't let it.

Her fate had changed rapidly, and it could change again. She couldn't take this for granted.

D-4 stopped at a dual hatch. "Here we are, Sergeant Brito."

The hatches whisked open to another sprawling space. Inside, a group of twenty Eagles stood in gunmetal-colored armor that matched Jax's legs. There was a droid here too. Twice the size of a man both wide and tall. Every inch covered in T-Flesh. Unlike the former Corinn war droids, this battle bot didn't have a facial display, but a curved helmet with a human skull painted on the outside.

D-4 started out toward the group, which stood in front of a man in fatigues with a lieutenant insignia just below his collar.

"Lieutenant Apollo, this is Sergeant Jax Brito," D-4 said.

"We've met, you dumb shit," Apollo said. "Didn't you read her file?"

"The file is classified."

"Ah, got it."

Jax tossed up a salute as Apollo walked over.

"If you're wondering, I requested you," he said.

"Honored to be here, sir," Jax said.

Apollo waved her toward her new platoon.

At first glance, they looked different from the soldiers Jax had served with before. Harder. Hard faces. Hard gazes. Hard bodies. Exposed flesh showed scars and tattoos. These weren't soft Eagles like Krish, or so many others that had served Hatchet Platoon.

These men had seen action. Lots of it.

Almost everyone had a robotic limb. One Eagle had a robotic eye with a metal plate over half of his face.

Lieutenant Apollo was no different. He opened his mouth of cracked teeth as he walked over, using his tongue to pick out something stuck in a back molar. When he got right in front of Jax, he scrutinized her with a raised brow and cold blue eyes.

"Bet you got a hell of a story behind those metal kickers," Apollo said. "That part of your classified file?"

Jax looked ahead, feeling the eyes of her new platoon on her.

"Well? You gonna tell us?" Apollo asked.

"Lost them in combat, sir," Jax said.

"How?"

"Fire sword, sir."

"Bet that hurt."

"It didn't feel good, sir."

Some of the other Eagles chuckled, earning a glare from Apollo.

"You a funny gal, Brito?" Apollo asked. "I hope you're not going to make me regret my decision."

"You won't, sir."

Apollo watched her another moment, then stepped back. "File in, Brito."

Jax walked over into a spot.

"Welcome to Outlaw Platoon," Apollo said. "We all have unique pasts. Including Hippo here."

He jerked his chin at the bulky war droid that was built like one of the Earth creatures. The name now made total sense.

"Nice to meet you, Sergeant Brito," said the robot in a deep baritone voice.

"And you," Jax replied.

Apollo began introductions.

"This is Corporal Ivey," he said.

"We call him Meatball because of that head of his," said a sergeant with a robotic leg.

"Thank you for the commentary, Sergeant Hesh," Apollo said. "I should note, Hesh isn't quite right in his dome. Makes him stutter from time to time, especially when he gets spooked."

"I'm fine, just fine," Hesh laughed.

Next, Apollo pointed to a man with two robotic arms and a mohawk atop his sun weathered face. "This is Specialist Tir Nadia."

Jax nodded at each of the soldiers in turn.

"Staff Sergeant Vikus Satani," Apollo said. The dark-skinned man had thick black hair that formed a widow's peak above robotic red eyes. He nodded back at Jax.

Apollo continued the introductions but stopped when someone shouted, "Commander on deck!"

General Gabriel Jessup walked out into the cargo hold, flanked by two guards. He walked at a brisk pace through the gathering platoons of Dark Horse Company, his orange energy-cape flowing like a waterfall behind him.

He went straight to the sealed-off launch bay shield hatch. It slowly rose over a glass wall protecting them from the vacuum of space. But there was something out there. The Citadel was orbiting a planet. It looked unremarkable from this vantage, nothing but a brown ball with veins of lava.

There was another station out there, a massive gray honeycomb with giant glass domes over the habitats.

The general turned back.

"That ball of rock is Corinnia, the former home world of the Corinns," he said. "The hive-looking station is the Nest, their home since the Wrath invasion."

Jax had seen images of the gargantuan space station that housed the majority of the Corinn species that hadn't spread to other planets, hoping their home world would one day recover. Over ten million lived in the habitats. Hardly a dip in the bucket of their former ten billion.

"For the first time in over thirty years, humans will be setting foot on this apocalyptic hell, and we're gonna be the first," Gabriel said.

Jax felt her heart thump in anticipation.

"For decades the Corinns have been attempting to terraform their planets and restore them," Gabriel said. "We've been told these projects were working, but we now know those reports were not accurate. In fact, those projects have failed."

He stiffened.

"After the war, the Corinns built outposts on Eern and Corinnia to both house terraforming crews as well as to stop thieves from raiding their planet. Two weeks ago, pirate activity was discovered on the surface of Eern. It was just one of several events where new Wrath technology was found."

The general paced a few steps.

"The Corinns have shared much of this with CAID through a backdoor channel and have now asked for our help in lieu of major new developments, including increased seismic activity and the loss of several terraformers as well as entire outposts." Gabriel turned to the viewports. "As you can see, most of their personnel have been evacuated from the surface to the Nest."

Jax focused on tiny triangle shaped ships with burning

thrusters. Dozens of them fled the atmosphere on their way to the sprawling space station.

"In a few hours, the first of our advance teams will head to the surface with Corinn soldiers on a recon mission," Gabriel added. "Something's happening down there, and our job is to assist our allies in finding out what it is."

He looked back to Dark Horse Company.

"We will guard the gates of Hell and strike with the vengeance of a thousand worlds!" Gabriel shouted with a raised fist.

The entire room erupted with the motto, the words echoing as the general left. As soon as he was gone, Apollo shouted, "You heard him! Get your asses ready to deploy."

Eagles fanned out with Jax following, but Apollo called for her to stop.

"You getting used to your new pegs?" he asked.

Jax glanced down at her legs and feet. "Yes, sir, they work incredibly well."

"Good, because you're going right into the fray with us," Apollo said with a grin. "Burn and learn, my new friend."

The *Trash Squid* lifted into the orange clouds.

"I hope you know what you're doing," Luna said over the comm.

"I hope so, too," Axel replied.

He kept his gaze on the man he believed to be the Phantom, aka, Rangnar Soki. The infamous bounty hunter stood in front of a blast door built into the cave system, gripping a laser cannon that could turn Axel to pulp.

Axel took a step forward, crushing something squishy under his boot.

"Watch your step there," Rangnar called out. "Had a run in with the local wildlife."

Axel glanced down at a severed snake-like limb. Several of the wormy apparitions littered the rocky shelf.

"You gonna just stand there, or tell me what you want?" Rangnar said. "If it's my head, you best get on with it, boy."

"Boy?" Axel grunted.

He stepped over the chunk of scaly flesh on the rock and then carefully reached into a vest over his armor.

"Easy now, b—" Rangnar started to say.

"I'm not a boy, old man," Axel said. "And if you shoot me with that thing, you'll destroy what I came to show you."

Ever so carefully, Axel pulled the Wrath ball out of his vest. The spiked artifact glowed as he held it outward.

Rangnar squinted, clearly curious. "The hell did you get that?" he asked.

"Stole it from some very unhappy Corinn pirates," Axel replied.

"Corinn pirates?"

Axel wasn't sure if it was a question, or a confused statement.

"On Eern," Axel said. "Long story."

"I'm not going anywhere." Rangnar lowered the cannon, slightly. "Start from the beginning."

Axel explained about the contract, finding the ships in the asteroid belt, being attacked by the pirates, and tracking them to Eern. "It was a Corinn pirate named Kian Ka' Ki," he said. "Something might have happened to their ship before we escaped with this."

He tossed the ball up in the air, prompting Rangnar to reach out and shout, "Don't!"

Axel caught it and froze.

"What?" he asked. "It's not going to open a black hole or something, is it?"

"Damn, boy! Don't you know enough not to mess around with Wrath tech?" He lowered the cannon slightly, but Axel wasn't going to let his guard down.

"How'd you find me?" Rangnar asked.

"Another long story. Basically, I got a good crew."

"Or stupid crew, considering you came here."

Axel shrugged. "So you want to buy this from me, or what?"

Rangnar let out a deep laugh. "You got some balls, boy."

"I told you not to call me that."

Axel took another step forward.

"Stop," Rangnar said. "I don't want to kill you, but you made a mistake coming here. If you can find me, so can my enemies, and right now I got plenty."

"So let's get on with it then. Tell me what this is, or make me an offer."

Slowly, the two men came closer, stopping a few feet away so Rangnar could get a better look at the ball. "Interesting," he said. "It's Wrath, but of all the artifacts, tech and weapons I've collected over the years, this is the first time I've seen anything quite like it."

"How much would it be worth to you?"

"Worth?" Rangnar laughed again. "I don't even know what it is yet."

"Listen, I'm sorry for tracking you down and all, but I figured you were our best bet at getting rid of this thing."

"Unfortunate for you." Rangnar shook his helmet. Then he turned and started toward the blast door.

"Where are you going?" Axel called out.

"To get some sleep and wait for the people that will be here to kill me soon." Rangnar stopped at the door but didn't turn. "I suggest you leave before they come, if you value your life."

Axel followed Rangnar. "I'm not leaving until you tell me what this is."

"Then you're dumber than I thought. I already told you, I don't know what that thing is, and I don't want it. I got no need for anything Wrath related anymore."

Rangnar jerked the laser cannon, shooing Axel away with the barrel. Then he went to the door, tapping in an access code.

"What if I told you one of my crew discovered a message coming from this?" Axel said.

Rangnar lowered his finger. "Message?" he asked. "What kind of message?"

"I don't speak Wrath, do you?"

Rangnar swiftly turned and walked over until they were face to face, staring at Axel through his visor as if he was trying to read his soul.

Axel stared right back. "You can trust me," he said.

"I don't trust any man." Rangnar backed down. "Come inside, but don't get comfortable. I'll take a stab at figuring out what that ball is."

Axel thought about what the voice in his head would tell him. Probably something about how this bounty hunter would cut his throat from ear to ear, stab him in the back, crack his head open then steal the ball from him.

That was all probably true, but he decided to follow Rangnar into the caverns. The bounty hunter took off his helmet once the door shut behind them, shaking his dreadlocks out. Axel looked at the scar that traced his jaw from lip to the deep wrinkles that marred his forehead. One of his ears was completely gone.

This was the face of a man that had seen many things over the years.

"You started your career here," Axel said. "Hunting a Steward."

"Your crew is good indeed, they did their research," Rangnar said. He raised a brow, probably wondering if Axel was here to kill him after all. "I am a lot of things, kid—"

"My name's Axel, not *kid*, not *boy*," he interrupted, "Axel Finn."

"Okay, Axel Finn, but I ain't no liar, and I will tell you right now I'm not proud of those days," he said. "Guess that doesn't matter anymore." Rangnar paused again. "If you came to kill me, now's your chance. I wouldn't blame you for it."

Now Axel was the one to scrutinize Rangnar. He was different than Axel had expected. Not evil. Not good. Somewhere in between.

"I'm not here to hurt you," Axel said. "I'm here to sell this artifact."

"Come," Rangnar said.

They continued into a corridor that opened to a living space. Blankets and mattresses lay sprawled across the ground.

"My other comrades are gone, don't worry," Rangnar said. "They won't be returning. I sent them away when they detected your ship in orbit."

Axel understood now. The bounty hunter had been prepared to fight Axel to the death but didn't want his crew to get hurt.

Unless that was a lie.

Maybe there were other hunters in these tunnels. He certainly wasn't going to risk his own crew by having the *Trash Squid* land. As if on command, his earpiece sizzled with a message from Luna.

"Captain, what's your status?"

Axel stopped. "Still alive," he reported.

"You coming or what?" Rangnar asked.

A command room of displays showing live feeds was on his

left, but Rangnar went to a complicated looking blast door. After entering a series of codes, that door swung open.

"After you," Rangnar said.

"Yeah, I don't think so," Axel said. "You first."

Rangnar shrugged then entered what appeared to be a clean room. There were suits, gloves, and helmets. He picked up a set of gloves and put them over the ones he already wore. Then he fastened his helmet.

"What's on the other side?" Axel asked.

"Unburied treasure," Rangnar replied. "If you want to know what you have in your hands there, we have to go inside."

"What's inside?"

"Wrath, *stuff*, and an analyzer that might tell us what your artifact is."

Rangnar opened the next door as Axel put on his own helmet. The bounty hunter walked inside a space with motion activated lights. As they walked by, lights clicked on over dozens of smaller safes and vaults.

He crossed over to a smooth, free-standing table with a curved top. From what Axel could tell, this itself was some sort of Wrath technology. "Is that...?"

"A scanner of sorts." Rangnar smirked, "Put your ball on it."

Axel hesitated.

"Come on, kid, my life's short as it is. You want to know what it is, or not?" Rangnar asked.

Cautiously, Axel approached, agitated at being called a kid again. But curiosity got the best of him. He reached out to put the artifact on the curved top as an electric forcefield activated all around him. He whirled to see Rangnar waving at him with a remote control of sorts.

"The hell is this!?" Axel blurted.

Rangnar slowly backed away. "Just a precaution," he said. "I need to know what *you* are."

"What I am?" Axel tried to reach the *Trash Squid* over the comms, but there was only static.

"They can't hear you from here," Rangnar said.

"I trusted you."

"An unfortunate mistake."

Axel tried to move against the field, only to be zapped backward. "I should have known a bounty hunter would have no honor," Axel said.

"And you should have known coming here was a risk, like I told you at least twice before you followed me inside," Rangnar said. He indicated to the Wrath ball in his hands. "Now if you would, please kindly put that on the scanner."

Rangnar stroked his long beard. "Gotta tell you, I'm not sure what I'm more curious about," he said. "You, or that intriguing object you brought me."

CHAPTER 16

There was no time for Jax to get acclimated to her new platoon, or her new legs. They weren't flawless, and required some practice, but she was getting used to them.

The complete shift in her destiny still had her thinking none of this was real.

She had gone from disgraced soldier to an Eagle assigned to the infamous Dark Horse Company, the exact group of soldiers her mom and dad had feared.

As she stood in the launch bay of the ship, she thought of her family. They might not approve, but this was far better than them hearing she had been discharged and sentenced to a penal colony.

She could still go home a hero someday.

Assuming she could survive whatever was happening on the surface of Corinnia.

Strong and steady, she kept repeating in her mind.

At various troop holds throughout the gargantuan destroyer, the Eagles of Dark Horse Company prepared to climb into their tubes and fire down to the ruined Corinn planet. Jax waited in

Launch Bay 9 with twenty-five members of Outlaw Platoon and their war droid.

The human soldiers and their bot weren't alone today. For the first time in history, a Corinn was preparing to launch with them.

The tall, lean male alien had yet to say a single word besides his name, Zang Za Zi. Jax tried not to stare, but it was hard to not look at the creature. The Corinn stood with his hands behind his tight-fitting black suit, bright green eyes roving across the room with a slow and calculated curiosity. There weren't any markings on his clothing, as the Corinns didn't follow the human traditions of insignia or medals. The alien society valued individuals over groups, and thus only one Corinn was assigned to each of the Eagle platoons.

All Jax knew was the aliens were members of what humans called the Novanauts, an elite Corinn military unit authorized and trained for warfare. From what she understood, the species had rooted out almost all violence from their society before humans colonized the Hironia System. What little remained was suppressed by war droids. The Corinns had manufactured entire armies to subdue the Marka population on Eern, and to handle Wooly populations in their many mining operations across the system.

When the Wrath arrived, the droids were easily defeated by EMP weapons, leaving the Corinns all but defenseless until the Stewards arrived on the battlefield. Since then, the Corinns had trained millions of Novanauts to fight, including this one, Zang Za Zi.

The presence of the alien made Jax nervous, but she was more concerned about what they were going to find on the surface of the former Corinn home planet.

She glanced over at the launch tubes along the hull that would transport her there. Soon the Eagles would climb inside a pod not much bigger than a coffin. But first, they had a dozen safety checks to perform on their suits and T-Flesh rigs.

The crate in front of Jax contained her new armor which would bulwark her from head to toe. Inside was a helmet with the fiery skull paint of the company and the initials DHC. On the visor, two blazing eyes stared back at her as she picked it out of the crate.

While dressing, she listened to the banter around her from the other Eagles. These soldiers weren't like the men and women she had served with in Hatchet Platoon. In fact, there wasn't a single woman here, nor in the larger Company, besides Jax. There weren't any greenhorns like Krish, either.

None of these hard soldiers appeared to have the pre-launch jitters. Or maybe they were just hiding it behind their jokes.

"I doubt a Wrath has ever seen an Eagle with a head like yours, Meatball," said Staff Sergeant Satani.

There was no arguing with that. The red haired giant of a man had the biggest skull Jax had ever seen.

"If there are Wrath down there, you'll be the first to die, Satani," Meatball replied with a snort. "Although I guess you'll take a bunch with you. The minute you try to hump one of them, you'll deliver a good case of the clap—considering all the nasty bitches you've been boning."

The other men laughed.

"You wouldn't believe it, Brito," Meatball continued. "Satani has a penis like a heat seeking missile that locks onto the nastiest looking creatures you've ever seen."

"Still wouldn't do a ginger," Satani replied with a shrug.

More laughter broke out, and Jax found herself laughing along with them.

"Those new?" asked Specialist Tir Nadia. The tall, lean man with a thick mustache and two robotics arms was looking at Jax's legs.

"Yeah," Jax replied. "Only had them two days."

Nadia scratched at the side of his 'stache. "Guess you're gonna break 'em in real fast, aren't ya?"

"Took me a week before I got used to mine," said Sergeant Hesh. He raised his robotic leg, wiggling the metal foot on which he'd painted a decent reproduction of the DHC logo. "I love it, man, even named her the Stallion. You know, like a horse."

Jax recalled what Apollo had said about Hesh having something off about him. She could sense that easily as he showed off his prosthetic.

She noted quietly that nearly the entire company had modifications. Satani had scars around his eyes, which were fully prosthetic. Both pupils glowed red, making him appear like he was possessed by a demon. They were homed in on Jax now, scrutinizing her.

From what Jax had heard, Satani had a criminal background. They said he served five years in a space brig after killing two miners in a dispute.

Jax guessed a lot of them were given a choice like the one offered back on the Coffin: Prison or Serve.

The jokes continued as the Eagles began to apply their armored rigs. Jax clicked the T-Flesh pads around her robotic legs, connected her middle-section, then put her chest rig over her head.

"Okay, listen up," said Lieutenant Apollo. "We're blasting to what was once Casion. There's a Corinn outpost about ten miles from our LZ that went offline. Our first objective is to get there and figure out what happened."

"We have no idea what happened?" Satani asked. "How's that possible?"

Apollo regarded Zang Za Zi, but the Corinn didn't offer anything up.

"We know there's been increasing seismic activity, and electrical and magnetic interference make communications difficult," Apollo said. "Once we hit the surface, comms with the *Nexis* will be sketchy until we establish an FOB. Due to surface conditions, we won't have any armor on the ground until we clear the area."

"Clear the area of what?" Hesh asked. "Do we have targets?"

"Negative, nothing confirmed," Apollo said.

Zang suddenly strode away, talking in his native tongue which came through a series of clicks and clacks.

Apollo waited a beat until the alien was out of earshot.

"Remember, this is still their world. Apocalyptic or not," he said. "You'll all show respect. That means no—"

"No taking shits or pissin' outside your diaper, Meatball," Hesh said.

"You're the one that takes dinosaur shits," Meatball said. "Mine are perfectly formed pieces of art."

"Enough," Apollo growled. "We have no idea what's down there, and since you want to be a dumbass, I'm putting you on point, Meatball."

"I wasn't the one that started talkin' shit, LT."

"Hesh and you can switch off."

Hesh shrugged. "We'll be the first to get a Wrath kill then." He reached out with a fist and Meatball gave him a tap.

"Or the first to have your guts ripped out," Satani said.

"Yeah, don't get cocky," Apollo said. "We're not blasting down to annihilate some rebels that don't want to pay taxes. We don't know what we're going to find, so be ready for anything."

The men fell into silence. Several of the Eagles glanced at Jax, probably wondering if they could trust her. She didn't blame them. They had only known her for a little over a day. Trust took time and was often only established during combat.

Zang returned, moving swiftly, faster than the leisurely pace Jax had noticed earlier. The alien also had his arms at his sides now, indicating some agitation.

"Lieutenant Apollo," Zang said. "My superiors have authorized our deployment to Casion."

"Got it," Apollo said. The Eagles waited while the lieutenant opened a line to his CO for a secondary confirmation.

Jax noticed Zang was staring at her with his chilling emerald eyes that reminded her of a lizard. She could almost feel the Corinn trying to communicate with her through telepathy.

Jax didn't know much about how the species communicated, but she knew there was some sort of portal they used to connect to their ancestors.

The warning siren blared for all non-combat personnel to clear the launch bay.

"Okay, this is it. Get ready to blaze," Apollo said.

"Burn and learn, Brito," said Satani.

Jax secured her helmet and walked up to her assigned launch tube. Twenty-five hatches along the thirty opened. This was the fiftieth time in her career she had entered one, but the first for anything other than a training mission.

The jitters rocked her body as she climbed into the pod. The hatch sealed shut.

A countdown formed on her HUD, in sync with the other Eagles of Outlaw Platoon. On ten, she gritted her teeth. The pod fired, rocketing out into the darkness beyond the *Nexis* and toward Corinnia.

Jax thought again of her family as the pre-determined coordinates in her pod steered her toward the hellish surface. She was doing this for them, for all the peaceful species across the galaxy.

As she rocketed through the atmosphere, her mind transported her back to the ash root fields on Ruin. She was with her brother Nico, carefully but quickly harvesting roots.

"What do you want to be when you grow up?" she asked.

"I want to be a farmer." He had smiled at Jax. "This is the best life, how could you ever want anything else?"

Jax never understood how Nico could be so satisfied there—so content. As soon as Jax found out about other planets, she had longed to see them. And then, to help fight for them.

Jax gritted her teeth as her pod rattled fiercely through the atmosphere. She missed her brother. His smile. His kind demeanor, and his competitive attitude.

She missed their parents too. Warmth filled her heart, and gratitude that she had a second chance at serving.

Before she knew it, the parachute fired, jolting her pod and yanking it skyward, or so it seemed. It lowered to the ground where it slammed into the dirt. The hatch clicked, swinging open to darkness.

She checked her HUD, seeing the thermal regulators and exoskeleton working properly. As she got out, it didn't feel more than seventy-degrees, despite it being over one hundred and five degrees Fahrenheit outside. Nor did she struggle to move in the high gravity, lifting her rifle with ease.

Turning on the light, she swept the beam over a cracked, desert-like terrain. Not a single plant or tree showed across the barren landscape.

All around her, the other pods had landed. Eagles fanned out with their weapons aimed into the smoky haze. The curtain drifted across her field of vision, but her optics displayed a clear view of their landing zone. Jax checked the map on her HUD to make sure everyone was on the ground. All twenty-five members of Outlaw Platoon were moving, except for one.

She homed in on the location, seeing it was almost a mile away.

"Blake's chute didn't deploy, goddammit," Apollo said. "Everyone check in, check your gear, check your buddy's gear, and then follow me."

Hippo walked among the Eagles, scanning them and the environment with flashing lights.

"I'm picking up significant amounts of SO_2 out here," remarked the droid in a booming, synthetic voice. "Much higher concentrations than the last Corinn data we received."

Apollo looked over at Zang, but their alien guide said nothing.

"SO_2?" Hesh asked. "Is that bad, or what?"

"Sulfur dioxide is a gaseous air pollutant composed of sulfur and oxygen that forms when sulfur-containing fuel like oil, diesel, coal burns, or during volcanic eruptions."

"Makes sense," Apollo said. "Explains the weird clouds too."

"Yes, there are sulfate aerosols present in the stratosphere, but the levels on the surface seem higher than one might expect," Hippo replied.

"Why's that?"

"Maybe cause we ain't on Earth," Hesh said. "Just a thought."

"I must perform further analyses to ensure it is not harmful to the platoon," Hippo said.

"I'm sure the lab jockeys figured that in. Nice of them to share it with us, as usual," Apollo said. "Regardless of that, we have the best breathing filters the military provides, for what that's worth, so suck it up, all of you."

"Don't worry," Meatball said with a chuckle.

"Famous last words," Hesh said.

"For big fat fucks, you're sure being little bitches," Apollo said. "Now get on point with Hippo."

"Yes, *sir*," Hesh said.

The droid raised both cannons and began the hike through the blasted wastelands that had once been a vibrant ecosystem of exotic creatures and beautiful colors. Jax thought back to some of the images she had seen as a kid from this world. Purple forests, teal streams, and the magnificent bulls that once roamed fields of wildflowers.

It was all gone, incinerated by the Wrath during their invasion over thirty-five years ago.

As the platoon moved out in combat intervals toward the crash site, she saw no sign of the demonic aliens among the cracked rocks and charcoaled soil. Steam blasted out of vents across the terrain, fading into mist as it rose toward the hazy dark sky.

On the horizon, smoke drifted away from raging fires. The platoon was headed in the same direction as those flames. As Jax took in the sights through the optics on her rifle, the ground shook. She lowered the weapon, turning in all directions.

"The hell is that?" Meatball shouted.

"What it feels like, bird brain," Hesh replied. "An earthquake."

"Intel says they are frequent, but not to worry," Hippo said.

"Not to worry," Satani said. "Good one, big guy."

"Keep moving, we need to find Blake," Apollo said.

Fifteen minutes later, they found the pod.

Apollo and Hesh were the first to arrive. There was no doubt the crushed bullet tube had turned into a genuine coffin for the Eagle. Once the remainder of the squad caught up, they worked together to pry off the dented and torn hatch, but it was already clear by the extent of the damage that the corporal didn't survive. The inside wasn't going to be pretty.

Hesh wedged his fire sword into a gap and forced the hatch open. Sure enough, the body of Corporal Blake slumped out. He landed on his side, a hand still on his cracked visor. Both eyeballs were wide open, frozen in a stare of horror. Now they were cooking in the one-hundred and twenty-degree heat and gasses.

"Shit, man," Hesh said. He leaned down and pulled the tag from around Blake's neck, snapping it free. He handed it to Apollo.

Apollo took it, bowed his head, then slipped the tag into his vest pocket.

The first human casualty on Corinnia, and it was from a tech error.

Zang Zi Za walked over. "Unfortunate," he said. "My condolences for your loss."

"Yeah," Apollo said. He flashed a hand signal. "Let's move, Outlaws."

Rangnar sat in his control room staring at the results that had popped out an hour earlier for the scan of Axel Finn.

Human DNA

Corinn DNA

He had known this young man was different the moment he laid eyes on him, but he still couldn't believe it. Axel wasn't just different. He was a miracle. Something that should never have existed.

He was the son of a Steward.

So they aren't all dead after all, Rangnar thought.

He wondered if the kid even knew. If so, Axel probably wasn't even his real name.

Chances were good he used an alias, like Rangnar had for most of his life. Chances were also good this young man had come here to kill Rangnar because he knew about his past. How he had made a career hunting Stewards. Men like Axel's father.

A chilly wave ran through Rangnar.

What if Axel was the son of Lannon? What if the lad had come to avenge his father?

He would have killed me right away, Rangnar thought. *Right?*

The paranoid side of his brain took over. He tapped a comm button. "Axel," Rangnar said.

The young man glared up at the mounted camera, a growing fire in his eyes.

"Who are you?" Rangnar asked. "And I mean, who are you really?"

"Open that door and let me out, or I promise you'll regret it."

"Bold words for someone surrounded by an electric field and locked in a vault, Steward or no Steward."

Confusion passed over the eyes of the young man. "What?"

"I scanned your body," Rangnar said. "I know—"

Could he not know? Or maybe he's been tricking me all along?

"Who tricked who?" Rangnar whispered. He couldn't help but crack a sly grin. He may have broken his Death Rules, but he was still putting forth his A game.

Still, he had questions. First, what was this Wrath artifact?

Rangnar rotated the chair to the monitor that showed a feed from inside the vault.

Axel was still standing in the same position, but he wasn't screaming to be let out anymore. He was staring at the Wrath ball, which was glowing again.

His gaze swept over to the monitor connected to the Wrath analyzer. That machine had yet to decode the Wrath language illuminated on the spiked surface.

"Let me out!" Axel shouted. He slammed against the forcefield, jolting backward, and yelping in pain from the electric shock.

Rangnar shut off the volume on the monitor. He knew it would only be a matter of time before the crew of this Steward offspring came to search for him. He would have welcomed that, if he had any plan to leave this rock. Clearly Axel and his crew would be easy to outwit and destroy, seeing how easy it was to get Axel into the vault. Son of a Steward, or not, he wasn't getting out of there.

Didn't matter anyway.

Rangnar had given up on leaving the planet. He had accepted his fate. This was where he would die. Maybe not today. Maybe not tomorrow.

But the Eagles *would* come here eventually. They would find him, and they would kill him just like Rangnar had killed Lannon.

Unless...

A sudden thought seeded in his brain. What if he traded this Axel Finn for his own freedom? Surely CAID would forgive the charges against him if he handed them the only living Steward. *I could throw in whatever this ball is.*

He was tempted to do just that.

It would take a simple transmission to Captain Weston. His old friend may have sold him out, but that didn't matter if he had a way to get out of this mess. Offering up this kid and the ball would be a sure way to trigger the deployment of a Warhorse with some of the most hardened Eagles. The ship would be here within an hour, and Rangnar would have a way off this rock and back to his crew as a free man.

But what about Billy Bob? Gunned down by the Eagles on Optus. Could he really strike a deal with the same people that had killed his loyal friend in cold blood?

Fuck no, I'll never surrender to them!

THE LAST STEWARD

Rangnar turned his focus back to the Wrath analyzer. The machine should have decoded the message by now. Something was wrong. Maybe it would only reveal itself in the presence of a Wrath. Maybe only under a specific environment.

He could try burning it or putting it in a vault with the bones of a Spectre. There were plenty of options he could test out.

An alert chirped in his earpiece. He rotated to the bank of security monitors. An exterior camera had picked up movement outside. The shadow of a long, four-legged body that could only be a Marka bolted across the bony terrain above the bunker.

At first, Rangnar couldn't tell which hunter had returned. Then he realized it wasn't any of his hunters.

This Marka was wearing a black suit. The creature wasn't alone. Multiple security alerts popped up. The orange ship was back. And it had landed.

The crew was coming for their captain.

"Well shit," Rangnar said.

He put his helmet back on and turned away from the monitors. He pulled his hand cannon from a holster on his belt. He didn't want to kill a Marka, but he wasn't going to surrender and let them kill him. Or whatever it was they had planned. If Axel was the son of Lannon, and had come for revenge, there was no telling what his crew would do.

Rangnar rushed out of the command center, back through the living quarters, and into a corridor when an explosion suddenly rocked his shelter. The shock wave blasted through the tunnel, knocking him to the ground.

He got up and tried to shake it off but staggered from the impact. The blast had thrown him off, and there was still wine in his bloodstream. Adrenaline joined it, prompting a rush of heat through his body.

As soon as he got to the next corner, he halted with his pistol raised to listen for footsteps. What he heard over his auditory system sent a chill up his back. The rap of feet was identical to Blaster's. That meant he had vastly underestimated this crew. They had a Corinn war droid.

Fortunately for him, he knew exactly where to shoot one to drop it. But he would have to do it fast.

Holding in a breath, Rangnar moved around the corner to a view of smoke and debris across the ground. His advanced optics adjusted, showing a one-armed droid with T-Flesh striding through the mess.

Sighting up the droid at the kill-spot of center mass, he pulled the trigger. The bolts pounded the upper right part of the chest, just a hair off. In the split second that passed, he noticed this robot didn't have a cannon attached to its remaining arm. Nor did it have a weapon at all. That was odd, but good luck for him, as he now had a second chance to get his shot right. But before he did, a second set of steps hit his ears. Not a moment later, the Marka he had seen on the video feed came bursting through the smoke.

Rangnar had a choice, and only a heartbeat to make it. He either killed this alien before it ripped his head off, or let it rip his head off. As this impossible decision ticked in his mind, he thought of a third option. With the push of a button, the ceiling collapsed between him and the Marka.

A cloud of grit burst past him as he went back around the corner and toward the living quarters.

Screw this, he thought. *I am going to steal that hunk of garbage they call a ship. They just gave me back Death Rule Number 3—always have an escape route.* He rushed back through the bunker when he heard a beeping noise coming from the command center.

The scanner had finally finished deciphering the Wrath message. Curiosity tugged at him though his brain screamed that he didn't have time—that he had to get to that ship and flank the crew.

Curiosity won.

He rushed inside and hovered over a monitor, his heart pounding when he saw it had decoded the hieroglyphics into numbers. A countdown of some sort. The scanner had also detected an internal transmitter and communication device.

Head spinning, Rangnar considered the possibilities, quickly concluding this was some sort of beacon. That realization was enough to hit Rangnar like a Steward fist.

This thing wasn't some bomb, but it was just as dangerous in a way. And if the mobilization of the CANDF and new allied Corinn forces was any indication, they were preparing for the return of this evil alien race.

"Holy space nuts," he stammered.

Growling answered him, followed by the unmistakable scent of burning flesh. Before Rangnar could react, a powerful grip pulled him from behind, knocking the gun from his hands. He spun to find Axel Finn standing there, eyes red with rage. He snatched Rangnar by the throat, plucking him clean off the ground, not an easy feat considering the weight of his T-Flesh rig alone, not to mention that Rangnar weighed over two hundred pounds.

His eyes flitted down to see Axel's armor smoking.

Now he knew where the stink was coming from.

The force field would have killed an average man, but Axel, of course, wasn't just a man. The Steward offspring squeezed his throat.

"I know...what...it is," Rangnar choked out. "And I know...what...you are."

Axel squeezed harder, until Rangnar's vision faded into a narrow tunnel of red. He knew then it was over. That he had used up all his tricks. There would be no more escape routes or rules to keep him alive. No deals to save his hide.

Memories of his past haunted him as the Steward held him pinned, choking the life from his body.

It was a fitting end, a good end. An honorable end.

Death by a Steward.

The last Steward.

CHAPTER 17

Blind with rage, Axel was completely imprisoned by a vision. Once again, dressed in golden armor, caked with the ash blowing across a field of flowers ranging in color from a deep royal red to a soft lilac. That view rotated to a simmering city—not just any city—this was the once famous Corinn Crystal City on their home world of Corinnia. The metropolis lay like an amethyst dreamscape set against the brilliant horizon, its spires etched in scintillating violet that reflected the fiery glow of the Wrath invaders.

Fleeing the alien monsters were thousands of Corinns, their feet pounding a stone street embedded with fragments of shanor, the same radiant crystal integrated into their ethereal architecture. Dozens of Warhorses and Clipper transports rose toward the smoke-choked skyline, ferrying bellies full of Corinns.

The vision changed again to another army—hundreds of warriors in shining golden armor. Stewards.

They stood tall at the edge of the towering rock cliff. The heart of the Crystal City had been constructed to provide a spectacular view. Now it provided a horrifying view of the invasion in the sprawling city built around the bluff.

Wrath ships pounded the buildings into simmering debris that sparkled where shanor crystal lay in shards, reflecting the glow of burning fires.

"We guard the gates of Hell and strike with the vengeance of a thousand worlds!"

That gruff voice was familiar.

The warriors in golden power armor raised their laser cannons and telescoping fire spears, chanting and bellowing in war cries. They marched in perfect formation, the ground rumbling beneath their spike tipped boots.

"We must hold this bluff to buy the civilians time to escape the hordes of Wrath!" commanded the soldier in his gravelly voice.

The vision continued with the warrior stepping up to the very edge of the cliff and looking over the five-hundred-foot drop. The burning crater appeared too inhospitable for life, and yet, something was moving down there.

Thousands of tiny lights flickered like fireflies among the sea of charcoaled structures.

A closer look revealed the source—Spectres—five-hundred-pound alien beasts that were as big as Corinn bulls, with a rocky exterior covered in spikes and barbs that could shift and change to take on different forms. Right now, they had all taken on the same monstrous figure with an elongated tail anchored to a studded torso. Two arms hung off the front of that torso, each covered in chitinous spikes and ending in three hooked talons. Protruding out of the torso shell was a barbed neck connected an elongated head with a dozen misshapen fiery eyes, fueled by some internal biological engine.

The beasts employed a distinctive locomotion pattern when moving, shifting from a spider-like scuttling with their front limbs, to a serpentine slither with their spiked tails. Their fluid movements allowed them to move at great speed that carried incredible momentum and power.

"We hold them here!" shouted that grizzly voice. "We send them back to the fiery pits in which their hideous whore mothers birthed them from their flaming cunts!"

Cheers and shouts erupted.

Axel watched as the line of Stewards came together. They aimed laser cannons and rocket launchers down the nearly vertical cliffs at the approaching horde. The first of the beasts were already clambering upward, their flexible limbs contorting and blurring.

"Fire!" the rough voice screamed.

The Stewards unleashed their own hell from above, raining rockets and laser bolts into the climbing alien monsters. Shell bursts and screeches—not of agony, but of rage echoed upward.

Out of the smoky clouds, came a shrill piercing shriek of a Hydra.

"Shield wall!"

Curved, orange energy fields blossomed out over the Stewards as a sinewy frame, adorned with twisted, razor-sharp spines, sailed on four tattered membranous wings. They flapped and stretched with a ghastly grace, casting an eerie shadow over the warriors.

The high-pitched shriek resonated across the battlefield, emanating from the studded head of a behemoth Hydra as it unhinged its jaw, revealing a second jaw with thousands of saw-toothed daggers, each the size of a man. But it was the empty eye sockets that delivered the real death, squirting a lethal fog of green fluids toward the area where Axel stood in this dream. Orange forcefields fired around the warriors on his right but were destroyed instantly.

The world went topsy turvy as the warrior through which

Axel saw this scene fell to the ground. The Steward pushed himself up to his knees, glancing over at three comrades rolling on the dirt nearby, covered in the fluorescent flames that ate through their gold T-Flesh. Screams of horror lasted several moments before they trailed off to croaking cries, and then silence. The green blobs ate their bubbling armor and the flesh beneath until there was nothing but bones that turned to ash.

A pair of Bloodhogs rumbled across the horizon, drawing the warrior's gaze as he got to his feet. The fighters peppered the wings of the Hydra with laser bolts.

"Close gaps!" This time the gruff voice was confident and fearless.

The Stewards closed their ranks to make up for their lost comrades. A steady stream of lasers and rockets lanced down the walls, blasting away at the Spectres scrambling up the side.

But still they came, climbing with such incredible speed.

Axel watched through the eyes of this Steward as he fired calculated shots at the clambering monstrosities, their fiery eyes gazing upward through the smoke.

"Prepare to draw swords!" commanded that rough voice.

A trio of Clippers sailed downward, wing-mounted laser cannons raking back and forth. The rocky abominations flailed, their limbs blurring, as they tumbled back to the ground hundreds of feet below.

Through the clouds flashed a green hose of light, carving through the first Clipper, and cleaving it in half. The second tried to pull up but was completely consumed by a puff of green mist from the Hydra.

The beast swooped downward, extending its unhinged jaw and snapping through the ranks of Stewards. Every single one of the warriors stood their ground, unwavering, holding up their force fields, only to be knocked away or melted by jets of green fire. In one area, only a pair of boots, still firmly planted in the dirt, remained.

Green-hued clouds of mist hung over the area.

Slinging his rifle, the Steward drew two fire swords just as a Spectre launched into the air, opening its beak jaw rimmed with serrated teeth. He thrust in one of those swords, the serrated blade activating as it entered.

The head protruded farther out from the shell, swallowing most of the sword and part of his hand. He brought his other burning sword down on the chitinous neck, the teeth crunching through the rocky armor. Black, oily blood oozed out of the crack.

With a powerful kick of his boot, the Steward freed his first sword and sent the abomination back over the cliff.

Throughout the line, more Spectres mounted the crest, slashing with their razor-sharp blades and slapping outward with their barbed tails. Axel watched one of those tails wrap around a Steward, activating spikes that crunched through T-Flesh. He could hear the screams of pain that faded away as the monster launched the soldier into the air over the cliff with blood squirting from the fresh holes.

Axel saw another Spectre strike with the stinger on its tail to break through the top of a Steward helmet. It yanked upward with so much force it plucked the soldier's head and spine out of his armor. The headless corpse collapsed to the ground.

A shrieking Hydra pulled his vision skyward, where the winged abomination flapped into the darkness, chased by a single Bloodhog with a smoking wing.

The entire battlefield slowed in this dream that Axel couldn't seem to wake up from. The Stewards fought without fear despite the overwhelming enemy forces, breaking open Spectre shells in swift strokes that sprayed brilliant arcs of flaming black blood.

The beasts crashed into the shields, threatening to break through. Stewards had fallen where some did, but comrades closed in quickly, filling the gaps. An injured Steward missing an arm used his other to fire a pistol. He was helped up to his feet and rejoined the shield wall.

Bloodhogs and Clippers dipped down to provide covering fire against the single Hydra. A beast flapped an injured wing, tumbling as a flurry of missiles and lasers pounded it. In a desperate maneuver to escape, it dove downward toward the bluffs.

But this wasn't an effort to escape, Axel realized. It was a final attempt to kill.

The eye sockets glowed with a malevolent intensity. Within their depths flashed green orbs that vented outward, torching an entire squad of Stewards as the creature went down. It hit jaw first into the ground, skidding and pushing up a mound of scree before it came to a stop.

"Together!" the Steward yelled.

The shield wall clamped tightly where troops had been erased.

"Push! Heave! Push!"

The squad of Stewards worked together, one line using shields to push the Spectres, while a secondary line thrust telescoping fire spears into the monsters. In what seemed like a miracle, the fence of golden armor began to make headway, forcing the enemy back, and knocking them over the cliffs. Still, the beasts fought back, extending and slicing with their flexible limbs covered in barbs and claws.

Carmine exploded from the broken T-Flesh of Stewards. But even the injured continued to fight, working as one, and commanded by the voice Axel heard.

"With the vengeance of a thousand worlds!"

Smoke drifted across the dream, momentarily blocking his view as the line of simmering golden armor pushed the rocky demons over the edge.

A moment passed, then, "ALL HAIL STEWARD VICTORY!"

Shouts and cheers broke out all around.

When the smoke cleared, only half of the Stewards remained standing. The injured tried to get up, some with the help of others, including the leader Axel had witnessed this battle through.

The vision faded away, replaced by a new world. He heard that voice again.

"No one escapes!"

The giant soldier encased in golden armor stepped out on a cracked plateau with scattered bodies across the blasted terrain. The remains were neither the ash piles of dead Stewards nor the rocky shell of a Wrath. He stepped toward the corpse of a man wearing a mining suit and helmet. There were alien bodies too, short and stocky carcasses of Woolies.

But not all of them were dead.

In the distance, a group of the creatures waddled across a dusty field toward the entrance of a mine shaft.

A pair of Stewards chased them down, grabbing the helpless aliens and tearing off their limbs. Axel watched in horror as the guardians of the system slaughtered the mostly peaceful miners and the few humans who stood to fight.

Again, the dream changed, sending Axel to a busy market on a human world. A line of Stewards marched through the cobblestone streets of Hex Prime. Citizens gently tossed flowers at the boots of the warriors, offered prayers, and blew kisses. Children *oohed* and *ahhed* from the grip of their parents holding them at the sight of the God-like warriors.

Then came an image of another cobblestone street with an open market. Locals walked leisurely, filling woven baskets with fresh produce and fresh fish. Patrons sat outside of eateries, enjoying wine and beer. Suddenly, one of those wooden doors exploded off the hinges, and a large man with a beard crashed out onto the street.

Ducking below the door frame came the aggressor, an even bigger human—but not completely human. This was a Steward, face red with fury. He pummeled the downed man in the face, breaking his nose. Then he straddled him, hitting him again and again until his face caved in like a shattered flowerpot.

The Steward rose, blood dripping from his paws. He raised them above his head, and let out not a scream of fury, but a laugh.

Veins bulged in his neck as his maniacal laughter filled the market.

Children in the arms of their parents no longer stared with awe like they had in the former dream. There was fear in their eyes, and in the eyes of their parents as they fled the market.

The citizens that remained stood in shock.

Another Steward made his way through the chaotic scene, dressed in golden power armor. He shouted at the laughing maniac, as did the Steward from within which Axel was watching. Both men reached out to stop their insane comrade.

"Gingi, what have you done!?" yelled the familiar rough voice. "You must stop!"

Another voice came, but this one wasn't intended for the psychotic Steward, Gingi.

It was for Axel.

Demanding *he* stop.

"Axel, let him go!"

Axel blinked, trying to understand what was happening. He

felt stuck between reality and a dreamworld. It played in front of him almost like errant bits from videos he had seen in his lifetime, yet he seemed to be *in* the video. He would say they played like memories, but not his own.

"AXEL!"

The voice snapped him from a purgatory of confusion to the image of a woman.

For a fleeting moment, Axel thought it was his mother. The braided hair, kind eyes, and dimpled face.

But this wasn't her—this was Luna.

Axel focused his gaze on her as she tried to pry his hand away from a limp man in his grip. It took another moment to realize it was Rangnar Soki, the bounty hunter that had tricked him into a vault.

A glance around revealed he was in a command center. A monitor across the space displayed the results of two scans. One for the Wrath ball that made no sense to Axel. The other, a scan of his body that flashed: *Human DNA—Corinn DNA*.

Axel tried to make sense of that through the swarm of anger still attacking his mind.

He can never see a doctor. No scans. No tests.

Axel recalled what his mother had said all those years ago.

In a panic, he tossed Rangnar against the monitor, shattering it, and erasing the data. The bounty hunter slumped off the desk and onto the ground.

"Axel!" Cricket chirped.

He turned back to the door, seeing his crew had arrived. They all glared at him in shock and horror like the citizens had stared at the violent Steward in that market.

Brayton rushed into the room in a panic.

"We have to scat," he said. "They're coming."

"Who's coming?" Axel asked.

"Eagles. Two Warhorses full of 'em."

"What do we do with him?" Luna asked.

Panting, anger still surging through his veins, Axel looked down at Rangnar. He was curled up in a fetal position. The gruff voice in his head returned.

Kill him, don't leave him behind to rat you out!

Axel blinked, trying to focus. It was true that Rangnar knew something about Axel that he couldn't let get out. Something his mother had tried to protect him from for all these years.

But Rangnar also knew something else—he knew what the Wrath ball was.

Right now, the bounty hunter was more important to them alive, than dead.

Axel reached down and picked up Rangnar, lugging him over a shoulder.

"Grab the Wrath ball on the way out," Axel said. "We're going to need it."

"What is that thing?" Apollo asked.

Outlaw Platoon had fanned out around a gigantic spherical, tracked machine on the cracked, plateau. The thing had to be the size of a city block, and had the biggest tracks Jax had ever seen.

Rivers of lava snaked across the barren terrain behind the idle machine. Fimbriae-like apparitions tendrilled away from the alloy hull where they had burrowed into the ground. A tower in the center of the humped aft section had fallen, crashing to the ground over the river of lava. Branches draping off the tower had scattered across the plateau, one of them close to the platoon. From what Jax could tell, they had an array of large nozzles.

The machine kind of reminded Jax of an industrial root harvester she saw once as a kid. But this was no harvester, and it wasn't Wrath either.

Apollo turned to Zang. "You gonna tell us what that is, or should I blow it up to make sure it's not a threat?" asked the lieutenant.

"We call it a Ka-li," Zang replied, speaking slowly. "The human word would likely be *healer*."

Hippo had pushed on in front of the platoon, stopping about fifty feet from the base of one of the extended arms.

"So it's a Corinn terraformer?" Apollo asked.

"Correct," Zang said.

"My scans reveal this unit is offline and currently not functioning as intended," Hippo announced.

"If by 'intended' you mean bringing this fiery asshole of a planet back to life, you're damn right about that," said Meatball.

Zang regarded Meatball with a side glance but said nothing.

"Brace yourself for seismic activity," Hippo announced.

Jax stiffened as the rumble rushed under her robotic legs. She could feel the tremors throughout her body. It was the tenth quake that hour, and from what Jax could tell, they were becoming more frequent.

So far, there was no sign of Wrath, or anything else living. But there were still a lot of ways to buy it out here. Sink holes. Tar fields. Mini volcanoes that spewed lava fifty feet into the air. Not to mention the Sulfur Dioxide-rich atmosphere laced with traces of Methane. Without her breathing filters, Jax would die a slow and painful death.

Corinnia was a real-life Hell.

"Goddamn. I really don't like this place," Meatball said over a shoulder.

"Go with Hippo," Apollo replied. "But keep your mutant shaped head on a swivel."

Meatball grumbled something indistinct, but Jax picked up a few words, including guinea pig. That wasn't far from the truth. Either the Corinns weren't sharing intel with Command, or they didn't have any either. If Jax had to guess, it was the latter. Especially considering their mission was to locate the Corinn outpost that had gone offline. The surface conditions didn't help matters with electrical interferences, seismic activity, and, yeah, the lava.

If Zang Zi Za did know anything about the fate of his comrades, the alien still wasn't talking.

"Follow me, but please keep a safe distance," Hippo said.

"Don't have to tell me twice," Meatball said. He heaved his mini gun up and started after the droid. The belt fed weapon stretched over his shoulders into a pack.

The second Eagle back was Satani, his red eyes glowing in the dim lighting. He kept glancing back with those eyes to check on the platoon which stretched behind them in combat intervals among the scorched terrain.

Then came Hesh, Jax, Zang, Apollo, and the rest of the platoon. They had spent the past four hours looking for a path across a river of magma. The fissure it flowed through was thirty feet across. They marched along the right side, keeping about five-hundred feet away. Even at that distance, the temperature spiked to one hundred-and thirty-degrees Fahrenheit. If it weren't for the ventilation system in their suits, the Outlaws would be cooking.

It was hard to believe this was once a thriving world of the Corinn species. Jax tried to picture what it had once looked like before the apocalypse. She had seen images of the prodigiously fertile meadows, teeming with vibrant flowers the size of a man's head. And the forests timbered with towering spring trees that spouted blue canopies which appeared as a fountain. Gushing rivers had crossed through the dense woodlands and the meadows.

The only rivers now were flowing lava, and she had yet to see any sign of life.

Hunks of melted metal and charcoaled stone littered the ground along with shards of crystalline shanor, once forged in mines by Markas and Wooly workers, shimmering across the ground like large, castoff diamonds.

It was the only evidence that this was once the outskirts of the great city of Casion.

"Crazy to think anything once lived here," Jax said.

"The Wrath really leveled it," Hesh said.

"Not the Wrath."

Jax turned to Zang, who strode forward. "We destroyed our cities," said the alien. "Rather than letting the enemy seize them."

The Corinn guide trekked past Jax and Hesh, who looked at each other in turn.

"Let's move!" Apollo shouted.

The platoon pushed on through the plateau, leaving the terraformer behind. They came up on a sloping hill with a vast view beyond.

On the horizon, the jagged teeth of mountains reached for the brown clouds. Lava glowed on top of one of those peaks, slowly funneling down the side. For a fleeting moment, Jax was struck by the hostile view all around her. As a child, she had once sat on her father's lap while plowing a field of crops at twilight. A transport ship had lifted off in the distance, blasting into the jeweled sky.

"Where are they going, papa?" Jax had asked.

"To another world," her father had replied.

"Can we go someday?"

"You're a farmer, Jax. We don't go to the stars. We feed them."

That was the moment Jax had realized she wanted to leave Runi. But she had never expected this would be where she ended up. Trekking through an apocalyptic landscape on the same ground Wrath had trampled decades earlier in their genocidal war against their perceived enemies.

"LT, why the hell did they send us down here without a way across this damn lava?" Hesh grumbled over the comms.

"The fissure is new," Apollo replied.

"How new?"

"New, as in the past few days."

Zang confirmed this with a slight nod. "Our Doma continues to change frequently, in human time, every day," he said.

"Doma?" Hesh asked.

"It's what they call their home planet," Apollo said.

Jax followed the lieutenant up the hill that Meatball had mounted. Apollo moved for a better look with a pair of long-range binos. He pushed them up to his visor and raked them over the landscape, stopping on a land bridge that crossed the thirty-foot molten river.

"We must find another way," Zang Zi Za said in his slow, indifferent tone. "That way is not safe."

"I don't see another way, and we're getting farther off course," Apollo replied. "What's wrong with that bridge?"

"Take a look at the sides," Zang Zi Za said.

Jax switched her visor to infrared, noticing what the Corinn had seen that none of them had noticed. The bridge was elevated over the lava stream, not through it. When Jax zoomed in with her rifle scope, she saw it was propped up on four rocks that smoldered along the edges where the magma ate at the sides. It was hard to say how long the bridge would remain. One minute. One day. One year.

"Brito," Apollo said, gesturing.

Jax rushed over. "Yes, sir."

"Ready to show us how fast you can move with them fancy new legs?" he asked.

"Sir?"

"You're on point. Find us a way across."

"Okay, sir," Jax said.

The Corinn watched Jax as she strode out in front of the platoon.

"Your prosthetics will not survive the lava," said the alien.

"Then I better make sure I don't take a wrong step," Jax said.

This was her chance to gain some trust from her comrades.

Or die an embarrassing but quick death, she thought.

Jax started down the hill without another second of hesitation. Steam vented out of cracks in the ground at the bottom. She plotted her course carefully on the way across the two thousand or so feet to the bridge.

A few minutes in, and she could see that the vents were larger in some areas. She moved close enough to one to look down inside at flames burning about ten feet beneath in some sort of tunnel system.

She flipped on the channel to Apollo.

"LT, there are corridors in the rock beneath me," she said. "Open flames down there, over."

"Copy that, keep moving."

Jax did as ordered, realizing that she was walking over a section of city. She looked up for a second at the thick clouds, imagining the spiked ships lowering over the city as citizens walked out of their homes. From what she had read, the Wrath fired a type of bomb that incinerated everything in its path, then they released Hydras from the underbellies of the ships. The monsters flapped downward, launching their own green fire on the horrified civilians who had managed to survive the infernos.

Everything beneath her had burned thirty-five years ago. And it was *still* burning. Part of that, according to Hippo, had to do with the type of minerals in the soil. It would burn for another three-hundred years.

The temperature gauge spiked on her HUD as Jax got closer to the bridge, hitting one hundred-and-forty-degrees Fahrenheit. She was closing in on the bridge when she saw it wasn't a land bridge at all, but part of a building. Maybe multiple parts. Melted together in what looked like a deformed beam.

She could also see parts of it melting right off the sides and dripping into the flow.

This thing wasn't going to last forever.

Then you better get moving, Jax thought.

She picked up her pace, moving around a vent of steaming gasses. She slid partially but kept her balance. The connection to her new legs did seem to be completely seamless, just like they were her own. And there was no pain, even during strenuous activity like this.

"Easy, Brito," Apollo said.

Jax slung her rifle when she got to the sloped edge of the bridge in the meandering lava river. The temperature had spiked to one-hundred sixty-degrees.

Determined, she started the trek, keeping to the center, away from the melting sides. Halfway across, another quake suddenly shook the landscape. Their orders now made sense. The terrain was too unstable for armored vehicles. Aircraft too. Anything down here was at risk. And soldiers were the least expensive to replace.

She hurried the remainder of the way, seeing a decent ten-foot drop at the end. Lava tendrilled around the edges. To get across, she would need to jump.

She froze at the thought. This would be her first time with the new legs, but she remembered something the Med-droid had told her about how she would love using them to jump.

Here goes nothing, she thought.

A quake shook the bridge before she could move. Voices called out in the distance, one booming over the comm channel.

"Run!"

Jax turned in horror at the sight of the platoon fanning out around an erupting lava field. The tremors rattled the bridge, knocking her from her trance. Globs of gooey metal fell away from the edges.

The first of the Eagles made it to the other end as the vibrations continued. Jax ran toward them, waving.

"Come on! Hurry!" she yelled.

While the platoon fled the field of venting magma, she charged right for it back across the bridge. On her HUD, she could see the infrared tags of those still out there. Hesh, Satani, Nadia, and Apollo had halted. It took Jax another few beats to see why.

They were trapped on ledges of rock as steam blasted upward between their bodies. The ground had collapsed, and someone must have fallen into the hole.

"Hurry, get the cables!" Apollo shouted.

Satani worked on unraveling climbing equipment from his gear pack while Hesh bent down and reached into the opening.

As Jax made her way over, she noticed another soldier had fallen into the ground. But why wasn't this one showing up on her HUD?

Because it's not an Eagle! Zang was clawing at the ground with his long arms and hands, only his head and neck above a fissure. The rest of his body dangled downward into the steam.

The temperature spiked upward as Jax approached. Another geyser shot up out of the ground.

The Corinn planet seemed to roar from underneath as the ground split open. Fissures expanded and snaked outward, one almost eight feet wide separated her from Zang.

The thought of jumping with her new legs gave her pause, but she had no time to reconsider. Taking a few steps back first, she inhaled then started to run. She leapt over the fissure with ease, the robotic limbs giving her extra height and distance as she sailed clear over the other side then crashed to the ground.

Wasting no time, she scrambled over to the struggling alien. Zang saw her too, but said nothing. There was no call for help, no reaching out.

"Brito, the hell are you doing!?" Apollo shouted. "Get back across that bridge with the others!"

Jax ignored him and reached down for Zang.

"Take my hand," she said.

The Corinn hesitated for a moment, then extended his long fingers toward her. A wave of steam rushed upward at the same moment. A warning chirped on her HUD as Jax kept her hand out. She could feel the heat through her gloves, but she didn't pull back.

A finger gripped one of her own, she felt another, then she gripped an entire hand. She hauled the Corinn up out of the opening and onto the ground. Zang pushed to stand as Jax looked over her shoulder at a scream.

It was Meatball, his armor on fire while Hesh dragged him up—what was left of him. Everything from his torso down was gone. The surface suddenly split, and Hesh stumbled backward, losing his grip on Meatball.

"Meatballllllll!" he shouted.

The upper half of Meatball screeched and flailed—then he

was gone, collapsing with the entire ledge of rock into the ground that swallowed him whole.

A mechanical cracking, like a starship being crushed, rang out in the distance. Jax turned toward the plateau they had left behind. Meatball wasn't the only thing this place had swallowed.

The ground had opened up, devouring the terraformer whole, the last tendrils vanishing into the broken ground.

Chills ran up her back at a thought, that the Corinn's Doma had a mind of its own—and didn't want to be saved.

CHAPTER 18

Rangnar awoke to darkness. Pitch black.
Is this death?
He had expected flames. Lots of fire, lightning, brimstone.

But this wasn't Hell, unless there were spaceships in Hell. A consistent vibration under his body told him he was on a vessel. He didn't dare move when he heard distant voices coming over the tiny translators still woven into his hair. He turned the amplifiers up and listened closely, but his head hurt.

So did his neck. His lungs. His brain.

It took his utmost concentration to focus on the voices.

There was one he recognized.

Axel Finn. The offspring of a Steward, perhaps the only living offspring anywhere. And for some reason, he had let Rangnar live, even after Rangnar had admitted he had hunted Stewards, and after Rangnar had imprisoned him inside the vault of Wrath bones and artifacts.

Rangnar knew he should be dead. He had been ready to die and should have died back on Tecca. But if the message he had decoded from the Wrath artifact was what he thought it was, it might not matter.

The aliens were returning.

When they did, the entire galaxy would go up in flames.

Keeping as quiet as possible, he listened to the crew while pretending to be unconscious. This wasn't the first time he had played possum in his life, and he knew keeping his heartbeat low was key to remaining discreet.

"We really screwed up, he-heh," came a robotic voice.

Rangnar recalled the war droid from the corridor back in his bunker.

"Not totally screwed," Axel said. "We didn't get captured, and we're all alive."

A female voice replied, "Those weren't your average Eagles, either. That was a platoon from Dark Horse Company."

"Brayton, you're sure we weren't followed?" Axel asked.

"If we were, we'd know it by now," another man replied. "I've been monitoring the encrypted messages coming from those ships on Tecca, and thanks to Uga's handiwork, I don't believe they found anything."

A male Wooly barked in response, the message translated by Rangnar's system. "Nothing left of that place," he said. "I used the last of our charges to bury it forever."

Rangnar wondered why they didn't leave him behind to die in the blast, to erase all evidence of what Rangnar knew about this crew. There could only be one answer.

They needed him.

That gave him room to negotiate.

He knew Axel's secret, something Rangnar wasn't even sure Axel knew. His crew definitely didn't seem to know their captain was the son of a Steward.

"Capa, what are you going to do with the smelly old guy?" Uga asked.

Smelly? Rangnar thought.

"Perhaps venting him out an airlock would be a good idea," chirped a Marka. "Or perhaps launching him on a trash pod into the nearest sun, like you should have done with that egg."

Rangnar snorted. "It's not a fucking egg," he said. "Let me out and I might tell you what it is."

There was silence outside his crate or whatever it was they had locked him inside. Then came footsteps.

A moment later, a dark blanket lifted over the glass dome he was trapped under. He tried to sit up but hit his head at the top. The first person he saw was the son of the Steward, still dressed in armor, but without his helmet.

Axel hunched down, staring at Rangnar with brown eyes. But where there was curiosity and adventure the moment they had met on Tecca, there was anger now.

"What? You don't like being the one in a cage?" Axel asked. "Seems like you built your reputation on doing that, or worse."

"You know nothing about me," Rangnar said.

"Yeah? Then how'd I find you?"

"You're smart, I'll give you that, but you're also stupid, because the Eagles will burn you all alive if...*when* they find you."

"I covered our tracks," said a man standing with his arms folded over his chest. "I've been monitoring the transmissions."

Rangnar raised a brow. They were good, that was for sure, but CAID was better. And they had an unstoppable force with unlimited resources. If command wanted to find someone, or something, they would, it was only a matter of time.

He took a moment to look at the crew. The XO, a woman named Luna. The guy who claimed they were fine, Chief Engineer Brayton. A Wooly named Uga, and a Marka he had heard them call Cricket.

There was also the ex-war droid, Spartacus.

Rangnar could tell the crew had been through the wringer. Maybe part of that was his own fault, but he knew now they hadn't come to kill him or rob him. They had genuinely sought him out to figure out what that artifact was and try to sell it.

That told Rangnar that Axel wasn't the son of Lannon, and also confirmed his suspicion that Axel didn't know the truth about his genesis.

Rangnar almost felt bad for the kid. He had no idea what he was getting into with their banged-up ship and very dangerous cargo.

"We are not actually considering keeping this scoundrel alive, are we?" Spartacus asked. "He nearly killed me, Captain."

"My apologies for shooting you," Rangnar said. "I was defending myself. Is that not justified?"

Spartacus held up his one arm. "Yes, but for the record, I was not authorized to hurt you." He directed his arm at Axel. "Captain does not approve of violence."

So that's it, Rangnar thought. The son of one of the deadliest warriors ever to walk the galaxy was a pacifist.

He almost laughed at the irony. Especially considering the lad had nearly crushed his windpipe in the command center.

But he let you live.

"You still haven't told us what the artifact is," Luna said.

"Yeah." The husky little Wooly waddled over, a half-smoked cigar stick hanging from his black lips. "What's it say?"

Rangnar massaged his long beard.

"Well?" Luna asked.

"He isn't going to tell us," Brayton said.

"Yes he is, or he's worthless," Axel said. "Spartacus, prepare the airlock."

Rangnar snickered. "You're not going to fire me out of the airlock, Captain," he said. "Let's all be honest about that. You're bluffing. I know, because you need me."

Axel cracked his head from side to side. Perhaps a habit to keep his anger under control. Rangnar could only imagine how difficult that was for the kid.

"You want to know what the artifact is? You want to get paid? Take me to Hex Prime, where I sent my crew," Rangnar said. "I'll pay you there, take it off your hands, and you'll never see me again."

"He-heh, he thinks you are an idiot, Captain," Spartacus said.

"I guess so." Axel shrugged.

"Look, my crew is there," Rangnar said. "Markas, three of them. I would never do anything to hurt them. That's why I sent them away when you showed up."

Axel watched Rangnar for a while, then looked to Luna, who gave a subtle shrug.

"I have one final hideout, on Hex Prime, in a mountain village called Montrane. Beautiful place," Rangnar said. "But there are threats there, and we should go at night."

"So it's easier for escape for you?" Uga barked. "Capa, I should put boomsticks all over this filthy fella. Give him third butthole if he run. Major owie."

"Third?" Rangnar laughed. "Owie? What are you, a fucking toddler? Oh, I get it, my mouth is the second butthole, got it. Good one. I like you, Wooly."

Uga growled, then walked over, turned, and released a fart at Rangnar.

"Dammit, Uga," Luna said.

"Should I sound the klaxon?" Spartacus asked.

"Oh... *oh* God," Rangnar said as the stench hit him. His eyes burned, and by the time he reached up to clamp his nostrils shut, the garbage had filled his lungs. He coughed and then lurched.

"He-heh," Spartacus chuckled.

Axel sighed. "You good, Phantom?"

Holding up a hand, Rangnar nodded and glanced at Axel and Luna in turn.

"Listen," he said. "I'm a lot of things, but I'm not a liar, and I didn't deserve that from your pal Uga. But I digress. My crew's held up in a bunker nestled into the mountains. A bunker with loads of forgite bars..."

Uga pulled the cigar out and licked his lips. "Now we talkin'," he grumbled.

"Tell us what the ball is first," Axel said.

Rangnar nodded. He understood. That was fair. He would want to know too. But if he told this Steward sperm what he thought it was, the kid would flee, and Rangnar needed it for his freedom. The CAID would let him off whatever bullshit charges in exchange for it.

No, Rangnar couldn't tell the truth. He had to keep some secrets.

"Spartacus, get the airlock ready," Axel said.

"Wait," Rangnar said. "Just wait a minute."

"You got seconds, maybe. Not a minute."

"You want to know the answer to this secret, and the others I know?" Rangnar raised a brow at Axel, his attempt at saying, *I know what you are* perhaps too subtle.

Axel narrowed his eyes right back at Rangnar and shook his head.

"Ah." Rangnar understood. So the Steward kid knew the truth about his past, but the rest of his crew didn't. It was a secret between them, and for now, Rangnar would keep it quiet.

Otherwise, he risked getting shit out the airlock by the one-armed droid.

"Okay, the ball isn't an egg," Rangnar said. "It's not going to hatch some Hydras or Spectre or alien chicken. It's not a bomb, or a weapon. It's a message left behind by the Wrath."

He paused, but held Axel's gaze, knowing if he looked away the kid might get a read on his lie. "The artifact simply reveals the location of former Wrath targets," he said. "Due to the rarity of this find, I believe CAID would be very interested in it, and so am I."

Axel didn't say anything for a long beat. He finally glanced back to Brayton.

"Don't look at me, Captain," he said. "I have no idea if that's true or not."

"Spartacus?" Axel asked.

"I am skeptical but have no way of proving this one way or the other," replied the droid.

"If it's not big-ass bomb, I say we sell it, no?" Uga barked.

Axel narrowed his eyes on Rangnar.

"I'll gladly take it off your hands if you let me go," he said. "forgite bars, my friends, for each of you."

Cricket wagged his tails, and Uga sucked back some leaking drool.

"You could buy me that new arm, he-heh," Spartacus said.

Luna gave Axel a confident nod.

"Okay, set course for Hex Prime, Sparty," he said. "And if this smelly old bastard screws us, I give you permission to give him a freezing galactic vacation."

The flight to Hex Prime gave Axel plenty of time to think. He was in an impossible situation by keeping Rangnar alive, especially with the knowledge the bounty hunter possessed about his genesis, something that even Axel didn't quite understand.

How could he have Corinn DNA?

Axel winced as he sat down on his bunk and removed his armor. So far, none of his crew had asked him what had happened before they arrived in the bunker. And if any of them had seen the data about his scan, they hadn't mentioned it.

Everything was a blur, though.

Straining to think through the fog, he managed to recall breaking out of the electric field in a blind rage. That gruff, angry voice had taken over, commanding him to kill Rangnar.

He pulled off his gloves and checked his burned hands, hands that he had lost control of for several seconds, nearly choking Rangnar to death. The attack was only hours ago, and he was already healing.

He thought of what his mother had said: *You're different, Axel, special. People won't understand.*

It wasn't just his body. He could do things other people couldn't, and he had never known why—until now.

He had always thought he was crazy, that the voice was a demon inside of him. But that voice was the same voice from these last visions. Of the Steward fighting the Wrath hordes in the Crystal City on Corinnia.

But how was that possible?

Unless...

"No," he whispered, shaking his head. "It can't be."

He remembered what his mother had told him about his father. How he had fought the Wrath. The evidence was starting to mount that his father had been a Steward. One of the greatest warriors to ever live. They had all gone crazy after the war, lashing out and murdering across the system, killing those they had sworn to protect.

"No," he said again. "I don't believe it."

But it must be so.

His mother had hidden the truth about his father, because his father was a Steward. They were hunted down, slain by the very military that had designed them.

Was that the reason she had sent him into hiding, and fled herself?

You must kill Rangnar to keep your secret.

Was this the voice again, or was this his own?

Maybe it was both.

Axel rotated his chair toward a locked cabinet. Inside, he retrieved a tiny, beetle shaped piece of tech filled with artificial learning nano-cells. He had found it in an abandoned Eagle outpost almost a decade ago. According to Spartacus, the device was put on soldiers in hostile warzones where they might be captured and interrogated for top-secret info. A certain word, or words, activated the nano-tech that would tunnel into the heart and kill the soldier almost instantly.

This won't save you if he traps you, Axel thought.

"Maybe not, but I won't murder him in cold blood," he whispered.

A knock interrupted his thoughts.

"Hold on," he said. He put his burned hands in his pockets. "Come in," he said.

Cricket nudged the hatch open. He used his rear end to close it. Two steps in and he stopped to stare at Axel with his back eyes.

"What happened down there?" asked Cricket. "Are you hurt?"

"I'm good," Axel replied.

"Captain, I mean...Axel, you can talk to me, you can trust me. It pains me to think you don't feel like you can."

"It's nothing. I just...I'm a little out of my element right now, pal. Bit off more than I can chew with that ball, but we'll get through this." Axel gestured with his chin toward the bed on the deck. "Get some rest before we land. I'm gonna go for a stroll and clear my head."

Cricket hesitated, then went to his bed and curled up. Axel

turned and put his gloves back on. Then he left his quarters and went to the bridge. Brayton sat in front of his station, scanning data logs with his glasses pushed up on his sharp nose.

Luna sat in her chair, watching Uga working on repairing the hole in Spartacus's T-Flesh with three of his limbs. Seeing them not bickering was odd, but that didn't last for long.

"Careful with those stubby limbs," Spartacus said.

"You want help, or no?" Uga barked back, curling one back to smack the droid.

Axel stepped in before the fight escalated.

"I'm sorry," he announced loudly.

Everyone turned to look at him.

"This adventure has turned into far more than what any of you signed up for," Axel said. "I'm taking Rangnar to the surface. Alone."

Luna got out of her chair. "Permission to speak, Captain."

"You don't need to ask, Luna."

"I'm speaking as your XO right now, and I'm saying this is a bad idea." She paused. "As your friend, I'm telling you the same thing. Remember how money isn't important if we're dead? Well, in case you've forgotten, I'm reminding you."

Uga climbed down from the chair he had mounted, barking. "I agree with the beautiful, intelligent XO," he said. "At least one of us comes with, no?"

Brayton scratched the side of his freshly shaved chin.

"Well?" Axel asked.

"If we're gonna do this, you'll need help," Brayton said.

"Spartacus, what's your status?"

"He's fine, Capa," Uga said. "In perfect workin' order."

"Fine? Do I look fine?" Spartacus strode over, reaching up to the patchwork job covering the damage to his chest unit. "How many lives do you think I have, Captain?"

"That's why I won't make another mistake," Axel said.

Cricket trotted into the room. "Am I missing something?" he chirped.

Axel looked at his crew in turn. He hated the idea of further risking anyone on this quest that he had forced on them all. It was his fault they were almost broke. His fault they had chased down an artifact that nearly got their ship destroyed. His fault they had gone after Rangnar and now held a dangerous prisoner.

And if his suspicions were true about his past, then they were in great danger simply being part of his crew. The best thing he could do was send them away.

But deep down, he felt he still had control of this situation. If Rangnar was telling the truth, and would buy the Wrath egg, then maybe they could get the *Trash Squid* and Spartacus fixed and then lay low for a while. Then he could decide if staying with his crew or parting ways was the best thing to do.

"Fine, Cricket and Uga come with me," Axel said. "I want you two to stay here with Spartacus."

"But I'm all out of boom," Uga barked.

"If all goes to plan, we will be able to buy you all the explosives your heart desires," Axel said.

"And food, no? You say yes, Capa?"

"Yes, and food."

Uga danced, whipping his arms back and forth while hopping around. For once, he didn't trip and fall.

"Good, it's settled. I'm heading to the cargo hold," Axel said. "Hail me when we arrive at Hex Prime."

Axel went below decks as the ship set course for the human controlled planet. It was the last place he wanted to go, but according to the coordinates Rangnar shared, they were going to be far away from the capital of Aritrea and in a remote mountainous region.

He opened the hatch of the cargo hold and slipped into the

room to see Rangnar under the same glass dome they had used to store the Wrath egg. It was now in a case within a case across the space, along with some of the gear they had brought back from the bunker on Tecca.

Axel walked over to it and opened a weapons locker where Eagles had once stored their armament before the ship was decommissioned. Inside was their only laser rifle. He had never fired one, didn't even know how. But how hard could it be?

He pulled it out, brought the butt to his shoulder and aimed it at Rangnar. The man laughed. "Show me you've never held a rifle without showing me," he said.

Axel walked over toward the dome. "I thought I told you not to speak?" he said.

"Don't worry, I'm not going to spill the beans about you-know-what."

Axel looked over his shoulder, but no one was in here with him. But that didn't mean his crew couldn't hear him over the surveillance camera in this space.

"Relax," Rangnar said.

"I'll relax once we get rid of you, and I get paid."

"You will, you have my word."

"You still haven't told me what the Wrath artifact said."

"Do you really want to know? I'm not sure you do, kid."

"Call me kid one more time," Axel said.

"Okay, easy, easy, boss." Rangnar held up his hands.

Axel backed down a bit. "What are you going to do with it?"

"Not sure yet, but I won't reveal who I got it from, I promise you that."

Axel almost laughed. "You think I believe that?"

He returned to the locker and put the weapon away. He wasn't going to kill Rangnar in cold blood, and if he planned a trap, a rifle wasn't going to help him out there.

But the nano-beetle might. He pulled it out of his pocket.

"You say anything about me and my crew, ever, and it's the end of your galactic journey," Axel said. "I've already programmed this."

Rangnar shook his head, clearly aware of what the device would do to him. "Real peaceful of you," he said.

"It's a precaution, and it won't be me killing you, it'll be you killing yourself."

"Fair enough. Go ahead, do it."

Axel attached it to Rangnar's chest, directly over his heart.

The comms blared, echoing through the troop hold.

"Captain, we've been cleared for landing by the orbital transit authority," Luna said over the comm piece in his ear. "Prepare for entry."

"Copy," he replied.

The hatch opened and Uga waddled inside with Cricket. They got into their seats next to Axel. He buckled his harness, and then checked the ship's log to see the magic Brayton had worked.

According to their freshly forged records, the *Trash Squid* was registered as the *Wayward Raft*. He couldn't help but smile at the irony. He slipped his headphones on and closed his eyes as the ship rattled into the atmosphere.

Peace is my way.
I will not hurt what can't be healed.
I will not take what can't be replaced.
Violence only leads to more violence.
All life is precious.
I will be the peace that I want to see in the galaxy.

"Entering Hex Prime," Luna announced over the comm.

As soon as they were through the atmosphere, the heat shields opened over the port windows, providing a visual of a mountainous region. Moonlight illuminated the snow-capped peaks and vast forests hugging tree lines around shards of rock.

The ship lowered over a valley with a snaking stream of clear water that sparkled in the bright white rays from the moon. The view reminded Axel of the cabin he had hidden in with his mother and aunt when he was a child.

"Prepare for landing," Luna said.

They flew over a small city with modern buildings intermixed with some built from the rock of the mountains. Botanical domes dotted the hills, probably housing food and plants from Earth that needed special environments to grow.

The ship set down, and the hold doors slid open. Axel unbuckled his harness and walked over to let Rangnar up.

"Don't make me regret this," he said. "I spared you once, I won't spare you again."

CHAPTER 19

"I can't get through to the Citadel," Satani said.

"Keep trying," Apollo ordered.

The Eagle with glowing red eyes had them directed skyward with a handheld dish-shaped signal booster. He angled it toward the storm front. Swollen clouds quickened across the dark horizon. Forks of red lightning broke across the darkness.

Nearly ten hours after landing, Jax scanned the plateau for hostiles, still expecting a Wrath to clamber out of the cracked terrain. So far, the biggest threat was that terrain itself. It had killed Meatball and would have killed their guide Zang if it weren't for Jax. The alien hadn't even offered a thank you after she pulled him from the vent. But Jax had a feeling that was customary for Corinns. They were internal creatures, connected to their ancestors in ways she didn't understand.

Jax took a drink from her helmet straw and checked her HUD. The temperature, despite the sun being blocked out, remained at a balmy one hundred degrees.

"Can't get this piece of shit to work," Satani said. "Too much interference."

"Fuckin-A," Apollo said.

"We got bigger problems than that, LT," Hesh said. "The GPS is all broke dick, and everything looks the same out here."

Apollo turned to Zang. The Corinn was on his knees one hundred feet away.

"The hell is he doing?" Apollo asked.

"Praying? Who knows," Hesh said.

"We don't need prayers. We need some working tech."

Jax checked her HUD again. The environment was severely screwing with their equipment. Nothing was working correctly outside of their life support systems, which were battery powered. *And thank the Gods for that*, she thought.

Without life support, she would have been a corndog by now. She was rattled to her core but trying her best to hide it.

Apollo went over to Zang, but Jax hung back with Satani and Hesh.

"The guy is worthless if you ask me," Hesh said.

"Nah," Satani said. "You just don't understand him."

"Yeah, so what's he doing then?"

"Finding the path, man. He tried to warn us not to cross that field. We didn't listen. Meatball bit it because of that."

Jax thought back to the warning the Corinn had given Apollo, who had ignored it. They were lucky it hadn't cost them more than Ivey.

The alien suddenly shot up and faced Apollo. Then he directed an elongated arm and fingers at the horizon to what Jax knew was east.

"We're moving out!" Apollo shouted. "Let's go, Outlaws."

"See," Satani said. "He was having a vision."

"No way," Hesh said.

"They can see through the eyes of ancients from tunnels. I wouldn't expect you to understand."

Jax wondered what it was that Zang had seen. The aliens were a mystery in many ways, with mental abilities that went beyond anything humans were capable. From what she understood, they had a mental tunnel that connected them to memories of others, like a stored bank of knowledge that was passed on through birth to the next generation.

Maybe Zang was seeing through the eyes of his father or mother, or even of someone that had been here before.

The Corinn guide walked over to Apollo and said something Jax couldn't make out.

"Listen up, our friend says we're close to the outpost," Apollo relayed over the open comms. "Combat intervals and heads on swivels."

Rifles went up to shoulders, and the two Eagles carrying belt fed mini guns heaved them into position. Outlaw Platoon fanned out across the plateau. The skies opened up a moment later, dumping acid rain.

Only seconds passed before the charcoaled ground began to turn to a paste.

Jax listened for the enemy but heard only the groaning of distant quakes and the sporadic crack of thunder. The surface seemed to be alive underneath, a great beast stirring and trying to awaken. The hair on the back of her neck stood as they started through the smoke.

Hesh took point, sweeping his minigun back and forth. Jax wasn't far behind. Three more Eagles moved ahead of her, their black-winged shoulder armor making them appear as demons moving in the haze. The rain picked up, transforming into a torrential downpour. Water sluiced down her visor as Jax scanned her surroundings.

She nearly jumped when a hand reached out and touched her shoulder plate. She turned to find Zang.

"Sergeant Brito," he said in his emotionless tone.

"Yeah?"

"I'd like to extend my gratitude for your assistance," said the Corinn. "If the situation arises, I will do what I can to pay what you might call a debt."

Jax didn't know what to say at first. "We don't leave each other behind," she said after a pause. "The other Eagles would have done the same."

"That, Sergeant Brito, is not accurate," was all the Corinn said before walking off again.

Jax hurried after him in the downpour. Visibility became shittier by the step. Grit and debris floated in the air, kicked up by the lancing rain drops that pounded the ground like bullets. In the respite of thunder, she heard an odd noise. The amplifiers in her helmet helped her focus on what sounded like a distant vacuum.

Hesh suddenly came trotting back.

"Did I tell you to stop?" Apollo asked.

"I got to stop a minute," Hesh said.

"Why? What did you see?"

"Not what I saw, LT. I got to *go*."

"Go—"

Satani laughed.

"It's been ten hours, LT," Hesh said.

Apollo cursed. "Okay, but don't let the Corinn see you."

Hesh trotted off while Satani continued to chuckle.

"Think that's funny?" Apollo asked. "You take point, then."

"I'll go," Jax said.

Apollo glanced over. "Why so eager?"

"Just ready to get to our target, secure it, and get an FOB established, sir."

"Good. Go ahead and knock yourself out. Satani, you go with her."

Satani grumbled as he followed Jax. The wind picked up, gusting into their armor and whistling, but that wasn't the source of the noise Jax could hear.

All sorts of images surfaced in her mind during the trek. Jax pictured a Hydra, flapping enormous scaly wings that could take a direct hit from a missile. Despite all her efforts to remain calm, reality began to break down the walls. Fear bled through the cracks.

Strong and steady, Jax.

Jax kept her rifle up, the vacuum sound growing louder. She led the platoon across the muddy terrain, through the rain and smoke. Embers swirled through the air, puffing when rain hit them.

Ahead, Jax noticed a sort of barrier on the plateau. A ridgeline from what she could tell. The rain appeared to sizzle as it hit an invisible barrier.

She slowed her gait, trying to get a visual of what was making it. A violent gust of wind brought a wave of embers rushing over the ridge, reaching through that barrier and outward with an almost instantly dissipating tendril of fire.

Jax had never seen anything like this before in her life.

"This place is cursed," Satani called out. "That sound—it's the sound of millions of trapped souls screaming for release."

Together, they walked toward the bottom of the ridgeline. The temperature spiked to a high of one hundred and ninety degrees.

"It's a furnace out here," Jax said.

Satani reached the bottom of the slope to the ridge where the temperature peaked at two hundred degrees. Jax started up, digging into the loose rocks. It struck her that this should have been mud, but most of the rain had evaporated on the baking ground.

Steam whisked out of the ridge as Jax crested the top. She

stood there for a moment trying to see what was beyond the curtain of smoke below. Flashes of red lightning broke overhead, the thunder clapping a moment later.

She noticed the flicker of flames below. Large flames. And they appeared to be moving. Jax looked down at a sheer drop off. At the bottom, hundreds of feet below, a giant vortex of fire swirled across the ground. Not just one, but three. All tearing across the surface.

"This is it," came the slow, emotionless voice of Zang.

"The outpost?" Jax asked.

"Casion," replied the Corinn.

Jax turned back to a view of the gorge stretching as far as she could see. This crater was once the great Corinn city.

Apollo climbed up.

"We're here, according to our guide," Satani said.

"What? What do you mean? Where's the outpost?" Apollo asked.

He stepped closer, but Zang reached out and held him back.

"The outpost was destroyed," said the alien. He pointed to beams protruding out of the ground far below. Jax hadn't seen those earlier but could now make out what looked like debris from a base. There was a downed terraformer too, partially buried in ash about two hundred feet beyond the Corinn rubble.

She gripped her rifle tightly, scanning for any evidence of Wrath.

But just like everywhere else they had been, the monstrous aliens were absent. Not a single track. It seemed the planet was the culprit for destroying both the outpost and the terraformer.

"I don't get why your species doesn't just abandon this place like we did Earth," Apollo said to Zang. "There's no bringing any of this wasteland back."

"Giving that opinion is not your purpose in being here, Lieutenant," Zang said. "We are not human."

"Damn straight," Apollo grunted.

He stared over the crater for another few seconds, then turned to the platoon waiting below the slope.

"Make camp on this ridge and set up a defensive perimeter," he ordered. "Hippo, see if you can find a way down. And Satani, get me a goddamned open channel to the Citadel."

Rangnar had not been back on Hex Prime for over a decade, but he had funneled money monthly to the Marka caretaker of his hideout. And he wasn't staying long. As soon as he got back to his crew, they were getting as far away from this place as possible.

If he was right about the Wrath ball, the monsters were returning. Hex Prime would without a doubt be a target.

Moving quickly, Rangnar led Axel, Uga, and Cricket away from the field where they had set their ship down. The bafflers were active, camouflaging the dented hull in with the rocky and grassy plain.

He wasn't worried so much about Axel or his crew killing him now. He was worried about his own crew. Coming here put them at risk. But he had nowhere else to go and knew his Markas would be happy to see him.

As long as the Eagles didn't find this place too.

The thought chilled Rangnar to his core. He had already addressed this with Axel, who also knew of the possibility. But according to the trash pod drone Spartacus deployed before landing, there was no sign of any hostile ships in the area. In fact, the space port was only occupied by tourist ships and the basic transports that brought pilgrims to the famous temple in Montrane.

Rangnar filled his lungs with the clean mountain air,

helping ease his worries. The beautiful scenery didn't hurt either.

A full moon shone over the mountains, casting brilliant rays over the jay trees. Their changing canopies were beautiful in the glow, currently the shade of a blueberry. People from all over Hex Prime would come here in the cooling temperatures of fall to watch the jay trees turn from green to blue. They were at the peak of the season right now, and much of the forest looked like an ocean. Some of the large leaves had already fluttered to the ground, providing gaps in the canopy. Rangnar spotted the town of Montrane nestled in the hills at the base of Mount Norrick.

"We're almost to the city," he said.

Axel eyed him but didn't say a word.

Rangnar cared about one thing and one thing only right now and that was getting ahold of the Wrath beacon. It equaled his freedom. It didn't matter what he had done in the past. The Wrath message was worth more to the Colonial Alliance than a single person. More than even the Steward.

But he wasn't going to tell Axel that.

Rangnar took another deep breath as they came across the stone paved street that led to Montrane. The quiet town was just as he remembered it, with vendors set up in the narrow streets, selling both on-world and off-world food. They were famous for their poutine, fries smothered in gravy, cheese, and other toppings.

It was late evening, but there were plenty of people out in the streets. Some of them sat in eateries enjoying dinner, others were on their way home or shopping for fresh ingredients for the next day.

"You hungry?" Rangnar asked Axel.

"You kiddin'?" Axel asked. "Keep moving."

"The poutine's to die for."

The Wooly sniffed the booths they passed. "Ohhhhh, Uga

starving," he barked. "Been eating nothing but bugs foreva. Give belly owies."

Rangnar was hungry too, but he was more focused on scanning for Eagles. So far, he didn't see any out here. That didn't mean there weren't spies or bounty hunters.

Axel also scanned for threats. He whispered something into his headset to Cricket. Rangnar glimpsed the Marka on a tiled rooftop above them. The alien leapt to the next roof, silently, without disturbing the tiles.

The journey took them through the heart of the city, where a cathedral reached for the moon. Jay trees grew around the stone temple, their blue leaves fluttering in the wind. The three-hundred-year-old structure was built by some of the first pilgrims from Earth, and it continued to attract colonists.

Rangnar saw several robed men and women inside, kneeling in prayer or sitting in pews facing an altar. Candles burned in rows along the walls.

"Come join us," came a voice.

A bald man in a white robe with bronze bracelets gestured to Axel. "It's never too late to hear the word of the Lord," the priest said.

Axel ignored the man, and Rangnar kept his head down.

"There's always room in the house of the Lord for lost souls," the man called after them. "You are welcome here anytime."

Rangnar had always thought it would be nice to believe in something like an afterlife. To be able to have faith that there was something better than what he had here. In a way, he envied spiritual people with such a resolve. But religion had never been for him. He had seen too much death. Too much cheap killing to believe there was something after this.

A gust of wind rushed through the jay trees, plucking off

several blue-bodied leaves that fluttered to the ground. Rangnar crushed one under his boots.

He turned his back to the temple and the priest, taking a long stone pathway that wound up a steep hill of houses. Vines and moss clung to the stone exteriors, snaking around open windows. Shutters clicked in the slight breeze. Balconies filled with potted plants and flowers looked over the narrow street.

There were hundreds of the stone structures built into the hills all the way to the base of the mountain. Rangnar could see his hideout.

"Not far now," he said.

Axel suddenly pulled him into an alley with Uga. As soon as they were in the darkness, Rangnar heard the tap of heavy boots, something he had missed, even with his auditory system. A moment later, two Eagles marched by, cradling laser rifles.

Uga flattened his husky body behind Axel.

Their boots clicked away, but Axel remained. Again, Rangnar heard something he had missed. More boots.

Lots of boots.

An entire patrol of ten Eagles hurried past, making their way down to the heart of the city. Rangnar had never seen this many troops in Montrane before. A decade ago, there might be two stationed here.

They were looking for someone.

His blood cooled at the thought of the last of his companions fleeing here right into an ambush.

"I've been compromised," Rangnar said. "Go, get back to your ship and leave."

Before Axel could stop him, Rangnar took off down the other way in the alley. He ran through the darkness, using moonlight to guide his steps. The alley came out at another windy road. He didn't slow to see if there was anyone coming, because he didn't hear anyone.

Rangnar burst out and ran up the incline, seeing only two citizens, a man carrying a bottle of wine, and a woman lugging two baskets of fresh produce. He ran by them and kept up his pace.

A shadow leapt overhead. The near silent impact of Cricket landing on a tiled roof hit his ears, but Rangnar didn't look up. He did, however, glance over his shoulder, seeing Axel chasing him.

God, this kid doesn't give up.

The next block was a green space with a statue of a famous pilgrim. Rangnar cut through the park, crushing more blue leaves under his boots. The stone pathway jutted out in two directions. One led to a street and more houses above. The other to a lookout to the west, built on an overlook of the city and valley. His hideout wasn't far from here. Just over the next hill in a pasture of fenced off estates.

He started up the steps to the street, winded by the time he got to the top, which intersected a street. When he went to cross, a flash of motion came from the right.

He started to cross when a man screamed.

"Watch it!"

Rangnar jumped back to avoid a cyclist wearing dark clothing, happy that it was just a local and not an Eagle. He checked the street again, then hesitated. There was a dirt path through a wooded area that led to the ledge above, but bolting up there would be a vital error—if his bunker had been discovered.

Stay calm, stay calm...

He looked back down the stairs he had come up, seeing Axel had yet to crest them. Cricket was nowhere in sight, but Rangnar knew the Marka was out there somewhere.

With time running out to decide, Rangnar took off down the street, heading for another route to the lookout, hoping to not only lose Axel and Cricket, but to get a view of his hideout to see if the Eagles had indeed found it.

Statues framed the way along the path. When he reached the lookout, he went up another path to the top where a fountain bubbled. Keeping low, he went to the stone overlook and hunched down for the first view of the pasture.

Rangnar held a breath as he scanned the landscape. A road led through the flat meadows furnished with biodomes. Their glass roofs reflected the radiant moonlight. Beyond those, were the fenced estates of ancient homes, some of the first ever built in Montrane.

Trees shaded the stone and tile mansions from the light, but Rangnar could see the entrance to his compound.

He searched for Nuke, Lucid, Saber, and Blaster, but saw nothing moving in the courtyard outside the house. The windows were shuttered, blocking the view inside. There was no evidence of an attack, and no Eagles lying in wait that he could see.

That didn't mean they weren't hiding to ambush him.

Growling came from behind him. He whirled as Cricket pounced, knocking him to the stone ground, his maw clamped around Rangnar's neck.

Axel let out a low whistle then bent down as Cricket loosened his grip and backed away.

"You're the galaxy's biggest asshole, ya know that?" Axel asked.

"That's something to picture," Rangnar grumbled.

"Get up." He reached down, grabbing Rangnar by the jacket.

Cricket sniffed the air.

"What is it?" Axel asked.

He looked up and let go of Rangnar, who dropped back to the ground. As he did, three shadows leapt over the wall.

At first, he thought these were Eagles, but the shadows belonged to short, lanky bodies.

Now we're in business, baby! Rangnar thought gleefully.

On the third second of the ambush, his Markas took the son of the Steward to the ground. Lucid clamped her teeth down around his neck while Saber jumped on his back, holding down his limbs. Nuke had Cricket pinned to the ground.

"Let go of him or I'll kill you all," Axel growled. Lucid bit down harder until he could no longer speak, only snarl like a wild animal.

The tide had changed so fast Rangnar couldn't help but grin. Another surprise came from a distant barking. That had to be Uga, and Rangnar ran over to the ledge for a look, seeing Blaster holding the Wooly by the throat. The droid brought the creature up to the lookout.

Rangnar was in complete control. He held up a hand to ease off but stay on guard.

"Meet my crew," he said. "This is Nuke, Lucid, and Saber. Hunters, this is Axel Finn and his pal, Cricket. Blaster there is holding rude, got a 'tude, eat anything, Uga Booga."

"I eat your pube covered butthole face, and spit it out," Uga snarled. He squirmed but Blaster tightened his grip, forcing a bark-yelp. Axel gritted his teeth as he fought violently to get free. His face turned a cherry red, veins bulging across his forehead and in his neck.

Rangnar knew he had just seconds to defuse the situation before Axel transformed into a berserker Steward. This time, the kid would definitely kill him if he got the chance.

"Everyone relax," Rangnar said. "No one has to get hurt." He bent down in front of Axel. "I'll let your friends up if you promise you won't fight," Rangnar said.

Axel glared at him, his eyes practically bulging.

"Calm yourself, my man," Rangnar said. "For the sake of your friends."

He waited a few more seconds, watching Axel begin to loosen his muscles. Lucid kept her grip around his neck and Saber remained on his back.

"Good," Rangnar said. "Let them up."

"Boss, what?" Nuke chirped.

"I said let him go. We're all friends now. They brought me to you all, safely."

Axel glared at Rangnar, as if he didn't believe what he was saying.

The Markas hesitated, but only briefly. Blaster dropped Uga and lowered his cannons.

Axel shot up to his feet with Cricket by his side.

"We need to get out of here before someone reports us to those Eagles," Rangnar said. "Come on, follow me."

Axel didn't move.

"Sorry. I thought you wanted to get paid. Was I wrong?" Rangnar asked. He turned and started the trek up to his hideout. Under the cover of darkness, the group followed, making their way into a pasture between the ancient estates built at the base of the mountains.

Rangnar smiled when he saw the stone wall covered in vines and purple orchid-like flowers. He opened the wooden gate to lead them inside. "Stay here," he said.

The group remained in the courtyard while Rangnar went inside. He hurried down into the bunker where he removed a stone in the wall to reveal his stash of forgite bars. Stuffing six into a crate with a handle, he then returned to the courtyard.

"The ball," he said.

Axel went to Cricket and pulled the Wrath beacon out of the pouch on the Marka's back. He walked over to Rangnar, their gazes once again meeting.

Rangnar exchanged the crate for the ball, leaning in to whisper in Axel's ear to remind him who was in charge now and to give him some friendly advice. "Your secret's safe with me, kid," he whispered. "However, I would highly suggest taking these bars and getting far away from Corinn civilizations. Go retire somewhere nice."

Axel pulled back, his youthful eyes narrowed.

"Just do it, Captain Finn," Rangnar said firmly. "Trust me."

CHAPTER 20

"We're rich, Capa!" Uga barked. "Gonna eat. Gonna eeeeat!" He danced at his station, arms whipping back and forth in slow motion before picking up speed.

Axel stood on the bridge of the *Trash Squid* as they lifted off from the field on Hex Prime.

"Sit down, Uga, before you hurt yourself," he commanded.

Uga's arms fell limply to his husky body. "You used to be fun, Capa."

"Yeah, well, there are Eagles out there," Axel said.

He sat at the controls and took over. The ship blasted away with the bafflers active to disguise their escape from the planet. Axel looked out the viewport at Montrane nestled in the mountains, wondering if Rangnar and his crew would get out of there without being captured.

Deep down, Axel hoped they would. Not just because of the secrets Rangnar knew about him, but he didn't hate the guy. The bounty hunter could have killed Axel multiple times, and Axel could have killed him multiple times. They were bonded by a mutual respect.

"Good luck, old man," he whispered.

He pushed the thruster down, launching them into the atmosphere and racing for orbit. It wasn't long before they broke through the clouds with a view of a dazzling star field. The crew remained at their stations, watching their monitors, Brayton especially in deep concentration.

"I'm picking up no chatter from any rogue vessels," he said. "I think it's safe to say we weren't seen."

"We are clear," Spartacus confirmed.

"We celebrate now?" Uga asked.

Axel waited a few more minutes before unbuckling his harness. "Spartacus, you have the bridge. Everyone else, head to the mess."

Uga launched all his arms into the air like a furry porcupine. "All hail, Capa Finn!"

Cricket burst away from his station, chirping, and vanishing into the corridor outside to get a head start on food preparation.

Axel remained on the bridge for a bit longer, just to be sure.

"I have it, sir," Spartacus said. "Go enjoy your victory, Capa Finn, he-heh."

Axel allowed himself to smile. He left the bridge and joined his crew in the mess hall. Luna held out an empty glass.

"About time we open this," Uga said. In one arm he held a bottle of Rumsuckle they had been saving. It was from Cricket's stash. He loved the cherry tea that his species manufactured using a rum-like liquor.

Uga used his other limbs to grab glasses, setting them down, and pouring the tea into each. One by one, he handed the full glasses out.

"Cheers," Luna said, holding up her glass. "To you, Captain, for getting us this amazing score."

Axel raised his into the air. "Thank you for trusting me."

Uga climbed on the top of the table, or tried to, getting stuck halfway. Luna pushed his behind up and Uga stood where they had dumped the crate of forgite bars.

"Do you know how unsanitary that is?" Cricket chirped. "That's where we eat!"

"Capa's gonna buy us a new table," Uga replied. "Gonna buy us a new everything! Right Capa?"

Axel heard him, but he was focused on the last thing Rangnar had said to him about retiring. What did the bounty hunter mean by that?

He stood around the table, forcing a smile, but unable to fully participate in the celebration. As much as he wanted to, he felt a growing dread about the past that he still hadn't quite faced. And now, dread about the future.

They were out of the crosshairs for now, but what if someone had seen them over the past few missions? What if the Eagles discovered the truth about Axel? The journey the Wrath artifact had taken him on had opened his past up like peeling a scab off a wound. He thought of his mother and father.

He didn't want to believe he was the son of a Steward. The warriors were killing machines, not much different than Spartacus when he'd been in service.

But unlike the droid, the Stewards had evil inside of them, or so it seemed. That meant Axel had it too. He was broken. Damaged. The reasons his mother had sent him away were finally making sense.

Axel took a long drink of the Rumsuckle, savoring the sweet liquor the Markas had perfected. As it slid down his throat, he watched Uga tap dance on the table. He had a forgite bar in each arm, and brought each up in turn to kiss.

"Things are going to be okay," Luna said quietly to Axel. She stepped next to him, watching the spectacle. "We can fix the *Hammerhead*. Load up on supplies, food, and repair the exterior of the ship," she said. "Then we should take some time off, relax and enjoy the score."

He nodded but said nothing.

"We can buy a brand new Tech-N fighter," Brayton said. "Why waste time trying to fix up that piece of junk when we have the money to replace it?"

"Yeah," Axel said.

"I'll start looking for replacements on the black market, and then also the best ports to get this one fixed up as fast as possible."

"Find a new arm for Spartacus too," Axel said.

"You sure about that?" Luna smiled. "I'm kidding."

The celebrations continued with a second bottle of Rumsuckle uncorked.

"This Marka been hidin' this from us, no?" Uga asked.

"If I didn't, you'd have drunk it long ago," Cricket chirped.

"He's right!" Uga barked, already tipsy and stumbling as he chanted, "Uga eat, drink, eat, drink, then..." He turned and bent over, then grinned. "Just kiddin'!"

Brayton let out a long laugh with Luna.

"I got you all!" Uga said. "Should have seen dumb human faces! So funny!"

He tipped back his glass, slurped down a drink, then belched.

Cricket shook his head and sighed as he worked on a stew of ash roots and the last of their frozen barbs, a crustacean from Honi.

Even as the steaming, delicious platters were served, Axel couldn't seem to shake the awful feeling of knowing his true identity.

Luna leaned over, tapping him on the arm.

"Why aren't you happy?" she asked. "You just led us on a wild goose chase to the biggest score of our careers."

"I'm happy, just very tired. Been a long few weeks."

"Gotta say, I was worried for a while, but things are gonna get better. Better than ever before."

As he downed his third glass, he began to relax. They had evaded the Eagles on Hex Prime and there was no evidence that anyone but Rangnar knew the truth about his past. Axel had gone that extra step to make sure the old bounty hunter never said a word.

"What's the next adventure, after the ship's all fixed up?" Cricket chirped.

"I want to go home to Dari, see my mom and sisters," Uga said. "Been too long."

"You just want some Wooly food," Cricket said.

"Of course! Best grub in the galaxy." Uga rubbed his belly. "I can't wait. Capa, please, we go soon?"

Axel scratched the stubble on his jaw. The planet of Dari was a sovereign and isolated world on the Inner Rim. It was about the size of Earth, with similar gravity and atmosphere. The Woolies were human-like in that they had warred for resources and territory and tried to remain peaceful. Many of the clans didn't take kindly to outsiders, especially humans.

That's a good thing, Axel thought to himself.

CANDF mostly left the planet alone, only collecting taxes on imports and exports. Visiting the remote planet after they fixed the ship sounded like the perfect place to go for some downtime. He had never been there and had always wanted to meet Uga's family. Not to mention see the peaks. Dari boasted the highest mountains anywhere in the Hironia System.

Some climbing might do his soul good.

"I'll think about it," Axel said.

"That's basically a yes, no?" Uga climbed back onto the table and did his famous arm wave dance with all six arms.

The entire mess broke out into laughter.

"You're next, Captain," Luna said.

Axel was afraid she was going to say that.

"Come on," she said. "Don't be shy now. You certainly weren't when you first saw me dance. Remember?"

"Yeah," Axel blushed.

He recalled that day on the *Jabbith*, about a year before they went out on their own with the *Trash Squid*. She was a gymnast and had always loved to dance, often practicing in the cargo hold of the mining freighter when she wasn't on duty.

Axel had walked in one day while working on an electrical panel. He remembered how graceful she was—until she saw him watching.

Feeling less anxious from the wine, Axel decided to let loose a bit. He did the only dance he knew, the ancient robot move that he still busted out from time to time, like right now.

The entire crew chuckled as he moved stiffly in contrast with Uga's flailing.

"Look, I'm Sparty the mech-man," Uga barked. He retracted all but one arm to his side and mimicked Axel's mechanical movements. "I'm a funny guy, *he-heh*."

Even Axel laughed at that. Slowly, he relaxed and decided to celebrate their wins and face his past later.

For the next several hours they ate, drank, danced, and smiled together until everyone was exhausted. Axel raised his glass one last time.

"Congratulations to you all," he said. "Now get some rest." Axel headed back to his quarters, feeling great from the wine, until he hit his head on the hull.

"Axel! Captain, are you okay?"

He turned to Luna. She stood behind him, a look of concern on her shadowed face.

"Yeah..." he said. "Think I had too much wine."

"Me too."

She took a step toward him, eyes twinkling in the dim lighting. There was something there he had only seen a few times. Desire.

He felt it too.

Axel wanted to reach out to her and pull Luna into his quarters. To feel something with someone else. He hesitated as she took another step.

"Not again!" Spartacus shouted.

Yacking echoed into the corridor, followed by Uga barking. "Owie, stomach, boo—"

Luna and Axel walked around the corner where Uga vomited onto the deck. The Wooly wiped off his mouth with an arm, then stuck a half-smoked cigar back in his lips.

"Sorry, Capa, Sparty the Gladiator clean it up," Uga barked.

"I certainly will not! I am not a maid," Spartacus said.

Holding a limb up to his mouth, Uga held back a violent burp. "Stomach owie, and butt no feel good. I see you tomorrow, night, night."

"Night," Axel said. He chuckled with Luna as they headed back into the corridor of quarters. She stopped at her hatch and looked at Axel, longing in her gaze.

"Goodnight," he said.

"Goodnight," she replied quietly.

She closed her hatch, and Axel entered his room. With Cricket still in the mess hall cleaning up, this was his opportunity for some privacy.

He sat down at his desk and turned on his HoloMatrix pad terminal. Playtime was over, he had to know more about his past.

"Private search mode," Axel said.

His heart kicked as he pulled out the tap board. He looked at the keys, then tapped out, *Steward history*. Several documents emerged. He used his fingers to pull them apart, bringing each up onto the screen. The third he found was titled. *Stewards: Created by Titan Vector Labs under the order of Colonial Alliance Galactic Minister and the Corinn Novanauts during the Blood Years.*

Axel had read about that brutal time in the history of the Hironia System, almost one hundred years ago when the colonies were plagued by war and disputes between human factions and the Colonial Alliance. A 3D image of a half-naked male warrior that was designed to stop the widespread bloodshed came onto the screen. Bronze colored flesh defined by lean muscles from the traps to the ankles made up his body. An eight pack of abdomen muscles bulged. The emerald eyes of a Corinn defined the sleek facial features.

He scrolled through a few more articles but found nothing substantial. Most of the info out there had either been erased or was encrypted and lived on CAID servers. He wasn't a hacker like Brayton, and couldn't exactly ask the Chief to do this for him. So Axel sat there and dug through file after file. After an hour of searching, he discovered a collection of opinion pieces buried deep in a library system from Hex Prime. That sparked his attention enough to scan some posts. Finally, he found one post that caught his interest.

Stewards: Heroes or Demons?

Axel clicked on it, seeing the post was twenty-two years old, and written by someone using the alias Achilles. The post was narrated by a deep, synthetic male voice.

Standing seven feet tall and weighing two hundred and fifty pounds, the first Steward stepped out of a medical pod in the headquarters of CAID's Titan Vector Labs, buried deep under an undisclosed mountain on Hex Prime. This first remarkable specimen was cloned with human and Corinn DNA in a joint effort between the Colonial Alliance Intelligence Division (CAID) and the Corinn Novanauts over two hundred and thirty-one years ago. These hybrid soldiers were the best of both species, utilizing the rapid healing properties of Corinns and the strength and speed of human fighters. The brain was predominately human, but retained some of the Corinn properties, such as what became known as "the Tunnel."

To the average onlooker, these giant copper-toned men were simply overly muscular humans, but beneath their lustrous golden armor, they had Corinn physiology of robust tissue and flesh that hardened into armored scales. Steward brains were a combination of the two species, retaining the neurological pathway, or Tunnel, which connects them to their peaceful Corinn ancestors. This connection provided Stewards a window to events of the past. Some claimed to hear the voices of relatives. It was an equal marriage of the peaceful Corinn mind with the more violent, aggressive psyche of humans.

Axel stared at the screen and slowly placed a hand on his head. That voice. He now understood how it got through. So he *wasn't* crazy—he had a Tunnel—to his father.

His mind reverted to the dream, but it wasn't a dream. It was a memory of the rocky cliff where the army of Stewards stood their ground against the overwhelming legion of Wrath. He remembered something that voice, the voice of his father, had said years ago:

You can't run from your fate forever. You have the blood of a warrior. You belong on the battlefield!

Axel looked back to the post and kept reading.

In the beginning, the genetically modified warriors worked in harmony to secure trade routes, crush rebellions, hunt smugglers, and destroy anti-Colonial Alliance terrorist cells. Stewards became walking weapons that protected the weak. Through their brutal violence, the warriors successfully maintained an uneasy peace and kept the coffers filled for their joint handlers of the Colonial Alliance and the Corinn Empire.

But peace is seldom the natural state of life, and there seemed to be no end to the upheaval across the widespread trading sectors of the human and Corinn empires. War followed humanity after it fled Earth and the Solar System for the Hironia System with their new faster than light engines, five centuries ago. But for those in power, war wasn't necessarily a bad thing—if it could be controlled. Stewards became the gatekeepers of the ebb and flow of blood. Decade after decade, Steward genes were modified to suit their task of measured violence. Muscles were made more resilient, reflexes sharpened. Bones became so dense that they were stronger than the exotic materials used in the hulls of an Ironclad Naval Destroyer. A Steward's bare fists could smash through the thickest armor like two flesh hammers working hot metal against an anvil.

It was said that Stewards felt no pain. Bleeding from a dozen wounds, some missing an arm, a leg, or an eye, Stewards kept fighting, kept killing. One story told of a Steward that had been run over by an armored personnel carrier, gotten up, chased the vehicle down on foot, and killed everyone inside. Another fell from a three-hundred-foot cliff, tearing and snarling at a Lark drone the entire way down, and then killing the beast before crashing onto rocks. The Steward got up, staggered forward, shook his head groggily, and continued the battle.

The stories continued across the galaxy, saying nothing could stop them.

Until the Wrath arrived...

Axel looked away as memories surfaced in his mind. Hiding his entire life. His constant attempt to control his anger and rage.

Now he understood it all.

Understood that when the anger took over, it opened a tunnel to his father. To his memories, to his voice. Sometimes, though, when it was powerful enough, it allowed his father's influence to control his actions and come close to spilling blood.

Axel imagined what would happen if his father took full control.

He would become a killer, a violent artist, relishing in taking life wherever he went.

You can't let that happen, he thought.

"I won't," he whispered. "I'd rather die."

"We finally got through to the Citadel. They are sending equipment to our position as soon as possible," Apollo said. "In the meantime, anyone not assigned to patrol is to remain on full alert, no one rests, got it?"

Most of the Eagles fanned away, but Jax remained with a small squad.

"Yeah, like anyone's gonna get any rest out here," Satani remarked.

Lightning flashed over the plateau, storm clouds dumping more acid rain into the muddy soil. Red blow-up bivouac shelters with life support systems littered the rocky terrain where Outlaw Platoon had set up their FOB.

According to their AI engineer, Hippo, this was the most stable ground.

Stable, Jax thought. The entire planet seemed like it was ready to explode.

Along with Jax, Specialist Nadia, Sergeant Hesh, Sergeant Satani, Zang, and Hippo remained behind with the lieutenant while the other Eagles dispersed.

"Here's the situation," Apollo said. "Hippo located a trail that leads down into that crater. I'm sending you down there to look for intel on what happened."

"What *happened?*" Hesh stammered. "The outpost got fried by those f-fire twisters, LT."

"Are you fucking slow? Because this entire mission you've been acting like you got somethin' wrong with your dome and now you're stuttering."

"I resent that LT. It's just this place gives me the heebie jeebies, and after what happened to Meatball I'm pissed the fuck off and that makes me stutter sometimes."

"What happened to Meatball was fucked up, but you did what you could," Nadia said.

"Yeah, and I don't want to end up like him."

"Then quit your bitching," Jax said.

No one said anything, until Apollo chuckled. "Yeah, Hesh, you heard Brito. Now get your dinosaur ass moving."

Jax started walking with the squad, but Hesh remained behind a minute. He clearly didn't like what Jax had said, but Jax didn't really give much of a shit. It wasn't the best way to make friends, but the constant complaining was getting on her nerves, and it wasn't good for morale.

Hippo led the way across the bottom of the ridgeline bordering the crater, heading east from the camp. The last of the Eagle guards held security on top of the crest, their black armor with white-winged backs covered in ash from blowing drifts.

Both men stepped aside, saying nothing as the squad mounted the ridge for a view of the deep crater.

Three vortexes of fire spun across the bottom in different locations, swirling up grit and embers. The gusts had calmed some up here since Jax last stood on the rocky border, but the heat was still intense. Over one hundred-eighty degrees.

Hippo started down a rocky path that descended three hundred feet to the bottom. It didn't take long to see the tracks the droid had discovered earlier. Zang crouched down to look, but even Jax could tell the boot prints were from the larger and narrower feet of a Corinn.

"This was one of my kin," Zang confirmed.

He stood and walked ahead of Jax at a brisk pace, in the first show of anything remotely emotional since they landed. Jax too picked up her pace with Satani, Hesh, and Nadia all falling in behind. The rocky path was ten feet wide and was far too perfect to have been natural. The Corinns had constructed this path.

And good thing for that, considering the elevator was gone.

Jax scanned the vast fiery crater as they descended. If the Wrath were anywhere, it was down here. The chill of fear gripped her at what felt like an undeniable demonic presence.

You wanted this. You wanted to fight!

But this wasn't the battlefield she had pictured. There were no insurgents firing at her from mining trenches on distant moons or asteroids. There weren't terrorists trying to snipe her from windows in an urban sector.

There was only the fire, smoke, and the terror of what dwelled in the darkness.

Hesh was right to be afraid. Outlaw Platoon was filled with hard soldiers, but even hard soldiers feared monsters.

Jax raised her rifle, gripping it tightly. Hippo halted ahead, stopping to examine more tracks with a scanner. The mammoth droid pushed downward into the increasing temperatures.

By the time they reached the halfway mark, Jax noticed her HUD hit over two-hundred degrees.

"Wow," Jax said. "You guys seeing these readings?"

"Toasty," Satani said.

"What did you expect?" Hesh asked. "We're practically at the gates of Hell."

Jax checked her battery, which remained at eighty percent. The filter in her helmet, however, was at forty-one percent. If she was down here too long, she would have to replace it.

A crunching roared, drawing her eyes up just as Hippo vanished into the path. Dust and grit poofed up where the droid had stood a second earlier.

"Back, back!" Jax shouted.

She turned and hurried back up with the others as the path collapsed behind them. They halted as soon as the crashing faded away.

Turning, the group checked the damage. Hippo was gone, and so was most of the path.

"LT, we lost Hippo," Satani reported over the team comms.

Static crackled over the channel, but there was no response.

"Son of a bitch, must be too much interference," Satani said. "Brito, can you see where Hippo fell?"

Jax looked over the edge as cautiously as she could. Two hundred and fifty feet below, she could make out the bottom of the crater, but not Hippo. She didn't want to call out either, for fear of giving away their position to any potential hostiles.

Zang suddenly pointed down.

"You see Hippo?" Jax asked. She made her way next to the alien, following his long finger toward the crater. Sure enough, the droid was at the bottom, covered partially in rocks and debris.

"Well shit," Jax muttered. From what she could see, the ground had given way, and formed what looked almost like a slide down the slope of the crater.

Satani moving in for a better look. "Oh damn, no way we're getting to him without a Clipper."

"How much cable do you have, Hesh?" Jax asked.

Hesh, still standing in the same spot, shrugged. "Hundred feet."

"Take it out," Jax said. "I have an idea."

"You want to pull Hippo back up here?" Hesh laughed.

But Jax didn't laugh back.

"Wait, are you serious?" Hesh asked. "We call him Hippo for a fucking reason."

"I'm not pulling him up," Jax stated. "I'm gonna rappel down, secure the cable, and give you a safe way down."

That shut Hesh up for a few seconds. "Okay, you're a tough chick, I see that, knock yourself out," he said.

Hesh began to unravel the cables while Jax fastened a clip to her belt. She checked the crater that Hippo had fallen into. The slope was steep. Too steep to walk down without the path, unless you had climbing equipment.

Jax moved into position, turned around, and gazed at Hesh, who held the other end of the cable.

"Don't worry, Brito, I won't let go," he said.

With Satani, Nadia, and Zang there, Jax wasn't too worried. But she had definitely gotten on Hesh's bad side.

The guy may be a dick, but he isn't a murderer, Jax thought.

She began to back down, sliding almost right away. She righted her body and continued down. With every step, her temp gauge spiked another few degrees.

Smoke drifted away from the bottom of the crater from the open burning fires along pits of magma. The terraformer was easier to see in the glow. The alloy hull had melted around the base, making it appear like a gigantic, humped jellyfish.

The tornadoes had all vanished, thankfully, giving Jax a window to get down to Hippo and check the terrain.

She thought of Krish as she descended. If only the cowardly prick could see her now.

The thought that Jax was lying in a hospital bed a few days earlier, waiting to be dishonorably discharged and sent to a penal colony was still hard to grasp.

She forgot about all that during the last few feet of her descent. A thick layer of smoke drifted across her path. Her optics compensated, allowing her to see through.

When her boot hit the bottom, it struck hard, glassy rock. At first glance it appeared volcanic, but this wasn't a volcano—it was created by the weapons the Corinns had used on this city to destroy the Wrath, rather than handing it over to the enemy.

Jax unclipped from the cable and brought up her rifle, aiming in all directions. The life scanner detected nothing as she did a three-hundred-sixty-degree turn. But her other scanners were picking up even higher traces of SO_2.

She looked away from her HUD and began the trek to Hippo. The downed droid wasn't far, and all Jax had to do was follow the scree to the pile that had partially buried the droid.

"Sergeant Brito," came a voice.

Jax crouched in front of Hippo. All but one of his limbs was buried. The robot reached out with the left arm, trying to claw at the rocks.

"I am stuck," he said.

For such a beast of a machine, Jax was surprised it couldn't get up on its own. That told her it had taken some damage during the fall. "Hold still, I'll help you," she said.

The sound of voices came from behind as Zang and Satani finished descending.

"Help me get this debris off," Jax said.

Satani bent down and together they heaved the rocks off the droid. Jax lugged the biggest chunk to the ground with a thud. It was then she realized they hadn't felt an earthquake for several hours.

She also noticed their guide was suddenly gone. "Shit, where did Zang Za Zi go?" she asked.

Satani looked up. "Great," he said. "Hesh, Nadia, do you see Zang?"

The other two Eagles shook their heads as they walked over.

"Finish clearing Hippo," Satani said.

The four soldiers quickly uncovered the droid.

"Are you functional?" Nadia asked.

The massive robot pushed at the ground and propped itself up, staggering slightly, but then going stiff. "My system is fully operational," he said.

Jax turned to scan the shifting wall of haze but saw no movement. She switched on the bio scanner again, and now it ticked from a hit. Two hundred feet away.

"I think I see Zang," she said.

Hesh, Satani, and Nadia fell in with her, spreading out in combat intervals with their rifles up. Hippo moved with them, both laser cannons pointed at the heat signature Jax was tracking. It was a Corinn, judging by the lengthy form.

They closed in a few moments later. It was indeed Zang, but the alien was on his knees, and he was...

"Is he naked?" Hesh asked.

"The fuck, man," Satani said.

Jax approached slowly, trying to make sense of the sight not ten feet from her. Zang was on his knees, head bowed, body completely naked. His armor, suit, and gear lay in a pile by his side.

"The hell are you doing?" Jax asked.

Zang kept his head bowed until Jax ran around to look at him. His flesh was already starting to burn in the heat. Corinns could withstand far more hostile conditions than humans, but he wouldn't last long out here.

"STOP!" Zang shouted when Jax moved in front of him.

Jax picked up and held aloft a robotic leg and foot in the air, seeing what she had almost stepped on. She quickly stepped back from a dead Corinn. More than one. At least ten, some partially buried from drifting dirt and ash. The bodies were still clothed with suits burned from exposure. Their helmets, however, were all missing.

"What kind of voodoo is this," Satani muttered.

Jax noticed what her comrade had just seen.

Not a single one of the Corinns had eyes.

She looked out over the mass graveyard. There had to be a hundred bodies down here. Upon closer examination, the deep empty sockets weren't from exposure to the elements, but rather a sharp object. The eyes had been gouged out.

The corpses formed a halo around an opening in the crater. Jax brought up her scope and zoomed in on a rock structure that formed an arc. Around the border of the bodies, there were several poles sticking out of the dirt that seemed to be perfectly placed. Each had Corinn letters engraved in them. She brought up her translator, seeing one of the poles read: *Dig site 19*

"The Wrath must have done this," Satani said.

"No," Zang said. He stood and put his suit back on, ending whatever bizarre ritual he had just performed.

As he dressed, Jax took in the scene again. The bodies weren't torn apart like she would have expected, had this been Wrath.

"If they didn't do it, who did?" Hesh asked.

Zang put his helmet back on, then pointed. "They did this to themselves," he said.

CHAPTER 21

Twelve hours had passed since Axel and his crew left Hex Prime, and Rangnar still hadn't made a decision on what he was going to do with the Wrath beacon. It sat in a case on his desk, flashing the same symbols.

Could it really be a countdown to another Wrath invasion?

If it was, the Eagles would be the least of his worries.

Whatever the case, Rangnar knew he was on borrowed time. Eventually the soldiers would find him, and then it would be too late to make a deal. His only option seemed to be handing the ball over in exchange for his freedom. Normally he would reach out on back channels to Captain Weston, but his gut told him that bridge was burned. And that if Rangnar did see him again, he would slit his neck from ear to ear.

"Supper's ready," chirped Lucid.

Rangnar looked up to see her standing in the open doorway of the office. He got up and followed the female Marka into the dining room. A fire burned in the hearth of the stone fireplace.

Saber was setting the table with his tail, serving a vegetarian dish from their gardens.

A knock sounded on the door, and Rangnar pulled his laser

pistol from his holster. Lucid bolted over and looked through the window.

"It's Nuke," she said.

She unlocked the heavy wood door to let the Marka in.

"Just in time for dinner," she chirped.

Nuke trotted in, shaking off his leather coat. Rangnar gestured at the pillows on the floor of the low table. He smiled as he joined the three for a meal, something he never thought would happen again.

"To say I'm glad to be with you again is an understatement, my friends," he said.

"We're not happy about being jettisoned away," Nuke said. "You're lucky you made it back."

"I know, and I'm sorry," Rangnar said.

"What happened out there?" Lucid asked.

Rangnar took a drink of wine, then went into the details. Most of the details. He didn't share what he had discovered about Axel. If he had, he would be a dead man. A single word of truth about Axel and that nano-beetle would tunnel into his heart.

Game over for Phantom.

"So what's the plan now?" Saber asked.

"I'll be right back." Rangnar went to his office and returned with the egg. The Markas all stared at him and the artifact.

"I'm going to use this to buy our freedom," he said.

Nuke went over and sniffed the metal exterior. "What's so valuable about this one?"

Rangnar wasn't sure how to tell his hunters, but they deserved to know.

"It's a Wrath message," he said. "A countdown. Maybe."

"A countdown to what?" Saber asked.

"Their return, I believe," he said. "I imagine they'll come back in a fleet that will block out the sun with their spiked black ships, firing lasers on the cities of the Colonial Alliance and the Corinn Empire. They will disgorge Hydras that will incinerate anyone that survives the first wave. Spectres will crunch across the land, burrowing into holes where survivors hide, yanking them out and ripping them to pieces."

The Markas were all silent.

"That's why as soon as I hand the artifact over to CAID and guarantee our safety, we are going to take what forgite we have left and go find ourselves a very nice unpopulated planet to live on," Rangnar said.

"Wait, let me get this straight. You're going to give that to the very assholes that ambushed us back on Optus?" Nuke asked. He bared his teeth. "You know I respect you, boss, but I can't support that."

"Trust me, I wish there was another way, but there isn't. I do this, or we die, plain and simple."

"If the Wrath return, we're dead anyways," Saber said. "There won't be anywhere to hide."

"Saber's right," Lucid said. "If this is true, and those monsters return, they will come back in greater numbers and will likely attack more worlds."

Nuke growled. "I say we load up on weapons and prepare to fight. I'd rather go down shooting on all fours than curled up in a cave. With respect, I'm glad we're not on Tecca anymore, boss."

"I agree," Saber said.

Lucid didn't reply but Rangnar knew she felt the same way.

"Maybe the Eagles and Corinns can win," Nuke said.

"Without an army of Stewards?" Rangnar said. "No matter how much the Eagles and Corinns have prepared, they won't defeat the Wrath without the fierce warriors that stopped them the first time around."

"Okay, so how can we escape then?" Saber asked.

"We run as far as we can," Rangnar said.

"I thought you were sick of hiding and running?" Lucid asked.

"I am, but it's the only way to protect you," Rangnar said. "I was ready to die on Tecca, but this ball provided salvation for us all."

"Or death," Lucid said.

Rangnar let out a deep sigh. Maybe they were right. Maybe not. All he knew was these Markas were all that mattered to him. In the morning, he would leave and find Captain Weston in Aritrea. He would hold a blade to his throat and find out if he was the one that betrayed them. If he wasn't, then he would help arrange a hand off for the artifact.

"You've made your points," he said. "Thank you for your honesty. Now I need to think." He turned away and started out of the living space back toward his office. Halfway there he stopped at a door that led outside. What he needed right now was some fresh air.

"Want me to come with?" Lucid asked. She had followed him into the hall.

"No," he said. "Go eat with the others."

He listened to her paws trot away and then opened the door. Rangnar stepped into the cool night air. Clouds drifted overhead, shadowing the biodomes within the stoned off wall of the bunker. He went over to one of the doors and opened it.

Plants from a variety of planets grew in pots along the wooden tables. Some seeds had even come from Earth. He went to his favorite, a red-stemmed plant that had a closed head of purple petals. The petals curled at the top as his finger hovered over it. Suddenly, they all peeled back, revealing the green teeth and red mouth of the flesh-eating flower.

It was beautiful, even now. The last meal it had eaten still remained partially in its mouth, the tail of a mouse hanging out.

He went down the row, passing Earth roses, lilies, and

Corinn weeds called tripods. The three blue blades glowed in the dark at night, creating vast fields of radiant blue in the evenings. He recalled a picture of the millions of acres of burning Tripods during the Wrath invasion. The thought chilled him under his layers.

If the Wrath were coming back, he knew they would come back even fiercer. Worlds would burn, and colonies would be turned to dust. This time, the Corinns and Humans faced complete extinction without the Stewards.

That made him think of Axel. They were similar, he and Axel. Both seeking refuge among misfit crews. Both searching for adventure in search of freedom but being trapped all the same. They were survivors.

"You're not going to leave us again," came a voice.

He turned to find Lucid.

Saber and Nuke stood on either side.

"We go where you go," Saber said.

"If you want to try and find a planet to hide on, then we will honor that wish. If you decide to stand and fight, we will stand with you," Nuke said. "If you want to go find Captain Weston, I'll come with you, as long as you let me rip his throat out—if he was the one who betrayed us."

Rangnar smiled at his loyal companions. They were smart creatures. They knew he was planning on leaving them out of the action, just like on Tecca.

"Okay," he said after a few beats. "Tomorrow morning, Lucid and I are going to Aritrea," Rangnar said. "I will find Captain Weston and make a deal for our lives in exchange for this artifact. Unless he betrayed us, then, I'll be the one to rip his throat out."

Nuke snorted. "Even if he wasn't, how can you be sure he will help us?"

Rangnar had a plan for that too, but he couldn't take credit for it. This idea had come from another enemy. "Don't worry," he said. "I've got that covered. What happens after tomorrow, we can decide together. Deal?"

The Markas all wagged their tails in agreement.

"Saber, Nuke, stay here with Blaster and get ready to leave while we're away," he said. "Pack up weapons, forgite, and supplies. As soon as I return with Lucid, we're going a long ass way away from all humans, Corinns, and Woolies."

"I've got just the place," Lucid said.

"Yeah?"

"Tor, I got a brother there."

Rangnar had heard of the colony located in an asteroid belt along the outer edge of the Hironia system. Thousands of Markas had settled there after fleeing captivity on their home world, Eern. It was a treacherous place for humans, and Rangnar doubted there were many humans there.

He liked the thought of that.

In fact, a colony of Markas sounded exactly like the place he would like to retire. Or to die, if the Wrath were returning.

"Preparing to eject *Hammerhead*," Axel said.

He faced the viewports on the bridge of the *Trash Squid*, now registered as the *Wayward Raft*, complete with a forged history. The rest of his crew worked at their stations, oblivious to the information that Axel now believed to be true. That the voice of his father had haunted him all these years, compelling him to violence that his mother had always told him to avoid.

He shook away those thoughts and focused on the task at hand. Uga had jerry-rigged some fresh explosives on the Tech-N. Axel was conflicted about destroying it, but he had to listen to reason. Landing with the damaged fighter attached would draw unwanted attention. And with their newfound wealth, they could buy whatever fighter they wanted, barely denting the stash.

"On your mark, Captain," Luna said.

"Thanks for the adventures," Axel whispered. Then he turned and gave Luna a nod.

"Ejecting the *Hammerhead*," she said.

Clanking sounded as the smaller fighter was ejected and sent twirling through space.

Uga held up a remote in one arm, a cigar stick wobbling in his mouth. "Ready when you are, Capa."

Axel waited a few more seconds, then gave Uga a nod.

The Wooly tapped the detonator. Outside, the *Hammerhead* continued to rotate through the darkness.

"Dumb piece of junk," Uga said. He smacked the side of the remote to no visible effect on the fighter. Then he bit down on it with a crunch.

A bright explosion burst in space, flashing outward. Within seconds, it was over, nothing but cooling debris drifting in the sea of black.

Axel turned from the view and went to his chair. "Sparty, take us to Jolia," he said.

The thrusters fired, resuming their journey to their first stop, a small and cold world on the outer edge of the system. The Corinns claimed it as part of their empire, but allowed human colonies.

There was a spaceport at the northern tip where Brayton had located both a new Tech-N fighter being sold on the black market, and a scrapped arm for Spartacus.

Axel kept calm during the flight, but thoughts of his father filled his mind. He couldn't help but wonder what his name was, and rank, and...

He's a killer. Evil. You should forget about him. Axel

thought. But like that nagging anger in him, there was also curiosity.

"We're closing in on Jolia," Luna said. "Preparing to request permission for landing using our shiny new transponder and flight-data."

"Capa, are we ever going to be the *Trash Squid* again?" Uga asked.

"Someday, pal," Axel said. "For the time being, we're going incognito."

The frozen planet of Jolia slowly came into focus outside their viewports. For the majority of the forty-five-hour day, the northern tip was frozen solid. But for five hours, as the planet rotated into the sun, that ice melted, and the hardy trees sprouted their flowers and leaves, blooming to soak in that precious sunlight before retreating into their barky hides.

It was currently on the pole as they approached.

"We're cleared for landing," Luna announced. "There does appear to be a Clipper at the port. Bringing up visual from the port video feed I hacked into."

Axel leaned down to examine the video footage of the transport, which wasn't much bigger than their ship.

"You got any info on their business here?" Axel asked.

Brayton finished tapping at his screen and whirled in his chair. "Stationed for a week, probably protecting some transports."

Axel let out a discreet breath. "Okay, take us down," he said.

The ship blasted toward the port nestled along an ocean bay. As they slowed on descent, hundreds of boats came into view. Most of them harvested a single product that ran the economy—a sweet tasting fish known as honeyfin. These wrinkly, green creatures were larger than any shark had been on Earth before their extinction. But instead of jagged teeth, they had baleen teeth used to filter a flowery plant that grew in the depths.

"Bet you'd like to surf those waves," Cricket chirped.

"No time for that," Axel replied. "As soon as we touch down, Cricket and Uga will come with me to take a look at the Tech-N. Brayton, you stay here with Luna. If you get wind of any problems, you let us know."

"You got it," Brayton said.

"What about me?" Spartacus asked.

Axel shrugged. "Figured you'd go look for a new arm."

"He-heh, you figured right."

The ship lowered over their instructed spot on the tarmac between two transport rigs, both twice the size of the *Wayward Raft*.

"Prepare for landing," Luna said.

Dozens of civilian craft were parked near the water. For a smaller port, it was alive with activity. Hundreds of workers with their droid assistants unloaded and loaded up transports.

Their ship landed with a jolt.

"Okay, let's get this done asap, then we're headed for a buffet on Dari," Axel said.

Uga barked and did a little wave dance with his arms.

The cargo hold ramp lowered and Axel swapped out his sandals for boots. He wore a black windbreaker and tactical pants, hoping to blend in. Outside, the port was indeed bustling. Lark drones buzzed around the platform, unloading crates from a hulking box of a ship with rusted wings.

On the starboard side was a sleek white transport with a bright green logo of a wrinkly honeyfin painted on the aft wings. The bulbous cockpit read: *The Angry Honeyfin*.

Axel crossed the platform with Uga, Cricket, and Spartacus. "Stay close, and don't mouth off," he ordered.

"Why you look at me?" Uga barked.

"Looking at you *and* Sparty," Axel said.

"I will avoid the arena today, sire," Spartacus said with a slight bow.

Axel grinned but kept his guard up as they took a platform from the tarmac to the docks.

Waves lashed a shoreline to the west. To the east, a marina was packed full of boats. Some of them sported catches, with honeyfin hanging from their waved rails. There were no Eagles in the crowd of dockhands, anglers, and droids. No sign that Rangnar had somehow sold them out. Or that this was an ambush.

Axel started down the piers. Most of the commotion came from a butchering area with grinding saws. A crane with a hanging honeyfin lowered the green beast to the pier. Two droids with chain-saw arms cut into the fresh catch as soon as it was set down on a conveyer belt. Two more droids worked on placing fresh steaks into boxes. One of them dropped a slippery hunk of the green flesh.

"Be careful with that you dumb shitcan!" yelled one of the supervising human anglers. He was a large, pale man with a long beard, and a blue stocking cap.

"My apologies," replied the droid.

Uga and Cricket walked past the scene, but Spartacus stopped to observe what was a fairly normal interaction between humans and their robots.

"What ya lookin' at, one arm?" asked the bearded angler.

Axel motioned for Spartacus, sensing trouble. "Come on, Sparty."

"He-heh," Spartacus replied. "This will just take a second, Captain."

Two more men joined the big lug. A pair of Jukes slithered over on their tails, which propped up their torsos with a single jointed arm. The most intelligent native creatures to Jolia, they were the size of a human toddler with one big eye centered in their red fish-shaped face.

"I'd tell you to clean up, but I ain't got time to wait for a cripple," the man said to Spartacus.

"Hey, watch it," Axel said. He felt the first heat of anger in his chest.

"What? This 'bot your sister or something?" the man said.

Both Jukes cooed and slithered back.

"It is all right, Captain," Spartacus said. He held up a balled fist, and then cranked up the middle finger.

"Funny gimp shitcan without any manners, huh?" the man replied.

"He's aggressive, but means well," Axel said. "Now back off."

The hulking angler walked closer, but two of his comrades grabbed his shoulders. "T—forget these off-worlders," one of them said.

"A cripple droid, a fat rat of a squid, and a mangy looking Marka," T said. "You must be one helluva crew."

"Who you callin' fat, cheeseburger ass?" Uga barked.

T stepped toward the Wooly, but Axel moved in front of him, sensing the first hint of the metallic taste in his mouth. He swallowed and narrowed his eyes, trying to keep the rage at bay and the voice from taking over.

"You got something to say, boy?" T asked.

As much as Axel wanted to give this bully a good pop to the face, he knew it wasn't worth it.

"Well, what you gonna—" T started to ask.

Axel jerked his body as if he was going to throw a punch, silencing the man, who took a step back. The swift fake-out had the guy staring in shock.

"I'm gonna walk away with my crew, and you're going to

stay right here," Axel said. He stared deep into the man's eyes, a warning without words.

Axel turned and walked over to Cricket with Spartacus and Uga following. None of them looked back, but Axel did listen for footsteps, hearing nothing but a few chuckles and crude jokes. He drowned it all out and focused on controlling his breathing on the way to the hangars.

"For time's sake, I think we should split up," he said. "Spartacus, go buy yourself an arm. I'll go with Uga to purchase the new Tech-N. Cricket, you keep watch."

"Thank you, Captain," Spartacus said.

"Just stay out of the arena, like you said, okay?"

"There will be no blood on the sands today, Captain, you have my word."

They parted ways, with Axel and Uga heading toward a row of hangars that looked worse for wear. Uga motioned them with one of his furry arms toward Hangar 22 at the very end of the row.

The duo stopped outside of a massive garage in disarray. Rusted parts from boats, spaceships, and vehicles were piled ten feet high on the left side and in the center were two fishing boats and a truck on lifts. Axel almost chuckled when he saw two Woolies wearing stilts on their legs, the bear-like creatures barking at one another as they directed their headlamps to examine the undercarriage of the truck.

The translation came through in Axel's earpiece.

"Too big to hide much up there," one of them said.

"Plenty big," said the other.

Axel had no idea what they were planning to hide, but figured it wasn't good when they both turned to Uga. One was thinner than most Woolies and had gray streaks in his facial hair. The other was built like a mini-lumberjack, with muscular arms and legs, and his head a bald crown.

Uga waddled inside in front of Axel.

"Look at this chunk a monk," said the big Wooly.

"Chunk a monk?" Uga barked back. "What they call you? Bald nuts?"

The big Wooly snorted through pierced nostrils.

"Uga, take it easy," Axel said, walking past and moving toward the two mechanics.

"What you want?" said the thin, older Wooly.

"We're here to look at the fighter," Axel replied.

"And who are you?"

"Captain Michael Satchel of the *Wayward Raft*," Axel lied. He pulled out the new records. The older Wooly pulled a pair of glasses out of his vest pocket and propped them up on his gray furred nose.

"I'm Uga," Uga said.

"Yeah, I got that," said the thin Wooly. He studied the identification papers, glanced up at Axel, then handed them back, and said, "Napo, shut the door."

The muscular Wooly went and hit a button, the door grinding overhead.

"Well? You coming or what?" asked the big Wooly.

Axel and Uga hurried under the closing door.

"I am Manoi," said the older one. "This is Napo."

"Yeah, I got that," Uga said.

Axel sighed.

"This way," Napo barked. He led them through the maze of loosely organized parts to the back of the hangar. Napo ripped a tarp off a boat on the ground, then began to push it with a shoulder. The bottom shrieked over metal.

"Need some help?" Axel asked.

Napo grunted but shook his head. A few moments later, he had revealed a trap door that the thinner Wooly opened.

"Go look," he said.

Axel drew a flashlight and ducked down. Sure enough, the outline of a Tech-N came into focus.

He stepped onto the ladder, followed by Manoi.

At the bottom, the elderly Wooly flipped a light switch, illuminating lockers, tool chests, and crates hugging the walls of the underground chamber.

Manoi held out one of his many arms. "Old, like me, but flies like a virgin," he barked.

Axel walked around the small ship, running his hand on the exterior. She was in good shape from what he could tell, but there was one thing missing.

"Where are the laser cannons?" he asked.

Napo walked over to the long crates. He unlocked one and propped the lid. "It's all here," he said. "Every part."

"How much you want for her?" Axel asked.

Manoi massaged the gray in his beard.

"Fifty thousand deltas," he barked.

Axel raised a brow. That was far more than it was worth, even on the black market. While they could afford it, he wasn't going to overpay, out of principle.

"Mind if we run some diagnostic tests on her?" Axel asked.

"Be my guest," Manoi said.

Uga pulled out his kit and hooked it up to the exterior engine router. Axel continued to examine the fighter as the device went to work.

"She must be in very good shape for your price," Axel said.

"When word gets out about what's going on in Corinnia, prices will be going up," Napo grumbled.

"What do you mean?"

"The Eagles have amassed a fleet above Corinnia," Manoi said. "We hear rumors the Wrath are returning."

"Where you hear this?" Uga asked.

"A friend of a friend who services a Warhorse."

Axel froze, thinking of what Rangnar had said about getting far away from Corinn civilizations. He had figured that had to do with the fact Axel had broken their laws by going to Eern, but maybe Rangnar had been referring to something much worse.

The device beeped and Uga nodded at him. "All good, Capa," he said. "No problems."

Manoi went back to massaging his beard.

"I'm not even sure I want to sell this," he said. "If the Wrath are coming back—"

"You're right. This fighter won't do anything against them," Axel said. "Uga, didn't you say there was another Tech-N in the port for sale?"

"Yes, Capa, sure did, sure did, indeed," Uga replied.

Manoi grunted and waved Napo behind the craft where they barked at each other. They returned a few seconds later.

"Forty-five thousand deltas, and I will fuel her up," Manoi announced.

"Thirty-nine, and the gas, and we'll take that extra charger for the cannons we saw up front," Axel said. "Can't fight the devil in this, but that kind of money can take you far from the battle."

"The tall man is right," Napo said. "We have our ship to flee if needed. Why leave all this junk unsold? In meantime, I am spend many days at the poles."

Axel almost laughed thinking about the "poles," the Wooly version of a human strip club, and the multi-limbed, husky aliens dancing naked, twirling around on a stage.

Damn, they sure like to dance, he thought.

The two mechanics argued a bit longer but then Manoi came back.

"Forty-two thousand deltas and you have a deal," he said.

"How long 'til it's ready?" Axel asked.

"Couple days..."

"We need it by tomorrow for a salvaging job," Axel said.

The two Woolies went behind the craft again, barking.

"Do they know we can hear them?" Axel asked.

"Yes," Uga said.

Axel chuckled but grew serious as the two Woolies hurried back to face him. "Forty-three, it ready tomorrow," Manoi said.

"Great, it's settled," Axel said.

Napo smiled. "By the time the ice melts tomorrow, the cannons will be installed, and the ship ready to fly."

They left, but Axel had an uneasy feeling.

"Capa, what you think?" Uga asked. "About the Wrath?"

"I think maybe we should be focused on fixing our FTL drive," Axel said. "Then again, I'm not sure there's anywhere we could hide if they return."

"Dari is safe. You will see. We disappear into the mountains, poof. No more problems."

CHAPTER 22

"You better start talking," Apollo said.

Zang remained silent as he kneeled in front of the mass grave of his comrades. Jax looked away from the macabre sight to her HUD. Her air filter was on orange, giving her maybe another ten hours before toxins started breaking through. Hopefully she wouldn't be down here for that much longer.

"This is some demonic shit," Satani said.

"Did you get ahold of the Citadel?" Hesh asked.

"Yeah, command wants a SITREP, so I came down here to see for myself," Apollo said. "But what the hell do I report back if our guide here won't talk?"

Apollo stepped up next to the Corinn, who was still gazing out over the graveyard. All six Eagles stood on the barrier of the death, clearly rattled by the view in front of them based on their heart rates, which Jax had access to on her HUD. The hard warriors of Outlaw Platoon weren't as hard as they had appeared.

But then again, this would have rattled most soldiers. Maybe not Stewards, but Stewards weren't normal beings.

The grisly sight of dead, eyeless Corinns was on the border of a dig site. No doubt a place where they had unearthed Wrath tech, artifacts, bones—and something deadly. The truth had died with them.

Jax stood there trying not to think about what horrors the Corinns had found. Horrors that had apparently made them rip their own eyes out.

Even Hippo was out of sorts, but that was from the massive drop earlier. Sparks and grinding sounded from the droid working on self-maintenance. The pile of scree didn't seem to have left any major damage on it, but Apollo had ordered a second round of tests just to be sure. The war bot was one of their most important tools on the surface.

Apollo grunted and walked back to their Corinn guide, who remained on his knees.

"Zang, sorry to disturb whatever it is you're doing, but I need to fucking know what your people found in that tunnel," said the lieutenant.

The alien kept his helmet down.

Jax wondered if he was trying to open a tunnel or something, a window into whatever had happened. But that didn't make any sense to her. She waited, like the others, for the Corinn to speak. Apollo, it seemed, grew tired of waiting.

"Zang," Apollo said loudly. "This is some bullshit. Your people made an agreement with ours for us to help, but how can we help if you don't share info?"

"You forget to whom you speak." Zang lifted his helmet, and then gestured out toward the dead. "These Corinns were not warriors. They were Neurosabers, what your people call scientists."

Apollo took a step closer but stopped when Zang held up a hand.

"Only a Corinn may walk among the dead," he said. "Keep your soldiers here, I will make a path."

"Wait a second, where were your soldiers? What about droids?" Apollo asked. "Were these scientists left unguarded?"

"Inside, perhaps, I do not yet know the truth," Zang replied without turning. "My eyes too are blind, but soon I shall see."

Jax moved back with the other Eagles to watch as the Corinn trekked through the graveyard, slowly dragging the bodies aside to form a path.

"What about a droid? Can a droid walk the path?" Satani asked.

"I must do this on my own," Zang said. He got up and looked at the tunnel entrance. "Stay here."

The Eagles watched while the alien cleared the graveyard.

"What you thinkin', LT?" Satani asked.

"I think they found something down here so horrible they killed themselves, but who the fuck knows? Maybe Zang will find out and tell us," Apollo said quietly. "I'm going to go topside and request support. You guys stay here and watch him."

He turned away but hesitated when Hesh reached out.

"Sir, you want us to stay here?" he asked. "What if those twisters come back?"

"Then you run," Apollo said. "Fuckin-A, man. I've never seen you act like this."

"This place, Lieutenant. It's got me all fucked up. I mean shit, just look at these eyeless Corinn. You heard Zang, he said they did this to themselves."

"Yeah, and our mission is to figure out why, and what the hell happened here. I'd send you in there with Zang, but last thing I need is to piss him off."

"Yeah, I'm good with him going alone." Hesh raised his minigun.

Apollo left with the two Eagles that had accompanied him down the cable Jax had descended to get to the crater.

"We're official lab rats," Hesh said. "Want to know what else? I got a theory."

"I'm sure you're gonna tell us," Nadia said.

Satani shrugged. "Let's hear it."

Hesh paced outside the ring of corpses while Zang dragged them out of the way. At each one, he knelt and bowed his head, speaking too low for Jax to hear.

"I think the Corinns have been working this site for a long time," Hesh said. "I think they found something that they couldn't handle and asked for our help. Now they want us to go in and fight off whatever demons they awoke."

"So what if you're right? You didn't join the Eagles to sit on your dino ass, did you?" Satani asked. "You joined to kill shit, just like I did."

"No! I joined because I had no choice. It was this or a prison camp on some asteroid where rat shit is a delicacy and piss is the drink of choice."

"Oh that's right," Nadia said. "You're a convict. What did you do again?"

"Nothing. I'm innocent of all charges."

"Sergeant Hesh was charged with first degree theft of a level 5 Corvette from Marcus Cotis on Hex Prime," Hippo said. "He was also charged with first degree kidnapping of a civilian."

"I know," Satani said with a laugh. "How could we forget? Hesh 'borrowed' a Corvette from one of the richest guys in the galaxy, while his mistress was on board, coincidentally, and then he crash landed it into a lake before getting off the planet."

Hesh laughed. "It was her fault. She showed me her tatas and I lost all—"

"He's going down," Nadia interrupted.

Jax noticed the Corinn had finished with the bodies and

was walking through the stone arc and down a ramp into the scorched ground, vanishing.

Nadia shouldered his rifle, and Jax did the same. The four Eagles formed a defensive perimeter around the graveyard while they waited for their Corinn guide to return.

Hippo towered over them, scanning the area for life forms with red lights flitting back and forth. All sense of jocularity passed.

The minutes ticked by slowly, each one seeming to be longer than the last. Sweat bled down Jax's forehead. The temperature had dropped a few degrees but was still over one-ninety. A freaking sauna by any standards. The fact Zang had spent time out here naked without sustaining any injuries was baffling. The Corinns were simply astonishing creatures, physically and mentally.

"Alpha team, do you copy?" Apollo said over the short range comm channel.

"Copy, Eagle One, this is Alpha One, over," Satani replied.

"What's your status?"

"Zang went inside the tunnel a few moments ago."

"Copy that. Command's sending a Clipper to our location with supplies. Hold security outside the Corinn site and report back once Zang returns, over."

"Understood," Satani said. He shook his helmet and raised his rifle again. "Sounds like we might be down here a while, lads. How are your suits all holdin' up?"

"I'm at ninety percent battery, air filter at seventy," Hesh said.

Nadia confirmed high numbers too. Jax was the only one with a low filter reading.

"Must have gotten a broke dick mask," Satani said. "I'll request someone to take your place."

"No, I'm fine, just have them send a new one down," Jax said.

"You got some balls, no offense, or a death wish, don't ya?" Hesh asked. "I reckon that's how you got them legs of yours cut off. Maybe trying to prove yourself?"

"If you call not shying away from combat proving myself, then sure."

Hesh glanced away from his rifle scope. "And what are you, *insinuating,* farmer hick?"

"Give it a rest," Satani said. "You're giving me a migraine."

The ground suddenly rumbled.

"Shit, just what we need, another quake," Nadia said.

The temperature on their HUDs suddenly spiked a few degrees. Steam hissed out of fissures across the ground hundreds of feet away.

"I'm detecting a spike in CH_4 as well as SO_2," reported Hippo. He rotated. Red lights lanced away from his helmet into the darkness and smoke.

Satani bumped on the short-range comms. "Eagle One, this is Alpha One, do you copy? Over."

"Copy, go ahead, Alpha One," Apollo said.

"We're experiencing more seismic activity down here."

"Copy that. If it gets worse, proceed to FOB, over."

The rumble faded away, and the steam vents dissipated. Jax let out a sigh of relief. She shifted her position, trying to get a view down into the tunnel that Zang had gone into, but saw nothing but steam and smoke shifting out of it like the mouth of a dragon.

Maybe Hesh wasn't such a coward after all. Maybe they should all just flee while they had the chance. Jax turned back to the cable, hardly able to make it out from her position.

"Alpha One, SITREP, over."

The voice of the lieutenant crackled over the comm channels, but just as Satani replied, a whooshing roared in the distance. Jax turned to the east, seeing flames blasting out of the ground in the distance. The methane reader on her HUD ticked up.

"I think this is what the LT meant when he said run," Jax said.

All across the eastern field of the crater, flames erupted from the ground. Some of them began to swirl, like the twisters she had seen before.

"Detecting multiple threats, searching for escape route," Hippo said.

Jax held her ground, but only because she had no idea where to move. The vents of fire burst out of the rocky surface, creating new fissures. The world rumbled from the explosions.

"Behind us!" Satani shouted.

Jax turned just as more rocks blew into the air, a geyser of fire and debris raining down. In a matter of a heartbeat, she noticed a pattern to the bursts. The vents were erupting in a circle around the arc and tunnel entrance. Including the dead aliens. It was as if it was some sort of defensive weapon to protect the small tunnel.

But how was that possible?

"Zang!" Jax shouted. "Zang, come back!"

"Fuck this Corinn. I'm not dying for him."

To Jax's surprise, it wasn't Hesh, but Nadia. The Specialist took off running toward the cable resting on the dirt slope of the crater wall.

"Nadia, get back here!" Satani shouted.

"There is not adequate time to reach safety that route," Hippo said.

"We can if we move fast!" Nadia screamed. "Come on!"

Jax and Hesh stood at the ring of corpses with Satani, while the droid strode after Nadia. The immense power of the vents came together a thousand feet away to the east, where flames twisted in the gaseous air. The vortex was already spinning toward their location, expanding all the way to the slope. Grinding came from the enormous power of the growing twister.

Nadia reached the cable and began climbing, moving quickly.

"Here."

The voice was coming from behind Jax. Zang had reemerged at the lip of the tunnel. He raised a long arm, then motioned for them.

The cracked ground continued to break open, venting steam and gases into the air.

Static broke over the comms. "Alpha... the hell... down there," Apollo said. "Give... damn... SITREP!"

The vortex drowned out his voice, screaming louder and louder, like an Ironclad was descending over them.

"On me!" Satani shouted.

He led the way through the graveyard, between the corpses Zang had moved. Hesh lumbered next to Jax.

A scream came over the comms—or maybe that was in the distance.

Jax turned just as she reached the tunnel entrance, sighting up Nadia on the slope. He was halfway up, holding onto the cable when the vortex whipped toward his location. The inferno rose up the rocky side, blasting him off before it hit. A moment later he was completely consumed, gone in the blink of an eye. The edge of the twister reached out toward the arc, blasting the corpses.

"Come," Zang said again, still as calm as ever.

The three Eagles followed the Corinn guide into the tunnel, down a near perfectly sloped ramp that led deep into the ground. Glowing hieroglyphics marked the rock walls. Jax turned back to look at the slope. Hippo was partially blocking her view, but she could see the cable simmering in the dirt.

Nadia was gone. Nothing left at all.

Another quake rumbled across the surface as the superheated wind spun toward them. Jax thought there was something about this area that would be spared, that it was a weapon she couldn't understand. Now she wasn't so sure.

She followed the Eagles deeper into the tunnel, passing those odd glowing script carved into the rock. *Not rock*, she realized. They were inside of an alien construct.

The sound of the storm grew distant, as if they were entering a void. Jax almost didn't hear the voice over the comms.

"Help me!"

"Is that...?" Satani began to say.

Hesh suddenly ran by Jax, heading back up the ramp. "It's Nadia, he's still alive!"

"He will be dead soon," Zang said slowly. "You can't save him."

"Please... help..." Nadia said again over the channel.

Jax and Satani both reached out to Hesh, trying to hold him back. He fought to get out of their grips, but Satani used a boot to knock his knee out, taking him to the ground.

"Hippo, you go!" Jax yelled. "Go, find Nadia."

The droid started back up the ramp while they worked to control Hesh. On his knees, he squirmed, yelling to let him go.

"Hippo will find him, don't worry," Jax said.

Hesh relented, chest heaving in the glow of the odd hieroglyphics.

A whimpering echoed down the ramp a few moments later, like a wounded animal. Grinding followed.

Satani and Jax let Hesh up as Hippo returned, dragging a simmering block of metal somewhat shaped like a human. The legs and arms were at odd angles, the armor scorched.

"N-Nad-Nadia?" Hesh stammered.

He ran up as Hippo gently placed Nadia on the ground. Jax and Satani hurried over, finding the Eagle was somehow alive. How, Jax wasn't sure. The visor was cracked open, exposing a melted face.

"I can't see...I can't see...I smell something...something's burning!" Nadia mumbled.

Hesh bent down to help. "Ah, shit, ah shit man," he said as he tried to open the port on Nadia's left arm, but only ended up prompting a cry of agony.

That arm was broken, along with his other limbs.

"We have to do something," Hesh said. "Hippo, do something, goddammit!"

Satani stood back, probably thinking what Jax was thinking. There was nothing they could do but possibly make him comfortable.

Hippo bent down and accessed the med-port in Nadia's broken arm. A syringe spun out of the droid's finger. It stuck that into the port to administer morphine.

"Hold on, man," Hesh said.

"I can't see..." Nadia said, quieter now. "I can't..."

He took another few ragged breaths.

A "signal lost" notification activated across their HUDs. Jax swallowed hard.

Nadia was gone.

Zang sighed.

Jax had almost forgotten the Corinn was behind her.

Hesh shot up. "He'd still be here if you hadn't disappeared, you fucking weird motherless—"

"Back off," Satani said. He and Jax got in the middle between Zang and Hesh.

"My condolences," said the alien.

"Fuck your cond—"

Grinding cut Hesh off. He turned toward the ramp where an oval shaped door was rising out of the ground.

"Hippo, stop that from closing!" Satani yelled.

The droid lumbered up toward it and reached down to grab the bottom. It tried to lift it back up, straining, but not even the giant war bot could stop the door from shutting. Hippo stumbled back just as the oval piece closed shut with a thud.

The sound echoed like a gong through the tunnel, deeper and deeper.

Hippo stepped away, the red glow from his lights illuminating deep grooves on the otherwise smooth door. When the noise faded away, Zang held a long arm out, purple crystal spheres in his suit spreading light across the door.

There was no mistaking the marks on their side. Someone had tried desperately to get out. Zang either didn't notice or wasn't worried about it. He turned back toward the incline. A thin mist of gas flowed upward.

Jax checked her HUD, seeing SO_2 indicators through the roof.

"Guys, you seeing these readings?" she asked.

Zang started walking down into the cloud. "We must go down there to learn what my kin found," he said.

"Fuck that, and fuck you," Hesh said. "I'm not risking my neck for you another minute."

Jax noticed her filter warning suddenly flashing on her HUD. Her heart thumped faster. Without her mask, she was toast down here if they couldn't get that door open.

Strong and...

This time, not even her motto worked.

She went over to the door in a sudden panic, nearly tripping on Nadia's corpse. An idea blossomed, and Jax bent down.

"What the hell are you doing, Brito?" Hesh asked.

"My filter's red," Jax replied. "Nadia doesn't need his

anymore, and if we're going to be down here a while, I figured he'd be fine with me taking it."

Jax glanced up, but Hesh didn't protest and slowly backed away.

Footsteps echoed behind them as Zang began down the passage.

"Wait," Satani said. "Hippo will go first to see what's down there."

Zang hesitated.

"Move aside," boomed the droid. "I will report back shortly."

The hulking machine lumbered past Zang, vanishing into the cloud of gas.

CHAPTER 23

"You're sure the captain will be there?" Nuke asked.

Rangnar grinned. "If there's one thing I know about Weston, it's he never misses a drink after work. He'll be at the pub, and if for some reason he isn't, I'll find him."

"I've surveyed maps of the area," Lucid said. "The plan the boss came up with will work."

Saber and Nuke didn't look happy about staying back with Blaster. They stood with the droid in front of Rangnar and Lucid in the woods at the base of Mount Norrick.

Twenty-four hours had passed since they had purchased the Wrath beacon from Axel. He had it in a case, tucked inside a backpack slung over his duster coat.

In a few more hours, Rangnar would use it to negotiate his freedom with Weston, then meet the rest of his crew at a rendezvous in Aritrea.

From there, they would take the *Beak* to a new home without the fear of being chased. But now there was another threat, greater than any Eagle. The threat of the greatest enemy in the galaxy—the Wrath.

Rangnar hoped CANDF and Corinn militaries had a damn

good plan to defeat the Wrath again. But he wasn't taking any chances. He had picked a remote colony called Tor on an asteroid that was home to mostly Markas. Lucid had family there and spoke often of her sister and brothers. If they were all going to die in the invasion, at least Rangnar would die with the species he loved.

"Tomorrow we will all be together on Tor," Rangnar said. "Maybe we can get back to a normal life."

"What's a normal life?" Lucid asked.

"A life where we aren't always looking over our shoulders."

"What's the fun in that?" Nuke chirped, playfully wagging both tails. "I'm joking, boss. I'm good with some downtime. Might even find myself a mate."

"Good luck with that," Saber said.

Nuke growled back, his way of laughing.

"Good luck, sire," Blaster said.

Rangnar nodded. "Stay safe, all of you."

He and Lucid took their leave and headed up into the mountains. The climb gave them a breathtaking view of the jay trees. The blue canopy shifted in the light wind under the glow of the moon. Rangnar used it to navigate the treacherous landscape. Lucid had no problem out here, but he was an aging man. Now more than ever he felt the years and scars on his body.

An hour later, Lucid stopped at the foot of a vertical wall that formed a ledge jutting over five hundred feet above them. The mountain peaks towered over it, looming thousands of feet overhead.

"We're almost there," she said.

"You guys set the *Beak* down up there?" Rangnar asked.

"Don't worry, it's out of view."

"I was thinking more about the climb."

"Don't worry about that either, I'll throw a cable down."

"I like that idea."

Rangnar stood by while Lucid took to the wall, climbing it with near ease. She scrambled up like a squirrel on a tree, easily scaling the exterior of the rocks. Wind rustled against Rangnar, blowing his beard.

The sound of crunching leaves caught his ear. In an instant, he drew his hand cannon and swung the barrel at the forest. The blue leaves of a jay tree fluttered to the grass. He scanned the darkness, but his eyes were another thing aging on his body. Ten years ago, he would have been able to make out every shadow. Now he struggled to see in the weak lighting.

Clanking sounded, drawing him back to the ledge. The cable extended and Lucid looked down.

Rangnar turned back to the forest but heard nothing now. He holstered his pistol after another long moment of observation and then began the climb up the cliff. Halfway up, he surveyed the canopy of tree branches creaking and groaning below him. Beyond, the warm glow of lights from Montrane filled the view. The beautiful, ancient city tucked into the rocky hills was one he would miss.

He turned and kept climbing. At the top, Lucid was already removing the stealth tarp from the six-seater transport. Rangnar opened the hatch to the cockpit and settled into the worn leather. With a flip of two switches, the dual engines rumbled to life.

"Ready?" he asked Lucid.

"When you are," she replied.

Rangnar performed a final flight check, then grabbed the yoke. He gently moved it, pulling the ship off the rock. A magnificent view of the city came into focus.

"See you soon," he whispered to the other Markas. Turning the yoke, he rotated the ship then blasted into the clouds drifting over the mountains. He watched the radar, making sure their quick launch hadn't attracted any attention.

So far, nothing.

The flight to Hex Prime would take only ten minutes at max speed, but he took his time, hugging the mountains and keeping out of sight the best he could. Thirty minutes later, he eased off the thrusters, and waited for a view of the human capital city.

He recited his death rules in his mind.

Never trust a human. Never risk your life for loot. Always have multiple escape routes. Blend in. Be prepared for anything.

The last one was what he focused on the most today, even if it meant slitting Weston's throat for betraying him.

Lucid tapped the dashboard, relaying their forged flight data, and their requested destination to the control tower.

"Thank you, *Blue Tiger*, you're cleared for landing. Please proceed to auto-pilot mode," came the robotic voice of an AI.

That was good news. If it had been a human voice, that would mean they had attracted unwanted attention. Rangnar had done everything he could to cover their trails. He turned the controls over to auto and took in the view.

The distant towers of Aritrea rose across the horizon, their metal and glass tips touching the clouds. It was the perfect blend of human and alien architecture among the mountains. In the distance, he could make out the Bronze Keep.

The *Beak*, posing as the *Blue Tiger*, dipped toward the destination Rangnar had spent an hour deciding on before leaving the bunker in Montrane. The landing zone was in a field by a lake on the eastern border of the sprawling city. There were several other small ships and vehicles parked there.

As the transport lowered over the field, he saw the rows of biodomes he had selected as their rendezvous. In a few hours, if all went to plan, the other hunters would meet him and Lucid here and take the *Beak* to Tor.

The transport set down with a thud. Rangnar unbuckled his harness. Lucid opened the hatch and jumped out. They started right for a path that led out of the park. The passengers of the other ships and vehicles were enjoying the lake and flowers of the late hour.

He scanned for threats as he hurried with Lucid. She led the way, cutting through alleys and avoiding the main arteries, just like Rangnar had taught her when she was just a pup.

Aritrea truly was a remarkable city, unlike most Rangnar had been to over the years. The green spaces, flower gardens, parks for kids, and unique architecture was truly a prize of the human empire.

He hated to think what would happen if the Wrath reached this place. Shaking the thought away, he followed Lucid to a large courtyard with a bubbling fountain twenty feet tall. She stopped in an alley that overlooked the open space. Tables packed full of patrons were set on the stone terraces outside of eateries and bars. Most people had finished dinner and were enjoying cocktails or wine.

Rangnar searched for the bar Weston was known to frequent. He spotted the logo of The Bronze Mug, where they had met over a decade ago.

After a quick scan for Eagle patrols, he turned to Lucid. "If something goes wrong, you head to the rendezvous. Take the *Beak* to Tor," he instructed. "Do you understand?"

Lucid nodded.

He set his backpack on the ground and pulled out the Wrath beacon then tucked it under his duster. It bulged slightly, but not too bad.

"You sure about this?" Lucid asked.

"Yes," he replied.

"I got a bad feeling."

She nudged her large head up against his shoulder in an embrace. He stroked her furry back and tapped the coat over her back.

"I love you, Rangnar," Lucid said. "Thank you for everything you've done for me."

They were words Rangnar hadn't heard for many years. And they were words he hadn't spoken himself for even longer.

"I love you too, but don't worry," he said. "This is the beginning of a fresh start."

Then he was up and striding into the courtyard. Keeping his breathing calm, Rangnar focused on his surroundings and the mission.

When he saw Weston, he knew they were all that much closer to securing their freedom. Rangnar kept his head low, duster hood pulled up, and hand inside on the case, constantly checking for Eagles. The square, though, seemed like mostly civilians just enjoying a late dinner and drinks. Not a single Eagle patrolled in full uniform out here and he didn't see any undercovers.

Weston was by himself, sitting on a stool facing a bar with a smart wall displaying a bug match from the stadium in Hex Prime. He didn't even seem to notice Rangnar walking up or standing next to him.

The captain had gotten soft over the years, probably from being off the battlefield and inside an office.

"Buy ya a beer?" Rangnar asked. He took a seat on the stool with his back to the bar and eyes on the entrance.

Weston began to get up, but Rangnar nudged him with the barrel of his laser pistol under his jacket. "Not happy to see me?"

"Surprised, is all," Weston said. He glanced out over the courtyard before easing back onto his seat. "Brazen move, but you always were overconfident. You got a huge bounty on your head right now. Coming here is beyond—"

"That because of you?"

"What?" Weston stared at him and firmly said, "No."

Rangnar had heard many lies in his life, from the best liars in the galaxy. He knew Weston well enough to know this wasn't a lie. The old bastard would be shaking if it were.

Still, he kept the barrel pressed against his gut, ready to blast his insides over the bar.

"I'll make this quick, old friend. I have something that could get you promoted a few times over again," Rangnar said. "A Wrath device that I came into possession of which is unique in nature. Unlike anything we've ever seen."

Weston raised a brow and took a drink from his mug. "I'm listening," he said.

"It's a message in Wrath," Rangnar explained. "It seems to be a countdown."

Weston lowered his mug. "Countdown to what?"

"To their return, would be my guess, but I suppose there are lab jockeys at the CEI that would have a better idea than me."

"How long have you had this?"

"Not long."

Weston took another drink. "Why you bringing this to me?"

"Because you can get me a pardon, and I'm willing to hand it over to wipe my slate clean."

A patron walked by, eyeing them both, and snorting.

Rangnar held his pistol steady, waiting for them to pass.

"The Corinns want you too," Weston said. "The bounty is joint. You killed one of them on Optus."

"She was trying to kill me."

"Look, if that artifact is what you say it is, I'm sure CAID will be willing to turn a blind eye, but that means you got to trust me."

"Trust is earned, old friend." He slowly pulled the barrel back from Weston and handed out the case with the Wrath beacon. As Weston took it, Rangnar retrieved a nano-beetle from his pocket that he had taken from his bunker in Montrane.

Before Weston could react, he placed it under the Eagle's exposed wrist.

"The hell is that?" asked the captain, turning his forearm.

"A guarantee. You sell me out, you die a very painful death."

Rangnar would have to thank the Steward kid for this idea.

"Seriously?" Weston asked. "Come on man, this isn't funny."

"Don't be so dramatic," Rangnar said. "It will de-activate in five days, plenty of time to get that pardon. If you don't...well...been nice knowing you, partner."

Weston glanced up. "You're not a very likeable person, you know that?"

"I've been told such."

"I guess I do still owe you for saving my life."

"I couldn't let a dumb kid die, could I?"

Weston chuckled. "I deserved it for what I did that day."

"Rushing a Steward with a fire sword? Yeah, that was probably the craziest and stupidest thing I ever saw."

"I almost had him..."

Rangnar thought back to that moment when Weston had sparred with a Steward they had found hiding on a jungle planet. Back then, Weston was an excellent swordsman, but lacked the strength of the Steward, which gave the warrior an upper hand. Weston ended up head deep in the swamp, nearly drowned by the time Rangnar showed up on his mud crawler bike. He used it to slam into the Steward, knocking him into the mud. The rest of the platoon surged the downed warrior and took him captive.

"You stay in that chair for another hour," Rangnar said. "If you don't, and if I get any wind of you trying to report my position before I'm gone, I will have you shot by the Marka sniper watching us."

Weston frowned. "Really?"

"Don't try me," Rangnar said. "On this or the nano-beetle."

"If what you say is true, I need to get this artifact to my CO as soon as possible."

"An hour won't change the fate of the galaxy, but it will change yours."

"Guess you'd better get moving then." Weston reached out with his hand. Rangnar shook it, and then backed away. As soon as he was outside, he turned, and he didn't look back.

His heart had settled by the time he got into the alley. Lucid moved ahead and Rangnar smiled. He grabbed his bag and pulled out his helmet. Placing it over his head, he then brought up his HUD which connected to the camera Lucid had installed on a rooftop while he was talking to Weston.

The live feed revealed the captain was sitting right where Rangnar had left him. If he did betray them, at least Rangnar would know, even though there would be no sniper in place that would blast his face off.

"Okay, let's go," Rangnar said.

Lucid led the way back through the city. They made good pace through the back alleys and narrow streets. It was getting late, nearing midnight. Nuke, Saber, and Blaster would be at the rendezvous shortly with the last of their supplies.

Rangnar checked his HUD multiple times, confirming each time that Weston remained in his seat. Forty-five minutes after leaving the Bronze Mug, he was closing in on the biodomes with Lucid. They didn't have long, but it was enough to grab the crew and get to the *Beak* to blast off.

"Almost there," he said.

They came out of an alley at the street separating them from the park. On the hill, in the moonlight, were the glass sides of the biodomes. Lucid waited for his order to cross the road. A pair of trucks rumbled past in both directions while they stayed in the shadows. The park was mostly abandoned, but he saw a few couples holding hands and a random guy smoking a pipe of Corinn honey.

Rangnar checked the HUD one last time, seeing Weston still in his seat.

"Okay, go," he said.

Lucid darted across the road with Rangnar running after her. They took a path curving up through the green space, passing under a thick grove of jay trees and then a terrace bordered with barb bushes, a rose with purple petals and curved six-inch thorns.

When they reached the Biodomes, they still had ten minutes before Weston would get up. Rangnar figured he would take another few minutes if he was going to betray them. It was time to hurry.

Lucid trotted up toward the entrance to the first biodome in a row of five. The entrances were supposed to be closed to protect the plants from the cool temperatures that came with night. All of them were except for dome three. That was their rendezvous and meant his companions had arrived.

A grin crossed his face as he walked up to the door with Lucid. They entered to the chemical smell of fertilizer. Flowers and potted plants framed the dark round room. In the center of the space stood Saber.

The Marka was on all fours, looking right at them.

"You good?" Rangnar asked. "Where's Nuke and Blaster?"

Saber's eyes went to Lucid, then to Rangnar, and then back and forth.

A warning! Rangnar realized.

He sniffed in that chemical smell again. This wasn't fertilizer.

Saber suddenly went up in flames, burning right in front of Rangnar. He charged toward the creature, ripping off his duster and throwing it over his friend. Lucid chirped behind him, but it wasn't until he'd tossed the jacket over Saber that he saw figures rushing through the entrance at them.

Footsteps pounded the ground behind them. More men rushed into the room, all dressed in civilian clothes, including the one Rangnar had seen smoking Corinn honey.

Heart pounding, and mind firing like an automatic laser rifle, he patted Saber down, trying to stop the flames as the alien howled.

The flames spread, burning Rangnar too. He held on for another second before he was forced to drop the Marka. As he let go, Saber's body fell apart, turning to ashes with the coat.

Only one thing could do that, a Wrath dart. A weapon that paralyzed the victim before burning them alive.

His breaking heart flipped at the sight of another pile to the left.

"Nuke..." he whispered.

Rangnar pulled out his pistol and brought it up but didn't get the chance to fire. An electrical charge tore into him, knocking him to the ground and forcing him to watch as two of the men beat Lucid down with batons.

"NO!" Rangnar screamed. He fought the electrical current, but it was too much, causing him to jerk and foam at the mouth.

The men formed a circle around him, and now he saw the armor under their ripped clothing. These weren't thieves or pirates. They were Eagles.

"Where is it!"

The voice came from behind but walked in front of Rangnar. This wasn't just any Eagle. This was General Gabriel Jessup.

"Where is it!" he shouted again.

He held a deactivated fire sword and motioned for two of his men to bring Lucid to him. They dragged her over as she yelped, and squirmed.

"Let...her...go," Rangnar stammered.

The sword went to her neck.

"Tell me where it is, or she dies, then you die," Gabriel said.

Rangnar managed to push himself to his knees, feeling a laser barrel at the back of his helmet. He took it off slowly, trying to buy time.

"I won't ask you again, Rangnar Soki," Gabriel said. "Where is it?"

Rangnar glared at the scarred face of the leader of Dark Horse Company. The Steward killers and thugs of the galaxy. He knew the only way to save Lucid was to give him what he wanted.

"Let her go, and I'll tell you," he said.

"Come on, Phantom man, you know me well enough to know I don't negotiate. Now tell me what the fuck I want to know," Gabriel said.

Rangnar hesitated another moment, then admitted the truth. "I gave the Wrath beacon to Captain Weston an hour ago at the Bronze Cup," he said.

"*Beacon?* Don't fuck with me, old man. I don't have time for your tricks."

He angled the sword down closer to Lucid's throat.

"In three seconds, I'm turning this on," Gabriel said.

"No, stop, please!" Rangnar begged. "I'm telling the truth about the beacon."

"I'm talking about the Steward bastard! Where is he?"

Realization passed over Rangnar. The general wasn't looking for the Wrath artifact. He was looking for Axel.

CHAPTER 24

Green lights danced across the northern skies of Jolia. Axel thought back to his youth on Earth, when he had watched the northern lights. They were mesmerizing back then, but they paled in comparison to the magnificent display of green and purple rays glistening in the sky here.

He sighed as he stood on the platform in front of the *Trash Squid*, his breath fogging up the inside of his helmet. Without it and his suit, he would freeze to death. The temperature had plummeted to a negative fifty degrees Fahrenheit.

The only lifeforms still in the port were Jukes. Their scaly bodies had transitioned from red to blue, allowing them to endure the hostile conditions. Teams of three worked on picking up trash and cleaning the piers of now frozen flesh from catches of the prior day.

None of them seemed to notice Axel as he sat, his legs dangling off the platform of his ship, listening to ancient Earth techno music through the speakers in his helmet. They drowned out the cracking noise echoing across the port as the ocean continued to freeze.

The water had formed frazil, icicle-like shards on the

surface. Waves brought them to shore where they cracked against each other under the hoisted fishing trawlers. As the temperature continued to get colder, the spray from the waves turned to ice in mid-air, hitting the ground and shattering, building a shoreline of pale broken shards.

In a few hours, the water would freeze for as far as he could see, and then the sun would rise, and melt it all. The circle of life was a brutal one on this planet.

He should have been sleeping, but rest was difficult now that he had unlocked one of the biggest keys to his past. And while he had always longed to know about his father, he now feared what else he would find if he uncovered any more.

Still, the curiosity that had always driven Axel, itched in his soul. He turned off the music, and switched to the post from Achilles about Stewards. The synthetic deep male voice narrated the text into his helmet, starting where he had left off.

> *For the first time, the Stewards felt the excitement and pride of taking on a worthy enemy.*
>
> *But on first contact, in the purple fields of a meadow on the planet Corinnia, an entire squad of the so-called immortal Stewards walked into an ambush of hundreds of Spectres that had burrowed under the ground. Overwhelmed, they fell, one by one, their blood staining the alien soil to the last man.*
>
> *Another squad was blasted by waves of flaming radioactive juices from the eye sockets of the flying Hydras. When Steward reinforcements arrived, all that remained of the golden armor, muscles, and dense bones of their brothers was a black meadow of ash.*
>
> *Most stood their ground in the face of certain death in the battles that followed, but there were some that did the unfathomable—they retreated. It became apparent to the scientists the stock of genetically modified warriors had a flaw, a crack in*

the design. The human and Corinn leaders met in secret, deciding victory could only be attainable through extreme measures. Stewards would need to shed all access to human emotion. Fear would be erased, but so would mercy and forbearance. A secret serum was transported to the legions of warriors and given before the battle for the great Crystal City on Corinnia, under the guise of an added endurance booster. It was here they won their first solid victory, driving the Wrath back into a crater, saving countless Corinn lives.

Axel felt a chill run up his back. His father had been there, had helped lead that charge. Had helped the civilians make it out of the city.

For a moment, he felt a different emotion about his dad—a hint of pride.

Captivated, he continued listening.

The Stewards did not watch in silence, nor did they cheer in victory. Fleeing Corinns claimed they heard laughter from some of the warriors. It seemed something had changed in that victory, but at first, no one, not even the Stewards seemed to understand.

For months they adapted on the battlefield, learning about their new enemy. They fought valiantly against this invading horde until they gained the upper hand. The Wrath, having lost millions of their own, retreated from Corinnia and Eern. Their jagged, rocky ships fired back into the darkness of unchartered space, pursued by a single Steward vessel to ensure they would never return.

Weeks passed, months, then a year. The Wrath did not return. Nor did the Steward ship.

Peace was declared throughout the galaxy and the ten thousand surviving Steward warriors returned to Hex Prime where they were greeted as heroes. But what happens when the perfect killing tool has nothing left to kill? For the first time in generations, the warriors found themselves without a real enemy, and scientists had not the forethought to plan a life for their super soldiers in peace. The Tunnels connecting them to Corinn ancestors opened the floodgates to the next battleground for Stewards—their minds. The serum they had taken to make them fearless butchers had corrected a battlefield flaw but added new ones that surfaced in the absence of violence.

The Stewards had been created with a thirst for battle, a bloodlust so powerful, that once it was triggered, nothing could stop it. In the past, on a distant planet, in the midst of a dire war, the killing was glorious. No longer terrifying, but logical. There were rules. In a peaceful society, that military logic could translate to a dozen men slaughtered over a disagreement gone too far with Stewards in a bar, but it could also mean worse. Women, children, a group of civilians that got caught in the middle of Stewards on a rampage—anything living that was too close to flee might be wiped out.

When the "battle" was done and the Stewards stood among the bodies, covered in gore and wiping the blood out of their eyes, laughing maniacally, the fury would return over having no one left to kill. Like a malfunctioning robot, some shut down, collapsing where they stood when they realized what they had done. Upon awakening, they'd have no idea what had happened. Just an ominous sense of dread that something terrible had taken place, and that they had somehow been the cause.

It didn't take many incidents like that—a town square, a shopping district, a school—before the heroes who'd brought peace to the galaxy became the biggest threat to that peace. It was clear that such creatures were not fit to live in the society they had created. Some proposed sending them to a planet of their own, far away from the civilized worlds. Others wondered if they could be retrained somehow. Some suggested that if their genes could be modified for war, perhaps they could now be modified for peace.

No. That wouldn't work. It was a tragedy, but it was decided that the only possible solution was eradication.

Some Stewards volunteered, sunken in guilt and afraid of what they might do. Others fought as it was what they were born to do. Some tried to hide, but over time, most were found. How could such a monster hide?

All were hunted to the edge of the galaxy. It took decades, but eventually it was believed every single Steward had been eradicated.

"All except one," Axel whispered.

He watched the northern lights, thinking about what he knew about his father from all the visions. In them, he had seen everything that this narrative described. Stewards standing bravely against daunting odds, fighting and dying so others could live. But also the scene in the market where a drunk Steward bashed a patron's head in. Then at the mining colony where Woolies had been slaughtered, their limbs plucked off like shrimp tails.

Axel had never seen any in which his father had personally done anything but protect innocents, but that didn't mean he had seen everything. Or that his father was innocent of evil.

The only way to find out the truth was to open that Tunnel again. But that required anger...rage. No, he would rather not know than risk that.

Axel would continue to choose the path his mother had set him upon.

He exhaled and tried to refocus his mind. But doing so was nearly impossible. Not just because of the truth about his father.

Everything felt like it was closing in around him, from the human monsters his mother had warned him about, to the alien monsters that could very well be returning to finish what they started thirty-five years ago.

Try choosing peace when the Wrath show up, Axel thought.

A soft voice caught him off guard.

"Beautiful out here," Luna said. She walked up next to Axel, also dressed in a vacuum rated suit. "You want some company?" she asked.

"Yeah, sure." Axel nodded. "Can't sleep?"

"Worried about you, Captain." She sat next to him, dangling her legs over the raised tarmac edge.

"Why? I'm fine," he said.

"You're just out here star gazing?"

"Yeah."

"You know I can smell your lies like a Wooly fart."

Axel laughed. "I'm that bad, really?"

"What's bothering you? I know there's something you're not telling me."

"Worried about the Wrath."

"We've lived under the threat of their return our entire lives," she said. "It's something more than that. I've known you a long time. Be honest with me."

Axel looked over at Luna. She had always treated him with respect, since the day she found him digging through the trash compactor.

If anyone deserved honesty, it was her, but he still couldn't bring himself to tell her everything. Perhaps because he didn't even understand things.

"It wasn't just what the Wooly mechanics said, it was something Rangnar told me," he admitted.

"What?"

"To get away from civilization."

"Maybe he meant because we could be hunted by—"

"It was more than that, Luna."

She sighed and looked back up toward the sky.

They sat there in silence, enjoying the peace, each of them knowing this very well could be the calm before a very violent storm. A storm that could change the entire galaxy.

"You know, the day I lost my parents, I thought my life was over," Luna said. "You saved me from the darkness of that loss. We've been through a lot together, Axel, and whatever comes next, I'm with you."

"You saved me too."

She reached out, brushing her armored finger against his wrist. He could almost feel the warmth of her touch through his suit. For years, he had resisted his true feelings for her, feelings that could put their professional relationship in jeopardy, their friendship, and the entire ship, for that matter.

He imagined holding her hand, leading her back to his quarters. No matter how hard he tried, in moments like this he couldn't suppress the burning connection he felt. It was even more intense than that raw, angry voice in his mind.

Harder to fight, less reason to fight it.

Axel stood and looked up at the flashing greens and purples. Then he reached down to Luna. She took his hand and she stood next to him, turning right into him.

The voice of Brayton surged over the comms. "Captain."

Axel swallowed, still staring at Luna through his visor.

"Captain, you copy?" Brayton said again.

"Yeah, go ahead," Axel said.

He rotated to the *Trash Squid*, seeing Cricket in a porthole watching over Axel like he always watched. If any of the crew knew about Axel and Luna, it was the Marka.

"I need you back on the bridge," Brayton said, his voice laced with fatigue. "Need to show you something."

"This can't be good," Axel muttered.

They both hurried back to the ship. On the bridge, Brayton was rubbing the sleep from his eyes. He stood as Axel and Luna entered.

"What is it?" Axel asked.

"A high value target was captured on Hex Prime, in Montrane," Brayton said. "Didn't think much of it until I found this."

Axel walked over to look at a screen.

"Witnesses reported seeing Markas being killed by Eagles in undercover clothing," Brayton said.

Axel looked at Luna.

"You think it's Rangnar?" she asked.

"Brayton, any way to know for sure?" Axel asked.

"No, sir, but I would bet on it."

Uga stumbled into the room, pulling up his pants.

Spartacus was the next one to walk in, holding up his new arm, and studying it like a child might an insect.

"Captain, I cannot thank you enough," he said. "I am still working on the wiring, but it is close to perfection."

"Good, you might need it soon."

"You think so?"

"If that's Rangnar who was captured," Luna said.

The crew waited while Axel thought about what to do. In his mind, there was only one choice. "Lieutenant, get the ship ready to depart," he ordered. "Spartacus, Cricket, you're with me. We're going to get the Tech-N early while the rest of the crew heads to Dari."

The droid and Cricket both walked over to Axel.

"Wait, we're splitting up?" Luna asked.

"Yes, it's too dangerous to sit here any longer," Axel said. "You go ahead to Dari—"

"But—"

"That's an order, Lieutenant," Axel said. "You have command of the ship, XO."

"Yes, sir." Luna stood straighter. "Good luck, Captain."

"Same to you."

They exchanged a long glance. This time, there was no sense of peace in that look, as there had been on the shoreline earlier. This was all business. Their lives, and the lives of their crew depended on their professionality, another reminder of why they could never be together.

Axel turned and left for the cargo hold at a brisk pace. Along the way, he looked back to Spartacus.

"I've never said this before to you, but things have changed," Axel said.

"Correct. I have two arms now."

"And I was serious about you having to use them." Axel opened the hatch where he had stored the forgite bars. "Cricket, you take these and hold them until I tell you to bring them. Spartacus and I will head over to finish the deal."

"Got it, Commendatore," Cricket said.

Dressed in their suits, they opened the exterior bay doors. A ramp extended and the trio hurried down into the freezing night. They stepped onto the tarmac as Luna activated the engines on the *Trash Squid*.

"All systems green, ready for departure," she reported.

"See you on Dari."

By the time they got to the hangars, they had lifted off. Axel watched the ship blast into the night, for the first time in his career, with half of his crew.

"Outlaw 1, Outlaw 1, this is Alpha 1, do you copy, over?" Satani said.

Jax listened on the comm channel but knew there would be no response. They had spent the past three hours in the tunnel with no external contact. Hippo had headed deeper to explore and scan.

Zang stood with his blades drawn, looking down the slope in Hippo's direction. Jax went over to Hesh and Satani who stood near the sealed door. The marks looked too weak, too tame for a Wrath. They were more likely to have been left by Corinns. The same ones who had clawed their own eyes out, perhaps.

Something terrible had happened to them, and Jax feared the same would happen to her squad soon. She went from the scratch marks to the hieroglyphics on the wall.

"Yo, Corinn," Hesh said.

Zang turned slightly.

"Tell us how to open this door," Hesh said.

"I would if I knew," replied Zang. "This is a Wrath construct."

"Construct?" Hesh said.

Clanking rapped in the distance, echoing up toward them. All three soldiers raised their weapons and Zang moved out of the way. Jax couldn't deny feeling the hot stab of fear, especially now, knowing they were inside something built by Wrath. She tried to make out the rap in the oddly quiet passage. What she heard wasn't the scratch of claws or roar of monsters, but rather the tap of metal on stone.

The red glow of Hippo's helmet came into focus, and they slowly lowered their weapons.

"Well shit, I never thought I'd be happy to see the tin can," Hesh said.

"What did you find?" Satani asked.

Hippo halted right in front of them. "There is a large chamber one thousand feet below us. The atmosphere changed significantly the lower I proceeded," he said. "I detected higher levels of SO_2 and CH_4."

"What's the purpose of the chamber?" Satani asked.

"Inconclusive."

Satani checked down the tunnel then looked back toward the sealed door. "Help isn't coming," he said. "Far as the LT's concerned, we're dead, so we might as well see if we can find a different way out."

"Agreed," Jax said.

"What about Nadia?" Hesh asked.

"We'll have to come back for him later," Jax said.

Hesh shook his helmet, bent down, and said his goodbyes. As soon as he was up, the group started down the tunnel.

Beams from their suits and rifles lanced through the stale atmosphere as they marched down the smooth ramp. The tap of their boots sounded muffled on the path into the abyss. The quiet just made Jax tense up even more. She moved heel to toe, rifle at her shoulder, scanning the shadows.

About five hundred feet later, they came across a section of passage with Corinn crates scattered across the ground. Two of them were open, but the contents were gone.

Zang kept going.

There was more equipment on the way down, but what Jax noticed most was the increase in the sulfur dioxide levels on her HUD. She closed her eyes briefly and thanked Nadia for the new filter. The unit read eighty-percent and was undamaged.

Zang halted ahead. "Here," he said, holding out his arm again. The light from his jewels spread outward. Satani and Jax moved up with Hesh to the end of the tunnel which opened to the chamber Hippo had discovered.

The soldiers stood there with their rifles aimed outward, their tactical lights spearing across the black bowl, unable to pierce all the way through the wall of darkness.

"This place is massive," Satani said.

Jax walked over to the edge and angled her rifle down. The beam hit the bottom.

"Hey, wait up," Hesh said.

Zang was already taking a curving walkway down to the left. It was only four feet wide, just big enough for Hippo. He stayed put while the group went down the ramp in single file, their weapons raking back and forth. Jax noticed the chamber had the same smooth walls as the tunnel they had entered. But there was something else down here.

"You seeing this?" Satani asked.

"Yeah, what is it?" Hesh asked.

From where Jax stood, it appeared there was a jagged pillar rising from a layer of mist drifting across the bottom. There were four, from what she could see. Only they weren't connected to anything. When the soldiers got to the ground, it became crystal clear that the forty-foot-tall beams centered in the chamber were hovering *above* the mist.

"I've never been anywhere like this," Satani whispered.

There were more pieces higher above that they couldn't see from the ramp. Three curved sections and a single sharp object, like an arrowhead.

"Are those things really float—" Hesh began to say.

"Oh shit! Look at that!" Satani said in a voice just shy of a shout. He angled his light at something attached to the exterior of the hovering rocks.

Jax went directly underneath, narrowing her eyes at the most gruesome sight she had seen in her career as an Eagle.

Splattered against the smooth rocks were the body parts of Corinns, evident by what was left of long limbs and fingers, and elongated heads.

"That is some fucked up shit, man, fucked up shit!" Hesh said.

Jax looked up to Hippo. "This is what you saw earlier?" she called up.

"Yes, Sergeant."

"Thanks for the warning," Satani remarked.

Zang paced beneath it all while glancing up. The Eagles surrounded him, roving their rifles in all directions. The wall of red light from Hippo's scanners spread out, hitting the different alien body parts splattered on the rocks.

Jax angled her rifle up at a pillar, the light capturing more of the hieroglyphics engraved into the smooth rock. They slowly moved around the room with their Corinn guide.

"Zang, do you know what those rocks are?" Satani asked.

He didn't respond, but he was visibly disturbed as evidenced by his irregular gait.

"Hey," Satani said. "I asked you a damn question, and I'm sick of not getting any fucking answers."

The Corinn paused, then turned to Satani.

"I know as much—as little as you do," Zang replied. "To answer these questions, I need to locate the data my people left behind."

He pulled one of the blue jewels from his armor and held it up. The tiny device sprouted wings and zipped away, glowing a bright purple as it searched the room.

A clicking rang out, followed by a hissing noise.

"What was that?" Hesh asked.

"Hippo, you got anything up there?" Satani asked.

The purple device continued to fly across the room. It lowered, and in the bright emission, Jax saw it had discovered more Corinn crates and some sort of pedestal with tubes snaking away from it.

There was also something else lying in the mist she couldn't make out. Something metal, perhaps a droid. She turned toward another hissing sound that seemed to be coming from the floor.

Zang walked over to the equipment.

A low tremor shook the chamber. Satani raised a fist and the Eagles halted.

"Contact detected, contact detected," Hippo called down. The red light from its visor formed a solid line, firing right over to Zang. The Corinn bent down to a knee.

Jax and Satani raised their rifles at the Corinn, and Hesh strode over with his minigun leveled.

"What is it?" Satani called out. "What did you find?"

Hesh suddenly cried out and fell through the floor. Satani rushed over and grabbed him by the shoulders as he screamed. Jax joined them, her light shining down as she helped him haul Hesh back out.

The big man got to his feet, breathing heavily and shaking as he raised his minigun up. Jax crouched to look down into the hole, her HUD scanner reporting another spike in SO_2 and methane levels.

"Watch your steps," Satani said. "Come on."

They pushed through the rising cloud of gas over to Zang. The Corinn was still on a knee, half of his body illuminated in the red light from Hippo.

"Watch our backs up there," Satani said.

"Weapons online," the droid replied. "Standing by for orders."

Jax passed the metal she had seen earlier. It was a Corinn war droid, disabled, by the looks of it. But there was something else a few feet away, and this was still moving right in front of Zang.

He had his hands on the upper half of another Corinn, this one a female, judging by the braided hair with jewels woven into the thick mane. Jax halted when she got within view, unable to comprehend what she was seeing.

The alien had nothing left below her hips. But there were

no entrails, no stringy flesh or any blood present. Whatever had cut off the bottom half had sealed the wound and left nothing behind.

Zang had one hand on the back of the injured Corinn and the other on his helmetless head. Emerald eyes focused on Jax as she slowly approached.

"As LT says, Fuckin-A," Hesh said when he arrived.

Zang was whispering something to the other Corinn as she tried to speak out of pale lips. Satani raised a hand for the Eagles to fall back and give them space.

Jax stood there, trying to understand what was happening—trying to understand how she had ended up here. On a ruined planet in an underground chamber where supernatural physics had suspended tons of rock in the poisonous air with alien body parts glued to the sides, and half a Corinn who somehow still breathed.

The alien finally spoke, the words croaking out of her mouth.

"Destroy...ma—"

A fiery glow suddenly blasted the chamber from the walls. The heat skyrocketed on her HUD as Jax spun, her heart pounding. The walls glowed a bright orange, like a furnace was burning behind them.

Concussions rang out, violently shaking the floor and walls. Jax heard them, but she didn't *feel* them like she should have. The chamber seemed to be insulated from the blasts. All of the smooth, glowing walls and dome held, not a single crack forming. And those rocks just hovered above, each of them glowing like candles, pulsating around the pieces of Corinns.

Jax noticed a set of legs—the same legs that had once been attached to the woman Zang was crouched next to.

"Guys...guys are y-you seeing this!?" Hesh yelled.

Zang suddenly stood and pulled out both of his fire swords.

Skittering resonated into the chamber, but where from, Jax wasn't sure. She turned in all directions, scanning for life forms. She raised her rifle, moved her finger to the trigger, and prepared to kill whatever was out there.

But what she saw next made her question if that would be possible.

The lower half of the Corinn body *stood* in the center of the room, walked over to the woman and lay down. As if guided by an invisible surgeon, the leg section burned against her torso, reattaching.

Jax blinked twice and shook her head, but the view remained the same.

How could they possibly kill what had already died?

CHAPTER 25

Rangnar screamed as the electrical jolt passed through his body. Pain throbbed across his limbs, spread out into an X on a platform that could spin him like a wheel. It was centered in the middle of a small room with gray walls and a single recessed light in the ceiling.

He coughed and took in a scent of burning hair. His head fell to his chest, the tendrils of his beard smoldering against his tattered shirt. He had been in here for what seemed like hours now, but he wasn't exactly sure how much time had passed since he was ambushed on Hex Prime.

Rangnar flinched at the thought of Saber burning in his arms, and the pile of ash that was Nuke. He still wasn't sure what had happened to Blaster, but chances were good the robot had been scrapped for T-Flesh.

The only thing that kept him fighting the torture was Lucid, and the hope she was still alive somewhere.

A tear fell from his eye, plummeting to the ground as the hatch to the room hissed open.

The wheel turned, flipping him upside down to a view of the scarred face of General Gabriel Jessup.

Rangnar fought the restraints, earning himself another zap.

"You should take it easy," Gabriel said as he strode inside. "I don't want your heart to give out."

He tilted his head, studying Rangnar's body briefly while the pain from the shock dimmed.

"The legendary Rangnar "Phantom" Soki," he said deeply. "The man who kicked off a career by hunting Stewards. How ironic it must be for you to find yourself here now, your life hanging in the balance because you know where the last Steward is but choose not to reveal that location. All you have to do is give him up, and I make the pain go away."

Pain from torture or death by poison, Rangnar thought through the agony.

"I know you know where that Steward cum stain is," Gabriel said angrily. "We know he came to Tecca. We know he then brought you to Montrane, but my spies lost him there. They picked you back up in Aritrea, but found no sign of him."

Rangnar thought of how Axel had come to him honorably, spared his life, and let him go. There weren't many people—let alone a Steward—who would have done that. Most would have slit Rangnar's throat to keep him quiet forever and collected the bounty on his head.

Part of Rangnar wanted to protect Axel, but he also had Lucid to think about. If she was alive, he would save her if it meant giving up the Steward.

"Where's Lucid?" Rangnar mumbled. "I am not saying shit until I know she's okay."

"Alive, but how long she remains that way is up to you."

A shutter opened in the small quarters, revealing a glass wall. On the other side, Lucid was strung up like Rangnar on another wheel.

"Give her a jolt," Gabriel said to whoever was listening.

"NO!" Rangnar shouted.

Too late.

Lucid jerked and spasmed in the other room. She chirped loud enough he could hear her through the glass wall.

"Stop! Please, stop!" he shouted in an increasingly hoarse voice.

After another agonizing moment, Gabriel raised a hand. Lucid's fur sizzled, smoking in multiple spots. Somehow, she remained conscious.

Rangnar's head slipped down to his chest again.

Gabriel reached out and grabbed him by the cheeks, jerking his head up, pulling patches of scorched beard from his jaw. He squeezed until his knuckles were white.

"Tell me *where* the Steward went," he growled. "You have one last chance. The Marka dies next, then you." He pushed harder, his own face turning red, his black eyes staring deeply into Rangnar's.

The pain grew worse when Rangnar smiled.

"Suck Wooly asshole," he said.

Gabriel let go and backhanded him, knocking his head to the side. Lucid chirped in the other room. As Rangnar looked up, the general raised his hand.

A shock lanced through Rangnar, burning him inside and out. This one was more intense than the others. He gritted his teeth but couldn't keep his jaw closed. It popped open, releasing a shrill of agony.

Rangnar jerked against the platform, his body pressing against the restraints that burned into his skin. Then it was over, the electrical charge fading, and his voice cracking. He hung there, gasping for air. The scent of burned hair hit his nostrils, making him choke. His eyes felt like they were bulging as he looked up.

"Again," said the general.

The next jolt ripped into Rangnar with a powerful force

that snapped his head back. Blood vessels burst in his eyes, burning his eyes and blurring his vision. He fought the pain by thinking of Saber, Nuke, and all his crew.

They had suffered because of him. Because he had chosen this life. Perhaps this was what he deserved.

When the agony receded, his head slumped to his chest. His shirt had ripped over the scars beneath his frizzly gray hair.

His eyes went down to the small beetle on his flesh. The general glanced down at him, following his gaze before he could lift it away.

Gabriel reached out as Rangnar tried to pull back, but he was too weak, bound too tightly. The general tore his shirt fully open, exposing the nano-beetle.

"I'll be damned," he said.

He motioned for the hatch, and a technician came inside. "Bring me an EMP patch."

"Yes, sir," the man said.

He returned a few minutes later with a rolling cart that held a variety of instruments, including some clearly meant for torture.

"Far, but not too far," Gabriel told the tech. "I need to know what he knows."

The technician pulled up a stool and brought out a handheld scanner. He turned it on and held it up over the beetle.

Rangnar used the reprieve from pain to think. He didn't know where the kid had gone, but he did know how to find his ship. He also knew that if he gave up Axel, Gabriel would just kill the lad—he would eradicate his entire crew, including the Wooly, both humans, and the Marka. There was a better than even chance he and Lucid would still die. That information was the only thing keeping them alive.

Rangnar looked down as the technician suddenly stood.

"What is it?" Gabriel asked.

The man reached out with a pair of pliers and ripped the beetle off Rangnar.

"It's not active," the tech said.

Rangnar narrowed his eye at the tiny device Axel had planted on his body.

Through his pain wracked mind, he realized the kid had never intended to hurt him. It had been a bluff all along. The young Steward didn't have it in him to kill.

"Speak," Gabriel said. "You've wasted enough of my time."

Glancing up, Rangnar looked at Lucid. She writhed in pain, her fate in his hands. But helping this beast of a man who'd killed his other Markas would require Rangnar to make a deal with a true devil, one worse than any Wrath.

"I won't ask you again," the general said. "Where's the Steward bastard? Tell me, and you and your friend will be spared."

"I don't know where he went," Rangnar said.

Gabriel leaned back, breathing in deeply through his nose. "As you wish," he said.

"I know how to find his ship, though," Rangnar quickly said. "And if you want to find him, you're going to need me and Lucid."

"I don't need—"

"Really? Then why are you here personally, and not some jerk-off colonel or CAID freak?"

"You're clever," the general admitted. "What you don't understand is that finding him could help save billions of lives."

Rangnar fought his dimming gaze to look at Gabriel.

"As you probably know, we have intel that the Wrath will return," the general said. "We need the Steward to complete our preparations for a future attack."

"You're not going to kill him?"

Gabriel grinned. "Oh I'm going to slay him, but first I'm

going to dissect him. You see, when the Stewards were destroyed, we, perhaps recklessly, destroyed everything about them, including their DNA. I need every inch of this bastard to perfect the stock and breed a new army, a flawless army, without that damned tunnel that corrupted the former batch. An army that will listen to our every command."

He leaned in closer to Rangnar.

"You take me to him, and I'll let you and your pet go," he said. "If you screw me, I'll keep her alive while peeling off every inch of her flesh while you watch."

The general straightened back up and raised a brow to study Rangnar. He was slowly starting to feel his body again, and the pain, making him grimace.

"I hate having to be an asshole and hurt people, I truly do," Gabriel said with an exhale. "Perhaps a different type of motivation will encourage you to help me."

Glancing to a technician, he then nodded.

"I know you know a thing or two about betrayals," Gabriel said.

The view rotated, or rather, Rangnar rotated in the chair. He blinked, straining to see as a dark glass wall lightened, revealing yet another prisoner on the other side.

Rangnar narrowed his eyes on a freckled face he hadn't seen for over twelve years.

"Nolan..." he muttered.

"Sure is!" Gabriel said as if he'd given Rangnar a gift. "Your old business partner. Disabled your ship, cut off your ear, and left you to—"

"To die," Rangnar interrupted. Adrenaline masked the pain across his body.

Gabriel walked in front of Rangnar and folded his arms over his uniform. "You help me, and I'll help you get your revenge."

Rangnar blinked, his vision clearing enough he met the

battered gaze of his old partner. The Eagles had done a number on his face. Nolan had a broken nose, a wide gash on his cheek, blood dripping down his split lip. One eye was completely swollen shut, but the other was directed at Rangnar, and it wasn't filled with anger—it was filled with fear.

He pled with Rangnar for help.

For mercy.

Memories flashed in his mind of their youth in the slums. No matter how bad things got, Nolan always had that charming smile and contagious laugh. God *damn* had Rangnar loved him.

But he couldn't forgive him for what he had done. His heart had turned hard over the years, leaving little room for sympathy.

"Lock him up, and throw away the key," Rangnar said with a grunt.

"I know of just the place to send him," the general said. "Inferno, the penal colony on Furia."

Rangnar had heard of that hellish place, nestled in abandoned old mines where Woolies had once extracted forgite. Not far from the battlegrounds where a platoon of Stewards made their last stand against the Eagles that had come to wipe them out.

Gabriel had been there that day, Rangnar remembered. With his twin brother, Nathaniel, who had died in that battle. Both of them following commands from their father, now Admiral Rex Jessup.

"Okay," Rangnar said. "I'll help you find Axel, if you promise to grant me and Lucid a full pardon."

Gabriel nodded at the technician and the straps freed Rangnar. He fell forward from the contraption, but the general caught him, holding him firmly and staring in his eyes.

"We have a deal, Rangnar Soki," he said. "As long as we find the last Steward."

"The fighter's not ready," Manoi said. "We still need to secure the laser cannons."

"I'll take care of that," Axel said.

Manoi shrugged. "Okay, okay, meet us at dock G in one hour. It's the most isolated and will attract the least attention."

"Good," Axel said.

The Wooly closed the door to his mechanic shop. It was after midnight, but the two aliens had been up working on the ship when Axel arrived with Spartacus.

"Let's go," he said to the droid. "Tell Cricket to meet us at dock G, and to be on full alert."

Spartacus sent the message out to the prowling Marka.

They started the journey through the quiet port. Axel scanned the piers for any potential hostiles. The only life he saw were Jukes. One of them was performing maintenance inside an enclosed crane.

Spartacus turned slightly as they walked over the frozen ground. "You seem distracted, Captain. I sense you are struggling with some internal thoughts."

"Just anxious to get out of here," Axel replied.

"Judging by your quickening heartbeat, I believe it's something more. I can hear it pounding in your chest, sir."

Axel grunted.

"You do realize I am not stupid, right? I am far more intelligent than any other species on the *Trash Squid*. Especially Uga. And, with all due respect, even you, sir."

"Yeah, I know that."

"I understand why you keep the truth from your crew," he said without looking at Axel.

"Truth?" Axel asked in the least surprised voice he could muster.

"This month alone you have magically escaped serious injury numerous times. I witnessed you pulled out of the ocean on Honi, after surfing a record wave that should have drowned you, with only a lump on your dense skull. I have documented you breathing atmosphere on Tecca that should have rendered you unconscious. I see the severe burns on your hands, which are now healing faster than any human is capable of."

Axel halted within view of the docks where they were to meet the Woolies. "What's your point, Spartacus?"

"Your crew is concerned about you, sir. I know they would stand by you, even if they knew what it is you fear."

Spartacus walked away, leaving Axel to ponder that statement. He was sick of lying to his crew, and he was sick of lying to himself. Maybe Spartacus was right and his crew would support him.

Or maybe it would just put them at risk too.

The rumble of an engine cut through the night a few minutes later. Axel turned to an enclosed tractor rig with a raised snowplow. In the cab, twenty feet off the ground, were Napo and Manoi. The Woolies drove the rig down the road with an attached trailer that had a tarp, half-tied down. It was obvious to anyone close enough there was a small fighter on the back. They drove down a boat ramp and turned the tractor.

Axel almost laughed at the sight, especially when Manoi climbed down the ladder. The thin Wooly was dressed in a fur coat and wore a helmet over his face to protect his lungs from the freezing air. He went to the back and removed the tarp while Napo remained in the cab. From there, he used a crane to lower the Tech-N to the water's edge.

"There ya go, big man," Manoi said. "Isn't she a beauty?"

"Sure is," Axel said. He walked over to examine the ship. The laser cannons were both bolted down, but not operational. Not ideal, but whatever. He wanted to get the hell out of here.

Napo jumped down, also dressed in a thick coat that hugged his muscular features.

"Mind if I have my droid start it up?" Axel asked.

Napo pulled out a laser pistol from his coat, but kept it leveled at the ground. "Be our guest, but don't try any funny business," Manoi said.

Spartacus walked over and climbed up to the cockpit. He opened it and got inside for a diagnostic test. A few minutes later, the lid popped back open.

"All good, Captain," Spartacus reported.

"Cricket, bring the forgite," Axel said.

The Marka came bounding out from behind a warehouse on the shoreline where he had been hiding.

He set the bag in front of Manoi. The Wooly bent and unzipped it, then looked up at Axel. "Nice doing business with you."

"You too," Axel said.

Manoi and Napo climbed back up into the tractor, turned it, and drove back the way they had come. Axel watched them go with Cricket by his side.

"You got a name for it yet?" Axel asked.

"No, do you?"

"Hey," Spartacus said.

"Yeah? Do you have one?" Axel asked. He glanced up to the droid standing in the cockpit, but he didn't seem interested in naming the fighter. He pointed to the west, toward the tarmac. "Might be trouble," he said.

Lights speared the horizon. Axel tensed up as he tried to get a view of this new vehicle.

"I don't think it is Eagles," Spartacus said, climbing out of the fighter. "I think it is just a group of anglers."

"Why would they be out this early?" Axel asked.

Sure enough, the lights were from a large truck with an even larger boat mounted to a trailer on the back.

"We're moving now, come on," Axel said. He climbed up into the cockpit with Cricket, but Spartacus remained on the road.

"What are you doing?" Cricket asked.

"Yeah, get up here," Axel said.

"I am going to use my new arm, like you said," Spartacus said.

"Huh?" Axel mumbled.

Realization set in when the truck with the boat stopped, and a man climbed down. It was T, the hulking fisherman who had words with Spartacus the day before.

"Oh come on, we don't have time for this shit," Axel said.

"Nice lookin' fighter!" T called out.

Three more men got out of the truck. They were all dressed in thick coats and helmets with lights that illuminated their bearded features.

Axel exhaled, and then breathed in as he approached, holding up his hands. "Look, T—" he started to say.

"Tanner Backus is my full name, you should remember it. I got some questions for you about your cripple friend. Looks like it got a new arm. Must got *a lottttt* of cash to buy T-Flesh and a Tech-N like that."

"Spartacus, get in the cockpit now," Axel ordered.

The men all spread out wielding a variety of knives and batons. Nothing that could do much damage to Spartacus—except for Tanner, who pulled out an old-school sawed-off shotgun.

"What do you want?" Axel said. "Money?"

"Money? You gonna pay me more than that bounty on your head?" Tanner asked.

Axel narrowed his eyes. "You don't know what you're talking about."

"No? CAID just issued a bounty for the crew of a ship that coincidentally matches the description of yours. Where'd it go?"

Spartacus took a step forward. The men were circling the droid. A warm wave of adrenaline surged through Axel.

"Cricket, get ready to fly," he said quietly into his headset.

The Marka reached out to the yoke, and began flipping buttons with his tail, just like Axel had taught him on the *Hammerhead*. The ship rose off the ground, thrusters blasting the frozen ground and melting it.

"Kill those engines!" Tanner yelled.

"Don't do this," Axel said from the hull. "I'm warning you."

Tanner pumped in a shell and aimed the barrel at Cricket. The wave of anger turned into a tsunami that burned through Axel. A swarm of red glazed his vision, the potent taste of metal flooded his mouth. Every muscle tensed up, preparing for a fight —hoping for one.

He knew what was about to happen—the tunnel to his father was opening.

Feed his corpse to the honeyfin! came that rough voice.

Axel jumped down to the ground, holding up both hands. Tanner swung the barrel at his chest. He fought the rush of rage, but it warmed his cold body. It felt *good*. His fists balled and his chest swelled.

"Distract them, Cricket," Axel whispered into his comm.

The Marka jerked the ship backward, over the water, the thrusters searing into the ice. Tanner swung the shotgun up and fired a blast at the closing cockpit. His other men charged Spartacus, stabbing and slamming the droid with their batons. He parried the blows, sparks showering the frozen ground.

"Give me the order, and I shall erase all of these wannabee bounty hunter, nerdy shits!" Spartacus boomed.

Axel charged in a fit of fury, unable or unwilling to control himself. He saw a muzzle flash from his left. The blast hit him in the side with the force of a Wrath Spectre. He flew a few feet and landed in open water, right under the hovering Tech-N. The thrusters torched the ice around Axel as he sank.

Pain rollicked his chest, but there was also numbness. Almost like his flesh, muscles, and bones were freezing. He was on his back, looking up as the water crystallized around him. It struck him then, he *was* freezing.

He tried to move, but his limbs wouldn't respond to the mental commands.

Lights lanced over the ice.

He heard a muffled voice over the comms, but he couldn't make it out.

A blinding light fired above him, forcing his eyes shut.

Moments later, the crushing ice loosened. He felt pressure around his body and opened his eyes to see the metal frame of Spartacus. The droid swam with him through the icy slush, back to the shore where the Tech-N had set down.

Vision going in and out, Axel only saw blurred shapes scattered across the icy terrain around them, each of them surrounded by frozen puddles of carmine.

Blood, he realized.

Spartacus carried Axel in his arms over to the Tech-N as Cricket stood in the cockpit, chirping something that Axel couldn't make out. As his body began to warm, he felt wetness on his side. His eyes flitted down to what he assumed would be melting ice.

Blood gushed from a series of concentrated holes in his chest armor. Now he knew what Cricket was chirping about.

The fighter lifted off toward the brilliant starry sky, but even those dimmed to darkness as Axel returned to the freezing grip of what could only be death.

The cold didn't last.

His body warmed under a blazing sun radiating across a cracked, arid landscape. It appeared as if he had been transported from the ice and tossed into an inferno.

This is death?

He looked dimly upon a hellish landscape with jagged red rocks and a redder sky. He stood in front of a mining tunnel marked with a sign. He was at a dig site on Furia, a planet known for its forgite deposits. Miners, crews of Woolies and humans, worked during the night to excavate it, as the daytime temperatures were nothing short of a furnace.

And yet five Stewards stood in the blazing sunlight, their golden armor encasing tall, muscular humanoid shapes. Axel watched through his father's eyes as the man walked out of the mine entrance, passing the carcasses of dead Woolies that littered the ground, partially buried by sand.

He went to the five warriors, who turned and saluted.

"Our defenses are ready, Captain," one of them said.

Captain, Axel realized.

His father stepped up to the edge of a bluff overlooking what appeared to be an abandoned spaceport in a valley a click or so out.

Was this another dream about the Wrath invasion?

It didn't take long for the answer.

Clipper transport ships lowered over the space port, disgorging Eagle infantry troopers in black-clad armor. With his father leading them, the Stewards returned to the mining tunnels where more Stewards waited. They stood stiffly, like statues in the shadows.

Unlike the other visions, Axel understood what was happening as if he was in the mind of his father. He could even *feel* what his father was feeling as he paced and swept his gaze over every Steward. To his surprise, there wasn't overwhelming anger that the Stewards were known for, but rather a sense of love for each of these warriors. For their loyalty, bravery, and most of all, for their sacrifice.

They were friends. Brothers.

"The Galactic Minister has ordered CANDF and the Corinn Empire to end our kind, to hunt us down, to terminate our existence," he said in a raspy voice. "To burn us out of history. Perhaps they are right to do so. Perhaps we are tainted, and the galaxy will be safer without us."

"Let them come!" someone shouted.

"They have sent their best," replied Axel's father. "General Jessup and his twin sons Nathaniel and Gabriel are on their way to destroy us all. To eradicate their creations."

He paused for a long moment.

"This may be our last fight together, but we will die with honor. Whether we were right or wrong, or whether we will even be remembered, I can't say. What I know for certain is that when the Eagles come for us, we will show them the fury and bravery we showed the Wrath and all our enemies!"

Weapons were pumped into the air, and bloodthirsty Stewards rushed out of the mine onto the dusty, cracked plateau. Trenches waited for the soldiers, who hopped inside and pulled heat reducing cloaks over their positions.

As the boots of the Eagles trampled across the plateau, his father thought of a woman, Mira, and of an unborn son.

Me, Axel realized.

"I'm sorry, Mira. I'm sorry I can't be with you, my love," said his father.

Those boots pounded closer and closer, the trap rising above the howl of the dust storm. He flung the cloak up, letting it fly away in the wind. He clambered out and aimed his laser rifle at the legion of armored figures.

"Make them remember our names!" he boomed.

Laser bolts flashed through the cloud of grit, cutting the surprised Eagles down. He charged with his fire cutlass, slicing into the closest Eagle diagonally, the two halves sliding away from one another.

All around him, the Stewards formed a phalanx, ripping through and crushing the first wave of surprised enemy forces. But one by one, the Stewards fell, as waves of Eagles in black surged across the battlefield.

General Rex Jessup sent everything he had to kill the surviving Stewards. Though it had meant the sacrifice of one of his sons, Nathaniel.

Axel saw the young Eagle now in the vision. He wore a flaming red helmet and lunged at Axel's father with a fire spear, nearly skewering him. His father hacked downward, breaking the shaft. Nathaniel tried to step back, but he couldn't escape the two swords that scissored off his head.

Laser bolts flashed over his corpse, knocking Axel's father to the blood-soaked dirt. Two of his lieutenants pulled him away, dragging him behind a rock. The Stewards were forced to retreat into a mining tunnel.

Instead of sending in more Eagles, they had fired missiles. Rained them down from a Warhorse hovering far above the blasted landscape. Axel watched them sail across the sky.

Injured, and unable to stand on his own, two Stewards helped his father stand tall as those missiles streaked down.

The vision dimmed away until all Axel could see was black.

CHAPTER 26

The female Corinn was dead.

As soon as she drew her last breath, the tremors stopped, the walls cooled to their dull gray. Zang remained near the corpse but was focused on the equipment the scientists had left behind. There was a single three-foot-tall black terminal with a blue sucker shape at the top that opened to a screen. Zang had his hands shoved into the wet interface on the sides with his green eyes closed.

Jax went back to patrolling, eyeing the disabled Corinn war droid. The skeletal model was the most advanced she had seen, but something had taken it down.

She bent down to give it another look. From all indications, there was no sign of an attack. No laser bolts. No claw marks. No visible damage at all. Whatever had happened to it must have affected the interior circuitry.

Jax made her way over to Satani and Hesh. Both soldiers were checking the circular openings in the chamber floor.

"Where do you think these go?" Satani asked.

"I d-don't want to know," Hesh stammered, shaking his head.

But it was the floating pillars and arc plastered with the remains of Corinns that had him most spooked. There were also grooves in the walls that they had first noticed in the fiery light that appeared during the quakes. Something was back there, but they didn't have the means to check.

Hippo remained on the ramp leading down into the chamber, scanning for life forms and monitoring the atmosphere. The minutes ticked by, each one more agonizing than the last. They seemed to be trapped in some purgatory between Hell—and something even worse.

"I'm going to go back to the door to see if I can get ahold of the LT," Satani said. "Hesh, you and Jax stay down here with Hippo."

Jax nodded, and after a brief hesitation, Hesh did the same. They kept close to Zang as he stood over a terminal.

"Evil—it's all around us," Hesh whispered. He studied the floating columns. "I got a bad feeling we're never leaving this place."

"We're getting out of here. Just keep focused," Jax said. The guy was definitely starting to freak out after losing Meatball, Nadia, and being trapped in the Wrath construct.

Zang let out a long sigh and pulled his hands from the terminal. The interface cooled, dimming to darkness.

"Well?" Hesh asked. "Did you figure out what did this to your friends?"

"The equipment has a data-log that goes back fifteen human days," Zang explained. "The outpost crew monitoring this area for scavengers reported the seismic reactions and atmosphere anomalies we have experienced. A scientific crew was deployed, and they discovered the tunnel that led to this chamber."

"And?" Jax said after a pause.

"They put in a report through the proper channels to bring in additional resources before going offline."

"We're the additional resources," Hesh said.

"Yes, Sergeant Hesh, but as you can see, there was security assigned to the staff," Zang said. He indicated to the downed war droid.

"Lot of good it did."

"So what happened to her, and the others?" Jax asked. "And more important, what *is* this place?"

"I have seen enough to make a logical assumption—"

"Great," Hesh said. "He's gonna guess."

"Corinns do not guess. My conclusion is based on the evidence presented," Zang replied. "To understand, I must see what the others saw."

"Whatever they saw caused them t-to gouge their bloody eyes out," Hesh said.

"Not her," Jax said.

Zang went back to the dead female.

"Wait, what are you doing?" Hesh asked. When Zang didn't answer, he repeated his question, twice more. Still not getting an answer, he raised his minigun barrel. "Answer me, you alien fuck."

"Hesh, stand down, god dammit," Jax said. She took a cautious step toward Hesh as Zang slowly turned.

"To see, I must connect with her," said the Corinn.

Hesh looked over at the body. "But...she's dead."

"The body is deceased, but the mind may still be functioning on some level." Zang looked at them all in turn. "I will try to connect, but this will leave me weakened."

"Hold on there," Hesh said.

"I will not 'hold on.' This is our mission," Zang said.

"Yeah, Hesh, let him work," Jax said.

"Listen to your intelligent comrade. You are achieving nothing besides wasting precious time, Sergeant Hesh."

Jax smiled. She was starting to like Zang.

"I'll...we'll watch over you," Jax said.

"Yeah," Hesh grunted.

"Gratitude," Zang said. He went down on both knees and lowered over the head of the female, pressing his elongated forehead to hers. Then he placed both palms flat on her temples.

Zang closed his eyes and began to hum softly. His arms began to quiver, then his chest heaved.

"This is some j-jacked up alien shit, man," Hesh said.

Jax watched curiously, unsure. She recalled the Corinns had a tunnel to their ancestors, so maybe Zang was trying to open one to the brain of this woman.

A throaty groan came from the Corinn and his head suddenly shot upward. He chanted in the Corinn dialect, translating almost live in Jax's earpiece to:

Ancient strength, protect me.

Every passing second, Zang shook harder, and his voice became more strained. Whatever was happening had a severe effect on his mind and body.

"What's wrong with Zang?" Satani called out from above. He passed Hippo on the curved ramp leading down into the chamber, then halted.

The Corinn vibrated, still chanting, louder and louder.

"He's trying to connect to this corpse or some shit," Hesh said.

Satani watched, then pointed at the Corinn. "Tell him we're leaving! Door's open again."

"Fuckin-A, finally!" Hesh shouted. "Let's go, Zang!"

The Corinn made no indication that he'd heard the sergeant.

"Come on, Jax," Hesh said. "You heard Satani, let's get the fuck out of here."

"We can't leave him," Jax said. "We said we'd watch over him."

"Then you stay with him. I'm leaving this tomb." Hesh started to lumber off with his minigun.

"Come on," Jax whispered. She'd stepped toward Zang when she heard a whistling. A blue light boomeranged out of the rising gases. It zipped up the ramp where Satani let out a croak. His helmet toppled off his neck, and his body slumped down into a tight crumpled position.

Jax watched in what felt like slow motion as the helmet rolled down the ramp, clanking to a stop near Hesh. Out slid the head of Satani, his eyes still glowing red.

"FUCK!" Hesh shouted.

He spun with his minigun and Jax roved her barrel. Orange lights glowed again on the pillars above. But this time, it wasn't just the rock glowing. The body parts dislodged, hovered in the air a moment before flying across the room where they began to reassemble. Arms with torsos. Legs with groins. Heads with necks.

This can't be real, Jax thought. She blinked, as if that would somehow change the insanity happening before her eyes.

Zang stood, panting heavily. He slowly looked up as parts of dead Corinn "scientists" interlocked, forming full bodies from what had clung to the pillars.

A figure suddenly rose out of one of the tunnels in the floor of the chamber. Then two. Three turned into five. The tall, thin forms weren't the rocky abominations that Jax had seen during her many trainings. They weren't Wrath at all—they were Corinns, with elongated heads and long limbs. But something was different about these aliens. Their eyes, instead of emerald, flickered orange, as if reflecting raging fires inside their skulls.

Something had changed these creatures. Possessed them.

Five more fully reconstructed bodies dropped down to the floor, joining the other naked figures. Three of the aliens held fire sickles that they cocked back simultaneously as if controlled by a single mind. Then came the shrieks. Awful, shrill noises, like a dying animal being torn apart.

"Kill them!" Hesh shouted. "Kill them all!"

He fired, the whine of the minigun resonating right before it began spraying .50 caliber rounds. They cut through two of the aliens, blowing off limbs and popping a skull into carmine mist.

They were blazing fast on all surfaces. Four of them skittered up the wall to Hippo, who raised his own laser cannons and tracked the targets. Hesh cut down another ghoul that ran at him with its sickle in hand. The arm spun away with the weapon still gripped in its long fingers.

Jax fired burst after burst, too fast.

Strong and steady, Jax. Keep it steady.

She slowed down and focused on calculated shots. But the violent aliens were also fast and hunched down in the gas for cover, keeping low as they attempted a flanking move. Jax hit one from behind, blowing holes in its bony back that knocked it down. The creature hopped right back up, the body twisted and deformed.

Zang staggered, still weak.

"We have to go!" Jax yelled.

Another reanimated monster leapt out of the gases between him and Hesh. The big Eagle had his minigun raised in the opposite direction. Closing an eye, Jax led the creature and then pulled the trigger. The shot hit the tall creature in the chest, blowing out a glowing red hole that hardly slowed it down. A shriek burst from its mouth as it jumped and slammed into Hesh, mounting him with its long limbs.

Another abomination threw a sickle that boomeranged into Hesh's leg, cutting out the back of his heel. He went down on a knee, screaming and firing upward into the floating columns.

Jax aimed at the alien, but it was too risky with it wrapped completely around Hesh. The creature had taken out two fire knives and was thrusting them through his thick armor. Hesh stumbled and staggered, screaming and still firing.

A flurry of rounds lanced toward Jax, forcing her to the ground. She brought up her rifle and fired at another reanimated Corinn that charged her position. The bolts smacked into the head, dropping the possessed demon instantly.

She felt a hand on her leg, and spun to her back, aiming right at the head of Zang. The Corinn held up both hands then motioned for Jax to follow him.

Jax turned back to Hesh, who was on his knees now, still trying to fend off the two aliens that stabbed him over and over. His helmet turned toward Jax as she raised her weapon. She sighted up a skull and fired, scoring another headshot. Then she put a three-round burst to the chest of the other monster.

A whiny screech called out, this one in the Corinn language.

"No escape. Only death!"

Hesh stared at Jax for a moment, blood squirting from multiple holes in his suit.

"F-fuck me," he mumbled as he fell face first into the gas, vanishing.

A thud came across the room as Hippo crashed to the ground, his red light blinking off. The unworldly scream of the victorious aliens echoed through the chamber.

The fiery eyes all homed in on Jax.

In a split second, she had to decide.

Fight, or follow Zang.

Tucking the gun against her chest, she decided to trust Zang. The Corinn was the only one who could help her survive whatever hell they had descended into.

"Axel, you must wake up..."

The voice of his mother echoed in his mind. The strong, sweet tone pulled him back to reality.

He opened his eyes to the face of a woman hovering over him.

Could it be?

Had he somehow found her after all these years?

Axel blinked heavy eyelids, lifting them to the youthful face of not his mother, but Luna.

"Captain's awake," she called out.

Reaching down, she gently touched his arm. "You're okay," she said. "You're on the *Trash Squid*. Sparty and Cricket brought you here."

Axel blinked and focused on his crew as they surrounded him.

"What happened..." he muttered.

"You were shot," Spartacus said.

"Spartacus pulled you from the ice," Cricket said.

Axel looked down at the bandage covering his chest, memories slowly breaking through his muddled mind. Not just of the fight with the fisherman, but of the Steward battle he had witnessed in a vision after he was shot.

He had seen his father die, seen him destroyed by the Eagles commanded by the now Admiral, Rex Jessup, the commander of CANDF.

Good or bad, seeing the Stewards betrayed like this filled Axel with anger. His father had loved these soldiers, he had tried to save them, just like he had tried to save Corinns and humans and all other races across the Hironia system from the Wrath.

The Stewards weren't all evil.

"You should be dead," Brayton said.

"You lucky, Capa, no?" Uga barked. "Bad boo-boo on your

chest."

"Very lucky, indeed," Spartacus chipped in.

Axel glanced around at his crew as they stood there, clearly shocked that he was still breathing.

"How long have I been out?" he asked.

"Almost two days," Brayton said. "Spartacus got you here hanging on by a thread. Stopped the bleeding."

"Where are we?"

"We're almost to Dari," Luna said. "But we have a major problem."

She tapped a smart-pad and turned it for Axel to see a CAID bulletin featuring an image of a decommissioned Plasma-31 transport carrying a very familiar looking crew, their faces, captured by surveillance footage on what appeared to be Honi. Axel was carrying a surfboard under an arm in the shot of him.

"Oh man," he whispered.

"I look pretty badass, don't I Capa?" Uga barked.

"Not as badass as a one-armed droid," Spartacus said. "And now look at me."

He held up both arms.

"You two are happy about this?" Luna asked.

"Idiots," Cricket chirped.

Brayton snorted.

All Axel could do was swallow hard. He was lucky to be alive, yes, but his chances of long-term survival, and that of his crew, had dropped exponentially.

"Why the long face, Capa?" Uga asked. "You should have zero worries, 'cause we're almost to the safest place in the galaxy. My family protect us, no problem."

"From Eagles?" Cricket asked.

"Sure, we hates them," Uga spat and showed off his canines. The same facial expression as the image on the bulletin.

"I know Uga, but your hatred means nothing in a fight, big little fella," Cricket chirped.

Uga held up two hands. "If Eagles come to *my valley, my family* will hide us. For small fee." He pinched the end of an arm together to make what looked like two fingers.

"Small fee, right...good thing we have plenty of forgite," Luna said with a smirk.

"Plenty?" Uga said. "Hah. Do you know how much food we can eat? How much glorious, wonderful, delicious food? Mounds. Mountains! And Capa promised us all!!"

"But, won't that put your kin at risk?" Brayton asked.

Uga tilted his head, as if this was the first time he considered that obvious aspect.

"Pfsh." He swatted the air. "My people hide us. Fear not."

Axel trusted Uga, but he wasn't sure they would be safe anywhere, now that they were actively looking for them.

It had to be Rangnar, Axel thought. Maybe he had discovered the nano-beetle wasn't active. Or maybe the Eagles had found the beetle, removed it, and tortured the info out of him.

Axel hoped that wasn't the case. He wouldn't wish torture on anyone. If the Eagles tracked him down, he understood clearly that a horrific fate awaited him. There was no telling what they would do to him, but it would not include a swift death, and more than likely lots of testing.

"Captain, we're closing in on Dari," Brayton said.

"What are your orders, sir?" Luna asked.

Axel winced as he sat up and swung his legs over the side of the bed with a hand on his chest. "Sparty, find us a place to put down, then you and I will go with Uga to find his—"

"Nothing offensive, no? Only, my clan no big fan of droids," Uga said.

"Right," Axel said. "Cricket, you—"

"Uh...not really into Markas either," Uga said. "No offense you either, Cricket."

"Captain, hold on a second," Luna said. "You were just shot. You need to stay here and rest, let me go."

"No," Axel said firmly.

Luna stiffened, her mouth tightening, clearly wanting to argue.

"Uga and I will go alone," he said in a softened voice.

Uga shuffled slightly, suddenly nervous.

"I'll meet you on the bridge," Axel said.

The crew moved out as he got off the table. When they were gone, he pulled the bandage down. What he saw couldn't be real. Where there should have been multiple holes, he saw only new scabs forming.

He was used to healing fast, and knowing the truth about his genesis explained it. But even with that knowledge, seeing his rapid healing properties on a devastating wound like this was remarkable. In just two days, his body was practically healed.

His crew had to know he was different now. Not fully human. Despite all his caution, hiding things over the years, they had just been presented with incontrovertible evidence that he was far from a normal human man.

But had they guessed just how different he was?

Axel pulled the bandage up and carefully dressed into a new suit. A few minutes later, he joined his crew on the bridge.

He would tell them the truth, soon. First though, he had to get them to safety.

"SITREP, Sparty," Axel said.

"I have determined the best place to hide the ship is in a lake," replied the droid.

A holographic map bloomed above the central terminal of the bridge. "Uga's clan lives in the Four Peaks Mountains, which are accessible through the forest bordering this body of water."

Axel studied the map, then gave the nod to proceed. He stood near his chair but didn't take a seat as the ship closed in on Dari.

Uga dragged a stool over in front of the viewports for a better view, clearly anxious to be returning home after so many years.

The ship roared toward the surface, entering the atmosphere, and breaking through a light cloud cover. Crimson-hued mountain chains lined the horizon, an odd but beautiful sight. One of those gigantic peaks was Colossus, the snow-tipped summit reaching far into the clouds. It was the largest in the system—the daunting mountain that no human had ever climbed—and the one Axel had always dreamed of cresting.

But he wouldn't be doing any climbing any time soon.

Uga stood on the stool to watch as they lowered over the surface. He held an unlit cigar stick they had purchased on Jolia.

A teal serpentine river meandered through the lush mountain valley of blue trees, all of it a stark contrast to the blood-colored peaks above. They descended lower, blasting through a ravine toward a gigantic waterfall dumping into a lake.

"There," he said. "That's it. Home. My clan lives there. Best place in the universe. I miss very greatly, like stomach miss food."

He pointed at a chain of four giant mountains bordering the sprawling lake. Based off their size alone, it could only be the Four Peaks. Crystal falls cascaded down the rocks in the distance, feeding the deep blue body of water reflecting the glow of the brilliant setting sun.

"No contacts on radar," Brayton reported.

The thrusters eased as they hovered over the lake, slowly

lowering. The view of the mountains vanished as water swallowed the ship.

"Okay, Uga, let's go," Axel said.

Once in the cargo bay, Axel opened his gear locker to find his armor chest rig hanging inside. Holes had punched through in several places.

Brayton was right. He should be dead.

You must wake up and live the truth, said the unmistakable voice of his father.

But how?

Axel felt no anger, and he was wide awake, in the present moment next to Uga.

Was he hearing things now?

He shook it away and laced up his boots, wincing in pain from doubling over, grabbed his pack and nodded at Uga.

"Moving into position," Spartacus said over their headsets.

The ship purred through the water, lifting slightly as they approached the shoreline. They climbed a ladder to a dorsal hatch and scrambled up onto the hull, then walked down to the end of the bow, which was half surfaced.

Calm waves lapped at the rocky shoreline not twenty feet away. Axel checked the depth of the water below. It looked plenty deep for a quick swim.

"Ready?" Axel asked.

"For what?" Uga barked.

"To go for a dip."

"Uga not made to jump that far, Capa."

"Sure you can."

"Wait—" Uga said.

Axel gave him a slight "nudge" of encouragement. The Wooly fell over the bow, arms flailing. He landed in the water with a splash, popping back up with a broken cigar stick in his maw.

"Oh, crap. My bad. Sorry, Uga," Axel said.

Uga spat out the limp cigar as he struggled to tread water.

Anxious to feel the water on his skin, Axel hopped off. He pulled the Wooly to a shoreline of copper-colored rocks. Once safely on land, they turned to watch the *Trash Squid* retreat into the depths, vanishing under the crystalline water. Bubbles burst across the surface, then it was still as glass.

"Lead the way, my friend," Axel said.

Uga grinned from ear to ear, then he took off, waddle-running with his arms bobbing at his sides. Even with his injuries, Axel easily caught up. Together, they made their way up the shore and into the forest. The thick tree bark was a grayish black, under the canopy of blue leaves. Groundhog-like creatures with floppy blue ears scattered into burrows at the sound of their boots. A slug carrying a shell the size of the Wrath egg slithered across the ground, leaving a path of silvery goo.

"Hold on, hold on," Uga said.

"What?" Axel asked.

The slug went into the shell as Uga snatched it with one of his hands. He used a canine to pluck the slug out, crunching it just once before swallowing the creature. His body trembled.

"Ohhhhhhhh yeah, that hit the spot," he barked. "You want one, Capa?"

"Nah, I don't need to puke right now, pal."

Uga tilted his furry face, as if he wanted to ask a question, but then shrugged.

On the horizon, the sun was beginning to set over the mountains, shadows flocking out over the terrain in the wake. A flock of birds with hairy feathers cawed loudly and took to the sky as Uga began hiking up a slope, dislodging several rocks in the process.

The hike up the foothills of the mountains took an hour.

Finally, Axel spotted a ridgeline overlooking the jagged vertical cliffs of the Four Peaks. By the time they arrived, the sun was a final flaming streak.

"My clan lives up there. Penthouse," Uga said, pointing to ledges thousands of feet above them. A few trees grew on the exterior of the bluffs and cliffs, but Axel didn't see any structures.

"How the hell do we get up there without a ship?" he asked.

"No problem. Just around corner, gorgeous Wooly ladies with velvet cushions carry your injured ass up cliffside,'" Uga said. "Come, they know we here. We will find a guard soon."

Axel followed Uga but the Wooly halted.

"Oh," Uga said. "Capa, you keep your hands at your sides. And don't talk until we find a guard." He took another step then turned again. "Then, don't talk."

"Understood," Axel replied.

He cautiously made his way up the rocky slope toward the mountains with Uga still leading the way. They came up to the crest of another slope, this one with a view of a five-hundred-foot gap between the vertical walls. A red banner hung from a tree on their right, displaying four mountain peaks, each of them burning.

The flag whipped in the breeze coming down from the mountains. The sound of cascading falls echoed out of the opening they approached.

"Almost there," he said.

The Wooly marched through the middle of the rocks, into a small valley about three times as wide as the opening. Waterfalls cascaded down both sides of the cliffs framing the path. Wind whistled above, rising and falling like an alarm might.

They passed the waterfalls and started up a steep, narrowing path chiseled out of the rock.

Axel paused when he heard something in the respite of the

howling wind. Debris and small rocks tumbled down the bluff on his right. He glanced up, seeing fog, or perhaps smoke. Something was moving up there.

All at once, shadows darkened the path and figures came bursting from above. Axel looked up as a dozen armored Woolies in harnesses attached to ropes came slinging down. They hit the ground, aiming laser pistols at the group. The largest wasted no time striding over to Uga. Standing five feet tall and built like a miniature Corinn rhino, this was the biggest Wooly Axel had ever seen.

The warrior wore a strap around his head and a gold T-Flesh rig around a bulky chest. He held four fire hatchets in his arms, each of them glowing blue as he walked up to Uga.

"Master Norn," Uga said, bowing. "Been a long time."

Norn growled, barring his teeth and looking from Uga to Axel in turn. Then he raised one of the hatchets at Axel. "How dare you bring humans here, Uga," Norn barked.

"I mean no disrespect," Uga said. "We come to see my family and seek refuge."

The warrior Wooly strode over, eyes flitting across Axel from his toes to his head before turning back to Uga. "Things have changed since you left," Norn said.

"Relax, Master Norn," Uga said. "This is a friend."

The Woolies closed in. Axel felt the itch that always came before the voice.

Norn lowered the hatchets and leaned down to Uga. "There are many whispers that have reached our lands," said the warrior. "Rumors about the Wrath. These are dangerous times. Now you bring humans to our gates."

"Capa here is a man of peace, Master Norn."

"It's true, I mean you no harm," Axel said. "As Uga said, we're only seeking a respite."

A voice called out. Human. Female.

Oh no...

"Let me go!"

Axel whirled to see Luna, her hands bound, two Woolies escorting her by the arms. A third warrior had a fire spear at her back.

"Hey, get away from her!" Axel shouted.

Luna squirmed to get free as the Wooly guards pushed her over to Master Norn. She fell to her knees, glancing up at Axel.

"Sorry," she said. "I just wanted to make sure you were okay."

The skitter of falling rocks sounded above. Axel followed the small tumble of debris up to a reddish bluff overhead.

"What's going on down there?" came a croaky old bark.

Axel glanced up at a Wooly with a fully white beard and jeweled necklace. Four Wooly warriors in spotless white armor stared down.

"Uncle Cardia!" Uga barked loudly. "Please, don't kill my friends!"

The chief lowered eyes, clouded by cataracts, down at them, squinting in the brightening moonlight.

"Uga, is it really you?"

"Yes, Uncle! I was trying to tell Master Norn that we have come home to seek refuge," Uga said. "This here is Captain Axel Finn and Lieutenant Luna Gervasi. These are two of my bestest friends in the universe."

"From what do you seek refuge?"

Norn stiffened and regarded Axel with narrowed, black eyes.

Axel was about to tell the complete truth, but Uga cut in first.

"We hear the Wrath might be coming back," he said. "We come for shelter here, in the mountains, where we be safe."

Cardia glanced down with his cloudy eyes. "I've heard talk about the demons returning," he barked. "You will be safe here."

Master Norn grunted and looked up at Cardia. The chief sighed a long breath. "You must be hungry."

Axel felt Uga nudge him and realized the chief was talking to him.

"Say yes, Capa," Uga whispered.

"Starving," Axel said.

"We can't trust humans," Norn barked. "Chief Cardia, the last time—"

Cardia wagged a gray furry arm, cutting off the warrior. "Stop with this constant worry, Master Norn," he said. "You will only make yourself miserable. It's been far too long since I saw my nephew, and I'm excited to hear about his adventures."

Norn grunted, then sheathed his fire hatches.

"Gather the rest of your crew," Cardia said. "Tonight, we will feast in your honor."

CHAPTER 27

Rangnar sat in the cell aboard an Ironclad destroyer thinking about the deal he had made with General Gabriel Jessup. It had ended the torture session for him and Lucid, but it had secured a bad fate for his old partner Nolan, who was on his way to Inferno, a prison that lived up to its name.

The bastard deserves it, Rangnar thought.

He pushed aside what was done with Nolan and focused on what he had done to Axel and the crew of the *Trash Squid*. He had provided CAID with every detail of the ship and all he knew about her crew from when he was a prisoner aboard the vessel. If the Steward kid was smart, he would be long gone and hiding somewhere.

But hiding from the Eagles was going to be damn near impossible now, especially with the bounty they had posted across the galaxy. Every hunter out there would be looking for Axel and his crew.

Dread ate at his guts as Rangnar sat on his bunk ruminating on his betrayal. He had made a deal with the very same shit stains that had killed Saber, Nuke, and Blaster back on Optus.

Hours passed of being lost in his thoughts. There was guilt, and regret, too, about mistakes he had made in his life. He hoped this new deal wasn't going to be the top one on the list.

Finally, the windowless hatch clicked and opened. Rangnar stood to face two Eagles. Not the average grunt military police. These were both combat veterans, according to the burning wings on their helmets.

"Hold out your hands," one said in a muffled voice.

Rangnar did as ordered. The other guard clanked cuffs around his wrists. The red power meter in the middle confirmed they were charged.

"Let's go," said the first Eagle. He led the way, passing the other closed cells.

"Where's Lucid?" Rangnar asked.

Neither of the soldiers answered.

They marched him to an elevator and got inside. The doors clicked together. Rangnar stood between the two men, questions racing through his mind that he knew they would never answer.

Ten seconds later, the doors whisked open on the largest launch bay he had ever seen. The entire place was bustling with activity. Not three-hundred feet away, twenty Eagles in combat armor were prepping gear outside of a Clipper.

There were rows of the small transports parked across the bay. At the other end was a Warhorse, parked horizontally with both mammoth thrusters facing closed doors.

Everything was state of the art, designed for one purpose—to fight the Wrath.

Judging by the activity, they were getting ready for something imminent.

Rangnar halted to look out viewports at some distant planet that he didn't recognize right away. But he did recognize something else. An entire fleet of warships dotted the darkness. Ironclads, Warhorses, and a massive station he had never seen before.

"The hell are we?" Rangnar asked.

"Keep moving," said the lead escort.

He pushed on with the guards past twenty rows of Clippers. They didn't stop until they got to the Warhorse. A wide, long ramp led up into the belly of the huge transport. The last time Rangnar had been on one of these he was a young man. He remembered the feeling of excitement at being selected as a bounty hunter to join the hunt for Stewards. The irony wasn't lost on him as he walked up into the cavernous, dimly lit corridors.

He was here again, for the same purpose, with the same bastards.

The Eagle guards took him to the brig where two more soldiers stood sentry.

"Rangnar Soki," said the lead escort.

The doors opened to a room with a dark mirrored wall. Standing in front of it was General Gabriel Jessup.

"Leave him with me," he said.

The guards slipped away. Rangnar stepped into the dark room to face the general.

"Your info was right, it seems," Gabriel said.

"You already found Axel?"

"No, but we found someone that claims to have seen him very recently. I need you to verify that it was in fact, Axel." Gabriel gestured for Rangnar to approach before turning to the mirror. It suddenly lightened, and Rangnar found himself looking through a glass panel.

A husky man was sitting at a metal table on the other side, dressed in coveralls and stocking cap. He had a straggly beard and a black eye. One of his arms was in a sling.

"Who's that?" Rangnar asked.

"A fisherman named Tanner." He held up a comm link to his lips. "Proceed."

An Eagle entered the interrogation room and Rangnar listened intently.

"Am I getting this bounty or what?" Tanner asked. He stood up, but the Eagle, a lieutenant with slick gray hair parted on the side motioned for him to sit.

"We need some more information," said the officer.

"I already told you everything," Tanner said as he sat back down.

"Tell us again," said the lieutenant.

Tanner sighed rudely. "The Plasma-31 transport landed about four days ago, or something like that," he said. "I confronted a tall human captain with a crew consisting of a Marka, a Wooly, and smartass war droid not long after they set down."

"What was the droid's name?"

"Sartorius? And it had one arm the first time we saw him," Tanner said.

"You said you had words with this droid?"

"That's right. Cocky piece of garbage. Threatened me with violence."

Rangnar knew right away this was in fact Axel and his crew.

"And you said the Plasma-31 was missing its Tech-N when it landed?" asked the officer.

"That's correct, but when I saw the bulletin, I recognized the ship and their faces, so my crew and I followed them out to the piers where they were boarding a new Tech-N," Tanner said. "Got it from two Woolies that run a black market side biz in the port."

"Where was the crew going?"

"I told you, I don't know. But that uppity droid got a new arm and tried to kill me with it." Tanner explained a chaotic scene that included him shooting the tall human in self-defense, knocking him into the freezing ocean. "No one could have survived that, but when they pulled him out, he was still alive," he said.

"It was him," Gabriel said without looking at Rangnar.

Yeah, it is him, he thought.

The general went to the other mirrored wall, which also lightened to an interrogation room. Two Woolies stood there, one a large muscular creature, and the other thin and old with gray streaks.

The same lieutenant appeared in that room a few moments later.

"What do you bird men want?" asked the older Wooly.

"The location of the captain that bought your black market Tech-N," said the officer.

"We don't know what you speak of," replied the muscular Wooly.

"We're willing to offer you a deal to overlook all of your criminal activity. Perhaps." The lieutenant paced the room. "All you have to do is tell us where they might have gone."

The two Woolies looked at each other, then spat at the officer.

"This is a waste of time," Gabriel said. He said something into a comm and then turned back to Rangnar.

"You're up next, *Phan*tom," he said. "Tell us where he might have gone and help me find this Steward."

Behind the general, the interrogation with the Woolies continued, but had transitioned from a talk, to a more heated conversation. It seemed Gabriel believed the aliens knew something, and he was willing to do whatever it took to get it out of them.

Rangnar watched as the two aliens were strapped onto tables, squirming, spitting, and barking. Unlike with Rangnar and Lucid, the Eagles used fire on the two creatures, who were deathly afraid of flame. They shriek-barked in agony as the torches burned the fur off their skin and seared their flesh.

"They would tell you if they knew something," Rangnar said.

"Perhaps," Gabriel said. "Doesn't matter. We have spies deployed all over, looking for them. It's just a matter of time. If he's injured he might be laying low, but not for long, is my guess."

Rangnar tensed up at the thought of helping further.

Gabriel motioned for Rangnar to follow him out of the room. From there, they went to his office where he opened a box with a single Wooly cigar. The finest in the galaxy.

"I've been saving this since Furia," he said. "When Captain Leon Kahr and his Stewards killed Nathaniel. We were going to smoke it to celebrate dispatching the last of those psychotic bastards."

He took a whiff.

A body suddenly jettisoned out into space, drifting past the viewport. Rangnar squinted to make out the clothing of the fisherman, his face contorted and frozen in shock as he tumbled into darkness.

Next came the brutalized, burned bodies of the Woolies.

All confliction about helping vanished at the sight when he pictured Lucid drifting by. There was no doubt in his mind now that Rangnar and his last Marka friend would suffer the same fate if he didn't help them.

Gabriel leaned against his desk. "Soon, the last of the Stewards will be nothing but a memory, replaced by a truly great warrior that I can control. Once we have the location of this Axel Finn, you will accompany me to track him down and ensure he doesn't escape."

"What? Why me?"

"Because he let you live, which tells me he trusts you."

Four, fifty-foot-tall wooden doors blocked off the entrance to the bluff. A burning mountain peak was engraved about halfway up each. After hours of trekking, and then a few hours of waiting, almost the entire crew of the *Trash Squid* had reached the entrance to the Great City of the Four Peaks. Cricket and Brayton were here now too, but Spartacus was still back at the ship.

Axel looked back at Luna, who had disobeyed his orders earlier. Suddenly he felt remorse for not trusting her and bringing her along in the first place.

There was also the growing remorse for lying to his crew. He should have trusted them all with his past, as they did him. And now they had *all* lied to Chief Cardia, to whom they'd come seeking refuge. Uga, who knew about his dealings with Rangnar, thought it was better to keep their probable bounties a secret. Axel agreed he was right about that.

"This way," barked Master Norn.

The hulking warrior had led the way here with a small squad of his soldiers. Chief Cardia had vanished not long after meeting Axel. The leader and his entourage had boarded a pair of black sleigh-shaped hover ships that shuttled them into the mountains.

Master Norn barked up to two guards standing in turrets framing the door built into the peaks. Shards of red rock rose high into the clouds behind the entrance. Axel admired the view, picturing himself climbing the nearly vertical surfaces with nothing but chalk and spiked shoes, just like the old legends on Earth.

Master Norn turned to them, snorting a growl. "Speak when spoken to and only then. Better yet, say nothing."

Uga snorted right back. "That is no way to treat guests. Not how things were done when I—"

Norn stepped over, leaned into Uga's face. "You've been gone a long time," Norn said. "Things have changed."

Uga flared his black snout, clearly agitated. The cranking of the left door opening provided a welcome distraction.

Although he didn't care for the warrior's attitude, Axel respected him. He was trying to protect his clan, just like Axel was trying to protect his crew. But now he worried this place was the opposite of salvation—that the city of Four Peaks would be a prison.

But there was no turning back now.

The door slowly opened to reveal a mile-long canyon cut through the mountains with arched columns spaced over the top. They looked almost like the massive rib cages of the alien mud beasts on Tecca. Or giant fossilized ice worms that had once lived in the frozen oceans of Lium, a moon orbiting Honi.

As Axel followed Norn through the entryway, he realized the entire valley was carved out of the mountain, a tunnel with no ceiling. He marveled at the remarkable sight.

The Wooly were legendary miners, masons, and craftsman, their woven goods sought throughout the galaxy. Giant rock statues of noble looking Woolies and some type of animal with antlers running up its skull like a Mohawk were carved into the exterior of the walls. The alien creature kind of reminded Axel of an elk he had seen as a kid in the mountains.

Across the cliffs, small Wooly homes salted the rock. They had used a type of concrete-like plaster to construct the light blue dwellings. Each had multiple windows with wooden shutters and stone chimneys. Metal and wood bridges connected the hundreds of ledges.

A meandering teal river ran through the bottom of the valley, feeding gardens and rows of crops framing the banks.

"Your home is beautiful," Luna said.

"For one thousand years my people have lived in this valley," Uga barked. "We survived countless attacks from rival clans by utilizing these mountains."

Axel remembered Uga telling him there were thousands of miles of tunnels burrowed deep into the rock. It was the perfect place to hide and ambush enemies.

Most impressive was the stone fortress at the other end of the valley. Every inch had been hammered out of the vermillion rocks.

Cricket trotted next to Axel as the crew walked into the great city. Horns blared on their approach. Master Norn led the way, glancing over his shoulder plates with a perpetual snarl on his furry face each time he checked on them.

Hundreds of eyes followed them from open shutters in the homes built along the walls of the canyon. There were Woolies of all ages. From the old and frail, to a newborn that a female nursed against her furry chest.

The main path led down into a valley boasting trees with trunks of undulating curves, whimsically spiraling upwards to meet expansive canopies that burst forth in an explosion of fluffy purple fruit. Uga stared at them with saliva dripping out of his mouth. A team of farmers harvested the fruits, placing them into woven baskets.

They looked up and watched the small entourage.

Along the river, Woolies pulled nets out of the water, using their many limbs to pluck out entangled purple crustaceans. The anglers stopped to stare curiously.

Uga waved and patted his belly. "I can't *wait* for a skewer of river prawns."

Norn took a path bordering the village of ribbed silos, ten

feet tall, with luminescent nodules that emitted a soft, purple glow on the sides. They tapered at the top, bending gently in the breeze. From what Axel could tell, these structures were storage containers for their food, judging by the Woolies carrying in baskets of produce.

A herd of ten giant Tark'bas grazed in a field of purple flowers bordering the structures. The three hundred pound shaggy creatures had paddle shaped tails and three comically large eyes poking out of the overgrown fur on their small heads.

Two of the beasts slapped at each other with their tails, letting out trumpeting noises.

"Mating call," Uga said. "Quite the sight."

"I can imagine," Luna said.

The group was led past the village and into a market where stalls were set up for the morning trade. Tomorrow, Woolies would barter some of the most famous goods in the galaxy. There would be carts of fresh food, pots of soup simmering with spidery limbs inside.

The river twisted through the fortress, running under a bridge and vanishing under the rock into the mountain. A bridge connected the valley to the castle built into the final mountain.

Uga suddenly grew silent as he looked up at small holes drilled into a vertical shelf. Engravings and names were chiseled under each.

This was a graveyard, a tomb, Axel realized.

Norn waved them onto the bridge where four Wooly guards in white armor stood with axes on shafts as tall as they were. The weapons formed two sets of Xs, blocking the way. They pulled them apart as Norn approached.

The bridge connected to a closed metal gate and a courtyard outside the castle. They were led through the gates into a vast terrace with flowers and trees growing inside of rock planters.

Fountains cascaded down the side into pools of water with tiled edges.

A second set of gates, then doors that opened to a passage sloping upward into the castle. Bright blue lights formed a dancing glow across the interior passage, reflecting off streams of water running on both sides of the corridor.

Aromas of baked goods and cooking meat drifted into the hallway lined with rock statues in various poses. It ended at a chamber with vaulted ceilings and crystal blue lights dangling down from cables over a round table in the center of the room.

"The Marka stays here," Norn said.

Axel looked over at Cricket, who went down on his hind legs in the hallway.

"It's okay, buddy," Uga said. "I'll bring you lots of food later, best stuff."

Cricket grunted his disapproval of being left behind.

Axel hated leaving his friend, but it seemed they had no choice. Luna, Brayton, and Axel followed Uga and Norn into the large chamber. Axel hoped the rock walls wouldn't block out any transmission to Spartacus if they needed help. Of course, if they did, they were going to need more than the war droid.

Dozens of heavily armed Woolies stood guard around the elevated throne. Sitting on that throne was Chief Cardia. In the center of the chamber were more Woolies, but these were dressed in ceremonial attire, colorful outfits and jewel encrusted forgite cuffs.

"Uga!"

A middle-aged female wobbled over with all four of her arms out. Two additional female Woolies shuffled up to Uga.

"These are my sisters," he barked. "Goli, Tonia, and Cree. This my Capa. He not married."

They all held out a single arm, interlocking the ends and coming together in a circle.

Goli stopped a foot away from Uga, standing a good three inches above her brother. Then she pulled her dress up to her furry ankles and started tapping at the floor with her paws. Tonia and Cree did the same.

The Wooly tradition prompted barking from the species, while Axel tried his best not to laugh. He didn't want to offend the chief or piss off Master Norn.

Once the dance was complete, a fourth female Wooly walked out of the gathered crowd. This one was much older and used two canes to walk.

"Mama," Uga said.

"Uga," she barked back. She handed him the canes, and did her best to dance, stumbling a few times, right into her son's arms.

Any trace of jocularity was gone now. Axel felt something deep inside of him awaken at the sight of son and mother, embracing in front of him. He thought of his own mother, his heart nearly bursting with pain at the loss, which, despite the years, was still raw in so many ways.

"Let us celebrate the return of Uga and welcome his new friends!" Chief Cardia called out. "Time to feast!"

"Feast, feast, feast!" Uga barked.

Axel and his crew took spots around the table. Brayton and Luna sat next to him, looking up as servants brought in plates of steaming food. River prawns, orange fruit split open, and loaves of warm bread.

The Woolies dug right in as Axel took in the scene. Apparently it wasn't just Uga that had a lack of manners. Before Axel had even picked up a utensil, the aliens had torn into their servings, using their limbs to swipe items off the platters, and occasionally off their neighbor's plate.

"Tell us about your journeys, Captain Finn," Cardia said as he chewed. Breadcrumbs burst from his open maw.

"Well, we've been all across the galaxy," Axel replied. "Mostly doing salvage runs, which required improvisation many times. Uga here was always the one to come through when we got ourselves into a bind."

"He's always been a good pup."

"Not a pup anymore," Uga said, chomping on the shell of a river prawn, then slurping out the sweet meat. "They named the ship after Uga, did you know that?"

He tossed the shell on the floor.

"No, do tell," Cardia said.

Master Norn watched from the side of the table, standing without taking a single bite. His hard eyes swept over Brayton, Luna, and Axel.

As Uga told stories, servants came back in and took plates away.

Axel, stuffed to the brim, wiped off his mouth.

"That was excellent, Chief Cardia," he said. "Thank you very much for your—"

"That was nothing," Cardia said. "You better have room for the main course."

The doors swung open, and four servants carried a fully roasted spider with ten charcoaled legs.

"Rock spider!" Uga shouted.

They dumped the dead beast off onto the table with a crunch. Cardia ripped a leg off and handed it to Axel. Uga glared at him as if to say, *you better eat that.*

Axel took the meaty limb with prickly burnt hairs. He brought it up to his mouth, the Chief watching him intently, nodding.

"Just like chicken," Luna said quietly.

Axel took a bite, but the burned, rubbery meat tasted nothing like chicken. He forced the chunk down then smiled.

"He likes it!" Cardia barked loudly.

The room erupted in applause, multi-limbed arms smacking together in unison.

Axel wiped his mouth off, then took another bite to act the part.

The evening turned to night, with more courses then dancing. The moon glowed outside the windows at its lowest arc, casting shadows in the chamber. In every lower part of the Great City of the Four Peaks, darkness quickly fell.

"Time for the festivities," Uga said. He got out of his chair and stepped back. Then he flexed his arms, kissing one arm, then another. "Who's first? Norn, how about you? Where'd ya go?"

Axel looked around, but the warrior had left the chamber.

"Guess he's scared of me, no?" Uga said. "Brayton, you scared, too?"

"Of what?" Brayton asked.

"Wrestling! It's our after-meal activity. Burns fat and provides room for more food."

Luna laughed.

"I'll pass," Brayton said. He raised a glass. "Thanks though."

"Captain Finn, how about you?" someone asked.

Axel looked over to see it was Uga's mother.

"It would bring us great honor for you to wrestle my son," she said.

Luna elbowed Axel under the table. "Don't hurt him, champ," she whispered.

Uga took another bite off a spider rock limb, then tossed it aside. Axel got up and went straight to the floor. Before he was even set, Uga had swiped at his ankle with an extended arm, hitting him hard in the shin and knocking him down to a knee.

A second arm smacked him in the chest, then a third wrapped around his neck, yanking him backward. Axel went down, surprised.

"Watch his ribs," Luna said.

Uga loosened his grip and Axel went to push himself up when he saw multiple armored legs surrounding them. He felt the cold metal of a blade suddenly on the back of his neck.

"Don't move," came a familiar bark.

The bark of Master Norn.

There were two additional guards pointing laser pistols at Luna and Brayton. Behind them, another armored warrior held Cricket in a tight grip.

"What's the meaning of this?!" Cardia roared.

"Uga lied to us," Norn said. "They are all wanted by the Eagles for stealing some Wrath tech."

"Is this true?" Cardia asked.

"I'm sorry," Uga said. "We just need a little time to figure things out, please. Please, uncle, let us stay."

"Maybe if that was all you were wanted for," Norn barked. "But your captain here is also wanted for *murder*."

Gasps and barks came across the room.

"What?" Axel said. "That can't be—that's not—"

"That's impossible," Uga said.

"Shut your jaw," Norn said. "Or I'll cut you down—"

"Stop this!" Cardia said.

He waddled over and looked down at Axel. "Who's he accused of murdering?"

"A group of fishermen on the planet Jolia," Norn said. "And two of our race, Napo and Manoi."

"I didn't hurt any of them," Axel said.

"What do you have to say?" Cardia asked Uga.

"Capa Finn never kill no one," Uga said. "Capa is man of peace, and has always walked path of—"

"*Men* can't be trusted," Norn said.

"Capa can be," Uga said.

"He did not kill them!" Cricket chirped. He had burst away

from his guard and was in a defensive stance with his tails both down.

"The word of a Marka holds no weight in this chamber," Norn said.

Cardia looked at Axel then to Uga before shaking his graying face wearily.

"It matters not what is truth," Cardia said. "If the Eagles say it is true, then your fate has already been decided. You must leave these halls with the sunrise."

"There isn't time for that, Chief Cardia," Norn said.

"Why is that?"

"Because I've already contacted our Eagle liaison to report we have Captain Finn and his crew. They will be here soon."

CHAPTER 28

Jax crawled through the tunnel she had fallen into hours earlier, with Zang moving ahead of them. They were being hunted, and they were lost.

The underground corridors formed a confusing matrix of catacombs beneath the central chamber. To make it even worse, steam vented through cracks in the walls.

But something had activated inside of Jax, masking her fear. An inner confidence and fuel drove her as she moved. She remembered her training. In combat, you never stop. You push ahead, fight, and move.

Staying put meant death.

Jax had no illusions about this enemy. Those Corinns weren't Corinns anymore. This place, this construct, had changed them into something evil.

The synthetic voice of one of those creatures echoed through the tunnels.

"You will never leave this place!"

Jax turned to look behind her. There wasn't enough space to raise her rifle, which was slung over her back, forcing her to carry her laser pistol. She held it in one hand and aimed it into the yellow, swirling gas.

A faint scratching hit her ear, but she couldn't tell how close.

She waited a moment, then another before turning back to Zang. As soon as she did, skittering resonated, and it sounded like it was coming from behind!

Jax turned around to see the burning eyes of a deformed Corinn. Raising her pistol, she aimed and squeezed the trigger. A bolt slammed into the ceiling, then the wall as the beast clambered through the narrow passage.

She fired again, hitting the creature in the shoulder. Steaming blue blood peppered the ground, but the Corinn kept coming. Jax aimed for the domed head and fired multiple times. Two of the lasers clipped the skull, shearing off flesh, bone, and brain.

The alien came sliding to a stop, gore slopping out of the cracked head where a flap of scorched skin rose up like a tongue.

The same voice they had first heard in the chamber called out in the distance.

"There is no escape!"

Jax turned and kept going, moving on her palms and knees. Zang was stopped ahead, looking in her direction. As Jax approached, she heard what sounded like a whistling noise. Not much different than the vortex they had heard in the crater when the fiery twisters burned across the rocky surface.

Zang held up a hand as Jax approached.

"Why are you stopping?" she whispered.

Then she saw the passage had ended. A cloud of gases drifted across the view below them in what appeared to be another chamber.

She rotated and aimed her pistol into the tunnel. "What did you see?" Jax whispered. "When you touched them?"

Zang remained quiet.

"It's just us now, and if you want to live, I need to know everything," Jax said quietly.

Still, the Corinn didn't answer.

"Look, Zang. We have to trust each other," Jax said. "Do you understand what that means?"

Zang nodded.

"Okay, good, so please, tell me what you saw," she insisted.

"I saw death."

"Death? Like, as in—"

"Burning worlds. And... something inside of worlds."

"*Inside?*"

Zang shook his head. "I'm unclear about that vision. However, I am certain that I saw human worlds and a Wooly world burning like this planet."

Jax tried to understand, but that didn't make sense. Zang couldn't have seen the future? That was impossible, right?

"I believe you were correct when you said we should abandon this world, that there is no hope of restoring it," Zang said. "I will report that to my superiors when we escape."

When? Jax thought.

She had a hard time believing they were going to escape from this place. Between the floating columns and black magic technology that had pieced the dead Corinns back together, it didn't seem likely she would see the surface again. She had to at least make sense of what they knew.

"It's as if those former Corinn scientists have become guardians of this place," Jax said.

"Yes, this Wrath construct has somehow taken control of their minds inside the chamber, and forced those outside to kill themselves—"

A distant scratching sounded, silencing him.

Jax kept her pistol aimed into the darkness, waiting for the next alien demon to emerge, but nothing came.

"We have to find a way back up to the chamber," Jax said. "Then find a way outside to link back up with my platoon."

"If we go back up that way, we die. But perhaps there is another way out."

Jax shivered as Zang turned to the chamber below them. The light haze of gases blocked her view of what was down there. Reaching down, the Corinn pulled out a blue jewel and tossed it in the air. Wings sprouted before it zipped away. The blue glow vanished, swallowed up by the darkness.

Another shriek resonated down the perfectly smooth rock tunnel. Jax couldn't hear much beyond the whistling noise coming from the chamber.

She flinched as Zang pulled her shoulder.

When Jax turned, she saw the winged device had returned, and below it, the darkness was chased away by a pulsating orange light.

Jax scooted over for a better look. There was something down there alright, a lot of somethings. From her vantage she couldn't make them out well, but the glow seemed to be coming from bioluminescent shells in a misty cavern.

"What are those things?"

"I'm unsure," Zang replied.

The Corinn moved slightly to the side, allowing Jax to squeeze up closer. The pulsating lights were coming from shells attached to drooping rows of stalks across the cavern below.

Jax had leaned down for a better look when she heard scratching. By the time she turned, it was too late. A fire sickle boomeranged toward her, nearly taking off the top of her helmet. She ducked down and brought up her pistol.

The freak alien that had thrown it was clambering toward

them on all fours, now just five feet away. Jax fired, hitting it in one of the arms as it lunged through the tunnel headfirst. The crest slammed into her chest, knocking her backward, right into Zang. The Corinn let out an *oomph* that turned to a yell that faded away.

There was no time to help, nothing she could do as Zang fell into the chamber. All she could do after landing on her back was try to beat the demonic alien away with her pistol. That did little good as it climbed over her body, pinning her to the rock. She squirmed under the weight, staring in horror at the monstrosity with fiery eyes. The pale head was connected to a neck with a black line tracing across it.

She tried to maneuver her pistol, but it was under the creature, stuck between them. She couldn't be sure whether the shot would hit her or the abomination.

Instead, she slammed the top of her helmet against the open mouth, shattering teeth. The creature roared back, but then it grabbed her by the neck with its long fingers, squeezing hard. She glanced down, seeing the barrel was indeed aimed at her own stomach.

The beast grabbed her head in both hands and slammed it to the tunnel floor, her vision going out like a light clicking off. It turned back on instantly to a view of those fiery eyes, but now she couldn't look away. She felt her mind being transported, like the creature had entered her thoughts.

She saw a burning sky with raging electrical storms over green fields. The image intensified, bringing her to the ground level where she stood in a field of ash roots. The tiny tree-like plants stretched across the horizon where smoke tendrilled over ridges covered in purple flowers.

Realization passed over her.

She was back on Runi, at her family farm. She turned and saw their house with solar panels on the roof. Her mom, dad, and brother were standing in front of the porch, looking up at the sky where a spiked ship lowered out of a lightning storm.

A flash burst from the hull, and the farmhouse vanished in a green explosion.

"NO!" Jax tried to scream.

Her voice croaked as the vision cleared back to the underground tunnel. The alien was still on top of her, eyes burning as it choked the life out of her. With only seconds before she slipped into the darkness, she worked on freeing her hand with the pistol.

The thought of her family helped give her a burst of adrenaline. She had to get out of this place, had to survive to fight the Wrath.

She finally angled the barrel up. The monster snapped at her face as she pulled the trigger. A laser bolt tunneled into the naked belly of the beast. It let go instantly, gripping the wound.

She brought in her other hand, holding the pistol in both and aiming at the face. The burning eyes flashed right before she pulled the trigger in rapid succession.

The burst erased the carved-up face of the monster, the head exploding like a ripe fruit. Gore peppered Jax but she pushed the creature off, searching the darkness for another hostile.

Seeing nothing, she crawled to the edge and looked down for Zang. Steam and gas drifted across the view, rising up from the spiked bulbs clinging to the wall. She moved closer to the ledge, still not seeing him.

A screech rang out behind her.

There was no time to react, other than to rotate enough to see the naked, stitched up body of a Corinn clambering toward her. The monster slammed into her, knocking Jax out of the opening. She fell sideways, plummeting face first downward.

The glowing, spiked constructs on the ground rose up to

meet her as she tried to reposition her body to land on her metal legs.

She closed her eyes, focusing on home. She wished she was back there now with her family, enjoying the beauty of a sunset over their crops, and the peace of their homestead.

In those final seconds of her life, she pictured their farm burning, knowing this vision would become reality unless she could live to prevent it.

Her body suddenly stopped, jerked to a halt, but there was no pain.

Jax opened her eyes to see she had never hit the ground. She twisted to look over a shoulder at Zang, holding onto one of the bulbs with one hand, and Jax's foot in the other. The arm the Corinn held her by was twisted at an odd angle, no doubt snapped out of the socket.

He let go, and Jax twisted as she fell the ten feet down to the floor. As soon as she regained her balance, she unslung her rifle and aimed it above.

Zang climbed down with her into a layer of the sulfuric gases drifting over a moist, fertile floor. They both looked up at the ledge, at the demented face of the Corinn mutant that had knocked Jax down. She moved her finger to the trigger, then fired a burst.

The bolts hit the top of the tunnel, narrowly missing the face. The monster snarled and shrieked, "You will never leave this place!"

Then it skulked back into the hole.

Jax kept her rifle aimed at the opening.

"Thank you," she said quietly. "You saved my life."

Zang nodded as he gripped his limp arm, still looking up. He suddenly snapped the arm back into its socket, holding in a muffled cry. He took another moment, and then motioned for

Jax to follow. Jax looked over her back at the tunnel above one last time before turning to the cavern.

"What in the world..." she whispered.

Rows of the curved black stalks rose off the squishy, moist floor. Jax bent down to examine the ground with a finger, scooping up thick, black viscera. She peeled an entire section up that connected to a tendrilled limb coated in an array of bristles at the bottom, surging upwards twenty, maybe twenty-five feet. They filled the chamber like a ghastly forest, and attached around their fleshy sides were pale orbs, their outer covering fine and translucent, like an eggshell, gently pulsing with a soft glow.

"Are those batteries?" Jax wondered. "Maybe some sort of tech left behind?"

"Perhaps," Zang replied.

They advanced through the gas, navigating the stalks and keeping far away from their barbed bases and the orbs drooping from the top.

Clicking resonated through the brooding chamber as they advanced.

"This place is massive," Jax said quietly.

Zang suddenly stopped under a stalk, glancing up at slime dripping from an orb far above them. Jax flinched as the semi-transparent shell flashed with movement—something bulged out from the gelatinous sphere: A hand maybe? Or a foot.

These weren't batteries or lights or some sort of tech.

They were eggs.

Was this place a Wrath nursery? A hatching ground?

Her mind wandered to the ramifications of what she was seeing. The discovery was unprecedented, an affirmation of the unthinkable.

"The Wrath aren't *returning*," Jax stammered. "They never left."

She stood in awe, looking out over the mammoth alien growfield.

"This is what I saw in my vision. These abominations have been feeding off the planet," Zang said. "Growing their legions, nurtured by the ash of my ancestors."

Jax hurried toward the wall.

"Where are you going, Sergeant Brito?" Zang asked.

"We know the way out is up there," Jax said. "The fate of both our species rests in our hands. We have to warn them, even if it means killing every single monster in here."

The Corinn nodded. "Then I shall help you slay them."

She nodded back. "Strong and steady, my friend."

We have to get out of here, Axel thought.

He stared out the window of the castle prison cell at the bare slip of moon lingering on the horizon, the clock-ticking closer toward his fate. Soon, Warhorses would soar over the Four Peaks Mountains, packed full of Eagles with one purpose —to kill him.

Just like they had killed his father, and every other Steward.

He had made a vital error coming here, but he had made an even worse error by bringing his crew. They would never let him be taken without fighting. Now their fate would be tied to his own, unless they could find a way to escape.

Axel grabbed the bars, testing them. They rattled slightly, but they were secure. He wasn't sure he had the strength to break them, especially with his injuries.

A glance down confirmed the terrace was at least a thousand feet below. Small, multi-limbed furry figures moved in the glow of burning torches.

He looked up, but all he saw were fluffy clouds drifting

across the mountain peaks. He pulled an image from when they had arrived, thinking of distant views of the castle. If he was correct, then the prison was at the top of the fortress, and directly connected to the peaks overhead.

Even if he could break out, he had injured ribs, a full belly—and no rope. The Woolies had made sure climbing would be impossible for one of their own, let alone for men.

But Axel was not an ordinary man.

That was their first mistake.

The second mistake was putting a Marka in the same cell.

Cricket lay on the stone floor, head on his front paws, waiting for Axel to give him orders. Luna and Brayton were standing in the adjacent cell. They too looked at him in anticipation of a plan.

Uga had been taken somewhere else, and Axel wasn't counting on the Wooly to help them now. If they couldn't escape, their only hope was Spartacus. Problem was the droid had no idea they were in trouble because the Wooly guards had taken his transmitter.

And even if Spartacus did know they were imprisoned, what could he do to rescue them? They were locked inside cells at the top of the fortress, guarded by two Master Wooly warriors in white armor, holding a variety of weapons in their many limbs.

The only way out, it seemed, was up.

"You have to let us go," Luna said to the guards. "What the Eagles said is a lie! They will come here and kill all of us, including you."

Both the Wooly guards remained stone-faced.

"Don't bother, they don't care," Cricket chirped.

She looked across at Axel.

"We can prove you aren't guilty," Brayton said. "We know the truth."

"The truth," Axel mumbled. "I should have told you the truth long ago, but I feared you wouldn't understand."

"Understand what?" Brayton asked.

"Wait, you did kill those men?" Luna asked.

"No," Axel said. "But it doesn't matter. They're hunting me because of what I am."

The three crew members looked at each other.

"What are you, Captain?" Luna said softly.

Axel felt the shame and guilt of his secret eating him from the inside.

He grinded his teeth in anger. Not at the situation, but at himself. At his past. He had lived with this curse his entire life.

"Axel?"

"I'm not who you think I am," he said.

Brayton smiled and scoffed lightly. "Neither was I, and you still took me in."

"You were there for me through my darkest years," Luna said. "You rescued Cricket and took in Uga. You fixed Spartacus. Fixed us all."

"Accepted us," Cricket said.

"We're a crew of misfits, and that's what makes us special, but I'm not like you all," Axel said. "I'm dangerous."

Luna narrowed her gaze, clearly wishing there was something she could say to ease his mind.

Barking echoed through the prison.

Female barking.

The translator Axel wore relayed some of it.

"Come here, handsome. I have something to show—"

The two guards turned at the end of the hallway.

"Hey! You're not supposed to be here," one of them said.

Axel glimpsed three female Woolies stride into the hallway. He recognized them immediately. These were Uga's sisters. They all turned and wiggled their furry asses at the guards, who instantly softened. But this wasn't a seduction, it was a distraction.

An object flew out and knocked one guard to the ground then came a second whistling rock that hit the other sentry in the head. He crumpled next to his comrade, forming a twisted pile of furry, armored bodies.

Goli, Tonia, and Cree pulled their skirts down, chuckling in low barks. Uga rushed between his sisters while waving at them to retreat. "Well done. Now go. Go home," he barked.

"Uga!" Cricket chirped.

He stood on all fours, both tails wagging.

"No time for wagging. That dork Master Norn be back in a minute," Uga said.

"How do you know?" Axel asked as he grabbed the cell bars.

"Big head Master Guards went with Chief Cardia to meet those Eagles." Uga pulled out a key and unlocked the cell holding Luna and Brayton.

"Hurry," he barked, turning to unlock Axel's cell.

"Wait," he said. "We should split up. Uga, you get the others to the ship. We'll meet there."

"What? No, Axel." Luna shook her head. "We should...we *must* stick together."

"There's no time to argue. Splitting up gives us the best chance of—" Axel said.

"No worries. We go into the mines on the eastern face of the valley," Uga interrupted. "Then we take a river boat to the lake, find the *Trash Squid*—well, hopefully still hidden."

Axel nodded and the group hurried down the hall, back toward the two unconscious guards. He bent down and pulled one of their fire hatchets from its sheath.

Luna took a laser pistol and Brayton armed himself with a fire knife.

"Good luck," Axel said. "Cricket, you're with me."

Luna nodded and lingered for one more moment before fleeing with Uga and Brayton.

Wasting no time, Axel activated the fire hatchet and began chopping at a barred window facing the exterior of the castle. He broke through three of the bars, grabbing them and pulling with everything he had.

Axel grunted as he pried at the bars, his ribs burning. They slowly bent apart enough that he leaned through. The castle exterior was vertical, as he had expected, but the climber in him saw plenty of hand and footholds.

Groaning sounded, and Axel rotated as one of the Wooly guards stirred awake. The dark, confused eyes flitted up to Axel, and realization set in, but not before Cricket used a tail to wrap around the furry neck, yanking his head into the wall with a thud. When the sentry awoke again, the Wooly would sound the alarm, and Axel would lead the troopers into the mountains, *hopefully* allowing his crew to get back to the *Trash Squid*.

But after that?

Axel could think about after, later. He had to focus on the right now. And that meant climbing. He moved back to let Cricket out first, and the Marka immediately started climbing. Then Axel pulled himself up and onto the ledge, bracing against the freezing wind. A strong gust whistled against his body, rippling his suit and hair.

Once it passed, Axel reached up to the stones, and pulled himself up after Cricket, his tails hanging behind him like ropes.

Axel reached up to a sliver of a ledge, found scant purchase, and pulled his lean body up. Normally, the free climbing would be easy, even with the wind, but his upper body ached, and his ribs throbbed. Thankfully, adrenaline flooded his system the higher he climbed, masking some of the pain.

In a few minutes, Axel could hardly see the escape window below.

He kept his gaze on the vertical shards of red rock rising into the clouds.

Careful what you wish for, he thought, remembering that he had fantasized about climbing these walls when he'd first arrived, never imagining he would get the chance. Now, getting to the top without being knocked off or shot would determine whether he could stay ahead of them and his friends might survive.

His heart flipped when he heard the roar of engines.

The Eagles were coming. Just like they had come for his father.

But now he was ready, and if it came to it, he would fight to protect his crew.

An internal fire ignited. He didn't think about what ledge or hold to grab next. There was no struggle to breathe or burning of muscles. He felt nothing but the cold wind in his hair.

They were almost to the cloud cover, far above the Wooly fortress, when the first Eagle transport blasted over the valley, landing gear deploying as it swooped down over the river.

Axel pulled up to the next rock. A sharp piece stung his freezing fingers. He held on as a gust battered his body, threatening to whip him off the ledge. He swung his other arm across to brace, his wound feeling as if it was going to tear back open from the swift motion.

The pain, he told himself, was a natural process. Just like breathing. Or eating.

Pain was part of living.

Cricket chirped down at him, and he glanced up to see the Marka sitting on a bluff hanging over the top of the fortress. They had made it.

Axel grabbed one of the tails, and Cricket heaved him up.

Side by side, they crouched to look over the valley. A single

Clipper had landed near the river. Eagles hopped out, six, then an entire unit.

Barking sounded from the fortress below.

The guards had woken, or perhaps these were new warriors.

"We must keep moving," Cricket chirped.

Axel went to move but stopped when he noticed a figure among the Eagles. A tall man not dressed in combat armor. While Axel couldn't see the man's face, he could see a long, distinctive beard.

Rangnar.

It appeared the old bounty hunter had come out of retirement to help hunt Stewards again.

Axel gripped the axe on his belt.

"You better hope our paths don't cross old, man," he said. "If they do, peace won't be my way."

CHAPTER 29

Rangnar stepped away from the Clipper with ten Eagles in black-clad armor. All the soldiers were armed to the teeth with laser rifles and sheathed fire swords strapped over their armored plating.

General Gabriel Jessup led the squad through a green field.

Overhead, a single Warhorse hovered above the mountain peaks, ready to deploy troops at a second's notice. Lucid was up there, her fate tied to whether or not they captured Axel, and whether Gabriel kept his end of the bargain.

A contingent of Wooly soldiers moved out of a forest separating the fields from a gigantic fortress carved out of the rock. They outnumbered the Eagles ten to one, but Gabriel walked away from the Clipper without a weapon in hand, clearly not concerned.

It was a smart move to not enrage the Woolies. Clans like these valued their independence and privacy. But it seemed they had willingly given up Axel for the bounty.

Not that Rangnar was surprised.

Woolies were fiercely loyal to their kin and clans, but not to outsiders—and all but Woolies were outsiders. Axel had made a vital mistake coming here with the contract on his head. Not that the Woolies giving him up made Rangnar feel much better about betraying Axel, as he followed the Eagles across the grass.

The river carving through the city of Four Peaks sparkled in the moonlight. Birds chirped in the cool night air, and small animals poked out of their dens to look at the strange newcomers.

Everything looked serene in the valley, but Rangnar knew all hell could break loose at any moment. The Eagles had taken his cuffs off, but he was without any blast armor to protect him from potential crossfire.

A group of six Woolies wearing white combat armor that overlapped like scales of a dragon, walked out of the forest. The chest pieces, the bulwark of the suits, were embossed with the emblem of the Four Peaks, the same design gracing a flag whipping on a pole held by one of the warriors.

As Rangnar marched across the lush grass, he surveyed the valley. Waterfalls cascaded down the rocky vermillion walls. Bridges draped over different levels of the mountain sides, connecting to homes built into the sheer cliffs. From them, hundreds of furry faces with curious eyes watched the Eagles.

There were also guard posts up there, and Rangnar was sure there would be far more out of sight. But still, these short, husky fighters would be little match for the Eagles, if the Warhorse deployed Clippers packed full of troopers.

He directed his gaze back to the envoy ahead. There was no sign of Axel or his crew. The armored Woolies shifted in the center, disgorging a gray-haired Wooly wearing a robe with golden cuffs. His short stride was matched in unison by two of the Master Warrior guards.

"Greetings," Gabriel called out.

The chief Wooly held up a shaky hand.

"You have entered the Great City of the Four Peaks," Cardia barked. "State your business."

The general took a step closer, towering over the small alien. "I am General Gabriel—"

"Jessup," said the Wooly. "I know who you are. I am Chief Cardia of the Four Peaks tribe, and I did *not* authorize your landing."

Gabriel, clearly growing agitated, sniffed the air. "Tell me where the Steward bastard is, and we will leave you in peace."

"He isn't here," Cardia barked. "Not anymore."

The general raised a brow. "Then where is he?"

"He was taken prisoner and he escaped."

Gabriel reached up to his nose, squeezing the bridge between his thick eyebrows, clearly frustrated. "When?"

"Not very long ago," Cardia said.

"And his crew?"

"They are under my protection."

"Is that so?"

"You will not take the crew, but I will hand over Captain Axel Finn once my Master Warriors have hunted him down."

Rangnar felt his pulse racing.

"You lost him once," the general said. "If your troopers manage to find him, it will likely be the end of their lives. He is not *what* you think he is."

"He is a man, like you."

Gabriel shook his head and sighed. "Why must things always be so difficult with you Woolies?"

Cardia bared his front teeth and his guards took a step forward.

"Maybe Axel didn't escape. Maybe you're hiding him," Gabriel said. "Either way, you're wasting my precious time. What do you want? forgite? A herd of Corinn bulls? How about some Torqs to bathe in your nice little meandering river here?"

"I want you to get back in your fancy ship and take off into the clouds. I will deliver this man to you once he is located."

"Is that so?"

Gabriel gave the valley a quick scan, then he turned to look at a lieutenant. His eyes flitted over to Rangnar, and Rangnar thought he saw a sly grin. In a swift movement, he raised a finger.

A dazzling light show burst around them.

The guards with Cardia had no time to react before laser bolts punched through their armor. All but Cardia slumped over, their furry bodies burning. The chief looked around with his cloudy white eyes, calmly taking in the scene of violence in a slow swoop. When he pulled a fire hatchet from a sheath, it was anything *but* slow. Unfortunately, it was too late. He brought it up just as Gabriel swung a flaming fire sword down, the serrated black easily lopping off the arm gripping the hatchet, and then skewering the chief through his chest.

Return fire blasted from the forest and cliffs.

Eagles closed in with their energy shields, forming undulating curves to deflect the incoming fire. A missile streaked away from the Clipper as the pilots lifted off. The projectile hit a tower in the forest, bursting in a brilliant explosion. A burning Wooly, his limbs aflame, cartwheeled through the air.

The Clipper rotated, unleashing missiles in all directions.

More came tearing from above, the Warhorse launching on pre-chosen targets. Shield generators absorbed some of the destruction, and return fire blasted out of turrets hidden in the cliffs, but Rangnar knew this clan would be no match for the Warhorse firepower.

He dropped to the ground, hugging the dirt as laser bolts streaked overhead. On his stomach, he began to crawl away from the Eagles. He looked for a weapon, something to try and kill Gabriel with, but there was nothing within easy reach.

He got up but then dove to the ground as an explosion burst in the air behind him. The Clipper was spinning out of control, round and round, until the starboard wings clipped the ground. Pieces of shrapnel whizzed through the air, metal shards flinging everywhere. The machine went down hard on the field, pushing up a hump of dirt right in front of him.

Rangnar ran from the earthen wave as fast as he could. At the edge of the riverbank he jumped into the water, splashing in and going under. The current sucked him outward, but he kicked up to the surface, gasping for air.

He hated water.

Ears ringing and vision blurred, he looked toward Gabriel, who was standing over the impaled chief, not fifteen feet away.

"You are a demon," Cardia barked in a low tone, the life fading from his old body. Despite that, the chief swiftly brought up an arm gripping a knife that Gabriel caught in a gloved hand. He pushed the hilt of his sword deeper into the chest of the downed Wooly, prompting a final howl of agony.

The general said something that Rangnar couldn't make out. Whatever it was, Cardia spat in response.

Gabriel wiped it away and then plucked the knife free from Cardia's furry arm. He bent down and traced it across the Wooly's throat.

Enraged barks resonated from the valley, forming a chorus of angry voices.

Lasers pounded the shields around Gabriel. He activated his helmet and strode away, rifle in hand, as his men flanked him.

"Find the Steward bastard!" he shouted. "Kill everyone in your way!"

Rangnar stared back up at the Warhorse, knowing then he wouldn't be able to save Lucid with the deal he made. The

Eagles would never honor it. The general was a murderer, intent on finding Axel, no matter what the cost.

That left Rangnar with one option—kill Gabriel Jessup.

He searched one last time for a weapon, anything to end the life of the madman in front of him. As the general turned in his direction, he ducked down, pushing away from the bank of the river, and letting the current take his body.

This wasn't over, but for now, he was free.

The Wrath invasion wasn't coming—it had already started.

Jax examined the bristling bottom of the organic tower that drooped, leaning toward the wall of the chamber. It looked sturdy enough to climb, but that meant climbing past the Wrath eggs. There were thousands of them down here, but no way out, from what Jax and Zang could tell. That meant they were going to have to go back the way they had come.

Jax scanned the tunnels in the wall above them, searching for the possessed Corinns that had become guardians of the unhatched offspring. The sulfuric gas flowing from the many tunnels above made it difficult to see, forcing Jax to rely on infrared scans.

She wasn't even sure if they would work on these Corinn zombies, if she could call them that. There had to be some sort of scientific explanation for the abominations, but whose science?

After a few moments of further surveying the wall above, Jax nodded to Zang. The Corinn guide started up the stalk, using the bristles as rungs. He climbed while Jax held security, roving her rifle across the tunnel openings.

About halfway up, Zang stopped and motioned for Jax to follow.

Slinging her rifle, Jax stepped on the first egg with her metal legs, fearing it would burst under the weight of her feet. But the hide, despite its translucence, was thick and scaly. She glimpsed a spidery beast squirming inside the amniotic fluid, or yolk, whatever it was floating in. From what little she could see, the liquid was viscous, like thick oil.

A rumble suddenly shook the construct as she moved up to the next egg. She grabbed a spike on the leathery hide of stalk and held on.

Jax looked up to Zang, who was still climbing despite his injured arm and the disruptive tremors. The quake shook the chamber violently. Jax held on and closed her eyes. She was exhausted, starving, and terrified of dying down here, not so much because she feared death, but because of what would happen if she and Zang were killed before warning their allies about what was happening on the planet.

Jax remembered something from training.

Fear is fuel you use to fight.

Thoughts of the vision she had when the Corinn connected to her mind snapped her free of that fear. The beast was up there somewhere, and she was going to kill it, along with every other monster hiding in the tunnels separating them from the chamber with the floating columns. From there, they would fight their way out and head back to the entrance.

Chances were good that door was closed again. If that was the case, Jax wasn't sure what they would do, but she had a few ideas. The nuclear option was to remove Hippo's power-cell, plant it at the door, and remotely detonate it.

It was the best plan Jax could think of, but she knew executing it would be dangerous. Still, there was no choice. She could allow nothing to stop her from getting out of here. They had to get the message to command.

Jax pressed on as the quake passed. She reached up to the

next bulb, grabbed a spike, and moved her leg up to a new foothold. Zang was almost to the closest tunnel entrance.

"Hold on," Jax called up.

She climbed to right below the Corinn and pulled out her pistol.

"The fate of both of our species could rest in our hands," Jax said. "We can help save them, together, but only if we fight as a team."

He nodded.

"I'll go first," she said.

Zang moved to the side, allowing Jax to check the inside of the tunnel. At first glance, it appeared clear. She prepared to leap from the stalk into the opening when she heard a distant clanking.

It seemed to be coming from below.

No!

Jax glanced up as a Corinn with a single burning eye skittered down the chamber wall, snatching her and pulling her up into a tunnel. The creature slammed her head into the side of the wall inside, then against the ground.

Stunned, Jax lay paralyzed from the pain, unable to fight as the monster grabbed her by the neck, intent on crushing her windpipe.

The elongated jaw opened, releasing a shriek. A blue light flashed through the tunnel and that fiery eye suddenly winked off. The head slid off the neck, thumping against Jax's chest armor.

She reached up and pried the hands off, sucking in a deep breath. Zang crawled into the tunnel and yanked his fire sickle out of the ceiling.

"We must move," he said, handing her the pistol she dropped.

Jax sat up, shaking from the shock. She took the weapon and crawled over the corpse of the dead Corinn.

In the combat situations Jax had experienced in the past, she would have exchanged a nod, or some heartfelt words with her comrades. But the Corinn wasn't like the humans she had served with on distant planets.

Still, she felt a bond with this alien. A bond she didn't even feel with the other Eagles.

"Thank you, Z," she said.

"I will watch over you, Sergeant Jax Brito. Strong and steady."

She smiled and nodded.

The Corinn turned back to the tunnel without another word, and began the climb. Zang moved fast, and Jax did her best to keep up. Ten minutes of moving at a brisk pace got them to their first sloped shaft entrance.

Jax waited for Zang to clear it, then followed him up into it. The top intersected with another level passage. It was there the distant sound of hissing monsters resonated downward. It was clear these noises were coming from the main chamber.

"Get ready," Jax said, heart pounding as they pulled their bodies up into the chamber floor. The first thing Jax saw was the columns overhead. Two of the arcs had connected with one of the pillars.

Zang was looking in the opposite direction, and when Jax turned with her rifle she saw three sets of fiery orange eyes. She took a few steps back with her rifle butt against her shoulder plate.

Three more sets of eyes flickered to life.

"Six hostiles," Jax said.

She came back-to-back with Zang, who held the fire sickle. The bluish-purple blades created a calm glow against the demonic flicker of fire in the walls. The beasts closed in from all directions.

Together, Jax and Zang started backing toward the ramp that led up to the entrance. They made it a few steps before the shrieks rang out. Then came the monsters, rushing all at once through the fog, wielding nothing but their arms and hands. Jax sighted up a head, aiming for those burning sockets.

In that moment, she felt no fear, only duty.

This was for her family.

She squeezed off a burst of bolts that sizzled through the head. The other two abominations went down on all fours, fanning out to avoid her shots. She led one of the clambering beasts with her barrel, firing right as it changed course. That burst hit it in the side, sending it sliding across the floor.

The final possessed Corinn on her side was only ten feet away and closing in fast. She missed her next few shots as the beast leapt into the air. In what seemed like slow motion she saw those burning eyes that sought to penetrate her mind again. She closed her eyes and pulled the trigger rapidly.

A meaty body slammed into her, knocking her away from Zang. She fell on her back and rolled away from the creature which crashed to the ground, limp and dead from a pair of holes in its head.

Jax pushed herself up to find Zang battling in close combat with two of the other mutants. He used his fire sickle to open the guts of one of the monsters. Black entrails sloshed out. The thing stumbled back, and Zang took off the head with a swift stroke.

The last monster thrust a fire knife into Zang's back just as Jax aimed her rifle. She fired a single shot into the head, blasting off the jaw, ending a shriek. The creature turned toward her and she finished it with a shot to the forehead.

Zang fell to his knees, the knife sticking out of his back. He reached over a shoulder and plucked the blade free.

After quickly clearing the space, Jax rushed over.

"Can you move?" she asked.

"Yes."

"I'll help you," Jax said. She bent down and got under Zang's armpits to get him on his feet.

Jax began the search for Hippo in the area where she had seen the droid drop to the ground. She found the hulking war machine a few moments later.

"Cover me," Jax said, handing her rifle to Zang.

Bending down, Jax went to work removing the back T-Flesh plates. She trusted her ally, but it was hard not to look up as she worked on carefully removing the power-cell.

"Got it—" Jax started to say.

Brilliant orange flashes burned up the walls around them as a quake rattled the interior of the construct. The pillars above burned from an internal source, growing brighter.

Jax stood with the power-cell gripped against her chest. She pulled out her pistol and started toward the ramp leading topside. Zang limped after her holding the laser rifle.

Vibrations rumbled over ground which felt to be rising.

"There is no life, only death."

Jax stopped right before the ramp.

Out of the swirling gases came the hulking, armored frame of Hesh and his prosthetic metal leg. The sergeant grabbed Jax by her helmet and slammed her into a wall, holding her there, forcing her pistol and the power-cell from her grip. They clanked to the ground as Hesh raised Jax higher against the wall.

Behind the monstrous warrior's cracked visor, eyes burned with the same fire that had possessed the Corinns.

This was no longer Hesh, and he was no longer stuttering.

A deep growl came from his throat.

Zang rushed over but was kicked away by Hesh's robotic leg. He grabbed Jax by her other hand, pushing inward with both large paws.

She fought to get free, using her own metal legs to kick at Hesh. The possessed, zombified warrior squeezed harder. Crunching and cracking sounded as the massive Eagle crushed her helmet like it was nothing more than a can.

A warning went off on her HUD as Jax tried to free one of her hands pinned against the T-Flesh chest plates. She gritted in pain from the intense pressure on her skull.

*Not like this...*she thought.

Zang came rushing back with a fire sickle. He slashed at Hesh, cutting deep into his right arm where the burning blade became stuck.

The giant former soldier removed a hand from Jax's helmet and smacked Zang away. The movement freed Jax's arm and she used the opportunity to reach down and pull out a fire knife.

She activated the handle and stabbed Hesh in the wrist of the hand he was still holding her with. The beast let out a roar, dropping Jax to the ground.

Zang rushed back over with another fire sickle as she stumbled away.

"Go," he said. "Blow the door."

Jax searched for the power-cell she had dropped, trying to shake the pain from her pounding head. Her alien friend slashed at Hesh, keeping the half-dead freak at bay.

Jax scooped up the cell and staggered to the ramp. By the time she reached the top, her full vision had returned. She managed to run inside the corridor, all the way back to that smooth door with claw marks on the exterior.

She crouched right in front of it with the cell, going through the steps to start the self-destruct countdown. It was something they taught Eagles in their basic training, but nothing she had ever thought she would need.

How long until it exploded, she wondered.

A minute? Thirty seconds? That part, she couldn't recall.

As soon the light turned red, she got up and bolted back toward the chamber. Halfway back, she saw orange eyes.

Hesh lumbered forward, the sickle still stuck in his arm. Blood oozed from multiple holes in his armor where Zang had struck him with the other blade. The Corinn, it appeared, had lost the fight.

Cornered, Jax had no choice but to fight.

She reached to her holster but realized she had lost the gun back in the chamber with Zang.

With nothing but her fists, she strode toward her former comrade.

Hesh snorted and hissed like the dying boar that Jax had killed on the farm when she was just an adolescent. She would never forget the primal, guttural cries of that dying creature after she had shot it in the stomach. It was the first animal she had ever killed.

Jax let out a cry of her own as Hesh charged.

Another scream answered as a figure leapt onto the back of Hesh. It was Zang, an arm wrapped around the neck of the giant man. He thrust a fire knife into his helmet just as Hesh reached up to pry the Corinn free.

The fiery glows winked out, and the big man crumbled to the ground, pinning Zang beneath him. Jax ran over to help, knowing she had only seconds before the detonation.

"No," Zang said. "Go. You must go."

Jax grabbed a boot and pulled, ignoring her friend. She

tugged, using all her strength, partly freeing Zang. The alien used a long arm to knock Jax backward.

"Go!" he shouted.

A flash burst as Jax fell to the ground.

The walls shook, the ceiling growled, and a tidal wave of fire surged down the passage.

CHAPTER 30

Crouching in the peaks with Cricket, Axel and his friend stared in horror at the battle—or rather massacre—below. Explosions boomed across the cliffs, destroying Wooly dwellings in blasts of stone.

A dozen Clippers had lowered from the Warhorse, destroying all alien air-defense systems in a matter of minutes using Lightning Missiles before disgorging Eagles on the ground.

Axel filled his lungs with the chalky scent of smoke and—burning fur.

That wasn't the only thing burning.

Anger flamed through his insides and the taste of copper hung in his mouth.

You must stand and fight these Eagles!

The voice of his father tugged him toward violence. He clenched his jaw, ready to embrace it, to make these bastards pay. The rampaging Eagles were here for one thing—Axel. Hunting him down just like they had hunted his father on Furia, killing anyone in their path.

And he could only blame himself. He had caused this. It

was *his* fault the Woolies were dying. Soon, if the Eagles didn't stop their assault, his crew would also be located and killed. They were somewhere to the east, hopefully in the mines, preparing to take a boat to the *Trash Squid*.

But what if they didn't make it?

Only he could stop this. Only he could save them.

There was only one way to end this.

Yes, you must become the warrior you know you are inside.

Axel wanted to listen, wanted to fight, but how could he fight so many?

"I have to give myself up," he said to Cricket.

"No," replied the Marka. "The Eagles will kill you."

"If that's what it takes to stop this slaughter."

"Axel, you're my best friend, and that's why I've got to speak my heart." Cricket whipped a tail over, wrapping it around Axel's shoulders.

"You giving yourself up won't stop the blood, nor will it make up for what's already been spilled," said the Marka. "I need you. The crew needs you—"

Axel heard a humming right before Cricket chirped a warning. A Clipper roared over the peak above them. This was his chance, raise his hands into the air and call out to be taken—or run.

"Axel, come on!" Cricket chirped.

Axel chased the Marka across a ledge of rocks that curved to the east. A thousand feet below was the entrance to the mines where the rest of their crew would hopefully be hiding, ready to escape. It was a long descent, when the entire valley had erupted into a war zone.

Smoke billowed out of a rocky ledge ahead. Axel climbed sideways in that direction, spotting the smoldering Wooly guard post. The stone lookout had taken a direct hit from a missile. A smoking lump of fur and armor lay under a pile of scattered rocks.

Axel climbed over to the ledge. He bent down to check for a pulse but could tell without turning the warrior over that he was dead. A search of the debris revealed a destroyed rocket launcher, a mangled but functional fire spear, and a burned laser pistol.

He handed the gun to Cricket.

"You know how to use this?" Axel asked.

"Does Uga know how to eat?" Cricket replied.

Axel plucked the twisted fire spear out of the ground. He broke off the bottom quarter of the mangled shaft then gripped the solid weapon in both hands. Humming broke over the wind.

He hunched down as another Clipper soared toward them from the clouds, rotating a laser cannon at the bluff.

"Run!" Axel shouted.

Laser bolts pounded the rocks as the Marka leapt away.

For the first time in his life, Axel didn't even consider peace. Something inside of him activated, like the final tick of a time-bomb. He let out a war cry in a voice he didn't recognize as he charged the aircraft hovering ten feet away from the cliff, laser cannon flashing.

The voice of his mother surfaced in his mind.

Peace is your way.

The conflicting rage-filled voice answered.

War is the only way to peace!

With the spear in hand, he picked up speed. At the edge of the bluff, he leapt into the air, sailing toward the open troop hold where a harnessed Eagle fired the laser cannon.

I will not hurt what can't be healed, he thought.

Then you will lose everything!

Axel released the spear mid-air. The blade punched through

the heart of the Eagle, knocking him back, his harness lurching him forward. Axel plucked the spear from the limp Eagle and crashed into the troop hold, landing in a hunch. Three more Eagles stood in their seats. Two had already pushed up the levers.

The two standing soldiers pulled out their swords, one of them fumbling, but the other man drawing it swiftly.

I will not take what can't be replaced.

You must! You or them! You or THEM!

Axel slashed with the spear, tracing the blade across their throats. The other three all pushed up their crossbars to free themselves. Axel shoved one of the dying Eagles behind him into the still trapped soldiers.

Violence only leads to more violence.

Only violence will end violence!

Axel moved without thought, everything based completely on instinct, allowing his brain to be possessed by the voice of his father. He pulled a laser pistol from the holster of a dead Eagle and fired at one of the pilots, who turned with a pistol of their own. The bolt hit him in the visor, tunneling through an eye.

All life is precious.

Your life is precious, not the life of your enemy!

All three Eagles in the seats were free now, and all of them were drawing their swords. Axel grabbed the arm of the closest man, breaking it with a quick snap. He then snatched the sword and thrust it into the heart of the next standing soldier. Plucking it out, he brought it down with both hands over the helmet of an Eagle who had dropped to their knees.

"No, no!" the soldier shrieked.

Axel brought the sword down with all his strength, splitting the skull in half like chopping wood. When he pulled it away, arterial blood squirted out of the neck. The dark carmine flow joined a pool on the deck.

Chest heaving, Axel looked to the cockpit where the last pilot held up both hands.

"Holy shit, holy shit, please don't," he begged.

Axel started up toward him, but only made it two feet before the man opened a side hatch and leapt out. The craft continued to hover as he turned back to the sound of scratching nails on metal.

Cricket stood in the open troop hold at the aft of the craft, taking in the massacre with all four of his eyes, then the front pair centered on Axel.

See what you're capable of now?

"Commendatore," Cricket chirped. "What have—"

Axel again felt the horror of violence. This time, violence from his own actions.

All the Eagles lay crumpled, their bodies limp and dead. An image surfaced in his mind, a memory from the tunnel, from Furia.

The dismembered, black-armored corpses of Eagles lay across the cracked plateau, surrounded in pools of blood. Standing among them were hulking Stewards, all of them raising their weapons into the air and shouting, "Lion! Lion! Lion!"

The image faded away, and his vision cleared to the inside of the Clipper. To the death inside—death he had caused.

Axel wasn't sure what to feel as the anger slowly receded like a melting hunk of ice. His mind went to the vision, to the Stewards chanting, "Lion!"

Was his father the Lion?

Crackling from the radio snapped him from the trance.

"Osprey 4, do you copy? We're in pursuit of hostiles heading into the caverns, and requesting aerial support, over."

Axel pulled the dead pilot out of his seat and dropped him to the deck. Cricket got into the other open seat.

Grabbing the yoke, Axel lowered over the valley, picking up speed. The battle on the ground seemed to be nearing an end, and most of the Wooly forces had retreated into the fortress and the cliff caves.

A sudden flash came from the sky. Axel knew right away it was from the Warhorse. Not a beat later, a massive explosion burst across the valley. He didn't need to turn in that direction to know the Eagles had fired a Razor Missile into the main fortress.

Uga's home was gone, the ancient castle carved out of the mountainside crumbling into a pile of scree. Axel glimpsed the statue of Chief Cardia cracked in half, the upper part tumbling into the river reflecting the moonlight and fires.

Anger spiked through Axel, an anger he had never known. An anger that made him want to rip off the limbs of his enemy and use them to beat them all down.

"There," Cricket chirped.

Axel followed the Marka's paw toward the cliffs on the eastern side of the valley. Two Clippers hovered outside the mouth of a cave. Their laser cannons suddenly blazed to life, cutting down Wooly defenders that stood to guard the entrances. Furry bodies exploded and burned over the shelf of rock.

"Osprey 4, Osprey 4, do you copy?"

Axel shut off the radio and scanned the display board. He located the missile controls, flipped the switch, and then grabbed the yoke.

"Strap in, Cricket," Axel said.

He activated the thrusters, flying toward the two Clippers. He tried to lock onto both, but a warning flashed on the screen.

Friendly contact. Disengage. Disengage.

"Not anymore," Axel said. He switched off the auto-targeting system, but by then both the Clippers had rotated their aft laser cannons.

Axel pushed down on the yoke, blasting toward the two enemy ships. They opened fire as he closed in, painting the sky with laser bolts.

"Commendatore!" Cricket chirped.

Axel jerked away from the fire and loosed a missile that forced both the hostile crafts to pull away. The projectile slammed into the mountain above them, exploding and showering rocks onto the Clippers.

One spun out of control, but the other righted itself and fired at them. The lasers pounded the armored hull, punching through the starboard side. Alarms wailed as sparks showered down over the dead Eagles in the back. Smoke billowed away from open flames in the troop hold.

Axel spotted movement on the ledge. Three Woolies had run out, two of them were carrying some sort of rocket launcher.

Another flurry of bolts pounded the Clipper as Axel swerved and jerked. He followed the attack ship with his naked eye, trying to line up a manual shot with the missiles. But it was too close to these Woolies. If he fired now, he would kill them all.

Instead, Axel pulled away, losing sight of them. He also lost control of the craft. He pulled on the yoke, but nothing worked. The Clipper began to spin.

"Can't...control..." Axel tried to say.

He caught a glimpse of the attacking transport, which was also going down. The Woolies had hit it in the belly with their rocket, blowing out the thrusters. The Clipper slammed into the mountain, bursting and showering debris over the rocks.

Axel tried to pull away, as they were about to be next. He unfastened his belt, kicked open the hatch, and grabbed Cricket.

The transport continued to spin, nearly striking the mountain side.

On the next pass, he tossed Cricket onto the cliff where the Woolies had fired their rocket launcher. The Clipper rotated again, and Axel waited for his chance to jump. When it came, he was dizzy, but alert enough to see he had already passed over the ledge. With no other choice, he jumped out, smacking against the jagged vertical walls.

Shards ripped through his suit and sliced open his palms. His boots slammed into a protruding rock, slowing his body enough to grab a handhold. As he clung for life, the Clipper crashed into a bluff one hundred feet below him.

An inferno rose up, licking at the sky. The heat rushed over his body and shrapnel speared through the air. A simmering piece of metal struck the back of his thigh, ripping through flesh.

He let out a shriek of pain.

There was no time for that. He had to start climbing. Clenching his jaw, he plucked the piece out then he reached up and started pulling his body toward the ledge above. A furry face suddenly appeared from above.

"Commendatore!" Cricket chirped.

Axel climbed higher, scaling the jagged rocks despite his aching leg. When he was just below the ledge, Cricket dipped both tails down. He grabbed on and the Marka pulled him to safety.

As soon as he was up, Axel saw the two Woolies that had saved them. They lay next to the rocket launcher they had used to bring down the enemy craft.

One of the inured creatures was still alive and letting out a mournful death moan. Both legs were blown off along with two arms. Axel nodded at Cricket, who put the warrior out of his misery.

Another group of six aliens waddled out of a cave entrance.

Axel prepared to defend himself, but these Woolies weren't wearing armor. These were civilians and stopped to stare at Axel and Cricket.

"Come with us," barked a gray female in ash covered clothing.

The group went back inside the tunnel where dozens of their clan were huddling in packs in the rock corridors. The anger surging through Axel dissipated at the sight of the shaking Woolies. Some of them were just chubby little children with big, scared eyes.

A female clutched her baby against her chest, trying to nurse the sobbing infant while a father kept his arm around her shoulder.

Cricket trotted with Axel deeper into the cave systems where more of the Woolies had wobbled in to escape. The sound of the battle waned as they worked deeper and deeper. Crashing water masked the distant noises.

The corridor came out in a sprawling circular chamber with a central waterfall down the middle. Platforms surrounded it, with access to five more tunnels into the mountain. Hundreds of Woolies were here, moving in and out of them in an organized fashion.

"Axel!" a voice shouted.

He looked across to see two humans among the mass of furry refugees. It was Luna and Brayton. They pushed through the fleeing aliens.

Axel and Cricket went toward them, but Luna halted when she approached, looking him up and down. It was then he realized he was covered in blood.

"Are you..." she started to say.

"It's not his," Cricket chirped.

Axel swallowed at the memory of the massacre. He had

killed with such ease, taking what could not be replaced. The voice of his father had finally taken over, guiding his hand.

Uga pushed through the crowd, but he moved past Axel. Barking came from a connecting passage to the left. Three Wooly warriors waddled into the opening. A Tark'ba with shaggy locks of brown hair strode down the tunnel with a stretcher attached to its paddle tail.

Axel turned to find it was Master Norn and two other Master Warriors on the stretcher. Norn had a bandage over half his burned-off face. He directed his one eye up at Axel.

"Wait," Norn said.

The Tark'ba halted, and Axel tensed up as the Wooly warrior extended a burned arm of blistering flesh.

"I made a mistake," he barked. "I should never have told them to come here."

"You did what you thought would protect your clan," Axel said.

"I doomed them. This is my burden now. Go to big waterfall, Uga, where we played as kids," Norn said. "The city is lost. We will blow the entrances and head to our other home."

Norn reached out with two of his arms. "Help me off this blasted thing."

Axel bent down and gently removed Norn from the stretcher. The Wooly staggered as Axel set the husky alien down, but then stood stiff and proud.

"Get Uga to safety and find your crew, Captain Finn," he said. "I will hold the demon men back as long as I can."

Axel got to his feet, hearing the distant crack of gunfire. He knew in order to survive what came next, he would need his father to guide his hands in battle.

He would become a lion, the apex predator.

CHAPTER 31

Dripping wet, Rangnar used the cover of darkness to climb a ladder up to a bridge. He could hear a labored snort, like the breathing of an injured Wooly over the rush of rapids below.

"Contact on the bridge," came a muffled voice.

The rap of Eagle boots echoed as a squad of five, by the sound of it, crossed the wooden planks. Two bolts chattered from a laser rifle.

The labored breathing fell silent to the rapids, and then the rap of those boots.

Rangnar held to the ladder, keeping low as the squad of Eagles hurried across the planks. When they were gone, he climbed up to find the deceased Wooly. Smoke fingered away from the two holes in his furry chest.

Crouching, he scanned the carcass for a weapon, but this had been a civilian.

"I'm sorry, pal," Rangnar whispered.

He got up and pressed on into a cluster of homes built into the cliffs opposite the river. Remaining in a hunch, he scanned the dwellings for any hostiles, human or alien. Out here, he was a target for both.

But there were no survivors left to worry about. Black and gray furry humps peppered the area in all directions where the Eagles had slaughtered the citizens.

Rangnar had seen death like this before, but not for many years. The bloodshed was hard to understand. To capture the last Steward, General Gabriel Jessup was hellbent on leaving a mountain of innocent bodies.

The sight of a dead Eagle stopped Rangnar. The soldier had crumpled behind some rocks on the side of a path. His squad must have left him for extraction after the battle was over.

Four dead Wooly warriors formed a halo around the Eagle. Rangnar ran over and dragged the corpse over to patch of trees and bushes, using them for cover to strip the dead Eagle of armor...only, the soldier wasn't dead. When Rangnar pulled off his helmet, frightened eyes locked onto him.

The man moved his neck and head, but that was it, indicating he had a severed spine. He couldn't talk either, probably the reason he hadn't been able to radio for help.

His mouth could move though, and he lipped for mercy.

Please...please...

Had the Eagle shown the same mercy to the Woolies?

This man deserved no quarter. The soldiers of Dark Horse Company knew what they signed up for by joining the infamous unit.

But Rangnar wasn't an Eagle, and he hadn't signed up for this.

Grabbing the man by the head, he granted him mercy with a strong twist of his neck, severing it from his brain.

"Trust me, pal. You're better off," Rangnar whispered.

He removed the black armor quickly. Within minutes, he

was wearing it, smirking at the irony. Now he was an unofficial member of Dark Horse Company.

He grabbed a laser rifle and set off toward the sounds of battle. All the shots and blasts were coming from the caves above him, where most of the Wooly population had fled during the attack.

The helmet gave Rangnar access to the team-comms. It sounded like the battle was still on the ground, with reinforcements on standby in the Warhorse far above the mountain peaks.

Rangnar looked up at the monster ship protruding from the cloud cover. Lucid was up there. His heart swelled in his chest at the thought of her being tortured.

She was all he had left.

But he wasn't delusional. He knew the chances of rescuing the Marka and getting her out alive was impossible. None of the Death Rules or strategies would save them.

All he could do was kill the man responsible for their pain.

Gabriel wasn't long for the galaxy—nor was every Eagle Rangnar could find along the way to slaying the general. He would avenge his team.

A radio message crackled over the comm.

His first victims were close.

"Target has been spotted..." White noise broke up the message. "Waterfall...follow the river."

Determined, Rangnar ran across another bridge to a second level of houses. Entrances to the caves were just beyond the structures. Moving at a hunch in the moonlight, he prepared to enter it when a blast rocked a ledge hundreds of feet above him.

Rangnar flinched at one and then two explosions bursting in the vertical cliffs high above the tunnels chiseled into the mountains. Rocks spewed outward, some of them already raining down. He made a run for the nearest entrance, wondering if it would suddenly explode.

Boulders pounded the ground behind him seconds after he made his way into the large tunnel. A wave of dust and grit slammed against his back, smashing him to the ground. He slid over the rock right into something soft and squishy.

Rangnar raised his helmet to see it was a body. Multiple bodies. All Woolies. And all dead. He pushed himself up, turned on the tactical light attached to the rifle and strode into the tunnel.

The distant sound of rushing water hit his ears. He ran toward it, the beam from his light bobbing up and down.

A voice suddenly called out, "Hey, stop!"

Rangnar saw two Eagles guarding the massive doorway that opened to the vaulted cavern carved from the interior of the mountain. Water cascaded down the far wall.

"Fellas, hey, I got separated from my squad," he said.

Both men walked toward him, their weapons cradled. "Jason, that you?"

Rangnar moved into the light of the helmets when he was ten feet away.

"Nah, man. Jason didn't make it," he said.

The Eagles raised their weapons a second too late. Rangnar blasted them both in their chest plates, sparks flying off. As they slumped over, he ran past, stopping to find the vaulted cavern was hollow in the middle, forming the opening the waterfall dumped through. A circular path surrounded the flow.

Multiple doorways led into the catacombs of tunnels. Rangnar ran toward the sound of laser fire. He had to be getting close now. A winding corridor snaked down into the mountain. Keeping his rifle up, he moved cautiously down into the rocky bowels. He halted at the bark of a Wooly, and the chatter of laser fire.

The creature howled in pain.

Two more shots silenced the cries.

Then came the muffled shouts of human soldiers. "We almost got them, move, move!"

Rangnar slowed his gait as he got to the bottom of the winding passage. He cleared the landing and peered into another corridor that intersected ahead with three tunnels. Two more Woolies lay on the ground, limbs scattered.

An Eagle lay face down not far from them, his helmet crushed and gore oozing from the broken faceplate.

Cautiously, Rangnar walked into the intersection, clearing the passages before looking straight past the dead Eagle. Another Wooly warrior had fallen in the entrance, this one dressed in white Master armor caked with streaks of soot. He was a big bastard for a Wooly, with muscular limbs, two of them still gripping fire hatchets.

A wood stretcher was shattered against the adjacent wall but was still connected to the paddle tail of a Tark'ba. The shaggy beast had curled up into a fetal position.

Rangnar stepped around the creature, seeing blood running out of its mouth. Two laser holes still simmered in its furry stomach.

A message crackled over the team comms.

"We have the target within sight. Orders are to take into custody, over."

Rangnar stepped away when a furry arm grabbed his ankle. He jerked away from the Wooly in white armor just as he tried to swing his axe. The fire blade came an inch from striking his leg.

The alien rolled over, letting out a final bark. His chest rose once, but then went flat. Rangnar hurried away, knowing there was nothing he could do to help.

For the next few minutes, he ran through the tunnel toward

the sound of rushing water. The rocky cavern brightened from distant moonlight.

He stopped at a corner to listen to an Eagle shouting orders.

"You're surrounded! Get on the ground, NOW!"

Rangnar carefully looked around the edge at six Eagles in a defensive position, rifles all aimed at Axel and his crew of Brayton, Luna, Uga, and Cricket.

They had nowhere to go.

A waterfall cascaded down across the end of the corridor. Rays of moonlight bled through the crystal-clear water. Five wooden rafts waited at the edge, about ten feet from Axel and his friends.

Ten feet too far.

A lieutenant had his pistol out and continued to yell orders for them all to get down.

Rangnar moved back behind the wall for cover, breathing hard, trying to come up with a plan. There was *no* way he could kill seven fully armored Eagles of Dark Horse Company.

Unless...

He looked down to the two plasma grenades on the duty belt he had stripped off poor Jason. A perfectly placed one behind these soldiers would definitely disable them for a few key moments.

Rangnar plucked one off his belt and stalked into the corridor.

"You all murderers!" Uga barked. "You killed my people!"

"On the ground. I won't ask again!" said the lieutenant.

"Call your forces back," Axel said.

"As soon as you are secure."

"Don't do it," Luna said.

The lieutenant aimed his rifle at her, and Axel raised a hand.

"Okay, okay, I'll come with you," he said.

Rangnar hesitated with the plasma grenade at that statement. Was the kid really going to surrender?

Not if Rangnar had any say in the matter.

He lobbed the plasma grenade directly behind the men. It tumbled across the ground, stopping at the boot of an Eagle who turned to look. The explosion sent him cartwheeling through the air and knocked the entire group down in a shockwave of blue.

Rifle butt against his shoulder, Rangnar strode out, looking for a target. The lieutenant was on his feet, shaking his head. He raised his pistol at Axel who charged.

Rangnar squeezed off three bolts that punched into the winged back of the officer. He crashed in front of Axel. Two of the other seven were already back on their feet, dazed but raising weapons. Two well-placed shots to their visors took them out of the fight.

Axel seized the moment, barreling into another soldier, smashing him to the ground.

As Rangnar searched for another target, roaring engines blasted into the tunnel. The brown bow of a ship pierced the waterfall.

Oh shit, Rangnar thought.

He aimed at the viewport but realized a beat later this wasn't a Clipper. It was the *Trash Squid*. A synthetic voice fired from exterior speakers.

"He-heh, I am SPARTACUS!"

"Sparty!" Brayton yelled.

"Mech-man!" Uga barked.

Rangnar fired another burst into an Eagle that had turned toward him, blasting holes into his chest armor. Another standing soldier got off a flurry of bolts at Rangnar. One of the lasers hit him in the helmet, knocking it clean off.

He fell to the ground, his head hitting the rock. The pain

was immense, blurring his vision with red. Practically blind, he scrambled for cover.

"Get to the ship!" Axel shouted. "Leave while you still can!"

Rangnar found a boulder and kept down for a moment as the chatter of laser bolts echoed through the passage. Blinking, he looked over the rock at the viewports of the *Trash Squid,* where Spartacus stood behind the glass. A ramp lowered, and the crew ran toward it. All of them but Axel.

He charged the Eagles, ducking under laser bolts, and jumping over rocks. A bolt hit him in the shoulder, but barely slowed his assault. He leapt into the air then plowed into two Eagles with his shoulders, knocking them to the rocks.

With only his fists, he went to work pummeling their helmets.

"Captain, get to the ramp," Spartacus said over the external system.

"Axel, come on!" Luna shouted.

Rangnar knew it was too late to pull him back now. The Corinn tunnel had opened, connecting him to his ancestors with a grip stronger than T-Flesh.

Axel slammed a battered helmet against the rocks in a blur of motion until the entire thing cracked open like a Lark egg. Another Eagle ran over with a drawn fire sword.

"Axel!" Rangnar yelled.

He twisted in just the right moment, his eyes red with rage. The glowing blade sizzled down toward his neck, but he ducked underneath it then reached up and grabbed the wrist of the Eagle, snapping it like a fishbone.

A muffled scream rang out.

Axel had the sword now—not good for the surviving Eagles, all of them injured.

The clap of boots hit Rangnar's ears. He rolled to a side to see another squad advancing down the tunnel.

And leading them was General Gabriel Jessup.

Rangnar lay still, playing dead as the group passed him by and surrounded Axel as his crew still pleaded with him to flee.

Shaking, Axel slowly stood in front of the scene of gore, his body covered in blood, the sword in his hand.

"Leave!" he screamed.

"Come with us!" Luna yelled back.

"*GO!* That's an order, Spartacus!"

The *Trash Squid* hovered outside the waterfall with Luna shouting on the still retracting ramp next to Brayton. Uga huddled between them, along with Cricket.

"No hurt Capa!" Uga barked.

Axel turned toward the approaching Eagles.

"Let them go and take me!" he shouted.

Gabriel strode forward carrying a fire sword in each hand. His visor surveyed the scene. "I was told you're a man of peace," he said. "Guess I never learned my lesson about listening to bounty hunter scum."

Rangnar searched for his missing rifle in the dust as Gabriel moved closer to Axel.

"I've wasted a lot of time tracking you down, boy," he said.

"Axel, don't do this!" Luna shouted.

"Come with, Capa!" Uga barked.

"Run, Commendatore!" Cricket chirped.

Tremors shook Axel, as if he was resisting a demon trying to control his body. Eyes bloodshot from fury, jugular vein bulging, chest heaving—Rangnar could tell he was losing the fight.

"This very moment, your father's voice is in your head probably telling you to crush my skull and piss on my corpse," Gabriel said. "That's the corrupted part of you, but your breed can be salvaged, if we correct the stock."

"No, that's not true," Luna said. She leapt off the ramp to the ground.

Rangnar finally spotted a weapon about five feet away behind a rock. He slowly began to crawl over to it. Down the passage, the Eagles all had their rifles aimed at Axel, but Gabriel lifted a sword for them to hold fire.

The general stopped an arm's length from Axel. "Your crew doesn't know, do they?"

Axel turned his head partially, long hair covering half his face as he glared back at Luna.

"He's the son of a Steward!" Gabriel said with a raised sword. "One of the most efficient and insane killing machines ever born! Connected by a tunnel to the infamous Captain Leon Kahr, the Lion of the Galaxy!"

Luna stared at Axel, but there wasn't fear in her eyes. There was something else, something that Rangnar hadn't felt for so long ago, he hardly recognized it.

Love.

"He isn't a killer, he's a good man!" Luna yelled.

Axel looked to her with relief and trust in his eyes, but also regret.

Rangnar reached his dropped rifle, taking it in his grip. He knew he would only get one shot at Gabriel.

Now was his chance.

He rose onto a knee, aimed, and fired.

An energy-cape flowed out of the port on the general's back, glowing orange as it deflected the bolts. The other Eagles turned toward Rangnar, and opened fire.

He dropped to the ground, noticing some of those bolts flashing to his right and left. These soldiers weren't aiming poorly—they had other targets.

The war bark of Woolies resonated a moment later.

Lasers ripped back and forth, narrowly missing Rangnar as he flattened his body on the ground. On the ramp, Brayton and Cricket fired weapons scavenged from the first Eagle squad.

Uga tossed a plasma grenade at the general and his squad. Just as he prepared to launch a second grenade, a laser lanced by his furry face, knocking off his aim.

"Owie, *fucking*, boo-boo!" Uga roared. He used a telescoping front arm to toss the grenade at the squad. The grenade hit an Eagle in the helmet, bouncing off to the ceiling where it wedged in the rock.

Right above Gabriel.

"Oh son of a bitch," he grumbled as he glanced up.

The explosion burst at the top of the corridor, raining rock on the Eagles. The general held up a shield that gave out under the onslaught of boulders. An avalanche crushed him to the ground, burying his armored body.

The *Trash Squid* pulled back as half of the ceiling came crashing down right on the bow.

"Hurry!" Spartacus yelled over an intercom. "I can't hold us!"

Another round of explosions clapped outside the waterfall. Rangnar heard the crack of glass on the *Trash Squid*. The ship had taken damage. Severe apparently. He glimpsed the hull in the moonlight as it went not up, but down.

Cascading rocks blocked the view, dumping into the exit of the cave and crushing two of the boats. The debris kept coming, until almost the entire tunnel had been blocked off. And the collapse wasn't over yet. A tsunami of grit and dust rushed toward Rangnar as he tucked his head down. The last thing he saw was Luna falling in the onslaught.

When the roar subsided, the groans and moans of the injured filled the void.

Woolies waddled quickly past, barking on their way toward the few boats that remained in a section of accessible waterfall. Fearing he would be mistaken for an Eagle, Rangnar stayed down, watching as the dust cleared.

Screaming rose over the frightened barks.

"Luna! Luna!"

It was coming from Axel, who furiously tossed aside rocks. Rangnar rose up slightly, spotting limbs sticking out of the rubble.

As the Woolies rushed away and took the boats, he got up and went to help Axel. By then, Axel had already cleared the debris. He was on his knees, holding Luna in his arms, despite two laser wounds to his back, and a third to his arm.

Rangnar moved closer, his step masked by rattled breathing as Luna fought for air. He knew that sound too. Her ribs were crushed, her body broken beyond repair.

Lowering his head, Axel put his ear to her mouth as she whispered her last breaths. When her head slumped to the side, Rangnar knew she was gone.

He slowly approached Axel, holding up his hands.

"I'm sorry, I tried to stop them," Rangnar said.

Axel glanced back at him with eyes clouded by rage. Rage that could rip Rangnar apart.

But the Steward's son directed his gaze back to Luna. His entire body seemed to soften, his shoulders slumping with defeat.

Rangnar looked at the mound of rocks, seeing the crushed helmet of Gabriel Jessup. As much as he wanted to defecate on it, he remained with Axel, putting a hand on his shoulder as gently as he could.

"I'm really sorry," Rangnar said. "I tried to kill—"

The sound of laser bolts echoed closer as more reinforcements surged through the tunnels. There was no time for Axel to grieve, or for Rangnar to celebrate the death of Gabriel.

"You should get out of here while you still can," Rangnar said. "I'll stay here and hold them back, try to buy you and your crew some time."

Axel shook his head, long hair flicking blood off the strands.

"There's not much time, man," Rangnar said. "You better get while you can."

"No." Axel gently put Luna down and rose to his feet. "You want to help?"

"Yeah," Rangnar said.

"Then go find my crew and protect them. They will need you."

Rangnar was going to ask what Axel had planned, but it was obvious. The captain walked toward the approaching rap of boots, hands balled and muscles flexing across his injured body.

"There's only one way to end this," he grunted in a rough voice.

Lights glowed at the end of the tunnel. Power-armor batteries burned orange like candles as the cautious Eagles advanced.

"Find my crew," Axel said. "Stay with them and make sure they are safe."

He looked back at Rangnar one last time, then ran toward the enemy.

CHAPTER 32

"This is Sergeant Jax Brito, does anyone copy?" Jax stammered into her comm.

Static crackled into her helmet, silencing the alarms on her HUD for a fleeting moment. They kicked back on, showing Jax she was in a world of trouble. She had a compromised suit and could feel burning atmosphere against her back.

Coughing into her helmet, she reached up and removed a hunk of rock. The power-cell had blown the door open down the corridor, but also collapsed part of the tunnel. That had knocked her unconscious, until just now.

Zang was severely injured, a broken arm, two shattered legs, and multiple stab wounds to his back. If Jax didn't get the Corinn out of here soon, he would die. Not even the genetically superior alien would be able to hang on forever.

Jax pulled another rock off the pile and tossed it to the side with a clank. The charcoaled armor of Hesh lay beneath the pile. The corpse of the possessed Eagle that had tried to kill them had actually helped protect them from the inferno.

Perhaps more ironic, Jax was the sole human survivor of the

fire-team that was sent to investigate the Wrath construct. Only she and Zang possessed the knowledge of what had happened in the construct, and what was still down there.

She had to get out of here and warn the Eagles topside.

Jax pushed a rock off her body, coughing again from the strenuous motion. She gasped for air, trying to fill her lungs. With each breath, she inhaled toxins and gases that had gotten past the filters in her breathing apparatus.

She focused her mind on her family and their farm on Runi. The burning ash root fields in her vision surfaced. Stopping that from happening and saving her family fueled her motions.

Adrenaline dumped into her bloodstream. Over the next few minutes, she removed enough rocks to free herself.

"Zang," she said. "Zang, can you move?"

The Corinn groaned as Jax shook him gently. She bent down and tried to pick the alien up, but could tell right away she wasn't going to be able to lift him. Certainly not over the pile of debris ahead.

"I'll come back for you," Jax said.

She climbed up onto the pile, then slid down the side of scree. Stumbling, she sucked in another breath that burned her lungs. The sensors on her HUD spiked.

The potent scent of sulfur filled her nostrils.

She staggered a few feet, drawing closer to the destroyed door. Each step was harder than the last, her muscles locking up.

Strong and steady. Come on, Jax, strong and steady.

In a final attempt to reach safety, she tried to run for the opening. Just a few more steps and she would be there, out into the crater bottom, and would hopefully be able to get a transmission out.

The darkness of the crater shifted, transporting her to the ash root field. She ran through the plants under a sunset the color of a bruise. Her childhood dog raced ahead, barking and wagging his tail.

The view went black, and then cleared back to reality.

She was in Hell.

Jax collapsed in front of the broken door. Her limbs twitched, out of her control. Her feet and hands wouldn't respond to her commands.

There was no more strong and steady left in her. She lay there, dying.

Thoughts of her family drifted into her mind. Her brother Nico trying to outrun her in the fields. Her father, the Ox, shoveling faster than a harvest droid. Her mother bringing them water and egg sandwiches.

Suddenly, Jax was moving.

Through blurred vision, she thought she saw someone carrying her. Was it Zang? Had the Corinn somehow managed to get up, despite his severe injuries?

The sense of movement continued, even as her vision darkened again.

At some point, she heard voices. Distant, muffled, but human.

She struggled to open her eyes. A bright light beamed across the ground, hitting her. More rays speared back and forth. The glow captured Eagles trekking toward her location.

"Over here," Jax whispered in a croak.

She tried to lift her hand.

Two soldiers ran over and bent by her side.

"We got a live one!" one of them yelled.

More Eagles rushed by, heading into the tunnel.

Jax tried to reach up to stop them, but was too weak, her hand falling back down.

"Wrath," she whispered. "You have to blow it."

A familiar voice answered: "Brito, where the hell's the rest of your team?"

It was Apollo, and he crouched next to Jax. A medic bent down and pulled out a breathing unit.

"Sergeant, we need to hook this up to your helmet," said the medic.

Jax rotated again and heard the hiss of a new oxygen tank being hooked up. She felt the cool flow and inhaled it into her scorched lungs.

"You're gonna make it, Brito," Apollo said. "Get her to the evac."

The lieutenant stepped away as Jax raised her hand again. "No...wait..."

Two Clippers flew over the crater, lowering to the ground and setting down. Their troop hold hatches opened, and more Eagles poured out.

"No," she said, grabbing the medic's hand. "The Wrath are down there. You can't send them—"

"Take it easy, Sergeant."

"You have to listen." Jax tried to sit up, but the medic held her down on the stretcher. "Zang will tell you."

Jax struggled to rotate her head both ways, looking for the alien who had saved her life. But the Corinn wasn't within sight. Turning, Jax almost fell out of the stretcher for a better view.

"Sergeant, please," said the medic.

Apollo ran back over. "Brito, what the hell happened down there?" he asked. "I'm getting a report of a bloodbath. Hesh, Nadia, Satani..."

"Corinns," she muttered, recalling their burning eyes. "Turned into monsters...they are protecting the...the eggs."

"Eggs?"

"Wrath eggs. They have been feeding on the planet...You *must* destroy them."

Apollo looked back toward the tunnel and said something into the comms.

"Zang will tell you," Jax said.

Another medic rushed over with a stretcher.

"Wait, hold on," Apollo said.

He leaned close to Jax.

"Zang will tell you," she said again.

"Hate to break it to you, Brito, but the Corinn's dead. Two scouts already found his body."

"What?" Jax gazed back at the tunnel. Somewhere in her oxygen deprived brain she realized she had somehow crawled out here on her own. But how? Had the alien somehow connected to her mind, taking over her body when Jax couldn't move on her own?

At this point, she would never know. Zang was gone. Another lost comrade.

She felt a prick and looked down to see a syringe had been inserted into the port on her armored right arm. Warmth flooded her system.

"No," she mumbled.

"Get her out of here," Apollo said.

The medics lifted Jax off the ground in the stretcher and started toward the Clippers.

"Blow it...they have to blow it," Jax whispered.

"Okay, Sergeant," said one of the medics.

Her vision dimmed as her body relaxed under a cool, soft wave, like she was lying on a cloud. The medics loaded her into the Clipper as two Bloodhogs roared over the crater. Three more transports descended from orbit with tanks and APCs attached to their hulls.

Seeing the firepower helped further relax Jax. Dark Horse Company was going to charge in and annihilate the eggs before they could hatch. Runi would be saved. Her family and everyone else would be saved across the vast system.

By the time she was secured in the Clipper, the first tank was on the ground.

Jax looked out a viewport as the transport lifted off the crater, thinking of Zang.

"Goodbye, my friend," she whispered.

Closing her eyes, Jax exhaled deeply. She lingered on the edge of consciousness, drifting in and out.

"Sergeant," someone said. "We're here."

Jax opened her eyes to see she was being unloaded from the Clipper inside a cargo hold of the Citadel space station. Three Knight attack cruisers were docked in the mammoth circular structure outside the viewports of the hold.

"Did they blow the construct?" she asked.

The medics didn't answer. She was carried out into a launch bay alive with activity. Bloodhogs being prepared for strafe runs. Eagles loading into Clippers. And another transport with a group of six Eagles personally assigned to Admiral Rex Jessup, judging by their light red armor.

They escorted a tall, muscular man with wild hair and hands bound by electric cuffs, wearing nothing but a jumpsuit. He didn't appear all that dangerous. But two war droids that looked like Hippo were accompanying the Eagles.

The soldiers moved cautiously, as if they were guarding a dangerous, feral animal.

They passed under an overhead light and Jax noticed this man was caked in blood. His hair, his flesh. He looked like he had taken a bath in it.

"Crazy. I heard that guy is a Steward," one of the medics said.

Jax raised a brow as she was carried out of the hold. In the corridor, one of the medics looked down at her.

"You found Wrath eggs, huh?" he asked.

Jax nodded. "Thousands upon thousands."

The medic shook his head and smiled. "All those gases must have had you seeing things, Sergeant."

"What do you mean?" Jax replied.

"Just heard over the comms the recon unit didn't find anything down there besides a bunch of dead Corinns and what was left of your squad."

"I love you. I've always loved you."

Luna's final words filled Axel with an emptiness he hadn't felt in a very long time. Not since he was just a young, scraggly kid trying to make his way without his mom. Living on a Junker ship all alone, always wondering what monsters were out there looking for him.

For years he thought the monster was inside of him, and he spent most of his life trying to control it. But now he knew the truth—the monsters were the Eagles that had hunted him since birth, as they had hunted and killed his father.

The Lion, Axel thought. General Gabriel Jessup had confirmed what Axel had suspected. His father's full name was Captain Leon Kahr. The *Lion* of the Galaxy.

Maybe if Axel had listened to his voice earlier, he could have saved Luna—maybe he would have found his mother, too.

No. He knew that wasn't true.

Nothing could have saved either of them. Not with the Eagles out there. He was glad he had stopped running and hiding and was proud to have finally stood up and fought.

At least the rest of his crew had escaped with Rangnar. The gritty bounty hunter would give them a chance at survival.

Head up, Axel shuffled down the ramp of a Clipper. Hands

and feet bound by electric cuffs, he staggered between a group of ten Eagles and two war droids gripping poles attached to his cuffs.

They escorted him across a cargo hold that was one of hundreds in the largest space station he had ever seen. Not only was the thing gigantic, but he had noticed thrusters and anti-grav technology on the flight in. This space station could *fly*.

Currently, it was above a dead brown planet, along with a fleet of Ironclads and Knight attack cruises. Dozens of Warhorse transports and the smaller Clipper troop carriers were buzzing to and from the massive station.

The Eagles pushed past dozens of docked Bloodhog space fighters. Mechanics and droids swarmed around the fixed wing fighters, preparing them for what Axel could only guess at.

This planet, whatever it was, seemed to be important in a way he didn't understand.

After crossing the sprawling hold, he was taken into a corridor and then into a freight elevator that rushed downward. When the doors opened, the guards shuffled out, and the droids pulled him into a vaulted chamber with a protruding round viewport overlooking the wasteland of a planet.

Standing in front of that view was an Eagle in ceremonial attire. Crimson Admiral Wings hung from his shoulder plates.

The Eagles around Axel came to attention, but the head of CANDF remained with his gaze on the planet.

The droids pulled the poles attached to his cuffs, yanking Axel forward. He stood his ground and pulled back, resisting both of the four-hundred-pound monstrosities.

All the Eagles closed in with drawn fire swords.

The droids both pulled back at the same moment, yanking him to the ground. He fell on his knees, his long hair covering his eyes. He whipped it back as the admiral turned from the viewport.

"You killed my son, Gabriel," he said.

Axel stared with realization—this was Admiral Rex Jessup, the commander of CANDF.

"And you killed my father," Axel said. His muscles tensed across his blood-stained flesh. "You used my dad and the Stewards to defeat the Wrath and then discarded them when some of them malfunctioned."

"You aren't wrong."

Axel lifted a brow.

"Your father, Captain Leon Kahr stood down there against the Wrath when they invaded thirty-five years ago," Rex said. "He fought with thousands of Stewards against the hordes and fiery legions of the enemy, saving millions of Corinn lives as they escaped."

Axel looked out the viewport at the planet. Now it made sense.

This dead world was Corinnia, the former home world of the Corinns. And the big metal honeycomb station far above the planet was their new home—a space station housing millions of the survivors.

"Your father was a brave man, and a good man," Rex said. "I took no pleasure in following orders to hunt him and his loyal Stewards."

Axel tensed up, eyes roving from soldier to soldier. He felt the warm surge of fire in his veins as the tunnel prepared to open. His father's voice, filled with raw rage echoed in his mind.

That's a lie. Get up and gouge his old eyes out!

"Why?" Axel asked. "Why did you kill all the Stewards if they weren't all bad?"

"Because many of the Stewards became uncontrollable after they'd served their purpose. We couldn't predict which soldier would go off next." Rex stepped closer. "War is a business."

"So your product was corrupted and you decided to destroy it and create a new one."

"In essence, yes." Rex shook his head and sighed. "That decision cost us both dearly. I lost my own son Nathaniel when we tracked your father to Furia. My other son, Gabriel, never forgot that day. He made it his mission to hunt down every single Steward."

Axel continued to scan the room as discreetly as he could to find a way out of here. If he could escape, maybe get to a ship... No, that would never work.

But he couldn't surrender to their will. He would never allow them to use his blood to make new Stewards. His cursed bloodline would end here.

With him.

Axel closed his eyes, summoning the strength from his father's voice.

Rage fueled his body, shaking it like the FTL engine had once rattled the *Trash Squid* before jumps. A tremor rumbled down his arms. He thought of his mother sending him away when he was a child, then of Luna's crushed body in his arms. The two most important women in his life had been taken from him and for what?

Show them what the last Steward can do! Break free!

Axel flipped his eyelids open and let out a war cry.

It was time to become the monster they all feared.

He jerked back on the two poles, prying them from the droids. He caught both rods and smacked the closest Eagle in the helmet, shattering his visor. Then he swept the leg out from the next closest.

With his next strike he smacked a plasma grenade off a duty belt. Sliding to the ground, he grabbed it and held it up as ten fire swords angled down toward his head.

"Back off!" Axel shouted. "I won't let you use me to create a new army."

The droids both raised laser cannons at him, ready to erase him in pulpy blasts of gore.

"Don't shoot!" Rex shouted.

The two soldiers Axel had maimed both pushed themselves up while the others held their ground.

"Axel," Rex said. He walked closer, unafraid of the plasma grenade. "The Colonial Alliance and the Corinn Empire need your help."

"Don't come any closer!" Axel shouted.

The admiral moved even closer, despite his guards trying to block his passage.

"Sir, please stay back," one of them said.

"Out of the way," Rex said.

The Eagle moved aside, and the old admiral walked within ten feet of Axel.

"You helped kill one of my sons, and I helped kill your father," he said. "That makes us enemies, but right now we must look past that. Right now, the fate of the entire galaxy rests in your hands."

"I said I won't let you use me!"

"There's no time to breed a new army, Axel. We know the Wrath will return within six months, and it's not just here they will be coming. That artifact you stole from the pirates on Eern, well here are more just like it. They all have the same countdown that we believe will activate a beacon inside once that countdown hits zero."

Axel didn't want to believe it, but deep down, his gut told him this was true.

"The seismic activity across Corinnia and Eern has dislodged Wrath tech long since buried, and we believe there is something else down there. We already have units on the ground searching, with the help of Corinn guides."

"What else is down there?" Axel asked.

"We will know soon, but we realize now we know little about our enemy still, about their forebearers, and their weaknesses," Rex said. "Fortunately, the Stewards left us a final gift."

The admiral held up a device. With a click, a hatch in the deck grinded across the chamber. A platform rose through the opening holding a white ship about the size of the *Trash Squid*.

"This is the *Vengeance*," Rex said.

The sleek, bullet shaped vessel sported three wings on each side with attached laser cannons. Fins protruded off the aft section and stern. Gold trim detailed the bulbous cockpit of the spotless ship.

"Thirty-five years ago, we deployed the *Vengeance* to follow the Wrath ships that fled into unchartered space," Rex explained. "It returned a few months ago, but we haven't been able to open it. Only a living Steward can unlock its secrets."

"So this is why Gabriel wanted my DNA?"

"My son was on his own mission, following a private agenda. He didn't know about this, and I didn't know about you."

Axel slowly rose to his feet, unsure if this was a lie. The Eagles all stepped back, but Rex stood his ground, unflinching.

"I swear to you, this is the truth," he said.

Axel studied the man. He was the leader of a ruthless military that had committed atrocities across the galaxy. The massacre of the Four Peak clan of Woolies was yet another stain in their bloody history. An attack that had killed countless innocents, including his Luna.

Anger began to grip his quickening heart.

Help this man?

Axel wanted to *smash* him into atoms.

He gripped the plasma grenade, eyes flitting from the admiral, to the Eagles, to the Steward ship. In his mind, there was sudden confliction that broke through the rage.

The admiral wasn't lying about the vessel, or the Wrath.

He thought of the Eagles in the Clipper that he had slain while listening to his mother and father's voices, at odds in his mind.

Maybe his mother wasn't wrong about peace and maybe his father wasn't wrong about war. If Axel could control the killing machine inside of him, then he could ascend to something greater. A calculated, feared, but ethical warrior who protected the weak, and cut down evil.

Evil like the man in front of him.

His parents had tried to shape his path their way.

But his destiny was his own to make.

An idea formed in his mind as he looked at the ship. If it was that important, they would never destroy it. If he could get inside, maybe he could escape.

"Back," he said, raising the plasma grenade. "All of you!"

Rex held up both his hands and then directed the soldiers to step back from Axel.

With the plasma grenade in hand, he made his way to the ship.

"Wait," Rex said. "There's something else you should know."

"What?"

"I know where your mother is."

"Where?"

"She's on Earth."

"No. She's not there." Axel shook his head as he remembered. "I searched for her."

"Not well enough. I know for certain she was there very recently, but now I'm not sure."

"What do you mean, you're not sure?"

"We've lost contact with our last outpost on Mars," Rex said. "The final transmission was an SOS, and described a barbed, rocky ship."

A chill ran through Axel.

"Yes, it's true," Rex said. "The Wrath aren't just interested in this system. I believe they intend to spread across the universe, destroying everything in their path."

The words seemed to echo through the chamber.

"Our only hope is to destroy their forebearers," Rex said. "To take the fight to their home."

He raised an old but steady hand to the *Vengeance*.

"Unlock the secrets of this vessel and help us before it's too late," Rex said.

Axel thought on it for a long moment, knowing this could all be lies. Part of an elaborate plan to use him for sinister purposes.

Or it could be real.

"I do this, and you grant me two things," Axel said. "One, I take this ship to Earth to find my mother, if she's still there. And two, you leave my crew alone."

Rex studied Axel, and Axel studied him right back.

"If that's what it takes," the admiral said with a nod.

Axel nodded back and walked over to the ship.

The Eagles crowded around with their laser rifles up, and the group that had arrived in hazard suits moved up with their white packs and flamethrower style weapons.

Axel held up a hand to the bio-scanner which glowed a cool blue. White light glistened in a circle centered in the hatch. It slid open to a clean, white interior. A set of golden armor plates, still shiny, lay on the deck.

Still holding the grenade, Axel stepped inside, looking for the remains of Stewards, but saw nothing. The ship appeared to be abandoned.

He wondered if his father had ever seen this vessel.

War is the path to peace, came the voice of his father.

It was friendly now. Intellectual. Encouraging.

Don the armor, Axel. Get to Earth. Find your mother.

"If you're lying about any of this, no amount of distance will keep me from killing you," Axel said to the admiral. "I will hunt you, like you've hunted my kind."

"I'd expect nothing less, Axel Kahr," Rex said.

Axel turned to the cockpit and the empty chairs, feeling a new determination inside of him. He had made a lot of mistakes. He had failed Luna. But he had a chance to make up for the past. For wasted years and wasted love. To utilize his genetics for a greater purpose.

There would be no more hiding. It was time to face the monsters.

Both men and Wrath.

End of Book 1

Standby for *Galaxy In Flames 2: The Last Ship*, flying your way summer 2024! Pre-order today to lock in a special early price.

ABOUT THE AUTHOR

Nicholas Sansbury Smith is the New York Times and USA Today bestselling author of more than forty novels with two million copies sold. Before his writing career, he served at Iowa Homeland Security and Emergency Management, a background that inspired many of his story concepts. A two time Ironman triathlete, he enjoys running, biking, and hiking. Nicholas also loves traveling, especially to his cabin in Northern Minnesota where he weaves his tales. He lives in Iowa with his wonderful wife and their son and daughter.

Visit Nicholas at
nicholassansburysmith.com

Made in the USA
Coppell, TX
31 October 2024